P

#1 *Ne* or

"Macomber nev

—*Library Journal*

"Macomber's patented recipe of idyllic small-town life with a touch of romance is sure to result in a summer best-seller."

—*Booklist* on *Cottage by the Sea*

"Romantic, warm, and a breeze to read."

—*Kirkus Reviews*

"Whether [Debbie Macomber] is writing lighthearted romps or more serious relationship books, her novels are always engaging stories that accurately capture the foibles of real-life men and women with warmth and humor."

—*Milwaukee Journal Sentinel*

"Debbie Macomber tells women's stories in a way no one else does."

—*BookPage*

"With first-class author Debbie Macomber, it's quite simple—she gives readers an exceptional, unforgettable story every time, and her books are always, always keepers!"

—*ReadertoReader.com*

DEBBIE MACOMBER

Evenings by the Fire

Bride on the Loose and *My Hero*

mira

mira™

Recycling programs for this product may not exist in your area.

ISBN-13: 978-0-7783-1219-2

Evenings by the Fire

This edition published by arrangement with Harlequin Books S.A.

For questions and comments about the quality of this book, please contact us at CustomerService@Harlequin.com.

Mira
22 Adelaide St. West, 41st Floor
Toronto, Ontario M5H 4E3, Canada
www.Harlequin.com

Printed in Lithuania

MIX
Paper from responsible sources
FSC® C021394

Also available from Debbie Macomber and MIRA

Blossom Street

The Shop on Blossom Street
A Good Yarn
Susannah's Garden
Back on Blossom Street
Twenty Wishes
Summer on Blossom Street
Hannah's List
"The Twenty-First Wish"
(in *The Knitting Diaries*)
A Turn in the Road

Cedar Cove

16 Lighthouse Road
204 Rosewood Lane
311 Pelican Court
44 Cranberry Point
50 Harbor Street
6 Rainier Drive
74 Seaside Avenue
8 Sandpiper Way
92 Pacific Boulevard
1022 Evergreen Place
Christmas in Cedar Cove
(*5-B Poppy Lane* and
A Cedar Cove Christmas)
1105 Yakima Street
1225 Christmas Tree Lane

The Dakota Series

Dakota Born
Dakota Home
Always Dakota
Buffalo Valley

The Manning Family

The Manning Sisters
(*The Cowboy's Lady* and
The Sheriff Takes a Wife)
The Manning Brides
(*Marriage of Inconvenience*
and *Stand-In Wife*)
The Manning Grooms
(*Bride on the Loose* and
Same Time, Next Year)

Christmas Books

Home for the Holidays
Glad Tidings
(*There's Something About Christmas*
and *Here Comes Trouble*)
Christmas in Alaska
(*Mail-Order Bride* and
The Snow Bride)
Trading Christmas
Christmas Letters
The Perfect Christmas
(includes *Can This Be Christmas?*)
Choir of Angels
(*Shirley, Goodness and Mercy,*
Those Christmas Angels and
Where Angels Go)
Call Me Mrs. Miracle
The Gift of Christmas
A Country Christmas
(*Kisses in the Snow* and
The Christmas Basket)

Heart of Texas

Texas Skies
(*Lonesome Cowboy* and
Texas Two-Step)
Texas Nights
(*Caroline's Child* and *Dr. Texas*)
Texas Home
(*Nell's Cowboy* and
Lone Star Baby)
Promise, Texas
Return to Promise

Midnight Sons

Alaska Skies
(*Brides for Brothers* and *The Marriage Risk*)
Alaska Nights
(*Daddy's Little Helper* and *Because of the Baby*)
Alaska Home
(*Falling for Him*, *Ending in Marriage* and *Midnight Sons and Daughters*)

This Matter of Marriage
Montana
Thursdays at Eight
Between Friends
Changing Habits
The Sooner the Better
Three Brides, No Groom
Summer Breezes
(*Fallen Angel* and *The Way to a Man's Heart*)
Seaside Springtime
(*For All My Tomorrows* and *Yours and Mine*)
Fairy-Tale Forever
(*Cindy and the Prince* and *Some Kind of Wonderful*)
Perfect Partners
(*Rainy Day Kisses* and *Love 'n' Marriage*)
Finally You
(*All Things Considered* and *No Competition*)
Winning Hearts
(*Laughter in the Rain* and *Love by Degree*)
Finding You Again
(*White Lace and Promises* and *Jury of His Peers*)
A Second Glance
(*Shadow Chasing* and *Yesterday Once More*)
Longing for Yesterday
(*Reflections of Yesterday* and *Yesterday's Hero*)
The Night We Met
(*Starlight*)
Time for Love
(*A Friend or Two* and *The Trouble with Caasi*)
Their Perfect Match
(*Promise Me Forever* and *Adam's Image*)
Married in Seattle
(*First Comes Marriage* and *Wanted: Perfect Partner*)
Right Next Door
(*Father's Day* and *The Courtship of Carol Sommars*)
Wyoming Brides
(*Denim and Diamonds* and *The Wyoming Kid*)
The Man You'll Marry
(*The First Man You Meet* and *The Man You'll Marry*)
Orchard Valley Grooms
(*Valerie* and *Stephanie*)
Orchard Valley Brides
(*Norah* and *Lone Star Lovin'*)
An Engagement in Seattle
(*Groom Wanted* and *Bride Wanted*)
North to Alaska
(*That Wintry Feeling* and *Borrowed Dreams*)

Debbie Macomber's Cedar Cove Cookbook
Debbie Macomber's Christmas Cookbook

CONTENTS

BRIDE ON THE LOOSE

One

It was one of those days. Jason Manning scrubbed his hands in the stainless-steel sink, then applied ointment to several scratches. He'd just finished examining and prescribing antibiotics for a feisty Persian cat with a bladder infection. The usually ill-mannered feline had never been his most cooperative patient, but today she'd taken a particular dislike to Jason.

He left the examining room and was greeted by Stella, his receptionist, who steered him toward his office. She wore a suspiciously silly grin, as if to say "this should be interesting."

"There's a young lady who'd like a few minutes with you," was all the information she'd give him. Her cryptic message didn't please him any more than the Persian's blatant distaste for him had.

Curious, Jason moved into his book-lined office. "Hello," he said in the friendliest voice he could muster.

"Hi." A teenage girl who seemed vaguely familiar stood as he entered the room. She glanced nervously in his direction as if he should recognize her. When it was obvious he didn't, she introduced herself. "I'm Carrie Weston." She paused, waiting expectantly.

"Hello, Carrie," Jason said. He'd seen her around, but for the life of him, couldn't recall where. "How can I help you?"

"You don't remember me, do you?"

"Ah…no." He couldn't see any point in pretending. If a cat could outsmart him, he was fair game for a teenager.

"We're neighbors. My mom and I live in the same apartment complex as you."

He did his best to smile and nod as though he'd immediately placed her, but he hadn't. He racked his brain trying to recall which apartment was hers. Although he owned and managed the building, Jason didn't interact much with his tenants. He was careful to choose renters who cared about their privacy as much as he cared about his. He rarely saw any of them other than to collect the rent, and even then most just slipped their checks under his door around the first of the month.

Carrie sat back down, her hands clenched tightly in her lap. "I—I'm sorry to bother you, but I've been trying to talk to you for some time, and…and this seemed to be the only way I could do it without my mother finding out."

"Your mother?"

"Charlotte Weston. We live in 1-A."

Jason nodded. The Westons had been in the apartment for more than a year. Other than when they'd signed the rental agreement, Jason couldn't recall speaking to either the mother or her daughter.

"Is there a problem?"

"Not a problem…exactly." Carrie stood once again and opened her purse, taking out a thin wad of bills, which she leafed through and counted slowly. When she'd finished, she looked up at him. "It's my mother," she announced.

"Yes?" Jason prompted. He didn't have a clue where this conversation was leading or how long it would take the girl to get there. Stella knew he had a terrier waiting, yet she'd purposely routed him into his office.

"She needs a man," Carrie said, squaring her shoulders.

"I beg your pardon?" The girl had his attention now.

"My mother needs a man. I'm here to offer you one hundred dollars if you'll take her out on a date. You are single, aren't you?"

"Yes…but…" Jason was so surprised, he answered without thinking. Frankly, he didn't know whether to ask which of his brothers had put her up to this, or simply to laugh outright. He couldn't very well claim he'd never been propositioned before, but this was by far the most original instance he'd encountered in thirty-odd years.

"She's not ugly or anything."

"Ah…I'm not sure what to tell you." The girl was staring at him so candidly, so forthrightly, Jason realized within seconds it was no joke.

"I don't think my mother's happy."

Jason leaned against the side of his oak desk and crossed his arms. "Why would you assume my taking her out will make a difference?"

"I…don't know. I'm just hoping. You see, my mom and dad got divorced when I was little. I don't remember my dad, and apparently he doesn't remember me, either, because I've never heard from him. Mom doesn't say much about what went wrong, but it must've been bad because she never dates. I didn't care about that before, only now…"

"Only now what?" Jason asked when she hesitated.

"I want to start dating myself, and my mother's going totally weird on me. She says I'm too young. Boy, is she out of it! I'm not allowed to date until I'm sixteen. Can you imagine anything so ridiculous?"

"Uhh…" Jason wasn't interested in getting involved in

a mother-daughter squabble. "Not being a father myself, I can't really say."

"The ninth-grade dance is coming up in a few weeks and I want to go."

"Your mother won't allow you to attend the dance?" That sounded a bit harsh to Jason, but as he'd just stated, he wasn't in a position to know.

"Oh, she'll let me go, except she intends to drop me off and pick me up when the dance is over."

"And that's unacceptable?"

"Of course it is! It's—it's the most awful thing she could do to me. I'd be mortified to have my mother waiting in the school parking lot to take me home after the dance. I'd be humiliated in front of my friends. You've just got to help me." A note of desperation raised her voice on the last few words.

"I don't understand what you want me to do," Jason hedged. He couldn't see any connection between Carrie's attending the all-important ninth-grade dance and him wining and dining her mother.

"You need me to spell it out for you?" Carrie's eyes were wide, her gaze scanning the room. "I'm offering you serious money to seduce my mother."

For a wild instant, Jason thought he hadn't heard her right. "Seduce her?"

"My mother's practically a virgin all over again. She needs a man."

"You're sure about this?" Jason was having a hard time keeping a straight face. He could hardly wait to tell his brother Rich. The two of them would have a good laugh over it.

"Absolutely positive." Carrie didn't even flinch. Her expression grew more confident. "Mom's forgotten what it's like to be in love. All she thinks about is work. Don't get me wrong… My mother's an awesome person, but she's so prim and proper…and stubborn. What she really needs is…well, you know."

Jason felt sorry for the kid, but he didn't see how he could help her. Now that he thought about it, he did recall what Charlotte Weston looked like. In fact, he could remember the day she'd moved in. She'd seemed feminine and attractive, more than a little intriguing. But he'd noticed a guardedness, too, that sent an unmistakable signal. He'd walked away with the impression that she was as straitlaced as a nun and about as warm and inviting as an Alaskan winter.

"Why me?" Jason was curious enough to wonder why Carrie had sought *him* out. Apparently his charisma was more alluring than he'd realized.

"Well, because…just because, that's all," Carrie answered with perfect teenage logic. "And I figured I wouldn't have to pay you as much as I would one of those dating services. You seem nice." She gnawed on her lower lip. "Being a veterinarian is good, too."

"How's that?"

"You've probably had lots of experience soothing injured animals, and I think my mother's going to need some of that—comforting and reassuring, you know?" The girl's voice became fervent. "She's been hurt…. She doesn't talk about it, but she loved my father and I think she must be afraid of falling in love again. I even think she might like another baby someday." This last bit of information was clearly an afterthought. Carrie cast him a speculative glance to be sure she hadn't said something she shouldn't have. "Don't worry about that—she's probably too old anyway," she added quickly.

"She wants a baby?" Jason could feel the hair on the back of his neck rising. This woman-child was leading him toward quicksand, and he was going to put a stop to it right now.

"No—no…I mean, she's never said so, but I saw her the other day holding a friend's newborn and she had that look in her eyes… I thought she was going to cry." She paused. "I shouldn't have said anything."

For one brief, insane moment, Jason had actually considered the challenge of seducing Charlotte Weston, but the mention of a baby brought him solidly back to earth.

"Listen, Carrie," Jason said, "I'm sorry, but this isn't going to work."

"It's got to," she pleaded urgently, "just for one date. Couldn't you ask her out? Just once? If you don't, I'll be humiliated in front of my entire class. I'd rather not even go to the dance if my mother drives me."

Jason hated to disappoint her, but he couldn't see himself in the role of rescuing a fifteen-year-old damsel in distress from her mother's heavy hand, even if Carrie did make a halfway decent case.

"Is it the money?" Carrie asked, her eyes imploring. "I might be able to scrounge up another twenty dollars…but I'm going to need some cash for the dance."

"It isn't the money," Jason assured her.

Wearing a dejected look, Carrie stood. "You sure you don't want to take a couple of days to think it over?"

"I'm sure."

She released a long, frustrated sigh. "I was afraid you were going to say that."

"Good luck." Jason held open the door. He had no intention of asking Charlotte Weston out on a date, but he he did feel sorry for Carrie. Although he hadn't been a teenager in years, he hadn't forgotten how important these things could seem. Things like the ninth-grade dance.

* * *

Charlotte let herself into the apartment at six that evening. She slipped off her heels and rubbed the tense muscles at the back of her neck.

"Hi, Mom," Carrie called cheerfully from the kitchen. "How was work?"

"Fine." There was no need to burden her daughter with how terrible her day had been. Her job as an executive assistant at a large insurance agency might have sounded high-powered and influential, but in reality it was neither. Charlotte worked long hours with little appreciation or reward. For six months, ever since Harry Ward had taken over as managing director, she'd been telling herself it was time to change jobs. But she couldn't give up the security of her position, no matter how much she disliked her boss.

"How was school?" she asked.

"Good. Tickets for the dance went on sale today." Her daughter looked hopefully at Charlotte, as though expecting her to make some profound comment.

Charlotte chose to ignore the pointed stare. Her stand on the dance issue was causing a strain in their relationship, but she refused to give in to her daughter's pressure. Carrie wasn't going on an actual *date*. She was interested in a boy named Brad, but as far as Charlotte was concerned, Carrie could attend the dance with her girlfriends and meet him there. Good grief, the girl was only fifteen!

"Mom, can we *please* talk about the dance?"

"Of course, but…"

"You're not going to change your mind, right?" Carrie guessed, then sighed. "What can I say to prove how unreasonable you're being? Every girl in my class is going to the dance with a *boy*. And Brad *asked* me."

Charlotte reached for an apron, tied it about her waist and opened the refrigerator door. She took out a package of ground turkey for taco salad. She wasn't up to another round of arguments over the dance.

"Did you buy a dance ticket?" Charlotte asked, forcing an artificial lightness into her voice.

"No. I won't, either. I'd rather sit home for the rest of my life than have my *mother* drop me off and pick me up. Brad's father said he'd drive us both… What am I supposed to tell Brad? That my mother doesn't trust his father's driving? You're making way too big a deal out of this."

Ah, the certainty of youth, Charlotte mused.

"Will you think about it?" Carrie implored. "Please?"

"All right," Charlotte promised. She hated to be so hardheaded, but when it came to her daughter, she found little room for compromise. To her way of thinking, Carrie was too young for a real date, even if the boy in question wasn't the one driving.

The meat was simmering in the cast-iron skillet as Charlotte started to wash the lettuce. The faucet came off in her hand, squirting icy water toward the ceiling, and she gasped.

"What's wrong?" Carrie asked, leaping up from the kitchen table where she was doing her homework.

"The faucet broke!" Already Charlotte was down on her knees, her head under the sink, searching for the valve to cut off the water supply.

"There's water everywhere," Carrie shrieked.

"I know." Most of it had landed on Charlotte.

"Are you going to be able to fix it?" Carrie asked anxiously.

Charlotte sat on the floor, her back against the lower cupboards, her knees under her chin. This was all she needed to make her day complete. "I don't know," she muttered, pushing damp hair away from her face with both hands. "But it shouldn't be that hard."

"You should call the apartment manager," Carrie said. "You've had to work all day. If something breaks down, he should be the one to fix it, not you. We don't know anything about faucets. We're helpless."

"Helpless?" Charlotte raised her eyebrows at that. The two of them had dealt with far more difficult problems over the years. By comparison, a broken faucet was nothing. "I think we can handle it."

"Of course we can, but why should we?" Carrie demanded. "We pay our rent on time every month. The least the manager could do is see to minor repairs. He should fix them right away, too." She marched over to the wall phone and yanked the receiver from the hook. "Here," she said dramatically. "You call him."

"I…I don't know the number." They'd lived in the apartment for well over a year and until now there hadn't been any reason to contact the manager.

"It's around here somewhere," Carrie said, pulling open the top kitchen drawer and riffling through the phone book and some other papers. Within a very brief time, she'd located the phone number. "His name is Jason Manning. He's a veterinarian."

"He's a vet? I didn't realize that." But then, Charlotte had only met the man once, and their entire conversation had been about the apartment. He seemed pleasant enough. She'd seen him in the parking lot a few times and he struck her as an overgrown kid. Frankly, she was surprised to learn he was a veterinarian, since she'd never seen him in anything other than a baseball cap, jeans and a T-shirt. Dressing up for him was a pair of jeans that weren't torn or stained and a sweatshirt.

"Are you going to phone him?" Carrie asked, holding out the receiver.

"I suppose I will." Charlotte rose awkwardly to her feet in her straight skirt. By the time she was upright, her daughter had dialed the number and handed her the receiver.

"Hello," came Jason Manning's voice after the first ring, catching her off guard.

"Oh…hello… This is Charlotte Weston in apartment 1-A. We have a broken faucet. I managed to turn off the valve, but we'd appreciate having it repaired as quickly as possible."

"A broken faucet," he repeated, and although she knew it made no sense, he sounded suspicious to Charlotte, as though he thought she'd purposely interrupted his evening. She resented his attitude.

"Yes, a broken faucet," she returned stiffly. "It came off in my hand when I went to wash some lettuce. There's water everywhere." A slight exaggeration, but a necessary one. "If you'd prefer, I can contact a plumber. Naturally there'll be an additional charge for repairs this late in the day."

He muttered something Charlotte couldn't decipher, then said, "I'll be right over." He didn't seem too pleased, but that was his problem. He shouldn't have agreed to manage the apartments if he wasn't willing to deal with the hassles that went along with the job.

"What did he say?" her daughter asked, eyes curious, when Charlotte hung up the phone. "Is he coming?"

"He said he'd be right over."

"Good." Carrie studied her critically. "You might want to change clothes."

"Change clothes? Whatever for?" Surprised at her daughter's concern, Charlotte glanced down at her business suit. She didn't see anything wrong with it other than a little water, and in any event, she couldn't care less about impressing the apartment manager.

"Whatever." Carrie rolled her eyes, returning to her homework. No sooner had she sat down than the doorbell chimed. Her daughter leapt suddenly to her feet as if she expected to find a rock star at the door. "I'll get it!"

Jason considered the whole thing a nuisance call. It didn't take a rocket scientist to figure out what Carrie Weston was doing. The girl had arranged this broken faucet just so he'd have a chance to see Charlotte. The kid seemed to think that once Jason got a good look at her mother, he'd change his mind about wanting to date her. Well, there wasn't much chance of that.

Apparently the girl thought he was something of a player. Jason might've gotten a kick out of that a few years ago, but not now. Not when he was nearing middle age. These days he was more concerned about his cholesterol level and his weight than with seducing a reluctant woman.

He probably would've ended up getting married if things had worked out between him and Julie, but they hadn't. She'd been with Charlie nearly seven years now, and the last he'd heard, she had three kids. He wished her and her husband well, and suffered no regrets. Sure, it had hurt when they'd broken off their relationship, but in the end it just wasn't meant to be. He was pragmatic enough to accept that and go on with his life.

Jason enjoyed the company of women as much as any man did, but he didn't like the fact that they all wanted to reform him. He was disorganized, slovenly and a sports nut. Women didn't appreciate those qualities in a man. They would smile sweetly, claim they loved him just the way he was and then try to change him. The problem was, Jason didn't want to be refined, reformed or domesticated.

Charlotte Weston was a prime example of the type of woman he particularly avoided. Haughty. Dignified. Proper. She actually washed lettuce. Furthermore, she made a point of letting him know it.

"Hi." Carrie opened the door for him, grinning from ear to ear.

"The faucet broke?" Jason didn't bother to keep the sarcasm out of his voice.

She nodded, her smile as sly as a wink. "Kind of accidentally on purpose," she explained under her breath.

Jason was surprised she'd admit as much. "I thought that might be the case."

She pulled a screw from the small front pocket of her jeans and handed it to him. "It was the only way I could think of to get you here to see my mother up close—only don't be obvious about it, all right?"

"Carrie, is it the apartment manager?" The subject of their discussion walked into the living room, drying her hands on a terry-cloth apron.

Not bad was Jason's first reaction. She'd changed her hair since the last time he'd seen her; it was a cloud of disarrayed brown curls instead of the chignon she'd worn a year earlier. The curls gave her a softer, more feminine appeal. She was good-looking, too, not trying-to-make-an-impression gorgeous, but attractive in a modest sort of way. Her eyes were a deep shade of blue, as blue as his own. They were also intense and…sad, as though she'd withstood more than her share of problems over the years. But then, who hadn't?

Her legs were attractive, too. Long and slender. She was tall—easily five-eight, maybe five-nine.

"She's not bad-looking, is she?" Carrie asked in a whisper.

"Shh." Jason slid back a warning.

"Mom, this is Dr. Jason Manning, remember? Our apartment manager," Carrie said, her arm making a sweeping gesture toward her mother.

"Hello." She stayed where she was, her fingers still clutching the apron.

"Hi. You called about the broken faucet?" He took a couple of steps into the room, carrying his tool kit. He'd have a talk with Carrie later. If this took more than a few minutes, he might be late for the Lakers play-off game. It was the fifth game in the series, and Jason had no intention of missing it.

"The broken faucet's in the kitchen," Charlotte said, leading the way.

"This shouldn't take long." Jason set his tools on the counter and reached for the disconnected faucet. "Looks like it might be missing a screw." He turned pointedly to Carrie, then made a show of sorting through his tool kit. "My guess is that I have an identical one in here." He pretended to find the screw Carrie had handed him, then held it up so they could all examine it. "Ah, here's one now."

"Don't be so obvious about it," Carrie warned in a heated whisper. "I don't want Mom to know."

Charlotte seemed oblivious to the undercurrents passing between him and Carrie, which was probably just as well. He'd let the kid get away with it this time, but he wasn't coming back for any repeat performances of this handyman routine.

"I should have this fixed in a couple of minutes," he said.

"Take your time," Carrie told him. "No need to rush." She walked up behind Jason and whispered, "Give her a chance, will you?"

True to his word, it took Jason all of thirty seconds to make the necessary repair.

"The bathroom faucet's been leaking, hasn't it, Mom? Don't you think we should have him look at that, too, while he's here?"

Jason glanced at his watch and frowned. If the kid kept this up, he'd miss the start of the basketball game. But he decided he had little choice: pay now or pay later. He gave Carrie the lead she was hoping for. "Or it'll need fixing tomorrow, right?"

"Probably." There was a clear glint of warning in the fifteen-year-old's eyes.

Charlotte turned around and glanced from one to the other. Crossing her arms, she studied her daughter, then looked at Jason as if seeing him for the first time. Really seeing him. Apparently she didn't like what she saw.

"Is something going on here I don't know about?" she asked.

"What makes you say that?" Carrie said with wide-eyed innocence.

Jason had to hand it to the girl; she had the look down to an art form.

"Just answer the question, Caroline Marie."

The mother wasn't a slacker in "the look" department, either. She had eyes that would flash freeze a pot of boiling water.

The girl held her own for an admirable length of time before caving in to the icy glare. She lifted her shoulders with an expressive sigh and said, "If you must know, I took the screw out of the faucet so we'd have to call Jason over here."

Once again Jason glanced at his watch, hoping to extract himself from their discussion. This was between mother and daughter—not mother, daughter and innocent bystander. He hadn't meant to let Charlotte in on her daughter's scheme, but neither was he willing to become a full-time pawn in Carrie's little games. No telling how many other repair projects the girl might turn up for him.

"Why would you want Dr. Manning here?" Charlotte asked with a frown.

"Because he's a good-looking man and he seems nice and I thought it would be great if you got to know each other."

It was time to make his move, Jason decided. "If you'll excuse me, I'll be leaving now."

"You purposely broke the faucet so we could call him down here?" Charlotte gestured toward Jason.

Carrie sent him an irritated look as though to suggest this was all his fault. "I wanted him to see you. For being thirty-five, you aren't half bad. Once he saw your potential, I was sure he'd ask you out on a date. I tried to talk him into it earlier, but—"

"You *what?*" Charlotte exploded. Color flashed into her cheeks like bright neon lights. Her eyes narrowed. "Tell me you didn't! *Please* tell me you didn't!"

Carrie snapped her mouth shut, about ten seconds too late to suit Jason.

"This is all a big joke, isn't it?" Charlotte turned to Jason for reassurance, which was a mistake, since he was glaring at Carrie, irritated with her for saying far more than necessary.

"I had to do something," Carrie cried, defending herself. "You need a man. I saw the look on your face when you were holding Kathy Crenshaw's baby. You've never said anything, but you want more children. You never date… I don't know what my father did to you, but you've shut yourself off and—and…I was just trying to help."

Charlotte stalked to the far side of the small kitchen.

"I can't *believe* this. You actually asked a man to take me out?"

"I did more than ask. I offered him money!"

Charlotte whirled on Jason. "Just what kind of man are you? Agreeing to my daughter's plans… Why…you're detestable!"

Despite himself, Jason smiled, which was no doubt the worst thing he could have done. "So I've been told. Now if you'll both excuse me, I'll leave you to your discussion."

"What kind of man are you?" Charlotte demanded a second time, following him to the door, blocking his exit.

"Mom…"

"Go to your room, young lady. I'll deal with you later." She pointed the way, as if Carrie needed directions.

Jason hadn't imagined things would go like this, and he did feel badly about it, but that didn't help. Charlotte Weston could think harshly of him if she wanted, but now Carrie was in trouble and Jason felt halfway responsible.

"She was just trying to do you a good turn," he said matter-of-factly. "Think of it as an early Mother's Day gift."

Two

With her daughter out of the room, Charlotte scowled at Jason Manning, angrier than she could ever remember being.

"You're..." She couldn't think of anything bad enough to call him.

"*Detestable* is a good word." He was practically laughing at her!

"Detestable," she repeated, clenching her fists. "I'll have you know I'm reporting you to..." The name of the government agency, any government agency, was beyond her.

"Children Protective Services," he supplied.

"Them, too." She jerked the apron from her waist and threw it on the floor. Surprised by her own action, Charlotte tried to steady herself. "According to the terms of our rental agreement, I'm giving you our two-weeks' notice as of this minute. I refuse to live near a man as..."

"Heinous," he offered, looking bored.

"Heinous as you," she stated emphatically. Then with an indignant tilt of her chin, she said as undramatically as she could manage, "Now kindly leave my home."

"As you wish." He opened the door and without a backward glance walked out of her apartment. He'd worn a cocky grin throughout, as if he found her tirade thoroughly amusing.

His attitude infuriated Charlotte. She followed him to the door and loudly turned the lock, hoping the sound of it would echo in his ears for a good long time.

When he'd gone, Charlotte discovered she was shaking so badly she needed to sit down. She sank onto a chair, her knees trembling.

"Mom?" A small voice drifted down from the hallway. "You weren't serious about us moving, were you?"

"You're darn right I'm serious. I'm so serious I'd prefer to live in our car than have anything to do with that… that…apartment manager!"

"But why?" Carrie's voice gained strength as she wandered from her bedroom to the living room, where Charlotte was seated. "Why are we moving?"

Charlotte had clearly failed as a mother. One more layer of guilt to add to all the others. "You mean you honestly don't know?"

"To punish me?" Carrie asked, her eyes brimming with unshed tears. "I'm really sorry, Mom. I didn't mean to embarrass you."

What Carrie had done was bad enough, but Jason Manning was an adult. He should've known better. True, her daughter had played a major role in all this, but Carrie was a child and didn't fully understand what she was suggesting. Her daughter had Charlotte's best interests at heart, misguided though she was.

Jason Manning, on the other hand, had planned to take advantage of them both.

"It isn't you I'm furious with, it's him." Charlotte pointed after Jason. To think a professional man would actually agree to such an idiotic scheme.

"Dr. Manning?"

"The man's a sleaze! Imagine, taking money from you—"

"He didn't."

Charlotte hesitated, the sick feeling in her stomach intensifying. "Of course he did," she argued, "otherwise he wouldn't have played out this ridiculous game with you."

"I was the one who took the screw out of the faucet, Mom. Jason Manning didn't know anything about it. When I asked him if he'd agree to take you out on a date, he refused. He was really nice about it and everything, but he didn't seem to think it was a good idea. That's when I offered him the babysitting money I've been saving, but he wouldn't take it."

A dizziness replaced Charlotte's nausea. Several of Jason's comments suddenly made sense, especially the hint of sarcasm she'd detected when he'd held up the missing screw. Yet he'd allowed her to rant at him, not even bothering to defend himself.

"But…"

"You really aren't going to make us move, are you?"

Charlotte closed her eyes and groaned. She'd had a rotten day at the office, but misplacing a file and getting yelled at in front of an important client didn't compare with the humiliation that had been awaiting her at home.

"I wonder how many fat grams there are in crow," she muttered under her breath.

"Fat grams in crow? Are you all right, Mom?"

"I'm going to be eating a huge serving of it," Charlotte grumbled, and she had the distinct feeling she wasn't going to enjoy the experience.

She gave herself an hour. Sixty minutes to calm her nerves, have dinner and wipe down the counters while

Carrie loaded the dishwasher. Sixty minutes to figure out how she was going to take back her two-weeks' notice.

"You're going to talk to him, aren't you?" Carrie prodded her. "Right away."

Charlotte didn't need Carrie to identify *him*. They both had only one *him* on their minds.

"I'll talk to him."

"Thank heaven." Carrie sighed with relief.

"But when I finish with Jason Manning, you and I are going to sit down and have a serious discussion, young lady."

Some of the enthusiasm left Carrie's pretty blue eyes as she nodded reluctantly.

Charlotte would've preferred to delay the apology, but the longer she put it off, the more difficult it would become.

Her steps were hesitant as she approached Jason's apartment. For some reason, she chose to knock instead of pressing the doorbell.

When he didn't answer right away, she assumed, gratefully, that she'd been given a reprieve. Yet, at the same time, she hated letting the situation fester overnight. With reinforced determination, she knocked again.

"Hold your horses," Jason shouted from the other side of the door.

Charlotte took one step in retreat, squared her shoulders and drew in a deep breath. He opened the door. He looked preoccupied and revealed no emotion when he saw her.

"Hello," she said, hating how shaky she sounded. She paused long enough to clear her throat. "Would it be okay if I came inside?"

"Sure." He stepped aside to let her into his apartment. One glance told her he wasn't much of a housekeeper. A week's worth of newspapers were scattered across the carpet. Dirty dishes, presumably from his dinner, sat on the coffee table, along with the remote control, which he picked up. The TV was instantly muted. He walked over to the recliner and removed a pile of clothes, probably things he'd recently taken from the dryer.

"You can sit here," he said, indicating the recliner, his arms full of clothes.

Charlotte smiled and sat down.

"You want a beer?"

"Ah…sure." She didn't normally drink much, but if there was ever a time she needed to fortify her courage, it was now.

Her response seemed to surprise him. It certainly surprised her. He went into the kitchen, returning a moment later with a bottle and a glass. Apparently he found something he didn't like in the glass because he grabbed a dish towel from the stack of clothes he'd dumped on the floor and used it to rub the inside. When he'd finished, he raised the glass to the light for inspection.

"Don't worry about it. I prefer to drink my beer from the bottle."

He nodded, then sat down across from her, leaning back and resting his ankle on his knee. He seemed completely relaxed, as well he should. *He* wasn't the one who'd have to plead temporary insanity.

"It's about what happened earlier," she began, gripping the beer bottle with both hands. "I talked to Carrie and discovered you hadn't exactly, uh, fallen in with her scheme. I'm afraid I assumed you had."

"Don't worry about it. It was a simple misunderstanding."

"I know. Nevertheless…"

"I'll place an ad in the paper for the apartment tomorrow. Would it be okay if I started showing it right away?"

So, he was going to make this difficult after all. "That's another reason I'm here."

"You've changed your mind about moving?" he asked conversationally, his gaze slipping from her to the television screen and back. Charlotte, however, wasn't fooled. Like any other man, he would enjoy watching her squirm.

His eyes wandered back to the silent TV. He made a fist, then jerked his elbow back in a gesture of satisfaction. Obviously things were going well for whichever team he was rooting for—much better than they were for her.

"I'd prefer not to move… Carrie and I like living where we do. The area suits us and, well…to be honest, I spoke in anger." This was all she was willing to give. If he was vindictive enough to demand she vacate the apartment, then so be it. She wasn't going to beg.

"Fine, then." He shrugged. "You're a good tenant and I'd hate to lose you." His gaze didn't waver from the television.

"Who's playing?"

He seemed surprised by her question, as though she should know something so elementary. "The Lakers and the Denver Nuggets."

"Go ahead and turn up the sound if you want."

He frowned. "You don't mind?"

"Of course not. I interrupted your game. If I'd known you were watching it, I would've waited until it was over." She took a swig of beer so he'd realize she intended to be on her way shortly.

He reached for the remote control with an eagerness he didn't bother to disguise. He pushed the volume button, dropped his leg and scooted forward, immediately absorbed in the game.

Charlotte didn't know that much about sports. Generally they bored her, but perhaps that was because she didn't understand the rules. No one had ever taken the time to explain them to her. Football seemed absolutely senseless, and basketball hardly less so.

As far as she could tell, basketball involved a herd of impossibly tall men racing up and down a polished wooden floor, passing a ball back and forth until one of them forged ahead to the basket to try to score. It seemed that whenever the contest became interesting, the referees would blow their whistles and everything would come to a grinding halt. She couldn't understand why the referees chose to wear zebra-striped shirts, either, since it wasn't likely anyone would confuse the short, balding men with the players.

"Who's winning?" That was innocuous enough, she decided. Such a simple question wouldn't reveal the extent of her ignorance.

"For now, the Lakers. They're up by four, but the lead's been changing the entire game."

"Oh." She watched for several minutes, then asked what she considered to be another harmless question. "Why do some throws count for three points and others only two?"

The thoroughness of his response astonished her, prompting several more questions. By the time he'd answered them all, he must've been aware that she barely knew one end of the court from the other. But if he was shocked by her lack of knowledge, he didn't let it show.

Soon Charlotte found herself actually enjoying the game. Now that it made a bit more sense, she began to understand why Jason liked it so much. The score was tied a minute before halftime and when the Lakers scored at the buzzer to take the lead, Charlotte leapt to her feet and cheered.

Jason raised his eyebrows at her display of enthusiasm, which made Charlotte all the more self-conscious. Slowly she lowered herself back into the chair. "Sorry," she mumbled.

"Don't be. I just didn't expect you'd be the type to appreciate sports."

"Generally I'm not. This is the first time I've had any idea what was going on."

A patronizing smile flashed in and out of his eyes. But that one instant was enough. Charlotte recognized the look; she'd seen other men wear the same expression. Men seemed to assume that because they could change their own oil and hook up a TV by themselves, they were naturally superior to women. Charlotte had run into that attitude most of her life.

Since it was her duty to defend womankind, and because she'd been fortified with a beer, Charlotte jumped to her feet. "Don't get haughty with me, Jason Manning!" she said.

Trying to recover her dignity, she sat back down, tucking one leg beneath her. "You think just because you happen to know a few sports rules, men are superior to women."

"We are," he returned wholeheartedly, without the least bit of reservation.

Charlotte laughed. "At least you're honest. I'm sick of men who pay lip service to women, then go into the men's room and snicker behind our backs."

"I'm honest to a fault," Jason agreed. "I'm willing to snicker right in front of you."

"Somehow I don't find that much of a compliment."

"Hey, admit it. Men *are* superior, and if you haven't owned up to it by now, you should. Don't forget, God created us first."

"Give me a break," Charlotte said, rolling her eyes.

"All right. If you can, name one thing a woman does better than a man, other than having babies, which is a given."

"I'll improve on that. I'll name…several."

"Several? You won't be able to come up with one."

"Okay, then," Charlotte said, accepting his challenge. "Women are more sensitive than men. Really," she added when he snorted in response.

"Sure, you cry in movies. That negates your whole argument."

"I'm not talking about crying." She frowned at him. "I'm referring to feelings! Women aren't afraid to face their feelings. Men are so terrified of emotion they hold it inside until they're totally bent out of shape."

Jason laughed, although grudgingly. "I suppose you think women are smarter than men, too."

"No," she said sincerely. "I'd say we're about even in that department."

"Go on," he urged, as though he suspected she'd depleted her list.

"Another thing. Women are better at multitasking than men. We're used to juggling all kinds of responsibilities."

Jason snickered.

"I'm serious," she returned. "If you think about it, you'll realize it's true. Women are expected to help support the family financially. Not only that, we're *also* expected to assume the role of emotional caretaker. Responsibility for the family falls on the woman's shoulders, not the man's. Have you ever noticed how rarely men put the needs of others before their own?"

"'Needs,'" Jason echoed. "Good grief, what's *that?* Some pop-psych buzzword."

Charlotte ignored him. "Frankly, I feel sorry for you guys. You've been allowed to remain children most of your lives. You've never been given the chance to grow up."

Jason looked as though he wanted to argue with her, but couldn't come up with an adequate rebuttal.

"Women handle pain better than men, too." Charlotte

was on a roll. "I've never seen a bigger baby in my life than a man who's got a minor case of the flu. Most of them act as though we should call in the World Health Organization."

"I suppose you're going to drag the horrors of giving birth into this now—which, I'll remind you, is completely unfair."

"I don't need to. Men have a hard time just dealing with a simple cold. If God had left procreation up to the male of the species, humanity would've died out with Adam."

"That's three," Jason muttered ungraciously. "Three is not several. Three is a *few*."

Charlotte shook her head. "It's enough. You don't have a leg to stand on, but you're too proud to admit it, which is something else a woman's more capable of doing."

"What? Standing on one leg?"

"No, admitting she's wrong. Don't get me started on that one. It happens to be a personal peeve of mine."

"You mean the others weren't?"

"Not particularly. I was just listing a few of the more obvious facts, waiting for you to come up with even one logical defense—which you failed to do."

He didn't seem willing to agree, but it was apparent from the smile he ineffectively struggled to hide that he was aware of his dilemma. He had no option, no argument.

"You realize you've backed me into a corner, don't you? I don't have any choice but to agree with you, otherwise you'll brand me as being smug and insensitive, unaware of my feelings and too childish to accept the truth."

"I suppose you're right." If anyone was wearing a smug look, it was Charlotte. She felt triumphant, better than she had all day. All week. Come to think of it, she couldn't remember when she'd enjoyed herself more.

Conceding defeat, Jason moved into the kitchen and

returned with a second cold beer for each of t
lotte hesitated. She'd never intended to stay this
Carrie might be concerned. After all the lectures sh
livered about being gone longer than expected, Char
felt she should go home now. But, to her amazement, s
discovered she didn't want to leave. Watching the rest of
the Lakers game with Jason appealed to her a lot more.

"Thanks, anyway, but I should get back to Carrie," she said.

Although she smiled brightly, some of her reluctance must have shown because Jason said, "So soon?"

"I stayed much longer than I'd planned to."

"But the game's only half over."

"I know, but…"

"Why don't you call her?" Jason suggested, pointing toward the counter where he kept his phone.

It seemed like a reasonable idea. Charlotte smiled and headed for the kitchen. She punched out her number and waited. Carrie answered on the third ring.

"Oh, hi, Mom," she said in an unconcerned voice.

"I'm watching the Lakers game with Jason."

"Okay. We're not going to move, are we?"

"No, Jason was kind enough to let me withdraw my two-weeks' notice."

"Oh, good. He's a great guy, isn't he?"

"Yeah." Charlotte was surprised by how much she meant it. Jason *was* a great guy. She hadn't stumbled on many in the past few—or was that several?—years. It was a treat to encounter a man who was candid, sincere and fun. But Charlotte had been fooled by men before, so she wasn't taking anything for granted.

"Well?" Jason asked when she replaced the receiver.

If she needed an excuse, he was handing her one on a platter. All she needed to do was make some vague reply about Carrie and she'd be on her way.

"Carrie says she'll call if she needs me."

"Excellent."

His smile was definitely charming, Charlotte decided.

"How about some popcorn?" he asked.

Charlotte nodded eagerly. She hadn't eaten much dinner, unnerved as she was by her discovery, knowing she'd need to confront him. Jason's offhand acceptance of her apology endeared him to her even more. If Jason was like her boss, he'd have flayed her alive. Instead, he'd just shrugged it off and given her a beer.

"Let me help," she said, following him into the kitchen.

"There's not much to do," he said, opening his microwave and tossing a bag inside. He set the timer, pushed a button and within a minute the sound of popping kernels filled the kitchen. The smell was heavenly.

When it was ready, Jason poured the popcorn into a large bowl and carried it out to the living room. Charlotte brought paper towels, since she couldn't find any napkins.

He placed the bowl in the middle of the coffee table and Charlotte joined him on the sofa. The game was about to resume. She tucked her feet beneath her as she'd done earlier, leaning forward now and then to scoop up some popcorn. It tasted wonderful, but that might've been because of the company. Or the fact that for the first time all day, she was feeling relaxed.

The Lakers scored twelve straight points and Charlotte rose to her knees, cheering loudly. Normally she was far more reserved, more in control of her emotions. It was as if someone else had taken charge of her mind. Someone more free-spirited and uninhibited. Someone who'd downed two beers on a near-empty stomach. Apparently, hearing that her daughter was bribing men to date her had that kind of effect on her.

Jason cheered, too, and they turned to smile at each

other. Their eyes met and held for the longest time. Flustered and unnerved, Charlotte was the first to glance away.

She hadn't shared such an intense look with a man since college. A look that said, I'm enjoying myself. I'm attracted to you. I'd like to get to know you better…a whole lot better.

Her heart was thumping as she forced her attention back to the TV. She took a deep swallow of beer to hide her discomfort.

Jason went strangely quiet afterward, too. They both made a pretense of being involved in the game. As time went on, however, it wasn't the Lakers who held their attention—it was each other.

"So," Jason said abruptly, "where do you work?"

"Downtown, for a large insurance agency. You might've heard of them. Davidson and Krier. They have a radio commercial that's played a lot." In an effort, weak though it was, to disguise her uneasiness, she sang the all-too-familiar jingle.

"I have heard of them," Jason said, nodding. His rich baritone concluded the song.

They laughed self-consciously. Charlotte wished she'd had the sense to leave at halftime. No, she amended silently, that wasn't true. She was glad she'd stayed. If she regretted anything, it was that she was so clumsy when it came to dealing with male-female relationships.

Maybe it wasn't so strange that Carrie had tried to bribe someone to ask her on a date. Charlotte hadn't been out with a man in three years. But she hadn't really missed the dating scene. How could she miss something she'd never actually experienced? She'd hardly dated at all since Tom left.

Tom. The accustomed pain she felt whenever she thought of her ex-husband followed on the heels of the unexpected attraction she felt toward Jason. The two didn't mix well. One brought back the pain of the past and reminded her that she had no future. The other tempted her to believe she did.

"I should be going," she announced suddenly, her decision made. She scurried to her feet as if she had a pressing appointment.

"The game's not over," Jason said, frowning. He didn't move for a moment. "Don't go yet."

"I'll watch the rest of it at my place. Thanks so much for the wonderful evening. I enjoyed myself. Really, I did." She picked up the empty popcorn bowl and the two beer bottles and took them into the kitchen.

Jason trailed her, his hands buried deep in his pockets. He nodded at his garbage can, which was overflowing. There was a semicircle of half-filled bags stacked around it.

"I've been meaning to take this out to the Dumpster," he explained, removing the bottles from her hands and throwing them into a plastic recycling bin.

"I appreciate how understanding you've been," Charlotte said as she walked to the door.

"About what?" he asked.

"Carrie and me and…everything."

"No problem," he said a few steps behind. He slipped in front of her and stood by the door.

Charlotte knew she was running away like a frightened rabbit. The trapped feeling had returned and it terrified her as it always had. She'd thought it would be different this time, but that had been the beer. Her fears would never change, never go away. They'd always be there to remind her of her shortcomings, how inadequate she was, how no man could ever be trusted. Tom had proved that. She was anxious to be on her way now, but Jason was blocking her only means of escape.

When she glanced up, some of the fear must have shown in her eyes because he hesitated, studying her.

There was a short silence, too deep to last long, but too intense to ignore. Charlotte held his gaze for as long as she dared before looking away. His eyes were so blue, so serious, so filled with questions. She'd perplexed him, she knew, but she couldn't explain. *Wouldn't* explain.

They'd laughed and teased and joked. But Jason was somber now. Funny, this mood was as appealing as the lightheartedness she'd sensed in him earlier. His mouth, even when he wasn't smiling, was perfectly shaped. Everything about him was perfect. His high cheekbones, his wide brow and straight nose. Too perfect for her.

The paralyzing regret threatened to explode within her, but Charlotte managed to keep it in check. How, she wasn't sure. It must've been her fear, she decided. Fear of what could happen, the happiness a relationship with him could bring—and the disappointment that would inevitably come afterward. The disappointment he'd feel in her. Then it would be over almost before it had begun.

She looked up one last time, to say goodbye, to thank him, to escape.

In that instant she knew Jason was going to kiss her. But one word, the least bit of resistance, and he wouldn't go through with it. Charlotte was completely confident of that.

Need and curiosity overcame the anxiety, and she watched, mesmerized, as his mouth descended toward her own. His lips, so warm and seductive, barely touched hers.

Charlotte closed her eyes, trembling and afraid. Her body, seemingly of its own accord, moved toward him, turning into his, seeking the security and the strength she felt in him.

He moaned softly and Charlotte did, too, slanting her head to one side, inviting him to deepen the kiss.

Yet Jason held back. The kiss was light. Sweet. More seductive than anything she'd ever known. It felt wonderful. So wonderful…

Charlotte didn't understand why he resisted kissing her completely, the way her body was begging him to. Restraining himself demanded obvious effort. She could tell by the rigid way he held himself, the way his hands curved over her shoulders, keeping her at bay. Keeping himself at bay.

Her head was full of the promise his lips had made and hadn't kept. Full of the possibilities. Full of the surprise and the wonder. She'd never felt like this before.

Once again his mouth brushed over hers, warm and exciting. Moving slowly—so slowly—and so easy, as though he had all the time in the world.

"Jason." It was a battle for her to breathe. Her heart sounded like a frantic drumbeat in her ears, drowning out coherent thought.

He tensed, then kissed her, really kissed her, wrapping himself around her, absorbing her in his size, his strength, his need.

They remained entwined, arms around each other, until Charlotte could no longer stand. She broke away and buried her head in his shoulder, her breathing heavy.

"Charlotte, I didn't mean to frighten you."

"You didn't." It was the truth; any fear she felt had nothing to do with him. "I have to go… Thank you. For everything."

But most of all for that kiss, she added silently. It was unlikely he'd ever know how much that single kiss had meant to her.

Three

He'd kissed her. He'd actually kissed Charlotte. An hour later, Jason still had trouble taking it in.

Oh, he'd kissed plenty of women in his day. But this time, with this woman, it was different. He didn't know how he understood that, but he did. He'd realized it long before he'd touched her. Perhaps because she was so different from what he'd assumed. He'd figured she was dignified, straitlaced, unapproachable. Then, as soon as he'd told her about basketball rules, she'd kicked off her shoes and was cheering as enthusiastically as he was himself. What a contrast he found in her. Prim and proper on the outside, a hellion waiting to break loose on the inside.

She intrigued him. Beguiled him.

At some point during their evening together—exactly when, he couldn't be sure—he'd felt an unfamiliar tug, a stirring deep within. The feeling hadn't gone away. If anything, it had intensified.

What they'd shared wasn't any ordinary kiss, either. Perhaps that explained it. They'd communicated on an entirely different level, one he'd never known before. It seemed their spirits—the deepest, innermost part of themselves—had somehow touched. He shook his head. He was getting fanciful.

No, this wasn't the kind of kiss he'd had with any other woman. He'd never gone so slowly, been so careful. Although she'd acted blatantly provocative, urging him to deepen the contact, he'd resisted. That same inner voice that had said Charlotte was different had also warned him to proceed with caution. He'd sensed how fragile she was, and the urge to protect her, even from himself, had been overwhelming.

Jason wasn't generally so philosophical. He didn't waste time deliberating on relationships or motivations. He wasn't sure what he was thinking right now. His reaction to Charlotte was unwarranted—wasn't it? Although it'd been a nice kiss, it wasn't so spectacular that his whole world should be turned upside down.

Yet it was—flipped over completely.

Jason felt almost giddy with sensation. These feelings weren't logical. It was as if God had decided to play a world-class trick on him.

Jason considered himself too old for romance. He didn't even know what romance was. Pure foolishness, he thought sarcastically. It was one of the primary reasons he'd never married, and never intended to. He wasn't a romantic kind of guy. A pizza and cold beer while watching a football game interested him far more than staring across a candlelit table at some woman and pretending to be overwhelmed by her beauty. Flattery and small talk weren't for him.

And yet…he remembered how good Charlotte's arms had felt around his neck. She'd held her body so tightly against his that he could feel her heart beat. It was a closeness that had transcended the physical.

By the time she'd left, Jason felt heady, as if he'd had

too much to drink. He didn't understand her rush, either. He hadn't wanted her to leave and had tried to come up with a reason for her to stay. Any reason. But she'd quietly slipped out of his arms and left before he could think of a way to keep her there. If he was witty and romantic he might've thought of something. But he wasn't, so he'd been forced to let her go.

Jason started pacing, the Lakers game forgotten. He needed to clear the cobwebs from his head. He wasn't any good at analyzing situations like this. All he knew was that he'd enjoyed holding Charlotte in his arms, enjoyed kissing her, and he looked forward to doing it again.

He sank down in front of the television, surprised to find the basketball game already over. Stunned, he stared at the credits rolling down the screen. He didn't even know who won. He waited, hoping the camera would scan the scoreboard, but it didn't happen.

He had a bet riding on the outcome of the game. Nothing major, just a friendly wager between brothers. Nevertheless, high stakes or low, it wasn't like Jason Manning to be caught without a final score.

The phone rang and Jason hurried to the kitchen to answer it.

"Hello," he said absently, keeping his eye on the television, still hoping to learn the final outcome.

"I knew I never should've picked the Nuggets," Rich muttered.

"You mean the Lakers won?"

"By eight points. Where have *you* been all evening?"

"Home," Jason returned defensively. "I had company. A tenant stopped in to chat."

"During a play-off game, and you didn't get rid of them?"

Actually Jason hadn't intended to tell his brother even

that much, but Rich had a point. Jason wasn't one to sit around and shoot the breeze when he could be watching a game. Any kind of game.

"It was business," he explained, unnecessarily annoyed. He felt mildly guilty for stretching the truth. Charlotte's original intent had been to apologize and tell him she'd changed her mind about moving. That was business. Staying the better part of two hours wasn't.

Ignoring Jason's bad mood, Rich chatted on, replaying the last half of the fourth quarter in which the Lakers had made an "amazing" comeback. While his brother was speaking, Jason glanced at the list of his tenants' phone numbers, which he kept by the phone for easy reference. The way his eyes immediately latched on to Charlotte's name, anyone might think it had been circled in red. He was so distracted by reading her name over and over in his mind that he missed most of what Rich was telling him.

When the conversation with his brother ended, Jason couldn't recall more than a few words of what they'd said. Just enough to regret that he hadn't been watching the game. Just enough to wish he'd thought of something that would've prompted Charlotte to stay.

Without a second's deliberation, he reached for his phone and dialed her number. Carrie answered before the first ring had been completed. She must not have recognized his voice, because she got Charlotte without comment.

"Hello."

"Hi," he said, feeling gauche. "The Lakers won."

"I know."

Apparently their kiss hadn't deranged her the way it had him. She must have gone back to her apartment, plunked herself down and watched the rest of the game, while he'd been walking around in a stupor for the past hour.

"I was thinking," Jason began, "about dinner tomorrow night. That is, if you're free."

"Dinner," she repeated as if this was a foreign concept. "What time?" she asked a moment later.

"Six."

"Sure."

His mood lightened. "Great, I'll pick you up then." He replaced the receiver and glanced around his kitchen, frustrated by how messy it was. He hated housework, hated having to pick up after himself, hated the everyday chores that made life so mundane. Every dish he owned was dirty, except the ones in his dishwasher, which were clean. It didn't make sense to reload it while there were clean dishes he could use in there.

Needing something to occupy his mind, he tackled the task of cleaning up the kitchen with unprecedented enthusiasm.

Jason's eagerness to see Charlotte again had waned by the following afternoon. A good night's sleep and a day at the clinic had sufficiently straightened out his brain. He'd behaved in a manner that was completely out of character. He couldn't even begin to figure out why.

Charlotte was a woman. There wasn't anything special about her. No reason he should be falling all over himself for the opportunity to take her out. He'd missed the last half of an important basketball game because his thoughts had become so tangled up with her. That would've been devotion enough for any woman in his life—only she wasn't in his life, and he intended to keep it that way.

Furthermore, Jason wasn't that keen on Charlotte's teenage daughter thinking he'd fallen in with her scheme. He could see it now. Carrie would give him a brilliant smile and a high-five when he arrived. The girl was bound to believe she was responsible for Jason asking Charlotte out. She might even try to slip him some of the money she'd offered him earlier. The whole thing had the potential for disaster written all over it.

If a convenient excuse to cancel this date had presented itself, Jason would've grabbed it with both hands.

The way his luck was going, they'd probably run into his parents, and his mother would start hounding him again about getting married. He'd never understood why women considered marriage so important. Frustrated, he'd asked his mother once, and her answer had confused him even more. She'd looked at him serenely without interrupting the task that occupied her hands and had casually said, "It's good to have a partner."

A partner! She'd made it sound like he needed a wife in order to compete in a mixed bowling league.

His parents weren't exactly throwing potential mates his way, but they'd let it be known that they were hoping he'd get married sometime soon. Jason, however, was intelligent enough not to become involved in a lifetime relationship just to satisfy his parents' wishes.

Whatever craziness had prompted him to ask Charlotte out to dinner had passed during the night. He'd awakened sane and in command of his usual common sense.

As the day went on he found himself actually dreading the date. The two of them had absolutely nothing in common. He'd go through with this, Jason decided grimly, because he was a man of his word. Since he told her he'd be there by six, he would be, but snow would fall at the equator before he gave in to an impulse like this again.

She was dressed completely wrong, Charlotte realized as soon as Jason arrived. Not knowing what to wear, she'd chosen a navy blue suit, not unlike the one she'd worn to the office. She'd attempted to dress it up a bit with a bright turquoise-and-pink scarf and a quarter-size silver pin of a colorful toucan. Jason arrived in jeans, a sweatshirt and a baseball cap with a University of Washington Huskies logo on it.

"Hello," she said, forcing herself to smile. A hundred times in the last hour she'd regretted ever agreeing to this date. Jason had caught her off guard when he'd phoned. She hadn't known what to say. Hadn't had time to think of an excuse.

Now she was stuck, but judging by his expression, Jason didn't seem any more pleased than she was. He frowned at her until she was so self-conscious, she suggested changing clothes.

"Don't worry about it," he muttered, tucking the tips of his fingers into his back pockets. They definitely made a pair. He'd dressed like someone visiting the amusement park, and she looked like a student of Emily Post.

Charlotte was grateful that Carrie had gone to the library with a friend. The other mom was picking them up, but it would give Charlotte a convenient excuse to hurry home.

"Where would you like to eat?" Jason asked once they were outside the apartment.

"Wherever you want."

"Mexican food?" He didn't sound enthusiastic.

"Fine." Especially since there was a restaurant close by. "How about Mr. Tamales on Old Military Road?"

"Sure," he agreed easily enough. He was probably thinking the same thing she was. The sooner they got there, the sooner they'd be finished and could go back to their respective lives instead of dabbling in this nonsense.

For the short time they were together, Charlotte figured she might as well enjoy herself. The restaurant was little more than a greasy spoon, but the food had earned its excellent reputation.

The place apparently did a brisk business on weeknights because there was only one spot available.

"I never would've thought we'd need reservations," Jason said, looking as surprised as Charlotte.

The hostess, wearing an off-the-shoulder peasant blouse and black skirt, smiled and escorted them to the booth. The waitress followed close behind. She handed them each a menu shaped like a cactus and then brought water, tortilla chips and salsa. Charlotte read over the choices, made her selection and scooped up a jalapeño pepper with a chip.

"You aren't going to eat that, are you?" Jason asked, staring at her as if she'd pulled the pin activating a grenade.

Charlotte grinned. "Oh, that's another thing I forgot to mention last night—women can eat chili peppers better than a man."

"Not this time, sweetheart. I was weaned on hot peppers." He took one, poising it in front of his mouth.

"Me, too," she challenged.

They bit into the peppers simultaneously. The seeds and juice dribbled down Charlotte's chin and she grabbed a paper napkin, dabbing it against her skin.

"You weren't kidding," Jason said, obviously impressed.

"I never kid." A five-alarm fire was blazing in her mouth, but she smiled and reached casually for another chip and some water. The water intensified the burning, but she smiled cheerfully as though nothing was wrong.

"Rich and I used to eat these peppers right out of Dad's garden."

"I take it Rich is your brother?"

"I'm one of five," Jason went on to explain, and she noted that his eyes brightened with pride. "Paul's the oldest, then there's me, followed by Rich. My sisters, Taylor and Christy, round out the family."

"Are any of them married?"

"Everyone but me. I'm beginning to lose track of how many nieces and nephews I've got now, and there doesn't seem to be a lull yet."

Charlotte had never had much of a family. Her father had deserted her and her mother when Charlotte was too young to remember him. Then her mother had died just about the time Charlotte graduated from high school. The insurance money was set up to cover her college expenses. Only the money hadn't been used for her. Instead, Tom had been educated on her inheritance; he'd robbed her of even that.

Charlotte lowered her gaze. It hurt too much to think about Tom and that bleak period of her life when she'd been so lost and vulnerable. So alone, with no family. Her ex-husband had used her and when he'd finished, he'd thrown her aside.

All the time she was growing up, Charlotte had dreamed about being part of a large, loving family. How she envied Jason his brothers and sisters.

"The story of my family tree is less about the roots," he said, grinning as he spoke, "than the sap."

Charlotte's laugh was spontaneous. She picked up her water, warmed by his wit and his willingness to laugh at himself. "I was an only child. I promised myself I'd have a houseful of kids when I got married so my children wouldn't grow up lonely."

"Lonely," Jason echoed. "I would have given anything for some peace and quiet. The girls were the worst."

"Somehow I guessed you'd complain about the women in your family."

"You know," he said, "I never thought I'd say this, but

I really miss Taylor and Christy. They're both living in Montana now, raising their families. We get together when we can, which isn't nearly often enough. It's been over a year since we saw each other."

The waitress came for their order. Charlotte asked for the specialty salad, which consisted of beans, rice, cheese, shredded chicken, lettuce and slices of tomato and jalapeño peppers. Jason chose the chicken enchiladas.

"Do your brothers live in the Seattle area?"

Jason nodded. "Paul's a journalist and Rich works as an engineer for Boeing. We see each other frequently."

Their orders arrived and they chatted amicably over their meal. Jason sampled her salad and fed her a bite of his enchiladas; both were delicious. Soon they'd asked the waitress for two additional plates and were unabashedly sharing their meals.

It was only seven-thirty when they'd finished, even though they lingered over coffee. Charlotte couldn't remember time passing more quickly.

All day she'd been worried about this dinner—and for nothing. She'd enjoyed herself even more than she'd hoped, but that was easy to do with Jason. He didn't put on airs or pretend to be something he wasn't. Nor did he feign agreement with her; their differing opinions meant a free and interesting exchange of ideas.

"I should be heading home," Charlotte said, although she could happily have sat there talking. They weren't at a loss for topics, but the restaurant was busy and Carrie would be home soon.

"Yeah, I suppose we should go," he said reluctantly, standing. He left a generous tip and took the tab up to the counter.

After talking nonstop for nearly an hour, both were strangely quiet on the drive home. Charlotte had been determined to enjoy herself from the start, but she'd expected to make the best of a bad situation. Instead she'd had a wonderful time.

She hadn't known how starved she was for adult companionship, hadn't realized how empty she'd felt inside, how deep the void had become.

As they neared the apartment complex, she realized one more thing. She didn't want this evening to end.

"Would you like to come in for coffee?" she asked as he parked his car. For half the ride home, Charlotte had been engaging in a silent debate. She was sure that if Carrie was home, she'd make a big deal about Jason's presence. But Charlotte would get the third degree from her daughter anyway, so she decided it didn't matter if Jason came in.

"I could use another cup of coffee," Jason told her, although they'd both had large mugs at the restaurant.

As luck would have it, Carrie wasn't home yet. Charlotte had been counting on her teenage daughter to act as a buffer between her and Jason. She half suspected Jason was thinking the same thing.

"Carrie's at the library with a friend," she explained. "But I'm sure she'll be back any minute."

"I wondered what she was up to tonight."

"I'll put on the coffee," she said self-consciously, going directly to the kitchen. "Make yourself at home."

While she scooped up the grounds and poured water into the pot, she saw that Jason had lowered himself onto her sofa. He reached for a magazine and flipped through the pages, then set it back and reached for another. Since it was upside down, his attention was clearly elsewhere. He noted his mistake, righted the magazine, then placed it with the others. Apparently *Seventeen* magazine didn't interest him after all.

There was no reason for him to be so nervous. It was

funny; they'd chatted like old friends at the restaurant, but the instant they were alone, they became uncomfortable with each other.

"I thought you might like some cookies," she said, as she carried the tray into the living room. She'd baked chocolate chip cookies that weekend, and there were plenty left over.

Being a single mother left her vulnerable to attacks of guilt—guilt that often led to an abundance of homemade cookies. There were so many things she didn't know about family, so much she'd missed out on. It bothered her more than she wanted to admit. Whenever Charlotte was feeling anxious or contrite about something, she baked. And with the ninth-grade dance hanging over her head, she'd been doing a lot of baking lately. The cookie jar was full. The freezer was packed, too. Even Carrie was complaining about all the goodies around the house. Too tempting, she said. Her daughter claimed Charlotte was trying to raise her cholesterol and kill her off.

More guilt, more need to bake cookies. It was a vicious circle.

"Homemade cookies," Jason said, sliding forward, far more appreciative than her daughter. "I didn't know anyone but my mother baked these days." He took one and downed it in two bites, nodding vigorously even before he'd finished chewing.

Charlotte smiled at the unspoken compliment and poured their coffee in plain white china cups. "There's plenty more where those came from."

Jason helped himself to a second and then a third.

Charlotte was pleased that he seemed to value her culinary skills. "I guess it's true, then."

He cocked one eyebrow. "What?"

"Never mind," she muttered, sorry she'd brought up the subject.

"If you're thinking the way to a man's heart is through his stomach, forget it. Others before you have tried that route."

"Several dozen, no doubt," she teased, amused by his complete lack of modesty. Not to mention his arrogance.

"I've suffered my share of feminine wiles."

"Feminine wiles," Charlotte repeated, trying hard not to laugh out loud. He acted as though she was setting a trap for him. She was about to reassure him that she had no intention of remarrying, then decided against it. She'd let him assume whatever he wanted. After all, he was helping her get rid of these cookies before they overran the apartment.

She did bring up another topic, though, one she couldn't help being curious about. "Why aren't you married?" She hoped he wouldn't be offended by her directness; based on their previous conversations she didn't expect him to be.

Jason shrugged and swallowed the last bite of the last cookie she'd set out. He seemed to be thinking over his response as he picked up his coffee and relaxed against the back of the sofa. "I learned something recently about the differences between a man and a woman. It's information that's served me well."

They certainly had a routine going with this subject. "Oh, what's that?"

"Tell me, all kidding aside," he said, his blue eyes serious, "what is it women want from a man?"

Charlotte thought about that for a moment. "To be loved."

He nodded approvingly.

"To be needed and respected."

"Exactly." He grinned, clearly pleased by her answer.

He was making this easy, and Charlotte warmed to her

ideas. "A woman longs to be held, of course, but more than that, she wants to be treasured, appreciated."

"Perfect," Jason said, smiling benignly. "Now ask me what a man wants."

"All right," she said, crossing her legs, holding the saucer with one hand, her cup in the other. "What is it a man wants?"

"Tickets to the World Series," Jason returned without a pause.

Charlotte nearly choked on her laughter. Fortunately she wasn't swallowing a sip of coffee at the time. "I see what you mean," she said after she'd composed herself. "There does seem to be a basic, shall we say, disconnect here."

He nodded. "It was when Rich gave up two tickets for a Seahawks football game that I knew he'd fallen in love."

"That's sweet," Charlotte said with a sigh, enjoying the romance of it all.

"Don't go all soft on me. It wasn't like it sounds. He gave the tickets to a friend as a bribe. Rich didn't want to date Jamie himself, he wanted someone else to fall in love with her."

"He bribed another guy to take her out?"

"Yup. He was in love with her himself, but like the rest of us, he's useless when it comes to romance. I figured it out before he did, and I know next to nothing about that kind of stuff." Jason grinned. "From that point on, it was all downhill for Rich. He's married and has a couple of kids now. A girl and a boy."

"I don't care what you say. That's sweet."

"Perhaps."

Charlotte was relaxed now. She removed her shoes and propped her feet on the coffee table, crossing her legs at the ankles. "Have *you* ever been in love?" At Jason's hesitation, she hurried to add, "I shouldn't have asked that."

"I don't mind, if you won't take offense at my answer—which is, I don't know. I thought I was once, several years back, but in retrospect I'm not sure. It hurt when we broke up, and I was sorry we hadn't been able to work things out, but I don't have any real regrets."

"What was her name?"

"Julie. She's married now."

Charlotte didn't understand where she found the courage, but she reached forward and brushed her index finger down the side of Jason's face. She wanted to ease the pain she read in his expression, the pain he discounted so casually. A pain she recognized, since she'd walked through this valley herself, with the cold wind of despair howling at her back.

Jason's gaze met hers and she felt immersed in a look so warm, so intense, that her breath caught. She couldn't remember a man ever looking at her that way, as though he wasn't sure she was even real. As if he was afraid she'd vanish if he touched her.

Jason removed the cup and saucer from her hands and set them on the tray next to the empty plate.

He was going to kiss her; she realized it in the same moment she owned up to how much she wanted him to. All night she'd been looking forward to having him do exactly this, only she hadn't been willing to admit it.

His mouth was gentle and sweet with the taste of coffee and chocolate. He kissed her the way he had the night before, and Charlotte could barely take in the sensation that overwhelmed her. She'd never thought she'd feel anything so profound, so exciting, again. She hadn't believed she was capable of such a rush of feeling....

She whimpered and wrapped her arms around his neck, holding on to him in a world that had started to spin out of control. His hands framed her face and he slanted his mouth over hers, answering her need with his own.

Jason kissed her again and again.

The sound coming from the front door barely registered in her passion-drugged brain.

"Mom…Jason…" was followed by a shocked pause, then, "Wow, this is great."

Charlotte broke away from Jason and leapt to her feet.

"Gee, Mom, there's no need to get embarrassed. People kiss all the time." Carrie floated across the carpet, then threw herself into a chair. "So," she said, smiling broadly, "is there anything either of you want to tell me?"

"Like what?" Charlotte asked.

Carrie shrugged with utter nonchalance. "That you're getting married?"

Four

On his way back to his apartment, Jason had to admit that Charlotte's daughter possessed a knack for the unexpected. Arriving when she did was only the beginning; introducing the subject of marriage had nearly sent him into hysterics.

Him married? It was downright laughable.

Thinking about it, Jason realized Charlotte had brought up the subject herself, wanting to know why he hadn't married, asking him if he'd ever been in love. Typical women questions.

Perhaps mother and daughter were in cahoots, plotting his downfall. No, that was equally laughable.

Jason simply wasn't the marrying kind. Not because he was a womanizer or because he had anything against the opposite sex. He liked women…at times and enjoyed being with them…occasionally. Liked kissing them… definitely. But he relished his freedom too much to sacrifice it to commitment and responsibility.

No, he told himself resolutely, Charlotte wasn't involved in any scheme to drag him to the altar. She'd been so embarrassed and flustered by Carrie's suggestion, her face had gone bright red. The woman's face was too open to hide her feelings. She had chastised Carrie, asked for and received an apology, and looked genuinely grateful when Jason said it was time he left.

Despite the episode with Carrie, Jason had thoroughly enjoyed his evening with Charlotte. He hadn't expected to. In fact he'd originally regretted having asked her out, but in the end their date had been a pleasant success.

Once again he was bewildered by the strong desire he experienced when he kissed her. He had ordained a hands-off policy for the night, but had shelved that idea the minute she'd sat next to him, gazing up at him with those pretty eyes of hers.

Actually, he'd known he was in trouble when he accepted her invitation to come inside for coffee. He'd thought of it as a challenge; he'd wanted to see how far he could push his determination. Not far, he concluded. When she'd looked at him, her eyes soft and inviting, he was lost. His hands-off policy had quickly become a hands-on experiment.

There was something about Charlotte Weston that got to him. Really got to him.

All that outward confidence she worked so hard to display hadn't fooled him. Beneath a paper-thin veneer, she was vulnerable. Any fool with two functional brain cells would have figured that out on the first date.

Only she didn't date.

Carrie had told him it'd been years since her mother had even gone out with a man. Undoubtedly she'd been asked—and if she hadn't been, why not? She was attractive, intelligent and fun. Offhand, he knew a half-dozen men who'd jump at the chance to meet a woman like Charlotte.

If she'd turned down offers, and surely she had, then there must be a reason. The question that confused Jason was: If she didn't date, then why had she agreed to have dinner with him?

Probably the same reason that had goaded him to ask, Jason concluded. The kiss. That infamous first kiss. It had rocked them both. Taken them by surprise, leaving them excited—and unsure.

As for the other questions that hounded him, Jason didn't have any answers. Nor did he understand everything that was happening between him and Charlotte. One thing he did know—and it terrified him the most—was that they were, in effect, playing with lighted sticks of dynamite, tossing them back and forth. The attraction between them was that explosive. That dangerous.

Carrie's arrival had been more timely than she'd realized.

All right, Jason was willing to own up, albeit grudgingly, that he was fascinated with Charlotte. He suspected she'd confess to feeling the same thing. To his way of thinking, if they were so strongly attracted to each other, they should both be prepared to do something about it.

In other words, they should stop fighting the inevitable and make love. That would get it out of their system—he hoped.

Naw, Jason mused darkly. Charlotte wasn't the kind of woman who'd indulge in an affair. She might wear only straight, dark business suits to work, but deep down she was the romantic type, which made her impractical. Most women seemed to be. If they were going to make love, they wanted it prettied up with a bunch of flowery words, a declaration of undying love and promises of commitment.

Well, Charlotte, along with every other woman, could forget that, he told himself. As far as he was concerned, romance and commitment were out of the question.

What he wanted in this relationship was honesty. If it

were up to him, he'd suggest they do away with the formalities, admit what they wanted and then scratch that itch.

He mulled that over for a few minutes, knowing it was unlikely that Charlotte would see the situation his way. He might not know her well, but Jason readily acknowledged that she wasn't going to be satisfied with so little. Women tended to see lovemaking as more than just the relief of a physical craving.

Well, he, for one, wasn't going to play that game. He liked Charlotte—how much he liked her surprised him—but he knew the rules. Either they dropped everything now, while they still could, or they continued driving each other insane. Sooner or later, one of them would have to give in.

Without a second's hesitation, Jason knew it would be him.

Charlotte affected him deep down. He couldn't bear the thought of hurting her or causing her one second of unhappiness. In the end he'd say all the words she wanted to hear, and he'd do the best job he could, because pleasing her would mean so much to him.

Then he'd get what he wanted; she'd make love to him willingly, with everything in her. He'd give her all he had, too. The problem was—and he knew it was inevitable—that before he'd quite figured out what was happening, they'd be talking about marriage, which was something he hadn't done since Julie.

Jason stopped right there. If he started thinking along those lines, everything would change. Soon Charlotte would be organizing his life, straightening up his apartment, making suggestions about little things he could do to improve his sorry lot. Women always saw his lot as sorry. He was happy living the way he was, but women couldn't accept that. They didn't believe a man could survive without them constantly fussing over him, dictating his life.

Bit by bit, Charlotte would dominate his world, eroding his independence until he was like every other married man he'd ever known—willing to change his ways for a wife. Picking up his socks, getting hassled about sports games on TV, the whole deal.

No, the domesticated life wasn't for him. Still, Charlotte tempted him more than anyone else had in ages, and he could *almost* imagine their lives together. Not quite, but almost.

He stared at his apartment door, wondering how long he'd been standing there mulling over his thoughts. He was light-years ahead of himself, he realized. Good grief, he was already trying to finagle his way out of marrying her and they'd only gone out on one date. He'd only kissed her twice.

But, oh, those kisses…

Like he'd told himself before, they were playing with explosives, and the best way to avoid getting hurt was to get out now, before they became too involved. Before he lost the strength to walk away from her.

"Aren't you going to *do* something?" Carrie demanded.

"About what?" Charlotte returned calmly, feigning ignorance. She glanced up from her novel, looking over the rims of her reading glasses with practiced innocence.

"Jason!" Carrie cried. "You haven't heard from him in a whole week."

"Has it been that long?" Seven days, two hours and three minutes, but who was counting? Certainly not her.

"Mom," Carrie insisted, hands on her hips, "you know how long it's been. You jump every time the phone rings. You keep making excuses about checking the mail and getting the newspaper. We both know you're hoping to run into Jason."

It hurt Charlotte's pride to learn she'd been so obvious.

"You like him, don't you?" Carrie asked. Her expression said that if *she* were in charge, this romance would be making far greater progress. Charlotte, however, had no intention of letting her daughter take control of her relationship with Jason Manning.

"I think Jason's wonderful," Charlotte admitted softly. She did like her landlord. Yet, at the same time, she was grateful he hadn't taken the initiative and contacted her again. If he had, she wasn't sure how she would've responded.

"If you're so crazy about him, then do something about it," Carrie said again.

"Like what?" Even if Charlotte had a drawerful of ideas, she doubted she'd ever find the courage to use any of them. She didn't know how to chase after a man and had no interest in doing so.

"You're asking me?" Carrie asked. "C'mon, who's the kid here?" She launched herself onto the cushion beside Charlotte. "What went wrong?" she asked, looking up at her mother with mournful eyes. "The two of you seemed to be getting along really well when I walked in last week."

Charlotte slid her arm around Carrie's shoulders. Despite her efforts not to, she grinned, remembering when she, too, had been so wise and confident.

"It might've had something to do with the subject of marriage—which *you* brought up. He seemed to get a bit green around the gills at that point."

"You think it frightened him off?" Carrie asked anxiously.

Charlotte shrugged. She'd brought up the subject herself, not quite as directly, but she *had* mentioned it. If ever there was a born bachelor, she decided, it was Jason Manning. Together, mother and daughter had managed to terrify the man. He must think they were sitting in their apartment ready to ambush him, tie him up and drag him in front of the closest preacher.

Charlotte wasn't sure what she wanted anymore. Perhaps she was protecting her ego by convincing herself that she wouldn't have gone out with Jason if he'd asked again. Perhaps it was just her pride. Charlotte didn't know because the opportunity hadn't come up.

She was embarrassed to admit it, but what Carrie had said about her hanging around the mailbox hoping to *accidentally* run into Jason was true. But she wasn't looking for a way to get him to ask her out, she told herself. She only wanted to set things straight. Since they hadn't met, accidentally or otherwise, Charlotte was content to let it drop. He apparently was, too.

Jason Manning had been a brief but pleasant interlude in her—she had to acknowledge it—humdrum life.

She was grateful for their time together. He'd taught her everything she needed to know about basketball. He'd challenged her in a battle of wits about male and female roles in society. Convinced her never again to eat a jalapeño pepper to prove a point. And most important, he'd kissed her in a way that made her believe, for those few minutes, that she was whole and desirable. It'd felt so good to surrender her fears and her doubts. If nothing else, she'd always be grateful for that.

"Maybe he's waiting to hear from you," Carrie said next. "It's your turn to ask him out, isn't it?"

"It doesn't work that way with adults, sweetie." Although Charlotte had no idea if that was even true.

"Then it should. I'm not going to sit home and wait for a man to call me. If I like him, I'll phone him. It's ridiculous to be a slave to such an outdated tradition."

Charlotte agreed with her daughter, but in this instance

she planned to do nothing at all. And that included hovering around the mailboxes.

It had been a long day, and Jason was tired when he pulled into the parking lot outside his apartment complex. He scanned the limited spaces, looking for Charlotte's car. The blue PT Cruiser was in the appropriate slot, so he knew she was home.

It wasn't that he was trying to run into her, but he wouldn't mind seeing her, finding out how she was doing—that sort of thing. He didn't intend anything more than a wave and maybe a friendly "I'm-fine-how-are-you?" exchange. Then he'd go about his business and she could go about hers.

Not calling Charlotte was proving to be more difficult than he'd ever expected. He thought about her even more now. He dreamed about her. Just that morning, the alarm had gone off and he was lying there in bed, trying to force himself to get up, when Charlotte casually sauntered into his mind. He couldn't help thinking how good it would feel to have her there beside him, how soft her body would feel next to his. He'd banished the thought immediately, angry about indulging in such a fantasy.

It had started the night before. When he'd arrived home from work, he'd found himself checking out the rear tire of Charlotte's car. From a distance it looked like it might be low on air. On closer examination, he realized it wasn't. He felt almost disappointed not to have an excuse to speak to her.

This evening he could tell from a distance that there wasn't anything wrong with her tires. Once again he wished there was, so he could talk to her.

Inside his apartment, he reached for the remote control

and automatically turned on the television. The six-thirty news crew made for excellent company.

As the forecaster gave dire warnings about the weather, Jason checked out the meager contents of his refrigerator. One of these days he'd have to break down and buy groceries.

As he suspected, nothing interesting presented itself, at least nothing he'd seriously consider eating. An empty cardboard carton from a six-pack of beer. A can of half-eaten pork and beans. A leftover taco, probably harder than cement, wrapped in a napkin, and a jar of green olives. He opened the jar, stuck his hand inside and fished out the last two, returning the container of liquid to the shelf. Chewing on the olives, he closed the door.

What he was really in the mood for was—he hated to admit it. What he'd really like was chocolate chip cookies. Well, he could forget that. The store-bought ones tasted like lumpy paste, and his mother would keep him on the phone with an endless list of questions if he were to call her and request a batch. Besides, it wasn't his mother's recipe he craved. It was Charlotte's.

Well, you can forget that, ol' boy.

A box of macaroni and cheese was the most interesting prospect his cupboard had to offer. He took it out and checked the freezer compartment of the refrigerator and brought out two frozen wieners wrapped in aluminum foil.

He was adding water to a pan when there was a frantic knocking on his door. Whoever it was pounded again before he had time to cross the apartment.

He saw Charlotte, pale and stricken, her lavender cardigan covered in blood. Her eyes were panicky. "A dog... someone ran over a dog...they didn't even stop. Please... can you come?"

"Of course." He kept a black bag at the house for just such emergencies. He grabbed that and hurried after her.

Charlotte was waiting for him, her eyes bright with tears. "He's unconscious."

"You moved him?"

"Only to get him out of the street."

"Did you see it happen?" he asked, trotting along behind her.

"No. I heard tires screech and a yelp, and that was it. By the time I got outside, a few kids had gathered around, but no one knew what to do."

Her pace slowed as they approached the injured animal. A group of neighborhood children had gathered around. Jason knelt beside the small black dog. He was a mixed breed, mostly spaniel, Jason guessed. He was badly hurt and in shock. Probably a stray, since he wasn't wearing a collar, and the poor thing looked mangy and thin.

"Does anyone know who he belongs to?" Jason asked.

"I don't think he belongs to anyone," a boy on a bicycle answered. "He's been around the last couple of days. I never saw him before that."

"I'm going to take him to my office," Jason said after a preliminary examination. He didn't feel too positive about the dog's chances.

"Is he going to live?" Charlotte alone voiced the question, but she seemed to be the spokesperson for the small gathering—each one wanted, indeed needed, to know. The children and Charlotte stared down at Jason, waiting for his response.

"I'm not sure," Jason answered honestly. "He's got a broken leg and internal injuries."

"I'll pay for his medical expenses," Charlotte offered, using her index finger to wipe a tear from her eye.

Jason wasn't even thinking about the expenses. Frankly,

he didn't think the dog would last the night. "Give me your sweater," he told Charlotte. Since it was already stained with blood, he figured they'd save time by using it to transport the injured dog.

She did as he asked, and he spread it out on the pavement, then placed the wounded dog on it. Jason carefully lifted him, using the sweater sleeves, and walked toward his car.

"I'll go with you," Charlotte said, while Jason placed the now-unconscious dog in the backseat.

"You're sure?" he asked. "This could take some time."

"I'm sure." Carrie came running up to the car. The girl had tears in her eyes, too. Mother and daughter briefly hugged before Carrie stepped away. She looked so mournful it was all Jason could do not to stop and reassure her. But he had no reassurances to offer.

His veterinary clinic was only a few blocks from the apartment complex. Charlotte followed him in. He set the injured dog on the stainless-steel examination table and turned on the lights above it. Charlotte's sweater was soaked with blood beyond the point of salvaging it, but she didn't seem concerned.

Jason examined the dog's injuries and it was as he'd feared: surgery would be required.

He told Charlotte and she nodded bravely. "Can I do anything? I'm not a nurse, but I'd like to assist—that is, if you think I'd be any help?"

Jason hesitated, uncertain, then decided. "You can if you really want to."

She nodded. "Please."

"You don't have to," he said. This wasn't going to be pretty and if she was the least bit squeamish, it would be better to sit out in the waiting room. He told her as much.

"I want to," she said confidently. "I can handle it."

Jason didn't take long to set up everything he needed for the surgery. They both scrubbed down and he gave her a green surgical cap and gown. He smiled at her before administering the anesthesia, taking pains to explain what he was doing and why.

The procedure didn't last more than an hour. When he'd finished, he transferred the dog to the hospital portion of his facility. There was a night-time staff member who'd watch over the spaniel and the other pets who required continuous care.

"What do you think?" she asked hopefully when he returned.

"It doesn't look promising," Jason told her. He didn't want to give her any false hopes or mislead her. "But he might surprise us. He's only a couple of years old and he's got a strong heart. The next twenty-four hours will be critical. If he survives until tomorrow night, then he should do okay. But he's going to need a lot of attention and love afterward."

"Carrie and I will make sure he gets it. Can we come see him?" She paused. "Do veterinary hospitals have visiting hours?"

"You can come anytime you like." He sighed and rubbed his hand along the back of his neck. He was tired and hungry.

"You were wonderful…." She seemed to sense his worry and exhaustion.

"Let's decide that in the morning."

"If Higgins lives, we'll owe everything to you."

"Higgins?"

"I thought it was a good name. Do you like it?"

He shrugged. He was too tired and too hungry to have much of an opinion on anything at the moment.

"You haven't had dinner, have you?" she surprised him by asking.

"No. How'd you know that?"

"You look hungry."

"That's because I am. You want to grab something?" he asked as if it were the most natural thing in the world.

She smiled. "Only this time I'll treat."

"Charlotte…"

"I insist. Please don't argue."

He didn't have the energy to protest, so he simply agreed. Since she was buying, he let her choose the restaurant. She decided on a nearby sandwich shop. He breathed in the scent of freshly baked bread as soon as he walked in the door.

It was the type of place where customers seated themselves and the silverware was wrapped in a red checkered napkin. The waitress, who looked all of sixteen, took their order, and promptly brought coffee. She came back a few minutes later with six-inch-high sandwiches, layered with sliced turkey, ham, roast beef, lettuce, tomato slices and onion.

"How have you been?" he asked casually after wolfing down the first half of his sandwich.

"Until the accident tonight I was just fine," Charlotte told him, her eyes flitting away from his. "I don't know what came over me. I'm usually not so emotional, but seeing that poor little dog on the road bleeding and hurt like that really got to me."

"It gets to me, too." The sight of an innocent animal suffering never failed to disturb Jason, although he saw it time and time again. The helplessness of the situation, the complete disregard for life that a hit-and-run accident revealed, angered him.

"I'm so glad you were home," Charlotte said, keeping

her gaze lowered. "I don't know what I would have done otherwise."

"I'm glad I was there, too." He reached across the table, taking her hand, linking their fingers. Her skin was smooth and soft, just the way he remembered.

His eyes sought hers. He smiled and she smiled back. Jason felt ridiculously, unreasonably pleased that they were together. For days he'd been fighting it, and now that they were together, he felt foolish for having put up such a struggle. He should quit worrying about the future, he told himself. Live for the moment. Wasn't that what all the self-help books said? One day at a time. One kiss at a time.

After what seemed like an eternity, Charlotte dragged her eyes from his.

"How about dessert?" he asked.

Charlotte picked up the menu and read over the limited selection.

"I was thinking more along the lines of homemade chocolate chip cookies," Jason said.

"They don't seem to have… Oh, you mean *mine?*" She raised eyes as blue as a summer sky.

He nodded enthusiastically. "I've reconsidered. It's true." His voice sounded slightly hoarse and, if he didn't know better, seductive.

"What is?"

"The way to my heart takes a direct route through my stomach."

"Oh." She blinked as if he'd caught her off guard. She was beautiful, he realized all over again. So gentle and caring. He'd missed her, yet he'd tried to convince himself otherwise, and had been doing a good job of it, too—too good, in fact.

The world seemed to stop. Jason knew his breathing did. He felt as if he were drowning in her eyes. He would've liked to blame it on how tired he was, but he'd only be lying to himself.

"You like softball?" he found himself asking next.

She nodded, obviously trying to keep her eyes averted from his. Apparently she was having a difficult time of it, because whenever their eyes met, it would be several moments before she looked away.

"I understand softball, more than basketball at any rate," she said, sounding slightly breathless.

"My brothers and I play on a team Saturday mornings. Do you and Carrie want to come and watch this weekend?"

Charlotte nodded.

"Good."

They were both silent on the way home. Jason knew he was going to kiss her again. He couldn't imagine *not* kissing her again.

Charlotte must have read his intentions, because her hand was on the car door the minute he shut off the engine. She reminded him of a trapped bird, eager to escape, and yet she didn't move.

His hand on her shoulder turned her toward him. His heart tripped wildly as she leaned toward him. He felt sure her heart was pounding as furiously as his.

Slowly, so slowly he wondered if he was dreaming it, Charlotte swayed closer. He lowered his mouth to hers. Jason wanted this kiss, wanted it more than he could remember wanting anything. It'd been over a week since he'd seen her and it felt like a lifetime. A thousand lifetimes.

Charlotte's hands were braced against his chest as he kissed her again, deeper, more fully. Again he kissed her, and again. Finally she broke away.

"Stop," she pleaded. The words were breathless and he could feel her shudder.

Reluctantly, Jason pulled back. Their eyes met again, and for the second time that night, Jason had the feeling she was frightened, although he didn't understand why. Wanting to comfort her, he traced a knuckle down the curve of her cheek.

"Carrie will be worried," she said.

He said nothing.

"I can't thank you enough. For saving Higgins. The dog."

Again Jason said nothing.

"Jason," she whispered. "Don't look at me like that."

"Like what?"

"Like you want to kiss me again."

"I do." He wasn't going to lie about it.

He saw that her hand was shaking as she opened the car door and climbed out. She seemed eager to make her escape now.

"Good night," she said with obvious false cheer.

"Little coward," Jason muttered under his breath, amused. "Saturday morning!" he shouted after her.

"What time?" She turned to face him again.

"Nine-thirty. Is that too early?"

"I'll be ready."

"I'll call you in the morning about Higgins."

"Please," she said, her eyes widening as though she'd momentarily forgotten the dog. "Oh, please do." She snapped open her purse and withdrew a business card, walking toward him now. "This is my number at the office. I'll be there after nine."

"Then I'll phone at nine."

"'Night."

"'Night," he echoed, returning to his apartment.

He wasn't there more than five minutes when his doorbell chimed. He certainly wasn't in the mood for company, but as the building owner and manager, he couldn't very well ignore a visitor.

He opened his door to discover Carrie standing on the other side, a covered plastic bowl in her hand. "These are for you."

He accepted the container with a puzzled frown.

"Mom asked me to bring you some chocolate chip cookies," she said, grinning broadly.

Five

"Mom, you look fine."

"I don't look fine…I look wretched," Charlotte insisted, viewing her backside in the hallway mirror. She must've been mad to let Carrie talk her into buying jeans. Fashionably faded jeans, no less. Not only had she plunked down ninety bucks for the pair, they looked as if they'd spent the past ten years in someone's attic.

"You're acting like a little kid," Carrie said, slapping her hands against her sides in disgust. "We're going to a softball game, not the senior prom."

"Why didn't you tell me my thighs are so…round?" Charlotte cried in despair. "No woman wants to be seen in pants that make her legs look like hot dogs. I'm not going anywhere."

Carrie just rolled her eyes.

"Call Jason," Charlotte told her daughter. "Tell him… anything. Make up some excuse."

"You can't be serious."

"Please do as I say."

"Mom?"

"We're meeting his *family,*" Charlotte cried. "I can't meet his brothers and sisters-in-law looking like this."

"Change clothes, then, if you're so self-conscious."

As though she had anything to change into. Charlotte's wardrobe was limited to business suits and sweatpants. There was no in-between. She couldn't afford to clothe both of them in expensive jeans. But after Jason had invited her out for today, she'd allowed Carrie to talk her into a shopping spree. Thank heaven for Visa. And thank heaven for Jason's generosity; he'd refused to accept any payment for the dog's care.

"I'm not calling Jason!" Carrie crossed her arms righteously. The girl had a streak of stubbornness a mile wide, and Charlotte had collided with it more than once.

Defeated, Charlotte muttered under her breath and fled to her room, sitting on the end of her bed. Before the shopping trip, she'd managed to put today's plans out of her mind and focus her attention on Higgins. Then the softball game had turned into the better part of a day, including a picnic, involving most of his family.

"Mom," Carrie said, approaching her carefully. "What's wrong?"

Charlotte shrugged, not sure how to explain her nervousness. "I wish I'd never agreed to this."

"But why?" Carrie wanted to know. "I've been looking forward to it all week. Just think of all the babysitting prospects. Jason's family is a potential gold mine for me." Carrie sat on the bed beside Charlotte. "We're going, aren't we?"

Charlotte nodded. She was overreacting, and she knew it. After shelling out ninety bucks she was wearing those jeans, no matter how they made her look.

"Good," Carrie said, leaping excitedly to her feet. "I've got the picnic basket packed. Honestly, Mom, we're bringing so much food, we could open a concession stand."

"I didn't want to run short." Charlotte didn't bother

denying that she'd packed enough to feed Jason's entire family. A fruit-and-cheese plate, sandwiches, potato salad, a batch of chocolate chip cookies and a variety of other goodies she'd thrown in at the last minute.

Jason had casually mentioned the picnic the day before, when she'd gone to the hospital to visit Higgins. The dog was just beginning to respond to them. He was recovering slowly, but according to Jason, they'd be able to bring him home within a week. Charlotte soon discovered that visiting her new dog was a dual-edged sword. Every time she was at the veterinary hospital, she ran into Jason. Usually they had a cup of coffee together and talked; once he'd suggested dinner and Charlotte hadn't been able to dredge up a single excuse not to join him. He'd even taken her and Carrie to a movie. Now she was meeting his family, and it terrified her.

Ten minutes later, as Charlotte was rearranging their picnic basket to find room for a tablecloth and paper napkins, Jason arrived.

Carrie answered the door and directed him to the kitchen.

"Jason's here," she said unnecessarily.

"Hi." Charlotte greeted him nervously, turning around, a tense smile on her face. She was watching him carefully, wanting to read his expression when he saw her in the tight jeans.

"Hi, I was just—" He stopped abruptly, letting whatever he meant to say fade into nothingness. He stood before her, his mouth dangling open. Slowly his eyes widened.

With appreciation.

At least she thought it was appreciation. She prayed that was what it was, and not disgust or shock or any of the emotions she'd endured that morning.

"I...I've got everything ready." She rubbed her suddenly

damp hands down her thighs. "Carrie says I've packed too much food, but I don't think so. I hope you like cantaloupe, because I just added one." She knew she was chattering aimlessly, but couldn't seem to stop.

"You look…fabulous."

"I do?" Charlotte hated how uncertain she sounded.

Jason nodded as though he wouldn't be able to take his eyes off her long enough to play ball, which had to be the nicest compliment he'd ever paid her.

"Carrie talked me into buying the jeans," she mumbled, tossing the napkins on top of the heap and closing the lid as far as it would go.

"Remind me to thank her."

He didn't say any more, just reached for the basket and brought it out to the car. Charlotte was so relieved, she wanted to weep with gratitude. Her spirits lifted—more than lifted—they soared as she and Carrie followed him. Carrie climbed in the backseat as Charlotte got in the front, hoping her jeans wouldn't split.

The ball field was several miles away, near the Southcenter shopping mall. Charlotte was grateful to Carrie for carrying the conversation. Thrilled with the outing, the girl had plenty to say.

Charlotte had never been to this park before, and when she saw it she was astonished she hadn't heard of it. It had several baseball diamonds, and an equal number of soccer fields. The Green River intersected the park, with several footbridges spanning its banks.

"I didn't mention I was bringing anyone," Jason told her after he'd parked the car. "Everyone's going to ask you a bunch of embarrassing questions. Do you mind?"

"No," she answered, having trouble meeting his eyes. "Don't worry about it." She was a big girl—she could deal with a bit of curiosity.

"I don't usually bring someone."

Charlotte stiffened, not because she was timid or dreaded the questions, but because it confirmed something she'd rather not deal with right then. Jason was attracted to her. As attracted as she was to him.

What did bring fear to her heart was that he might be taking their time together seriously—that he might really start to care for her. That would be disastrous. *You care for him,* her heart reminded her. Yes, but that was different.

Kissing was all they'd done; it was all Charlotte had allowed. A few innocent kisses didn't amount to much. Or did they?

"Uncle Jase!" Two boys—Charlotte guessed they were seven or eight—raced across the green lawn toward Jason. One glance told her the pair were identical twins.

"Hello, boys," Jason said with a wide smile.

They stopped abruptly when they noticed Charlotte and Carrie, their eyes huge and questioning. Suspicious.

"These are my friends Charlotte and Carrie," Jason said, motioning toward them.

"They're *girls,*" one of the pair muttered.

"I noticed that myself," a tall, athletic man said as he strode toward them. He was wearing the same uniform as Jason. Charlotte didn't need an introduction to know this was his brother.

"This is Paul, my oldest brother," Jason said, tucking a couple of baseball bats under his arm, along with his mitt. The task appeared to demand a great deal of attention.

In the next five minutes, Charlotte was introduced to Leah, Paul's wife, who was five months pregnant and chasing after a toddler named Kelsey. Jason's younger brother, Rich, his wife, Jamie, and their two children, Bethany and Jeremy, arrived shortly afterward, and there was another series of introductions.

Charlotte's head was spinning with all the names and faces. Everyone was friendly and helpful. Openly curious, too. Carrie, who loved children, was delighted when Rich's daughter wanted to sit in the bleachers with her.

The men were on the diamond warming up when Jamie sat next to Charlotte. Leah joined them, sitting on her other side. Charlotte smiled from one to the other. Their curiosity was almost visible. As the silence lengthened Charlotte frantically sorted through a number of possible topics, but try as she might, the most inventive thing she could think of was the weather.

Oh, what the heck, she decided. "I imagine you're curious about me," she said. After the morning she'd had, she wasn't up to a game of Twenty Questions.

"We didn't mean to be so blatant about it," Leah, the shorter of the two, murmured. She had one of the nicest smiles Charlotte had ever seen.

"You weren't," Charlotte lied.

"Yes, we were," Jamie said with a laugh. "We can't help it."

"Ask away," Charlotte invited.

"How long have you known Jason?" Rich's wife asked without hesitation.

Charlotte found Jamie Manning to be a study in contrasts. Rich, Jamie's husband, was probably one of the best-looking men she'd ever seen. Definitely *GQ* material. Yet, at first glance, his wife seemed rather plain. Charlotte soon learned how misleading first impressions could be. Five minutes with Jamie, and Charlotte was awed by her radiance. She had an inner glow that touched those around her.

"I met Jason about a year ago," Charlotte answered, when she realized both women were staring at her, waiting for her response. "My daughter and I live in one of his apartments."

"A year," Jamie repeated, leaning forward so she could exchange a wide-eyed look with Leah. "Did you hear that? He's known her a whole year."

Charlotte felt she should explain further. "Actually, I met him a year ago, but we've only recently started to, uh, know each other."

"I see." Once again it was Leah who spoke, wearing a subtle smile as though she was amused and trying to disguise it.

"You'll have to forgive us for acting so surprised, but Jason doesn't usually bring anyone with him on Saturdays," Leah elaborated.

"Or any other day for that matter," Jamie added.

"So I understand. I…I take it he doesn't date often?" Charlotte asked. In some ways she was hoping they'd tell her he went through women like water. But in her heart she knew it wasn't true. If anything, it was just the opposite. Charlotte didn't want to hear that, either, didn't want to know she was special, because it made everything so much more difficult.

"Let's put it this way," Jamie answered, crossing her legs and resting her elbows on her knees. "We've been coming out here for what, two, three summers now, and this is the first time Jason's ever brought a woman."

Charlotte drew in a slow, deep breath.

"I don't remember Jason bringing a woman to any family function, ever," Leah said, looking positively delighted. Her eyes sparkled. "I'd say it was about time, wouldn't you, Jamie?"

"About time, indeed," Leah's sister-in-law said with a grin.

From his position on the diamond, Jason could see his two sisters-in-law on either side of Charlotte. No doubt they were pumping her for information, wanting to know every minute detail of their relationship. The distance was too great for him to be able to read Charlotte's expression.

If he had half a brain, he would've realized what he was doing before he invited her to join him. Why had he asked Charlotte to this game? Clearly he needed his head examined. Only an idiot would thrust a lamb like Charlotte into a pack of hounds without warning.

He'd told her his family would probably be curious about her, but he'd said it casually in the parking lot after they'd arrived. It wasn't like he'd given her much advance warning.

His family was far too nosy. By the end of the afternoon, Charlotte would be so sick of answering questions, she'd never want to go out with him again.

He pitched the ball to Paul with enough force to make his oldest brother remove his mitt, shake his hand and cast Jason an odd look.

Jason was angry. But it wasn't the way Leah and Jamie had surrounded Charlotte that had set him off. He'd had no business inviting Charlotte and Carrie to this game. For one thing, they were playing the league leaders and likely to be soundly defeated. If he was going to ask someone to come and watch them play ball, it should be against a team that'd make him look good, not like a bunch of fools. The outcome could prove to be downright embarrassing.

Not only were they likely to get their butts kicked, but Charlotte was going to spend the entire time being interrogated. First by Jamie and Leah, and then, when the game was over, by his brothers. They wouldn't be subtle about it, either. The first woman he'd cared about in years was going to come away thinking his family had been trained by the CIA.

Even now, Jason wasn't sure what had prompted him to

ask Charlotte to come. But he certainly remembered the night he'd done it….

They'd been sitting in the car outside the apartment the night of Higgins's surgery. She'd been shaken by the accident, struggling to hide how much. He had known when he dropped her off that he was going to kiss her again. She'd known it, too. His lips had brushed hers. Lightly. Briefly. He had sensed she was still frightened—of him? Of their mutual passion? Of her own desires? Until she was at ease with him, he was content to proceed slowly. He'd never indulged in any kisses more sensual or seductive than those he'd shared with Charlotte.

He could tell she was a novice when it came to lovemaking. That surprised him because she'd been married. He'd never asked about her ex-husband, preferring to wait until she was comfortable enough to talk about it on her own. But from what Carrie had told him the day she'd come to his office, the marriage had been short and disastrous.

Jason was convinced Charlotte hadn't realized how much he enjoyed their kissing sessions. How much holding her satisfied him. How she left him feeling dizzy with need.

The same magic that had made him kiss her that night had encouraged him to risk inviting her to the ball game. Only now did he understand what he'd done. He'd dragged Charlotte into an impossible situation. Carrie, too. He was glad they were with him, but he wished he'd thought of some other way of introducing Charlotte and her daughter to his family. Some other time, when he'd be at her side to ward off their curiosity.

"Jase!" Rich's voice shot past his ear two seconds after a ball nearly creamed the side of his head.

Stunned, Jason took two steps backward.

"What's wrong with you?" Rich demanded furiously.

"You mean you don't know?" Paul shouted from the shortstop position. He looked pointedly toward the stands. "It seems to me that he's met his Waterloo."

After nearly getting his head knocked off by a fly ball, Jason focused his concentration on the game, which to his surprise wasn't going badly. Every now and then he could hear a high-pitched shout, which he'd like to think came from Charlotte. By the end of the seventh inning the score was tied.

Jason came to bat at the bottom of the ninth. The all-important ninth inning. The score remained tied and there were already two outs. Either he pulled off a hit or they were going into extra innings.

Charlotte was sitting in the stands almost directly behind him. He set the bat over his shoulder and eyed the pitcher. The first pitch was a fast ball and Jason swung, determined to hit it out of the field. More to the point, he was hoping not to be embarrassed in front of Charlotte.

He heard the cracking of the wood against the ball and he dropped the bat, then started running as though his life depended on making it to first base. It wasn't until he got there that he realized he'd hit a home run. He felt jubilant as he rounded the bases.

He cast his eyes toward the bleachers to find Charlotte on her feet, cheering and clapping. Her face was bright with excitement. In all his life, Jason had never felt such elation.

He crossed home plate and didn't stop. His brothers, his whole team, stared at him as he trotted behind the protective barrier between home plate and the viewing stands and headed straight for Charlotte. Excitedly, she launched herself into his arms.

Jason grabbed her around her waist, lifted her from the bleachers and swung her down. Her eyes shone with happiness and Jason thought he'd never seen a more beautiful woman.

Charlotte threw back her head and laughed. It wasn't for several minutes that Jason was even aware of the crowd that had gathered around them.

A bit self-conscious now, he lowered Charlotte to the ground, but kept his arm around her. Paul and Rich were the first to congratulate him, followed by several other teammates, who slapped him heartily on the back. One suggested Jason bring Charlotte again, since she was definitely his good-luck charm.

"You were wonderful," Charlotte said, smiling at him proudly. Jason found it difficult to pull his gaze away. The urge to kiss her was so strong, he had to fight to restrain himself. He would've done it, too, would've kissed her in front of everyone and ignored the consequences, if only his brothers hadn't been present. He held back more to protect Charlotte from embarrassment than to ward off any razzing he'd get from his family.

"I'm hungry," Ryan, one of the twins, announced once the excitement had died down. "When are we gonna eat?"

"Soon," Leah promised. Paul headed toward the parking lot.

"I'll be right back," Jason said and, without thinking, did the very thing he'd decided against. He kissed Charlotte briefly, before trailing after his brother to get the picnic basket in the trunk of his car.

Jason couldn't believe he'd done that. Neither could Charlotte, judging by the look of surprise that flashed in her blue eyes.

"Are you going to fess up?" Paul asked, holding a heavy cooler with both hands, studying Jason.

"To what?" he demanded, narrowing his eyes, hoping his brother would take the hint.

"Charlotte."

"What about her?"

"Don't go all defensive on me. I was just wondering how you met."

Jason relaxed a little. He was being too touchy. "She lives in the complex." He didn't think it would sound good if he admitted Carrie had offered him money to take her mother out.

"She seems nice."

"She is. Lay off her, though, will you?"

Paul's eyes went solemn, as if he was offended by Jason's remark. Then he nodded. "Whatever you want."

Paul must've said something to Rich, too, because when they sat down to eat, after pushing three picnic tables together, no one gave Charlotte more than a glance. It was as though she'd been part of the family for years. Which was just the way Jason wanted everyone to treat her. Heaven forbid she figure out how special she was to him. He'd already made a big enough fool of himself, simply by inviting her and Carrie to this outing.

Charlotte's daughter had won a few hearts all on her own, Jason saw, secretly pleased. Ryan and Ronnie had clamored to sit next to her at lunch, beating out Bethany, who cried with disappointment until Carrie agreed to hold the little girl on her lap.

"I think Carrie's made a conquest," Jason said to Charlotte, munching on a chocolate chip cookie. His fourth, and he was ready for another.

"She loves children. She's the type of kid who'd prefer to be the oldest of ten."

Jason watched as a sadness, however brief, flashed in Charlotte's eyes. It told him she wasn't speaking only for Carrie, but herself, as well. She must've wanted so much more from her marriage than she'd gotten. He remembered something else then, something Carrie had told him about Charlotte wanting more children. At the time he'd decided to stay away. A woman with marriage and children on her mind was someone he planned to avoid. Strangely, the thought didn't terrify him nearly as much now.

Still, he had to admit that the fleeting look of pain got to him. He'd experienced the desire to protect her in the past, to guard her from hurt, but only when she was in his arms. Only when he feared *he* might hurt her. Now, the need to keep her safe burned in his chest. He wanted to block out anything that would cause her pain. Most of all, he wanted to meet the ex-husband who'd walked away from his family, and he'd prefer it be in a dark alley some night.

Although he didn't know any details of the divorce, Carrie had told him she never heard from her father. What kind of man would desert his family? What kind of man would turn a warm, vivacious woman like Charlotte into a near-recluse?

"I like your family," Charlotte said, smiling up at him, distracting him from his thoughts.

"Did Leah and Jamie bombard you with questions?"

"A few, but they're so nice, I didn't mind."

"What did you tell them?" Jason was eager to know, partially because it might clear up a few questions he had himself. Maybe Charlotte could put into perspective what he was feeling and was unable to define.

She laughed, causing the others to momentarily look their way. "Are you worried?"

"No." The question surprised him.

"For a moment there, you looked as if you were afraid I might've told them something you'd rather I didn't."

"You can tell them anything you want," he said decisively, meaning it. If she chose to imply that they were madly in love, then fine, he'd deal with it. On the other hand, if she'd chosen to let his family believe they'd only just met, which wasn't so far from the truth, then he'd live with that, too.

"I told them we're friends…special friends."

Jason approved. He couldn't have said it better.

"Uncle Jase," Ronnie shouted, clutching a Frisbee. "Are we ready to play?"

"Play?" Jason didn't need to be invited twice. His favorite part of these family get-togethers was the time after lunch that he spent with his nieces and nephews. Chasing after Ronnie and Ryan and a Frisbee kept him young at heart, he told himself. Though he didn't care to admit out loud just how much he liked running around with a pair of eight-year-olds. The boys enjoyed it, too, and before the afternoon was over Rich and Paul invariably joined in.

As they did now. The two brothers against Jason and a handful of youngsters in a game of Frisbee football. A few minutes into the competition, Jason dived to catch a wild throw, catapulting himself into the air and latching triumphantly on to the disk.

Ronnie and Ryan cheered, and Jason felt as pleased with his small feat as he'd been with the home run. After an hour, the two teams took a break. Breathless, he reached for a cold soda, pulled back the tab and guzzled it down.

He turned, looking for Charlotte. The last time he'd seen her she was with Leah and Jamie cleaning up the remains of their picnic. He saw her sitting on a blanket under a madrona tree, bouncing Jeremy on her knee. Bethany and Kelsey were sprawled out, napping, beside her. She was playing a game with the baby, nuzzling his neck and making cooing sounds. Her eyes radiated a happiness he'd never seen. A joy that transfixed him.

"Jason, are you in or out?"

Jason barely heard the words, his gaze on Charlotte.

"In," he decided, tossing the empty can in the garbage and heading back to the field. A couple of minutes later he was completely engrossed in the game. Carrie had sided with his brothers against him and was proving to be a worthy opponent. Ronnie caught the Frisbee and lobbed it to his twin. Jason glanced toward Charlotte again and saw her lift Jeremy above her head and laugh up at him.

Jason's heart constricted. Watching Charlotte with his brother's child did funny things to his chest. She was smiling, happy. A powerful emotion seized his heart in a way that was almost painful.

One pain was followed almost immediately by another as the Frisbee hit him hard. The wind momentarily knocked out of him, he doubled over.

"Uncle Jase!"

"Jason!"

Paul and Ronnie were the first to reach him.

"You all right?" Paul asked.

Jason's eyes moved toward Charlotte and he shook his head. "No," he muttered, "I don't think I am."

Six

So this was what it meant to be part of a family, Charlotte mused, as Jason drove her and Carrie home from the ball field. This profound sense of belonging, of acceptance. She'd never experienced anything like it before. It was as though Jason's family had known and loved her for years. As though they genuinely cared for her. Charlotte couldn't recall a time when she'd felt anything as uplifting as she had that afternoon.

After the game they'd gathered together for a picnic. Charlotte didn't think she'd ever laughed more. There'd been good-natured teasing, jokes, games. Even now, driving home, laughter echoed in her ears. The cousins were as close as brothers and sisters, the older ones watching out for the smaller children. They fought like brothers and sisters, too, mostly over Carrie, each wanting her attention.

Carrie had beamed, loving every minute of it.

After the initial round of questions, Leah and Jamie had treated Charlotte like...well, like family. The women were obviously good friends, yet included Charlotte in all their conversations. Jason's brothers, too, had tried to make her feel comfortable. Neither Paul nor Rich had asked a single question about her relationship with Jason, probably content to have their wives fill in the gaps later.

"You're very quiet," Jason said, taking his eyes off the road for a second. "Anything wrong? My brothers didn't—"

"No," she assured him with a smile.

The only sound was the hum of the road. Carrie, usually filled with boundless energy, was exhausted after chasing the children around for most of the afternoon. She'd enjoyed herself as much as Charlotte had.

And perhaps her daughter was thinking the same thing Charlotte was—that she'd missed out on something important because they only had each other.

Jason parked the car, then carried the near-empty picnic basket into her kitchen. He hesitated after setting it on the counter. "You're *sure* nothing's wrong?"

Charlotte nodded. "Positive. I had a wonderful time. A fabulous time. Thank you for asking Carrie and me."

He didn't seem to believe her. "Did Leah and Jamie hound you with questions?" he asked for the second time that day, a pensive frown on his face.

"Jason," she murmured, resting her hands on his forearms and gazing up at him. "I meant it. Every word. This day with you and your brothers and their families was one of the happiest of my life. If I'm being introspective it's because...well, because I've never realized until now how much I've missed in life." Jason's questioning eyes sought hers, as if he wasn't sure he understood.

She managed to meet his eyes. She felt close to Jason just then, closer than she had to anyone, and that confused her. She was falling in love with this man and that was something she couldn't allow. Was it Jason she loved, or his family?

"Charlotte, look at me."

She ignored the request. "I was an only child, too," she told him, "like Carrie." She wanted to explain. "There were never outings that included aunts and uncles or cousins. This is a new experience for Carrie *and* me."

"Look at me," he said again, his voice low and commanding.

Slowly her gaze traveled the length of him, up his chest, over the width of his shoulders, to his eyes. She stared into them and felt a sudden sense of connection. It was a powerful sensation, powerful and exciting.

"Where's Carrie?" Jason asked, glancing over his shoulder.

"She's on the phone in her room. Why?"

"Because I'm going to kiss you."

Charlotte's heart tripped into double time. She was tempted to make some excuse, anything that would put an end to the craziness that overcame her with Jason, but she didn't trust her voice, let alone her heart.

Whatever she might've said was never meant to be. Jason's kiss saw to that. He gathered her in his arms, and lowered his mouth to hers. His lips were there, warm and moist, reminding her of sunshine. The kiss was chaste, yet curiously sensual.

Of her own accord she deepened their kiss. Jason responded quickly.

He moaned, or perhaps it was her own voice making those soft sounds. She melted into him, her body responding instinctively, naturally, to his.

"Charlotte." He brought her even closer, and their kiss went on and on. She grew hot, and hotter, then hotter still… until…

"No more…" she cried, breaking away, panting. "Please…no more."

Jason trembled with restraint, closing his eyes. "You're right," he murmured. "Carrie's in the other room."

"Carrie," Charlotte repeated, grateful for the excuse.

Jason drew in several deep breaths, then said, "I should be leaving."

Charlotte nodded, but she didn't want him to go. Her body was on fire. She wondered if he was experiencing the same kind of torment himself—and if he was angry with her for sending him away.

"Would you like to come with me again next Saturday?" The question was offhanded, as though he'd just thought of it.

Charlotte's heart soared at the prospect. "If you're sure you want me."

Laughter leapt into his eyes, melding with the fire that was already there. "Trust me, Charlotte, I want you."

With that, he was out the door.

No sooner had Jason left than Carrie appeared in the kitchen. "Did Jason leave?"

Charlotte nodded, too preoccupied to answer outright. She was trembling, and all because of a few words. *He wanted her.* He'd been honest and forthright as she'd come to expect.

"Mom, we need to talk."

"Go ahead," Charlotte said, as she unloaded the picnic basket. There was surprisingly little food left over. Ryan and Ronnie had discovered her chocolate chip cookies, thanks to Jason, and the three dozen she'd brought had disappeared in no time. She'd set out the fresh fruit-and-cheese platter and that had disappeared, too. There were a couple of sandwiches still wrapped, but they'd keep for her and Carrie to eat the following day.

"It's about the ninth-grade dance," Carrie said stiffly from behind her.

Charlotte froze. This wasn't a subject she wanted to discuss, not again. "I've said everything I'm going to say about it, Carrie. The subject is closed."

"I hope you realize you're ruining my entire life," Carrie announced theatrically.

"Dropping you off at the dance and picking you up myself is a reasonable compromise, I think."

"Then you think wrong. I'd...rather walk to school naked than have you drive me to the dance as if...as if there wasn't a single boy in the entire class who wanted to be seen with me."

She sighed. "I'll be happy to pick up Brad, too, if that'll help." That was more than she was really in favor of, but she supposed she could live with it.

"Then everyone will think I asked Brad to the dance. I mean, I know girls do that, but it's important to me that a certain girl find out that Brad asked *me.* How can you do this, Mom? Can't you see how important this is?" Her eyes were imploring, a look designed to melt any mother's heart.

Charlotte steeled herself. "You're too young, Carrie, and that's the end of it."

"You don't understand what you're doing to me!" Carried wailed.

"The subject is closed."

"Fine, ruin my life. See if I care." She stalked out of the kitchen, arms swinging.

With a heavy sigh, Charlotte watched her go. This argument was getting old. She'd been under the impression that her daughter had accepted her decision. But now it was apparent Carrie had only been regrouping, altering her tactics. Cool reason had evolved into implied guilt. Her fifteen-year-old made it sound as though Charlotte had done untold psychological damage by not letting her go on an actual date. Well, so be it, Charlotte decided. This issue was one she didn't intend to back down on any more than she already had.

Pulling out a kitchen chair, Charlotte sank tiredly into it, resting her face in her hands. She sighed again. She had trouble enough raising one child; she was insane to even contemplate having another.

A baby.

But she *did* want another child, so badly she ached with it. Holding Jeremy, Jamie and Rich's little boy, had stirred to life a craving buried deep within her heart. She attempted to push the desire away, rebury it, anything but acknowledge it. She'd had to repress this desire several times over the years.

A baby now was out of the question, she stubbornly reminded herself. She was too old; there were dangers for a woman on the other side of thirty-five. But age was the least of her concerns.

Getting pregnant required a man. Even more problematic, it required making love.

The sadness that weighed down Charlotte's heart felt impossible to carry alone. Tears blurred her eyes. If ever there was a man she could love, it was Jason Manning. But the thought of falling in love again terrified her. Charlotte was afraid of love. Afraid of all the feelings and desires Jason had stirred to life. He was wonderful. His family was wonderful. But it was a painful kind of wonderful, taunting her with all that was never meant to be in her life.

Charlotte had dealt with her share of problems. Finances. Isolation. Low self-esteem. Everything had been a struggle for her. She didn't know how to react to *wonderful.*

For the first time since her divorce, Charlotte felt the protective walls she'd erected around her heart being threatened. Those barriers were fortified by years of disappointment, years of resentment and pain. Now they seemed to be crumbling and all because of a man she'd never even seen without a baseball cap.

For now, Jason was attracted to her, but in her heart she believed his interest in her wouldn't last. It couldn't. The time was fast approaching when she wouldn't be able to put him off, and he'd know. That very afternoon, she'd seen the way he'd trembled in an effort to restrain himself. She'd watched as he'd closed his eyes and drawn in several deep breaths.

Soon kissing wouldn't be enough for him. Soon he'd discover how inadequate she was when it came to making love. She had never satisfied Tom, no matter how hard she'd tried. In the end he'd taunted her, claiming the day would come when she'd realize all the ugly things he'd said about her were true. She didn't have what it took to satisfy a man.

When Jason learned that, he'd start to make excuses not to see her again. He'd regret ever having met her, and worse, he'd regret having introduced her to his family.

She never should've accepted his invitation. It would make everything so much more awkward later....

The tears slipped from her eyes before she was aware she was crying. The soul-deep insecurity, awakened by the memories of her marriage, returned to haunt her. The doubts, the fear and dread, were back, taking up residence in her mind.

Covering her face with her hands, Charlotte swallowed the sobs beginning to spill out in huge swells of emotion. In an effort to gain control, she held her breath so long her lungs ached.

She heard her ex-husband's words—*you aren't woman enough*—inflicting injury all over again until she covered her ears and closed her eyes, wanting to blot them out forever.

Why should Jason fall in love with her when the world was full of whole, sexual women who'd gladly satisfy his needs? Passionate women who'd blossom in his arms and sigh with pleasure and fulfillment. She was incapable of giving a man what he needed. Tom had repeatedly told her so. She was inept as a woman, inept at lovemaking.

"Mom," Carrie said coolly from behind her. "I'm going to Amanda's house." She waited as though she expected Charlotte to object.

Charlotte nodded, then stood and resumed unpacking the picnic basket, not wanting Carrie to see her tears. "Okay, honey. Just don't be late."

"I may never come home again," Carrie said dramatically.

"Dinner's at six."

"All right," Carrie muttered and walked out the door.

It wasn't until later, much later, while she was in bed finding it impossible to sleep, that Charlotte's thoughts returned to Jason. She'd allowed things to go further than she should have. It was a mistake. One she had to correct at the earliest possible moment. She must've been crazy to let their relationship reach this point.

Crazy or desperate? Charlotte didn't know which. It had all started weeks earlier when she'd held a friend's baby. Funny how she could remember the precise moment with such accuracy. The longing for a child had escalated within her, gaining momentum, refusing to be ignored. She'd gone home and wept and although the tears had finally dried, inside she hadn't stopped weeping.

Shortly after the incident with Kathy Crenshaw and her baby, Charlotte had met Jason. He'd kissed her that first night and it had been… She hadn't tensed or frozen up and that had given her hope. Her confidence continued to grow when he kissed her again and again; he'd always been gentle and undemanding. He was special that way, and she'd be forever grateful for the uncanny gift he had of understanding her needs.

But Jason was a man of raw sensuality. He wouldn't be satisfied with a few chaste kisses for much longer. He had no idea how terrified she was of him, of any man.

No, it was only a matter of time before the best thing that had happened to her in years came abruptly to an end.

On Sunday, Jason wasn't in the mood to cook. Microwave popcorn for dinner suited him better than a frozen entrée. He popped a batch and sat down in front of the television to watch a bowling tournament. Not his favorite sport, but there wasn't much to choose from.

When his phone rang, he stood on the sofa and reached across to grab it from the kitchen counter. He was half hoping it was Charlotte.

It wasn't.

"Jase, I don't suppose you've got Charlotte's phone number, do you?" Paul asked cordially enough, only Jason wasn't fooled. As the oldest, his brother sometimes got the notion that he needed to oversee family matters. That didn't include Charlotte, and Jason intended to make sure Paul understood that.

"Jase?"

Of course he had Charlotte's number. "Yeah. What do you want it for?" Suspicions multiplied in his brain. Being a newspaper reporter, Paul was used to getting information out of people.

"Don't get all bent out of shape, little brother. Leah and I want to go to a movie."

"So?"

"So, we'd like Carrie to babysit. She was a real hit with the boys yesterday. You don't mind, do you? The girl's a natural with kids."

"Of course I don't mind." The fact was, Jason felt downright pleased. If Paul and Leah wanted Carrie to babysit, then Charlotte would be at home alone. He could come up with an excuse—Higgins would do—and casually drop in on her.

They needed to talk, and the sooner the better, although it wasn't talking that interested him.

He tossed what remained of his popcorn in the garbage, brushed his teeth and shaved. He even slapped on some cologne. He wasn't accustomed to using anything more than aftershave, but this evening was an exception.

He was whistling when he'd finished, his spirits high.

On the pretense of asking about next Saturday's ball game, he phoned his brother to be certain Paul had managed to get hold of Carrie. He had. In fact, he'd be picking her up in the next half hour. Allowing ten minutes for Paul to whisk Carrie out of the apartment, that left him with forty minutes to kill.

Forty minutes would go fast, Jason mused, as he sat back down and turned on the TV. But his mind wasn't on the bowling match. A far more intriguing match was playing in his mind. One between Charlotte and him.

Tonight was the night, he decided, determined to take Charlotte beyond the kissing stage. He didn't mean to be calculating and devious about it… Well, yes, he did, Jason thought with a grin.

He'd be gentle with her, he promised himself. Patient and reassuring. For years he'd been treating terrified animals. One stubborn woman shouldn't be any more difficult. He had no intention of pressuring her into anything.

Nor would he coerce her if she was at all uncomfortable. He'd lead into lovemaking naturally, spontaneously.

He glanced at his watch, eager now, and was disappointed to see that only ten minutes had passed. Half an hour wasn't *really* very long, but it seemed to feel that way to Jason.

"I'm leaving now, Mom," Carrie called out.

Charlotte walked out of the kitchen, drying her hands on a terry-cloth towel. She smiled at Paul, then looked at her daughter. "Do you know what time you'll be home?"

"Before ten. Don't worry, I know it's a school night."

"I'll have her back closer to nine," Paul assured Charlotte.

"Okay." She nodded. "Have fun."

"I will," Carrie said as they left, offering her first smile of the day. Actually, Charlotte had been talking to Paul, but she let it pass. Carrie was still upset about the school dance and had been cool toward Charlotte all afternoon.

Charlotte had just settled down with a book when there was a knock at the door. *Please, God, don't let it be Jason,* she prayed, but apparently God was occupied elsewhere. Just as she'd feared, she opened the door and came face-to-face with Jason, boyishly handsome in his baseball cap.

"Hi," he said, charming her with his smile. It wasn't fair that a man should be able to wreak such havoc on a woman's heart with a mere movement of the lips.

"Hello." She'd been dreading this moment all day. "I was going to phone you later." A slight exaggeration; she'd been planning to delay calling for as long as possible.

"Oh?"

"Yes…I won't be able to go to the ball game with you next Saturday after all."

"Don't worry about it," he said, making himself comfortable on her sofa. He anchored his ankle on the opposite knee and grinned up at her. "There'll be plenty of other Saturdays. The summer is filled with Saturdays."

It was awkward for her to be standing, while he seemed completely at home. So Charlotte sat, too—as far away from him as she could while still being on the same sofa. She angled her legs sideways, her hands clasped. "I'm afraid I won't be able to make it any other Saturday, either."

A pause followed her announcement. "Why not?"

"I…I…" She couldn't look at him. "I don't think it's a good idea for us to see each other anymore."

"Uh-huh." He didn't reveal his reactions one way or another.

Emotion seemed to thicken the air. He might not be *saying* anything, but he was feeling it. Charlotte was, too.

"Is it something I said?"

She lowered her eyes farther and shook her head.

"Something I did?"

"No… Oh, please, Jason, just accept this. Don't make it any more difficult than it already is." Her voice, which had remained steady until then, cracked.

"Charlotte," Jason said, moving next to her with startling agility. "For heaven's sake, what's wrong?"

She covered her mouth with one hand and closed her eyes.

"I'm not leaving until you tell me," he said.

"I can't."

"Why can't you?"

"Because!" she cried, leaping to her feet. "Everything would've been all right if you hadn't been so…so nice." She was angry now, unreasonably angry, and not quite sure why.

Jason stood, too, his gaze holding hers. "I'm not sorry I kissed you. Nothing would make me regret that."

His words made it all so difficult. She wasn't sorry, either.

Her expression must have told him as much. He relaxed visibly and reached for her, gently holding her shoulders. Slowly, he drew her forward. Charlotte had no resistance left, and walked right into his embrace.

She sobbed once, then hid her face in his chest and wept openly.

Jason stroked her hair and whispered reassurances in her ear, as if she were a small child needing comforting. In some ways, she was exactly that.

After several minutes he lifted her face upward to meet his mouth. Over and over again he kissed her, lightly, softly, gently. Her breathing grew shallow.

"Jason…"

"Yes?" He raised his head, his eyes meeting hers.

"You're doing it again."

His mouth curved into a deliberate smile. "I know."

Her hands were against his chest when he sought her mouth again. He was still gentle, but the kisses changed in texture and intensity. Their lips were fused together, the heat between them burning so fierce, she thought it might scorch her. Charlotte found it difficult to breathe, but she didn't care. Breathing wasn't important. She held on, her hands clutching his upper arms.

Jason led her back to the sofa, and without protest, Charlotte followed. He sat down and brought her into his lap. He didn't give her the opportunity to protest before he directed her lips back to his. When her mouth opened in exultant welcome, he moaned. He kissed her again and again, until she was panting. Until her heart seemed to stop beating. Until there was nothing in her world but him.

His hands were opening the front of her blouse even before she realized his intent.

"Jason, no," she said in a panic. "Please, no."

"All right." Jason twisted around and turned off the light. The room dimmed and shadows danced across the walls. "Is this better?" he asked.

Charlotte clamped her eyes shut. "I…I'm not very good at this," she whispered, close to tears. "I'm not… sexy enough." The only thing that kept her from springing free of his hold was fear. It held her immobile.

"You're beautiful," he whispered. "Charlotte, do you hear me? You're perfect."

She buried her hands in his hair. His cap was gone, but she didn't remember when he'd removed it. Or if he had. She sighed.

He kissed her again, his mouth hard and hungry. Charlotte understood his hunger, but she wasn't capable of satisfying it. "No," she whispered when she could.

"No?" How disappointed he sounded.

"No," she said a second time.

"You're sure of that?" he asked, sounding regretful.

"Y-yes."

He nodded, kissed her once more, then inhaled sharply. "I just wanted to check."

Seven

"Who told you that you aren't sexy?" Jason asked, relaxing on her sofa.

Charlotte's hands stilled as she poured coffee into two mugs.

How do you expect a man to get excited when his wife's such a cold fish? No wonder you're a failure at lovemaking. Are you sure you're even a woman?

Charlotte's heart reeled as Tom's words returned to haunt her. She'd laid to rest as much of his vindictiveness as she could, bound her wounds and gone on with her life. Pulling away the bandage, examining the damage now, just seemed pointless.

"Charlotte?" he probed gently.

"My ex-husband," she muttered.

"He's wrong, you know."

She nodded, rather than argue with Jason. For the moment he was infatuated with her, but his fascination wouldn't last, and eventually he'd feel the same way as Tom.

"You never mention your ex-husband."

"There's not much to say." She carried the two mugs into the living room. "Carrie was excited about babysitting Paul and Leah's children," she said, pointedly changing the subject.

Jason stood and took a cup from her hands, then sat next to her on the sofa, sliding his arm around her shoulders. His touch was warm against her chilled skin.

"You're perfect," he whispered and kissed her cheek. "You're lovely and sensuous and beautiful. Don't ever let anyone tell you differently. I'm not going to force you to discuss your marriage. Not now, but I want you to know I'll be ready to listen whenever you're ready to talk."

She smiled wanly, determined to steer the conversation away from the past.

Jason drank his coffee and left soon afterward, when it was apparent Charlotte wasn't in the mood to talk. She wasn't sure *what* her mood was, but she lacked the strength to analyze it.

Before leaving, Jason asked if she'd changed her mind again about the ball game on Saturday, and after a short hesitation, she nodded. Yes, she'd go, she told him. Jason smiled, obviously pleased, and headed out the door.

Something was happening to her, Charlotte thought, trembling. And it was happening against her will.

She'd made the decision earlier—she wasn't going to see him again. After careful deliberation she'd decided it was best to end everything now before one or both of them ended up hurt. It was a simple, cut-and-dried conclusion.

Yet…yet when she'd tried to talk to him about it, regret and doubt had consumed her until she'd dissolved in tears and pain.

Heaven help her, she didn't want it to end! Jason must've sensed that because he hadn't appeared too concerned when she'd told him.

His confidence was well-founded. Within minutes, he'd

broken through her resolve and was kissing her senseless. And Charlotte hadn't raised a single objection.

It was too late. Too late to walk away from him. Too late to go back to the way her life had been before Jason. She was trapped by her own weakness and would continue to be until Jason discovered the truth for himself.

Carrie arrived home soon afterward, full of tales about the twins and Kelsey. Seconds later, it seemed, she was in her room and on the phone. Her thoughts heavy, Charlotte appreciated the privacy.

It wasn't as though this was the first time Jason had kissed her. The impact he had on her senses wasn't startling or new. The man had the uncanny knack of stirring awake the part of her she'd thought had died the day Tom asked for a divorce.

She felt reborn, alive with hope. And yet she was more frightened than she'd ever been before. Everything was different with Jason. In his arms she experienced an excitement she'd never even known was possible. His tenderness, the loving gentle way in which he touched her, had given her cause to wonder, for the first time, if what Tom had said was true.

What if it wasn't? Could that be possible? With Jason she felt none of the dread she'd felt when Tom had kissed her. His lovemaking had always been so hurried, so raw, as if he were in a rush to complete the act so he could turn away from her. She couldn't imagine Jason being anything but compassionate and tender.

But what if all the things Tom had said *were* true? Her heart slowed with uneasiness. Jason Manning was an attractive, sensual man. A passionate man. And he'd expect—no, he'd need—a passionate woman.

Thinking of her years with Tom conjured up such ugly images in her mind. His taunts echoed like the constant sound of waves in a seashell, never stopping, never fading, always there to remind her of what a failure she was.

At ten, Charlotte turned out the lights, made sure Carrie was off the phone and went to bed. She should've guessed that sleep would escape her that night.

You're perfect, Jason had said.

Only she wasn't—Tom had made certain she knew as much. The need to weep welled up within her, tightening her throat.

She had loved Tom. She'd hated him.

He had stripped her of her pride when he left.

Her life had ended that day. Yet, in other ways, her life had begun.

She'd known for weeks, months, that Tom was involved with another woman, and she'd said nothing because she was afraid. Because she feared life alone. Because she was willing to do whatever she could to save her marriage, even if that meant denying the truth. So she'd chosen to believe his lies.

When he'd forced her to face reality, he'd come at her in anger and guilt…and hate. She hadn't cried. Not a single tear, not even when the divorce was decreed final. It wasn't until years later that she gave herself permission to grieve for the marriage, the fantasy she'd built in her mind of what might have been.

In the beginning she'd been too numb with shock, too dazed by that last horrible scene, to experience any emotion. Gradually, as time passed, Charlotte began to feel again, a little at a time. It was like an anesthetic wearing off. As the years went by, as the numbness faded, she had to deal with the pain. A throbbing, savage pain.

Her grief came in waves. Regret struck first, reminding her of all the might-have-beens; one fantasy led to another. By now they would've had more children, she'd told herself. Tom would be established in his career and she'd be living the life she'd been cheated of as a child.

Anger followed regret. How could she have given her heart to a man who'd ravaged her self-respect? How could she have loved him when he'd treated her so poorly? But love him she had, so much that she still ached at losing the life she'd dreamed they'd share.

But mostly, as the years went on, Charlotte felt an overwhelming sense of guilt. She knew it was unreasonable. After all, it was Tom who'd cheated on her, Tom who'd walked out on his family, abandoned his wife and child. It was Tom who'd forsaken their vows. Yet *she* was the one who accepted responsibility.

Sometimes the guilt was so overpowering, Charlotte found it intolerable. If she'd been a better wife, Tom wouldn't have sought another woman. He'd said so himself. If she'd been more enticing, more sexual, more attractive, more satisfying, he wouldn't have done it. She was too thin, too flat, too cold. The list was endless.

After years of telling herself that Tom had used her inadequacies as an excuse for adultery, years of struggling to repair her self-esteem, Charlotte gave up. Surrendered. She bought it all. The reassurances she tried to offer herself were empty. Null and void.

Everything Tom had said was true. She was a failure as a woman. A failure as a wife. No man would ever be satisfied with her. Not for long. Tom hadn't been and Jason wouldn't be, either. She might as well accept that now and stop fighting the inevitable.

The doorbell chimed just as Jason finished reading the latest issue of one of the veterinary periodicals he subscribed to.

"Yeah?" he said, opening the door, half expecting one of his tenants.

"Hi," Carrie said, striding purposefully into his apartment. "Have you got a minute to talk?"

"Sure." Jason led the way into the living room and sat down. Carrie started to pace in front of his television, hands behind her back. Walking in his apartment was dangerous with the week's worth of newspapers spread across the carpet.

"Is it Higgins?" he prompted, when she didn't speak right away.

She shook her head, eyes lighting up. "Higgins is doing great. He's eating and everything. I think he likes it with Mom and me."

"I'm sure he does." They'd lavished the dog with love and attention from the moment Jason had carried him into their apartment on Monday afternoon. One would've thought the mutt was some kind of hero. In a way he was, Jason decided. If it hadn't been for the dog, Jason didn't know how long it would have taken him and Charlotte to connect.

"What can I do for you?"

"It's Mom," Carrie said.

"What about your mother?" He saw that tears had pooled in Carrie's eyes, and she wasn't trying to hide the fact. Like most men, Jason was uncomfortable when a woman started to cry. No matter what the cause, he felt personally responsible. And he felt an overpowering urge to do whatever he could to rectify the problem.

He certainly felt that way with Charlotte—even more so. She'd look at him with her beautiful blue eyes and the instant he saw the slightest hint of tears, he'd be putty in her hands. He was putty in her hands, anyway, tears or not, but that was because it was Charlotte.

"My mother's ruining my life," Carrie was saying.

Jason was no psychiatrist, but he wasn't completely obtuse. "Does this have something to do with that dance?"

Carrie nodded. "There's this boy…his name's Brad. He's the cutest boy in class and the star of the track team. Every girl in school's crazy about him and he asked *me.* Me," she emphasized again, bringing her hand to her heart. "He asked me to the ninth-grade dance. When I talked to Mom, she said I could go, but when I said Brad's father was picking us up and…and driving us there, she went totally weird on me."

"I'm sure your mother has a good reason for feeling the way she does."

"She won't even talk about it."

"Carrie, listen. I'd like to help, but this is between you and your mother. I can't interfere with a parenting decision."

Carrie nodded, her throat working as she struggled not to cry. "I don't expect you to interfere… I was hoping that you'd help me—tell me what to say to make Mom understand how old-fashioned she's being. I haven't said anything to Brad about my mom not wanting me to be in the same car as him and his dad and…and the dance is next Friday night. There isn't much time left."

Jason rubbed the side of his face. "What's your mother's primary objection?"

"She thinks driving with him makes it a real date. And I'm not allowed to *date* until next year."

"I see. What if she drove you and Brad to the dance?"

"That won't work, either.… Everyone will think I asked him and…it might be silly, but I want Suzie Jennings to know otherwise." She wiped her eyes and took a moment to regain her composure.

"How about if Brad's dad drops you off and your mother picks the two of you up after the dance?"

Carrie dropped her hands to her side. "Picks us up?" she repeated thoughtfully.

"It wouldn't be considered a date then, would it? The two of you obviously need to be driven to and from the dance and this would simply be a means of transporting you."

"There's a party at Amanda Emerich's house right afterward, but it's directly across the street from the school and everyone's invited."

"I have an even better idea," Jason said enthusiastically. At Carrie's blank stare, he explained. "How about if your mother offered to chaperone the dance?"

Judging by the look Carrie gave him, she didn't share his enthusiasm. "That wouldn't work because she'd need a date. Chaperones at our school dances are always couples."

"I'll go with her," Jason said casually. As soon as he made the suggestion, he wanted to jerk it back. Him dancing? The last dance he'd attended had been his sister's engagement party. He'd rented a tuxedo and been miserable most of the night. Before then, his only other experience on the dance floor had been as a high-school junior. He didn't know how to dance then and he hadn't learned since.

"You'd do that?" Carrie asked, her voice rising. For the first time since she'd entered his home, her eyes sparkled with hope.

"Ah..." Oh, what the heck, he'd do it if it would help the kid. "Sure," he answered. "I'd volunteer to be a chaperone."

Carrie let out a cry of glee and raced across the room to throw her arms around his neck.

"Your mother might not be willing—"

"She will," Carrie said confidently. "Mom's crazy about you."

"Yes, but will she be crazy about the idea of Brad's dad driving you there and the two of us taking you home?"

Carrie mulled that over for a moment. "Of course she will," she said, revealing no doubt. "Why shouldn't she be? It's a wonderful compromise. We'll both be satisfied.... I mean, this plan isn't perfect—no one wants their mother chaperoning a school dance—but it'll work because Mom's going to agree when she knows you suggested it."

Jason was suffering from second thoughts when he rang Charlotte's doorbell an hour later. Carrie had devised a plan for approaching Charlotte with his idea. At the appropriate point, he was to suggest the two of them chaperone the dance and make it sound like a spur-of-the-moment idea.

He was rather proud of his compromise—not the part about chaperoning the dance, but the shared-driving idea. By the time Carrie had left his apartment, he felt like an expert. Raising children wasn't so difficult if you applied a bit of common sense.

Now, though, he wasn't entirely sure he should get involved. The dance was an issue between Charlotte and Carrie, and his instincts told him he was trespassing.

It would've been different if Charlotte had come to him for advice, but she hadn't and he doubted she would. There wasn't any reason for her to, at least not with regard to Carrie. Charlotte was the one with parenting experience, not him.

Despite his second thoughts over his role in this drama, he'd agreed to help Carrie—even though his instincts now told him he was going to regret this.

Carrie answered the doorbell and smiled brightly when she saw him.

Charlotte looked pleased to see him, too, but she also

looked like she'd rather not be. Jason was learning to read her quite well, and that skill was coming in handy.

"Hello, Jason," she said softly.

"Hi. I stopped by to see how Higgins is doing." A weak excuse, and one she was bound to see through in the next couple of minutes.

The black dog trotted toward him, his tail wagging slowly. Jason squatted beside him and affectionately rubbed his ears. "How do you like your new home, fellow?" he asked.

"Do you want a cup of coffee?" Carrie called out from the kitchen. Her voice was enthusiastic. The kid wasn't any better at disguising her emotions than her mother was.

"Please." Jason glanced up at Charlotte. He didn't know what was going on with her lately. She'd been avoiding him—that much he understood—but he was willing to give her the space she needed. For now. He was a patient man. She was attracted to him, fighting it as hard as she could, but her resistance wasn't strong enough to defeat him.

For the first time in his life, Jason had met a woman who needed him. Unfortunately she was too self-sufficient and proud to admit it. Charlotte Weston brought out all his protective urges. And his intuition told him he'd begun to bring out qualities in her—a sensual confidence and an ability to laugh, have fun—that she'd been repressing for years.

The woman was a puzzle, but slowly, surely, he was putting together the various pieces she revealed. Once he had the whole picture, he'd be able to scale those defensive walls of hers.

He strongly suspected Charlotte's problems revolved around her ex-husband and her marriage. She'd been badly hurt, and gaining her trust and her love would require time and patience. Where Charlotte was concerned, Jason had an abundant supply of both. Carrie brought him a cup of coffee, and Jason pulled out a kitchen chair, then nonchalantly sat down. Carrie did the same. Higgins ambled over and settled at his feet.

Charlotte glanced at the two of them and frowned. "Is something going on here that I should know about?"

The kid couldn't have been more obvious, Jason mused again. "Carrie came to me earlier this afternoon," he announced, deciding honesty was the best policy, after all. The way he figured, if they were forthright about *what* they'd discussed, then Charlotte might be willing to forgive them for discussing it behind her back.

"Jason," Carrie muttered a warning under her breath.

"Carrie came to you?" Charlotte demanded. "About what?"

"The dance," Carrie admitted sheepishly.

"You went to Jason about an issue that's strictly between you and me?"

"I needed to talk to someone," Carrie cried, pushing back the chair when she stood. She faced her mother, feet braced apart, hands on her hips. "You're being completely unreasonable and Jason agrees with me. He came up with—"

"Carrie." Jason could see he'd been wrong. In this case, honesty might not have been the best policy. "I didn't ever say I thought your mother was unreasonable."

His defense came too late. Charlotte whirled on him, her face red and growing redder. Her eyes, the eyes he'd always found so intriguing, were filled with disdain.

"Who gave you the right to intrude in my life?" she flared.

"Charlotte, it's not what you think." Jason could feel himself sinking waist-deep in the quicksand of regret.

"You're undermining my authority."

"Mom…please, hear me out."

"Charlotte, give me a chance to explain." Jason didn't have much of an argument; he should've listened to his instincts and stayed out of this.

"You may think because…because I've let you get close to Carrie and me that you have the right to express your opinion on how she should be raised, but you're wrong. What goes on between my daughter and me is none of your business. Do I make myself clear?"

Feeling all the more chagrined, Jason nodded. The best thing to do now was make a hasty retreat. "I can see I've—"

"Just go." Charlotte's voice trembled as she pointed to her door.

"Mom," Carrie shouted. "The least you can do is listen to him."

Charlotte ignored her daughter while Jason, calling himself every kind of fool, made his way out of the apartment. He paused long enough to cast an apologetic glance at Carrie, but he agreed with Charlotte. He'd butted in where he didn't belong.

After Jason's departure, Carrie went to her room, slamming her door with such force Higgins scrambled across the living room, frantically looking for a place to hide.

Charlotte was so angry, it was all she could do not to follow Jason and tell him she never wanted to see him again. She would have done it, too, if she didn't know she'd regret it later. And if she didn't need to coax Higgins out from behind the couch and comfort him.

The man had some nerve! If Carrie thought she was going to manipulate her into giving in by getting Jason to side with her, then her daughter was wrong.

"I hope you realize what you've just done!" Carrie shouted as she opened her door.

Still stroking Higgins, Charlotte ignored her.

"You've insulted Jason."

"He deserved it."

"Like hell."

"Watch your language, young lady."

Thirty silent minutes passed while Charlotte cooled her temper. Carrie was apparently doing the same thing. A short while later, her bedroom door opened again and she walked out. She was pale and her eyes showed evidence of crying, but she appeared to have composed herself.

The same didn't hold true for Charlotte. She was still furious. How dare Jason involve himself in her affairs!

"I've called Brad," Carrie announced, opening the refrigerator. She stared at the contents, took out a cold pop and pulled back the tab. After taking one long drink, she turned to face Charlotte. "Brad said he'd tell his dad you'd be driving us to and from the dance."

Of all the things Charlotte might have expected, this wasn't one. "Good," she said, feeling only a little better.

"I...was hoping you'd be willing to split the duties. Let Brad's father drive us there and you pick us up."

Charlotte mulled it over. That didn't sound so unreasonable. She'd have a chance to meet the boy's father when he came to get Carrie, and it wasn't as if the two kids would be alone in the car—or at the dance.

"I...I'd be willing to agree to that."

Charlotte thought Carrie would be grateful or relieved; instead she broke into giant hiccuping sobs. Her daughter slumped in a kitchen chair and buried her face in her arms and wept as if she'd lost her best friend.

"Carrie." Charlotte placed her hand on Carrie's shoulder. "What's wrong?"

She raised her head and brushed the tears from her face,

her shoulders heaving with the effort to stop crying. "You should never have said those things to Jason."

"Carrie, he intruded in my affairs."

"But I was the one who asked him to talk to you. If you're going to be angry with anyone, it should be me, not him."

Charlotte realized Carrie didn't understand the nuances of a male-female relationship. Frankly, she wasn't that well acquainted with them herself. She'd admit that she'd reacted in anger, but it was justified. Jason had simply assumed too much.

"But Jason didn't want to interfere," Carrie sobbed. "It took me forever to get him to agree and…and he only did it because I was desperate."

"He overstepped the bounds." Charlotte tried to remain adamant.

"You made him leave without even bothering to listen."

Charlotte said nothing.

"I like Jason—and you do, too," Carrie added unnecessarily. "He's the best thing that's ever happened to us. Higgins is alive because of him and…and he took us to meet his family. Saturday was the most fun day I've ever had. It…it was like we belonged with Jason and his brothers."

Charlotte had felt the same way.

"Jason wasn't minding your business, Mom, at least not the way you think. He…he was helping a friend. Me. And you hated him for that."

"I don't hate Jason." Far from it. She was falling in love with him.

"He's the one who came up with the idea of Brad's father driving one way and you driving the other. He…he suggested you chaperone the dance just so you'd feel comfortable about everything." She drew in a shaky breath. "When I told him you'd need a date for the dance if you were going to be a chaperone, he said *he'd* take you. I mean, Jason isn't the kind of man who dances…but he'd be willing to do it, for me, because he's my friend. And for you, too, so you'd be comfortable at the dance. And what did he get for being so nice?"

"My anger," Charlotte whispered, feeling wretched.

"You kicked him out of the house, and I don't think he'll ever want to come back. I know I wouldn't."

Charlotte sat down next to her daughter, feeling strangely like weeping herself.

"I wanted to go to the dance with Brad more than anything," Carrie admitted, "but now I don't care if I do or not."

"Carrie, this isn't the end of the world."

"I *really* like Jason," she said emphatically. "When I asked him if he'd ask you out, I did it for selfish reasons, and I apologize for that…but I'm glad I did it. You're happier when you're with him, Mom. You don't think I notice, but I do. Jason makes you smile and laugh and forget how much you don't like your job."

Charlotte folded her arms around her middle. What Carrie said was true. It was as if her life had started all over again when Jason first kissed her.

"I don't care about the dance anymore," Carrie murmured. "But I care what happens with you and Jason. Go to him, Mom. Tell him you're sorry. Please."

Her daughter's entreaty affected Charlotte more than any regrets she might feel about what she'd said and done. For one thing, she hadn't realized how fond Carrie was of Jason.

"Will you do it, Mom?"

It didn't take Charlotte long to decide. "Yes," she said. She would apologize, for not giving him the benefit of the doubt, for not being willing to listen to him and Carrie, but mostly for the rude way in which she'd told him to leave her apartment.

It was the second time she'd had to apologize to this man.

"When?" Carrie asked.

"Soon," Charlotte promised.

The opportunity came the following morning. After walking Higgins, Charlotte was on her way to the office, crossing the parking lot. She'd spent a sleepless night composing what she intended to say to Jason. She'd wait until that evening, go to his apartment and say what needed to be said.

She was halfway to her car when she heard her name. Her heart filled with dread when she saw Jason jogging toward her.

"Hello," she said, feeling wretched.

"I won't keep you." His eyes bored into hers. "I want you to know I'm sorry for what happened yesterday. I should never have gotten involved. This is between you and Carrie, and I was out of line."

"I should never have spoken to you the way I did."

"You were angry and you had every right to be."

"But you… Oh, Jason, I feel terrible."

He frowned. "Why should you?"

"Carrie told me how you were willing to help chaperone the dance and…and I didn't have the common decency to hear you out."

"It's probably for the best. I'm not much of a dancer."

Charlotte smiled up at him, knowing her heart shone in her eyes, and not caring. "Why don't you let me find that out for myself Friday night?"

Eight

"You need to borrow a suit?" Rich asked, looking smugly amused as he led Jason to the walk-in closet in the huge master bedroom. The home had been built several years earlier, when Jamie was pregnant with Bethany. Rich himself had designed the sprawling L-shaped rambler that overlooked Puget Sound, and he was justifiably proud.

"Yes, I need to borrow a suit," Jason muttered, not giving his brother the satisfaction of explaining. Already he regretted having volunteered to be a chaperone for this dance. No matter how hard he tried, he wasn't going to be whirling around a dance floor as if he knew what he was doing. He'd probably make a fool of himself in front of Charlotte and a bunch of smart-aleck ninth-graders.

As an engineer, Rich was required to dress more formally on the job than Jason was. Jason owned a suit, but it was outdated. Maybe if he waited a few more years it would become fashionable again.

If the truth be known, he wasn't even sure when he'd last worn it. Sometime in college, he guessed. He'd buy another one if he thought he'd get any use out of it, but that didn't seem likely.

"What do you need a suit for?" Rich asked outright.

"I wouldn't be borrowing one if I'd known I was going to face an inquisition."

Rich chuckled, clearly enjoying Jason's discomfort. "I just want to be sure you aren't going to run off and marry Charlotte. Mom would kill you if you pulled a stunt like that."

Jason snickered, hoping to give the impression that marriage was the furthest thing from his mind, which it was. Wasn't it?

"Hey, don't act like it couldn't happen," Rich said, pushing hangers aside as he sorted through several tailored jackets. "With our family's history, it wouldn't be unheard-of for you to elope."

Jason couldn't argue with that. It had all started with Taylor. A few years back, his sister had moved to Montana and within three months had married Russ Palmer. The decision to marry had apparently been impulsive—and it happened while they were chaperoning the high-school drill team in Reno. The deed was done by the time they bothered to contact any family.

Jason frowned. Taylor had been a chaperone, too, and look where it had led. This high-school dance was beginning to sound more and more dangerous.

Christy had married on the sly, too, again without telling anyone in the family. There were extenuating circumstances in her case, however. Well, sort of. His youngest sister had actually been engaged—to a lawyer, James Wilkens—when she'd gone to Idaho with Cody Franklin and married him. Their marriage had caused quite a ruckus in the family, but eventually everything had been smoothed over. Anyway, Christy was much better suited to Cody than to James, although the attorney had remained a good family friend.

Rich had followed suit, marrying Jamie with some idiotic idea of being a sperm donor for her baby. Jason had stood up for his brother, but he'd known from the beginning that the two of them were in love. He'd predicted that this sperm donor business wouldn't pan out, and he'd been right. Jamie had gotten pregnant, sooner than either of them had expected, and the process hadn't involved any artificial insemination, either.

Paul had been next. Diane, Paul's first wife, had died tragically, shortly after giving birth to Kelsey. Her loss had sent the family reeling. For six months, Paul had shunned his family's offers of help, attempting to balance his duties at home with his job and at the same time comfort his grieving children, all preschoolers. He'd been proud and angry. Leah, Diane's sister, had convinced him he couldn't continue alone. She'd given up her teaching position at the college and moved in with Paul and the children. Shortly afterward, they were married. But once again, no one in the family was informed of the ceremony.

The only single Manning left was Jason, and he didn't plan to get married. He'd decided that years before. It was unfortunate that his parents had been cheated out of putting on a large wedding, but those were the breaks. He wasn't marching down any aisle just to satisfy his mother's need to work with caterers and some florist friend she'd known for years.

"So, Jase," Rich said casually, breaking into his thoughts. "How are things with you and Charlotte?"

"Fine."

"Fine?" Rich repeated, with that smug look Jason found so irritating.

"You don't need to concern yourself with my affairs," Jason said, resenting the way Rich and Paul made his love life their business.

"Are you going to ask her to marry you?" Almost in

afterthought, Rich held up a well-cut gray suit coat. The tailoring was excellent and the material was top of the line.

Jason ignored the question and reached for the jacket, trying it on over his black T-shirt with *Seattle at Night* silk-screened across the front.

"What are your intentions toward Charlotte?" Rich asked with a pensive frown. He sounded oddly formal—and unusually serious.

"My intentions are my own, but since you asked," Jason said, turning around to admire his profile in the full-length mirror, "I'll tell you.... They're dishonorable, as always." He tried to make a joke of it, laugh off the attraction he'd been battling from the moment he'd met Charlotte Weston over a leaky faucet.

His joke, however, fell decidedly flat.

"Not this time, big brother."

"What do you mean by that?" Jason demanded. He didn't like his brother sticking his nose where it didn't belong, but he couldn't help being curious about Rich's remark.

"You're in love with her."

"Is that right?" Jason returned flippantly.

"It's the first time you've ever invited a woman to watch you play softball."

Rich made it sound as if that alone was enough to force him into a shotgun wedding. Jason refused to get into an argument with his younger brother. It wouldn't do him any good. Just because Rich and Jamie were so happy together, his brother seemed to think he was an expert on the subject of love and marriage. Jason didn't want to be the one to disillusion him.

Perhaps he did have some deep affection for Charlotte, Jason told himself. He'd be the first to admit he was strongly attracted to her, but marriage? Out of the question.

This was a familiar argument, one he'd worked through early in their relationship. It had worried him then, but he'd been so fascinated with her that he'd pushed his apprehensions to the back of his mind, deciding to take one day at a time.

He'd face one hurdle, he decided, before he confronted another. For now, the obstacle was their physical relationship. When she trusted him enough to put aside her fears and allow him to make love to her, it would be time to reevaluate what was happening between them. But not yet.

"Are you going to let me borrow the suit or not?" Jason asked stiffly. "If I have to stand here and listen to a lecture, too, I'd rather go to the rental shop."

He half expected Rich to jerk the coat off his shoulders and send him on his way. Instead, his youngest brother grinned, as if he knew something Jason didn't. It was another irritating habit of his.

"You're welcome to keep the suit as long as you like," Rich assured him. "You never know when you're suddenly going to need one."

Friday evening came, and it took Jason a full half hour to knot his tie correctly. He was out of practice, and getting it just right frustrated him. He should've borrowed the clip-on variety, but he hadn't thought of asking for one. No doubt Rich had plenty of each type.

Surveying his reflection in the mirror, he barely recognized himself. He was tall, besting his brothers by an inch or more, his shoulders were wide and, if he had anything to be proud of physically, it was that his stomach had remained flat. Haphazard meals and baseball did that for a man.

Charlotte probably wouldn't recognize him, either. If memory served, it was the first time she'd gone anywhere with him when he wasn't wearing a baseball cap. He brushed his hand along the side of his head, making sure his hair stayed flat. He carefully examined himself to see if he could find any gray hairs for a more distinguished look. When he didn't, he was actually disappointed.

He checked his watch. If everything had gone according to schedule, Carrie would have been picked up fifteen minutes ago for a pre-dance buffet. Since the dance didn't start for another two hours, Jason had suggested taking Charlotte out to dinner.

He didn't know what had gotten into him lately. He'd made reservations at an expensive restaurant, and ordered a fancy corsage to give her when they arrived.

Normally, his idea of a night on the town included pizza, beer and a Mariners' game. Drag an irresistible woman into his life, and before he knew it, he was forking out major bucks for dinner and flowers. The thing was, he'd come up with the idea on his own and was even excited about it, knowing how pleased Charlotte would be.

He'd seen this happen with his friends—his brothers, too—but he would never have believed *he'd* fall such willing prey to a woman's charms. It wouldn't have happened with anyone but Charlotte. Of that, he was certain.

At exactly seven, he walked over to Charlotte's apartment and rang the bell. She kept him waiting for several minutes before she opened the door—not a promising sign.

When she finally did come, Jason was about to complain. He was going to a lot of trouble for this blasted dance; the least she could do was be ready on time.

Whatever he'd intended to say, however, flew out of his mind when he saw Charlotte. For the longest moment of his life, he stood there immobile.

This was Charlotte! She was…stunning.

"I'm…sorry," she said, sounding flustered. "I didn't

mean to keep you standing out here, but I'm having a problem with this dress."

She was beautiful.

The word didn't begin to describe how breathtaking she looked. Her hair was done in a way he'd never seen before, swirled to one side, exposing the smooth skin of her cheek and her long, slender neck. Dangling gold earrings swung from her ears. Her eyes were a brighter blue than ever before, the color of the sky washed clean by a summer squall. Her dress was a paler shade of blue… Her dress… Jason's gaze slid over the sleeveless dress with its tight bodice and flared skirt, and an invisible hand seemed to appear out of thin air and knock him senseless.

"Jason." Her eyes implored him as she held one hand behind her back. "Is something wrong? I look terrible, don't I? Don't worry about hurting my feelings… This dress is too fancy, isn't it?"

It was all he could do to close his mouth. "You look… fabulous." Which was the understatement of the century. Jason felt sorry that he wasn't more sophisticated and urbane.

If he had been, he might have told her how exquisite she was. He might have found the words to say he'd gladly rework the knot in his tie for another hour if it meant he could spend the evening with her. For the first time since he'd donned the suit jacket, he felt no remorse for volunteering to escort Charlotte to her daughter's dance.

"I can't get the zipper all the way up," Charlotte explained. "I was so busy helping Carrie get ready before Brad and his father arrived that I…I didn't get dressed myself, and now I can't reach the zipper. Would you mind?"

She presented him with her back and it was all Jason could do to pull the tab up instead of down. If he went on instinct he'd have had her out of that dress, in his arms and on the way to the bedroom. He couldn't recall a time he'd wanted a woman more than he did Charlotte Weston right then and there.

"Jason?" She glanced over her shoulder when he delayed.

His hand felt clammy, and at first his fingers refused to cooperate, but with some effort he managed to do as she asked, sliding the zipper up her back.

"Thank you," she said. "You can't imagine what a madhouse it's been around here," she went on. "Carrie was so nervous. She looked so grown-up. I can't believe my baby isn't a baby anymore."

Jason returned her smile. "My mother felt the same way when Christy—my sister—attended her first big dance."

Even now, Jason was having trouble forming coherent sentences.

"The dress isn't mine," she told him as she searched for her evening bag, wandering from one room to the next until she located it. "I borrowed it from one of my friends at the office… It's too close to the end of the month to go out and buy one." She sighed, sounding breathless. "Even if I'd had the extra money, I doubt I would've been able to find one at the last minute. I'd feel dreadful if something happened to Cheryl's dress."

"I borrowed the suit from my brother." Maintaining an intelligible conversation, he discovered, wasn't as much of a problem as keeping his eyes off her.

Charlotte drew in a deep, steadying breath. "I know it's silly, but I'm as nervous as Carrie."

He smiled, trying to reassure her.

"The last dance I attended was in college," she said. "I…I don't know if I can dance anymore."

"I'm not exactly light on my feet, Charlotte," Jason felt

obliged to remind her. He'd warned her earlier, but he doubted she'd taken him seriously.

"Do you think we should practice?" she asked.

She was gazing up at him with wide eyes. Jason would've given everything he owned to find out if she was feeling anything close to the emotional havoc he was.

"Practice?" he echoed. "That's an idea." He swallowed, wondering exactly what he was inviting. Trouble with a capital *T,* considering the way his body was reacting.

Charlotte set aside her evening bag and walked into his embrace. "I'm afraid I'm not going to be very good at this," she murmured.

"Don't worry. Hey, as far as I'm concerned, those ninth-graders are going to dance circles around us anyway."

Charlotte's laugh sounded sweet and soft, and Jason's heart constricted. Could this be love? This pleasure he felt in doing small things for her—like the dinner and flowers? This need to hold her in his arms? This desire to be with her and her alone?

The feel of Charlotte's body against his was the purest form of torture he'd ever experienced. She fit in his arms as though she belonged there. Had always belonged there. He tried to ignore how right it felt.

And couldn't.

He tried to ignore the fragrance of wildflowers that whispered through her hair whenever she moved her head.

And didn't.

He tried, but failed.

Everything went fairly well for the first few minutes. At least he wasn't stepping on her feet. Then Jason realized their feet weren't moving and they were staring at each other more than they were dancing. Gazing at each other with starry-eyed wonder.

He shifted his hand upward, wanting to lessen the feeling of intimacy, but his fingers inadvertently grazed the skin of her upper back.

Either he kissed her now or he'd regret it the rest of the night. Either he continued the pretense or confessed openly to how vulnerable she made him feel.

He brought her closer to him. He could feel her heart racing, echoing his own. Once he kissed her, he knew there'd be no stopping. Not this time.

He lowered his head ever so slightly and waited.

Charlotte sighed, closed her eyes and lifted her mouth enticingly to his. He suspected she was unconscious of what she was doing, what she was seeking.

Frankly, Jason didn't care. He was so hungry for the taste of her, nothing mattered. His mouth found hers and he groaned. Charlotte did, too.

He hadn't touched her in days, wanting to give her time, give himself time to define the boundaries of their relationship. It had been too long. He felt so needy he trembled.

The kiss was long, slow, deliberate.

Slowly, reluctantly dragging his mouth from hers, he created a small distance between them. Her eyes slowly fluttered open and met his.

"Jason?"

"I want you, Charlotte." He couldn't be any plainer than that. "I need you."

Emotion flickered in her gaze. Was it fear? Pain? Jason found it impossible to tell.

"Do you want to stop?" His hands were in her hair. By the time she lifted her mouth from his, Jason was melting with a need so powerful it throbbed within him.

Charlotte sighed into the hollow of his throat. "Jason, will you be angry with me?"

He saw the emotions assailing her, but noted the dignified way in which she tilted her chin and the proud squaring of her shoulders.

"No, I won't be angry."

She relaxed. Visibly. "Didn't you tell me you made dinner reservations for seven-thirty?"

"Yes." He recognized her fear and tried to ignore his own disappointment.

Self-conscious now, Charlotte broke away, quietly adjusting her clothes, then retrieved her evening bag. It wasn't until she looked up at him that he saw the anguish in her eyes.

He didn't know what her ex-husband—he assumed it was her ex-husband—had done. Her gaze linked with his, regret and misery so evident it was all he could do not to reach for her again. To comfort, not to kiss. To offer her solace, not passion.

Now, more than ever, Jason was determined to discover how her ex-husband had hurt her so badly. Determined to help her recover and teach her how beautiful love could be.

Charlotte was shaken to her very core. The intensity of their kisses had grown fervent and passionate, near the point of no return. If she'd given him the least bit of encouragement, he would have carried her into the bedroom.

For one wild moment, she'd been tempted to let him. Then the haze of desire had faded enough for sanity to return.

She felt grateful that Jason had allowed her to regain her senses, had given her the option to stop or proceed. Not like Tom…

Charlotte was jarred by this latest exchange even more than the other times Jason had held her and kissed her.

He'd almost made her forget.

Since her divorce, Charlotte had been content in her

own small, secure world. The world she'd so carefully constructed for herself and Carrie. It had been the two of them, prevailing against all odds, forging a life together. The borders of her world had been narrow and confining, but Charlotte had made peace with that, had accepted its limitations.

Then a series of events had thrown her into confusion. It had all started at the baby shower for her friend Kathy Crenshaw. Charlotte had held the newborn in her arms and the longing she'd managed to ignore all these years had struck her full-force.

Shortly afterward she'd met Jason, and her life hadn't been the same since.

Because of Jason, she'd recognized how restricted her world had become. How limited. If that wasn't enough, he'd shown her glimpses of a life she'd never dared hope existed. He'd taught her to dream, to believe in the impossible.

Almost.

After a protracted farewell to Higgins, they went out to the parking lot. Jason opened the car door and helped her inside, then stood in the fresh air for several minutes, hands in his coat pockets. He closed his eyes and turned his face toward the night sky.

Charlotte knew it was difficult for a man to cut the love-making off as abruptly as they'd done. He needed a few minutes to compose himself.

She watched him as he climbed into the car. He hesitated after inserting the key into the ignition and smiled over at her. "Ready?"

Charlotte nodded. "Are you…all right?"

"Never finer," he assured her, then clasped her hand to kiss her knuckles.

Nine

Jason Manning was a romantic. Beneath that I-don't-give-a-damn attitude was a tenderness and warmth that left Charlotte feeling like a starry-eyed adolescent. The candlelight dinner at an elegant cliffside restaurant had been wonderful. There he'd given her a fragrant rosebud corsage that was so lovely, it had brought tears to her eyes.

The dance had been the best part of their evening. They'd had a delightful time, despite being surrounded by ninth-graders and forced to endure an earsplitting mixture of songs.

Jason and Charlotte had discovered early on that they weren't going to be able to dance to rap music. After a number of hilarious attempts, they'd given up. Several of their efforts had left Charlotte laughing so hard, her ribs ached.

Jason had been equally amused, and after their unsuccessful attempts to blend in with the kids, he'd reached for Charlotte, guiding her into his arms. She'd draped her wrists loosely around his neck and he placed his hands on her hips. Then they'd invented their own dance….

Although Charlotte knew Carrie had risked her "cool" status, her daughter had come to her, eyes bright with excitement, to confess it wasn't so bad having her mother chaperone a dance, after all.

After the dance, while Carrie and Brad attended the nearby party, Charlotte and Jason sat outside in the schoolyard, gazing at the stars, laughing and kissing. Not the passionate, soul-deep kisses of earlier, but tender, sweet ones. By the end of the evening the barriers surrounding her heart had started to crumble.

Charlotte and Carrie came home at a respectable hour, their heads filled with romance. With barely a word, they wandered off to bed, passing each other like sleepwalkers in the hall.

Several hours later, Charlotte, unable to sleep, wrapped her memories around her like a cloak. Not since her own schooldays had she been more at ease with a man. In the space of one evening, she'd come to realize—without doubt, fear or regret—that she was deeply in love with Jason Manning.

After an hour of savoring every moment, she found she could finally sleep, knowing she'd be with him the next morning when he picked her up for the game.

"You ready, Mom?" Carrie called happily from the kitchen. It was shortly after ten. "Jason'll be here any minute."

Charlotte sucked in her stomach and zipped up her skinny jeans. Then she reached for a clean sweatshirt and tossed it over her head. Jason was already in the kitchen, checking the contents of the picnic basket, when she sauntered in from her bedroom. Her heart did a little dance when she saw him.

"Good morning." She felt shy, and couldn't explain it.

He turned around and their eyes met before he sent her a wide smile. "'Morning."

Charlotte opened the refrigerator and withdrew a six-pack of diet soda to add to the cooler.

"Is that all I get—just a friendly 'good morning'?" he asked, keeping his voice low so Carrie wouldn't hear.

"What else do you want?"

"You should know the answer to that. I swear, Charlotte, leaving you last night was one of the hardest things I've ever done." He slipped his arms around her waist and nuzzled his face in the slope of her neck.

Charlotte twisted around and stared up at him. "It was?"

"The only thing that got me through it was knowing I'd be with you again this morning." He lowered his mouth to hers, and she parted her lips. The kiss was slow and deep and hot.

"Honestly, you two are getting ridiculous," Carrie said from behind Charlotte. "Even Higgins thinks so." At the last minute, Carrie had convinced her they should bring the dog. Charlotte wasn't sure he was healed enough to run around the park, but Carrie had phoned Jason and he'd felt it would be all right.

"You ready?" Jason asked, picking up the wicker basket, his hand around Charlotte's waist as though, even now, it was difficult to let her go.

"*I've* been ready for the last ten minutes," Carrie said pointedly, holding Higgins's leash and leading him to Jason's car.

On the ride across town, Jason put on a CD and the three of them sang along with Bon Jovi. But as they pulled into the massive parking lot, Jason's voice stopped abruptly.

"What's wrong?" Charlotte asked.

"Nothing for you to worry about." He tried to reassure her with a smile, but she wasn't so easily fooled. She glanced around, wondering what could possibly be amiss.

She couldn't imagine, unless it was a vehicle he happened to recognize.

"I'm going to take Higgins for a walk," Carrie announced as soon as she'd climbed out of the backseat. Charlotte knew her daughter was eager to show off the dog to Ryan, Ronnie and the other children.

When Jason was opening the trunk of his car and removing his softball equipment, Charlotte spoke.

"Is there someone here you'd rather I not meet? An old girlfriend, a former lover?"

He turned and his gaze met hers. He smiled, a smile that started with his eyes and worked its way down to his mouth. "Nothing quite so dramatic. My parents are here."

"I see," she said. "You'd rather I wasn't with you."

"No," he said vehemently, and she realized he wanted her with him as much as she wanted to be. A rugged sigh followed his response. "I don't like the idea of you having to endure another inquisition."

"I'm a big girl."

"You don't know my mother."

"I'd like to, though," Charlotte assured him. She couldn't help thinking Jason's parents must be exceptional people, to have raised such a wonderful family. Before meeting the Manning clan, she'd known so little of what it meant to be part of a family, one in which everyone supported and encouraged one another. Where joys were shared and grief divided. All her life, Charlotte had been on the outside looking in, yearning for that special bond.

"They're going to drive you crazy with questions," he said grimly.

"Don't worry about it. I know how to be evasive. You forget, I'm the mother of a teenage daughter."

Jason's laugh was automatic. He grinned over at her, tossed a baseball bat over one shoulder and reached for her hand, linking their fingers. Linking them in a way that would dissolve any doubts.

Charlotte's heart sang with a joy that radiated from her heart.

They strolled casually, hand in hand, across the freshly mowed lawn. Jason's steps slowed as they approached the playing field.

Charlotte glanced up to find his eyes on her. "I just pray I can keep from hitting a home run," he whispered.

Charlotte laughed as they walked toward the older couple talking with Paul and Rich. Jason made the introductions and Charlotte smiled warmly and held her hand out to his parents.

"I've been looking forward to meeting you," she said confidently. "After getting to know Jason and his brothers, I can't help thinking you two must be very special people."

Jason waited a restless twenty-four hours for the summons. It arrived Sunday morning, disguised as an invitation to dinner at his parents' house that same evening. Jason, however, wasn't fooled. His mother intended to feed him, but he knew he'd be obliged to sing for his supper.

He showed up promptly at six and was pleased to see that his mother had gone to the trouble of preparing all his favorites. Homemade rolls hot from the oven. Crispy fried chicken, mashed potatoes and gravy, fresh-picked peas. A molded gelatin salad rested in the center of the dining-room table.

Jason had always been a meat-and-potatoes man, unless he had to cook for himself, which unfortunately he did most evenings. His eating habits were atrocious and he knew it. A homemade dinner like this was a rare treat.

"We don't see nearly enough of you," his mother said, as the three of them sat down at the table.

Jason noted that she'd set out her best china and silverware, as well as linen napkins and a matching tablecloth. This was going to be a heavy-duty interrogation. And it didn't look as if he had much chance of escaping before his mother ferreted out the information she wanted.

His father handed him the platter of chicken and Jason thought he might have read sympathy in his eyes.

"Generally, when your brothers are here for dinner, I get so involved with the grandchildren," his mother said conversationally. "You and I don't have much of a chance to talk."

"We talk," Jason said, reaching for the rolls and adding three to his plate, along with a thick slab of butter and a spoonful of strawberry preserves. His mother would have to wait for her information while he enjoyed his dinner.

"Gravy, son?"

"Thanks, Dad." A look of understanding passed between them.

"I hardly know what's going on in your life these days," his mother continued, undaunted. "I haven't seen you in a month of Sundays."

"That's not true, Elizabeth. Jason was over two weeks ago. Now, let the boy eat. You can drill him about Charlotte later."

His father was nothing if not direct. His mother didn't even pretend to be affronted; she simply sighed and nodded. "If you insist."

"I do," his father muttered, ladling gravy over a modest pile of mashed potatoes. He set the gravy boat aside and shook his head. "I don't understand you, Elizabeth. You've been half starving me for months, claiming we've got to start eating healthier. I've been eating salads and fish and broiled chicken. Now *this*. I'm beginning to feel like it's my last dinner before facing the executioner."

"This is Jason's favorite dinner!" Elizabeth declared righteously.

"Don't be fooled, son," Eric Manning said, his elbows on the table. "Your mother's after something big this time."

"Eric!"

"Sorry, dear," Jason's father said contritely, then winked at him.

If his mouth hadn't been full of homemade bread, Jason would have laughed. His mother was in quite a mood. His father, too, but he was well aware of the love they shared. They had the kind of relationship he'd always hoped to have with a woman himself. For the first time in his life, he felt that might be possible.

They ate in relative silence with short discourses from Jason as he answered their questions about the veterinary hospital and his practice. He noticed how carefully his mother steered away from the subject of Charlotte and his social life.

No sooner had Jason and his father cleared the table than his mother brought out a deep-dish apple pie. Even the dessert was Jason's favorite.

While she dished up heaping bowlfuls and added ice cream, his father poured coffee.

"Now, Eric?" she asked, looking expectantly toward her husband.

"If you insist."

Jason glanced from his mother to his father, realizing his reprieve was about to end.

"I most certainly do. Jason," she said, shifting her attention to him, "as you probably know, your father and I are curious about you and Charlotte. *Very* curious."

"Yeah, I had that impression."

"We both liked her very much."

"She's a likable person," Jason said.

"How'd you meet her?"

He finished his pie, tipping the bowl on its side and spooning up the last of the melted ice cream. When he was convinced he'd gotten every drop, he wiped his mouth with the napkin, set it aside and reached for his coffee.

"She lives in the apartment complex."

"Widowed?"

"Divorced." He wasn't going to volunteer any more information than necessary.

"Are you in love with her?"

His mother was going for the jugular. Jason supposed she was entitled to the truth, since she'd gone to so much trouble with this dinner.

"Yes." The reaction he received was definitely satisfying. His mother's eyes grew huge, and she glanced excitedly at his father.

"I thought as much," she murmured.

"It's obvious the boy's in love, Elizabeth. I told you so, didn't I?"

"But it makes all the difference in the world that he's willing to admit it himself."

"Charlotte means a lot to me," Jason added without hesitation.

"Are you going to marry her?" His mother's voice had a breathless, hopeful quality.

Jason sipped his coffee. He was in love with Charlotte, no question. He woke in the morning and his first thoughts were of her. When he went to bed at night, she was there in his mind, following him into sleep. His whole day was focused on when he'd see her again. Kiss her again.

"Jason?" his mother urged.

"Yes, I'm sure I'll eventually marry Charlotte."

"Hot damn." His father slapped the table.

"Oh, Jason, I couldn't be happier." His mother dabbed

the corners of her eyes with a napkin. "I'm so pleased," she said with a sniffle, reaching for her husband's hand.

"I'm happy you two are so happy." Jason hadn't talked about marriage with Charlotte yet, but he'd do that in due course. They were still beginning to know each other, feel comfortable together. By next summer at just about this time, they'd be ready to take such a monumental step.

"Now this is important, son," his father said, his eyes serious. "Your mother and I want your word that you're not going to do what your sisters and Rich and Paul did. In other words, don't marry Charlotte without the family being there."

Elizabeth backed her husband up. "I've waited all these years for a family wedding and I refuse to be cheated out of my last chance. Do you understand me, Jason?"

"Don't worry," Jason said calmly. "When Charlotte and I get married, we'll do it up big, just for you. The whole nine yards."

"A reception, with a dinner and dance?" His mother's eyes implored him.

"As long as Charlotte agrees, and I'm sure she will. She enjoys that sort of thing."

"But will she mind…my helping with the arrangements?"

Jason shrugged. "My guess is she'd welcome it. She doesn't have any family of her own, you know."

"Personally, I don't care if your mother has her hand in the arrangements or not," his father muttered. "I just want to be sure you aren't going to marry Charlotte behind our backs."

"I already promised I wouldn't." Still, given their family's history, Jason could understand his parents' skepticism.

"So I have your word on this?" his mother asked anxiously.

"My word of honor. Only..."

"Only what?" His mother looked concerned.

"Nothing, Mom. Don't worry about it."

"What is it?" she demanded.

"Well, I was wondering... Once Charlotte and I decide to marry, would you show her how to make fried chicken like yours?"

It wasn't fair to bother Jason with her problems, but there wasn't anyone she trusted more, anyone's opinion she valued as much. Her day at the office had been one of the worst ever. Her boss, Mr. Ward, had been unreasonable and demanding in the past, but his abuse that afternoon had reached an all-time high. He'd shouted at her, called her incompetent, belittled her. And it had been over something that was completely out of her control. A client had left the agency due to a problem with accounting, not anything Charlotte had done, yet she'd taken the brunt of Mr. Ward's anger. Unfortunately the insurance agency wasn't large enough to have a Human Resources department, so there was no one to complain to, no recourse to speak of.

It wasn't the first time and it wouldn't be the last. For three years she'd been employed as an executive assistant at the insurance agency. In the beginning she'd enjoyed her job and thrived on the challenge. Then, six months ago, Mr. Beatty, her original boss, had retired, and she'd found his replacement to be the worst kind of supervisor.

She'd made her decision earlier that afternoon, prepared her letter of resignation and placed it on Mr. Ward's desk before leaving the office. Although she'd felt confident when she left work, she was vacillating now, uncertain that she'd made the right decision.

It always seemed to be like this. She'd become indignant, decide to leave, and later, after her anger had cooled, she'd change her mind. Mr. Ward would seem repentant, try to convince her that his outbursts weren't personal; they were just his way. She'd start to believe him, at least until the next time.

Then it occurred to her.

What kind of woman would allow a man to verbally abuse her like that? What kind of woman allowed herself to be swayed by cheap talk and empty promises? The kind of woman who'd stayed married to Tom Weston for as long as she had, that was who.

She needed a sounding board, someone who'd listen to her frustration and doubts without casting judgment, without anger. Someone whose self-esteem was strong enough to accept her decisions whether she took his advice or not. Someone like Jason Manning.

Jason answered the phone immediately, sounding delighted to hear from her.

"I…I had a crummy day," she said when he asked. "Do you…would you go for a walk with me?" She considered bringing Higgins, but he was curled up with Carrie on the sofa.

"I'll be right over."

As Charlotte left, Carrie was talking on the phone with Brad. She hadn't told her daughter about quitting her job, although she was sure Carrie would cheer her decision.

"Hello," Jason said, kissing her lightly on the lips when she stepped out the door.

Charlotte closed her eyes. They joined hands and walked in the direction of the community park several blocks over.

The evening was beautiful. The fragrance of rhododendrons filled the evening air, mingling with the scent of blooming azaleas. Birds chirped and several people were getting a start on their yard work.

"I…did something I'm not positive I should have done," she said, keeping her eyes lowered.

"Was it illegal?"

The question made her smile. "No."

"Then why look so grave?"

"Well…"

"Do you want to tell me about it?"

She nodded, grateful they'd arrived at the park. Jason steered her toward an unoccupied bench and they sat down, his hand still holding hers.

"I…I don't get along with my boss. I'm good at my job—at least I used to be. But now… Mr. Ward makes unreasonable demands and takes out his frustration on whoever's close at hand. Unfortunately most of the time that's me."

"It doesn't seem like a healthy atmosphere to be working in."

"It isn't." Charlotte wasn't the only employee who felt unhappy. Cheryl was on the verge of giving her notice, too, and so were a couple of the others. It wouldn't surprise Charlotte if half the office staff left with her.

"Then you should quit."

He made it sound so straightforward.

"I've never been a quitter. It's one of the reasons the divorce was so difficult for me. I—" She stopped abruptly. She hadn't meant to drag her marriage into this, lay it out for Jason to examine…yet, perhaps it was time.

"Go on," he urged.

Charlotte inhaled deeply, gathering her resolve. "I wrote my two-weeks' notice this afternoon and left it on Mr. Ward's desk and now…now I'm having second thoughts."

"Why? Do you want to continue working at the agency?"

"No."

"Are you afraid you won't be able to find another job?"

"Not particularly—there's always a high demand for executive assistants. It's just…I know what's going to happen in the morning. Mr. Ward will arrive and read my letter and call me into his office. He'll apologize the way he always does. He seems to know exactly what to say, and when he's through with the apology, he'll offer me a token raise."

"It'd be nice if he threw in a bouquet of flowers."

"He might. He has before."

"Are you going to be swayed by that?"

"No-o." Her voice trembled and she shut her eyes to hold back the tears that burned. "It's so much like my marriage."

"Having to deal with an angry unreasonable man?"

"Yes…but more than that. Mr. Ward treats me the same way Tom did, and I swore…I promised myself I'd never allow another human being to do the things he did to me. And yet I take it, day after day, and I hate myself for it."

Jason's arm was around her now, hugging her close as if he wanted to absorb her pain. She was thankful he wasn't kissing her; she couldn't have endured that just then.

"I feel so angry when I let someone manipulate me. I want so badly to believe that things will change…that they'll get better. But they never do. Sooner or later Mr. Ward will go back to doing exactly what he's always done…and I'll realize I've let myself be controlled again. I can't seem to deal with the truth…. I guess it's easier to deny everything than face the reality. Why is truth so painful?"

Jason waited a few minutes, his arm about her calm and comforting. "Is it your boss you're talking about or your ex-husband?"

"Both." Charlotte raised her head and wiped the tears

from her eyes before they had a chance to fall. "Tom…had an affair. I knew it for months but…I pretended I didn't. I made believe we were happy and in love, while doing everything I could to win him back. But it wasn't enough… Now I know nothing would have been enough."

Jason didn't interrupt her with questions; once again she was grateful. The effort not to weep had produced a lump in her throat, and talking was almost painful. She hesitated, head still lowered.

Jason's mouth brushed her hair. "Your husband was a fool, Charlotte."

She didn't respond; she couldn't. Jason didn't know the full story, didn't understand that there'd been a reason Tom had turned to another woman. Any healthy male would have, or so her ex-husband had vehemently assured her time and again.

"I'm stubborn and hardheaded," she said, her voice cracking. "I don't know when to let go and…so I hold on, no matter how painful…or damaging."

"I can't tell you what to do," Jason said after a thoughtful moment, "but don't judge yourself so harshly. Some people know exactly what to say to get what they want. Everyone needs to hear they're important, that they're loved and appreciated. But those are only words, and talk is cheap. You got out of your marriage at the right time and—"

"No," she sobbed, "I didn't…. I didn't *want* out of the marriage, don't you see? It was Tom who asked for the divorce, Tom who forced everything into the open. I would've gone on pretending forever if he hadn't. I won't do it again. I won't! I'm quitting my job, Jason. I'm walking out two weeks from now and I won't look back. I swear to you, I won't look back."

* * *

There was a message from his mother when he returned to his apartment. His mind was heavy with everything he'd learned about Charlotte's marriage and he contemplated waiting to return his mother's call, but she'd sounded so excited.

Sighing, he reached for the phone. His mother answered on the first ring.

"Jason, I'm so glad you called! I have so much to tell you. I talked to Taylor and Christy and they've both agreed to come."

"Come?"

"You can't imagine what a day I've had," his mother continued, her voice animated. "I called Barbara Johnson, you remember Barbara, my friend who owns the floral shop, don't you? We went to high school together a thousand years ago."

"Mom…"

"Let me finish." With barely a pause to breathe, she went on, "Barbara was the one who got things started. She suggested we contact the yacht club right away and book a date for the reception. They're booked at least a year in advance. A year, I told myself. I know you, Jason, and when you're ready to do something, you don't want to wait an entire year. Barbara was right. The earliest date was August the year after next. I can tell you, I was shocked. I had no idea we'd need to book the reception so early."

"Reception? What reception?" Jason was starting to get a frightening premonition.

His mother ignored his question. "That's when I learned there'd been a cancellation in July. This July! I couldn't believe our luck. Naturally I booked it that very instant. Then I contacted the caterers and, as luck would have it, they agreed to do the dinner, although it's only three weeks' notice. *Three weeks,* Jason. Three weeks. It sounds crazy to even attempt something of this magnitude, but we're going to pull it off without a hitch."

Jason's vague premonition was beginning to solidify. "Mom, what are you talking about?" he asked with growing anxiety.

Once again his mother disregarded his question. "That's when I phoned Taylor and Christy. They both called back to say they're coming. They've already made their plane reservations. Russ is coming, and Mandy, too. Remember Mandy, Russ's sister? She's in college now, you know."

"Coming? To *what,* Mother?" Jason demanded.

"Why, Jason, I've spent the day making the arrangements for your wedding to Charlotte. What else would I be talking about, for heaven's sake?"

Ten

"Mother, have you gone stark, raving mad?" Jason had difficulty keeping a rein on his anger. "How can you set a wedding date and hire caterers when I haven't even *mentioned* it to Charlotte? This is insane." He rubbed his face, wondering if he'd imagined this entire fiasco.

"Your father warned me you'd be angry, but, Jason, I know you. Once you and Charlotte decide to marry, you won't want to wait two years."

"Mom, I don't suppose it dawned on you that there are other places we could have a wedding reception—*if* we were actually having one. The yacht club isn't the only venue in this town."

"Frankly, no, it didn't occur to me," his mother returned calmly. "Since we're just going to have one formal wedding in this family, we're doing it up big, and the yacht club's the best alternative."

Jason could see he was losing ground. "Let me talk to Dad."

"But, Jason—"

"Mother!"

"All right, just a minute."

That minute seemed to take an hour. By the time he

had his father on the line, Jason was as angry as he'd ever been. The instant he heard Eric pick up the receiver, he shouted, "Has Mother gone crazy? Have you? How could you let things go this far?"

His father chuckled, apparently amused, something Jason most definitely wasn't. "I agree with you," his father said breezily, "your mother has gone a little crazy."

"Dad, listen, I know you and Mom mean well, but I refuse to let you run my life. Scheduling the reception, talking to florists, I can't believe you'd allow Mom to do all this without talking to me first."

"Don't forget, she's involved Taylor and Christy, as well. That's when I thought she'd stepped over the line. You haven't even asked Charlotte to marry you, and Elizabeth's got your sisters choosing bridesmaids' dresses. By the way, I don't suppose she told you about the honeymoon? Two weeks in Hawaii—it's our wedding gift to you."

Jason clenched his fist at his side and closed his eyes, trying to calm himself. It didn't work. The situation was absurd. And he was beginning to see that his father was in on this nonsense. "Two weeks in Hawaii…Taylor and Christy choosing bridesmaids' dresses. You've both gone off the deep end."

"To your mother's credit, she didn't intend for this to happen. It just did. I know you're upset now, and to be honest, I don't blame you, but once you get used to the idea, it doesn't sound so ludicrous."

Get used to the idea, Jason mused. He felt like he was in the middle of a nightmare. "You honestly think I should agree to this…this outrageousness?" He could barely speak.

"Answer me this. Are you in love with Charlotte?"

"Yes." That much was a given—he'd already told his parents so.

"Do you intend to ask her to marry you?"

His dad knew the answer to that, too. "Yes…eventually, in my own time and my own way."

"If you're planning to marry the girl anyway, then what's the problem?"

"I wasn't going to do it in three weeks!"

"Three weeks, three months, what's the difference?"

Jason couldn't believe it. His father was talking pure craziness.

"I realize your mother and I went about this wrong, but after what happened with your brothers and sisters, all I ask is that you cut us a little slack."

"A little slack," he snorted. "Marriage is a serious step. A man doesn't make that kind of decision one minute and march up the aisle the next."

"I used to feel that way myself, but it's pretty much what happened with Taylor and Russ, as well as Christy and Cody. They made up their minds, then went right ahead and did it."

"All right, all right," Jason muttered, willing to concede the point. Their weddings were spontaneous, to say the least. Same for Rich and Paul.

"I agree, marriage is a serious step," his father went on calmly, "but if you're in love with Charlotte and intend to marry her anyway, I don't see the harm in your mother getting the ball rolling."

The ball rolling. She'd started an avalanche. "Don't you think Mom's just a tad premature?"

"Perhaps," his father agreed amicably enough. "But you can't really blame her for that. She got caught up in the excitement of the moment. Once she talked to the yacht club, everything sort of fell into place. It makes sense once you analyze it. You've been a bachelor a long time, Jason. If you're as serious about marrying Charlotte as you claim, my advice is, just do it. If you wait, you might talk yourself out of it."

"Do it," Jason echoed. "You make marriage sound like taking up an exercise program." He could see he wasn't going to make any more headway with his father than he had his mother.

"Think about it, all right? That's all I ask."

"Aren't you forgetting something?"

"What?"

"Charlotte might say no."

His father laughed. "Charlotte's as much in love with you as you are with her. She'll marry you in a New York minute and we both know it."

"But, Dad…"

"Just think about it overnight. That's all your mother and I are asking. If you decide you'd rather not go through with this, then phone us in the morning and we'll put a stop to everything."

"I don't need to sleep on this," Jason argued. "I can tell you right now that I'm not going to agree. I've never heard anything more absurd in my life. A wedding in a few weeks! I was thinking more along the lines of two or three years!"

A heavy silence followed his words. "Then you must not be as much in love as your mother and I assumed. Give us a call in the morning," his father said and hung up the phone.

Jason was too furious to stand still. He paced his living room, jerked his baseball cap off his head and slapped it against his thigh. He tried to smooth out the crease in the bill, realized he couldn't and tossed the hat on top of the television.

Earlier that evening, he'd been talking to Charlotte about this very thing—people manipulating and controlling others. Well, he wasn't about to fall prey to it now. Especially not with his parents.

If he allowed his mother to schedule his wedding, there was no telling where she'd stop. The next thing he knew she'd be meddling in *all* his personal affairs. She'd be deciding when it was time for him and Charlotte to have a family.

He drew in a deep, calming breath to clear his head.

His assessment of his mother was unfair, he told himself a few minutes later. His parents hadn't interfered in his brothers' or sisters' marriages. From what he understood, they'd suggested Leah and Paul get married, but that was common sense. Leah and Paul should have seen it themselves. He knew his parents had debated long and hard about confronting them and had done so reluctantly, after much soul-searching.

But arranging his marriage to Charlotte was an entirely different matter. They'd stepped over the boundary there—although…although he did understand how easy it must have been to get caught up in the heat of the moment. Getting the date at the yacht club had set everything in motion, and before either of his parents were aware of it, they'd planned the whole wedding.

As he recalled from his dinner conversation the day before, Jason had told his mother that Charlotte would welcome her assistance in planning the wedding. She'd done a bit more than suggest what type of flowers to use in the bridal bouquet, however.

No, it was out of the question.

Jason flatly refused to be a pawn. When he was ready to marry Charlotte he'd…

Married. He and Charlotte.

He needed at least a year just to get used to the idea. A

man his age didn't surrender his freedom without plenty of serious thought.

Then he remembered the phenomenon of holding Charlotte in his arms, of loving her, and the simple pleasure he found in spending time with her. He tried to imagine what his life would be like without her and discovered he couldn't. So his belief that he wasn't ready flew out the window.

But marriage, he told himself, would take away his freedom. He'd never watch another game on TV again without feeling guilty—a wife would make sure of that. Women nagged and controlled, didn't they?

Charlotte was a woman, but she wasn't like the others he'd known. She'd been controlled and manipulated herself; she'd fought against it. Jason couldn't in all honesty believe she'd try the same tactics on him.

Once again his argument wouldn't hold.

All right, maybe there were more things to consider besides his freedom. But here, too, he was losing ground. He'd found freedom in Charlotte, freedom to be himself, freedom to look toward the future.

Charlotte wanted children.

Another contentious issue. Children. Carrie had said as much the day she'd stopped by his office to bribe him to take out her mother. If he married Charlotte, he might as well accept that a year or so down the road they'd have a baby.

So? Wasn't that what he wanted?

He hadn't thought much about a family until recently. He vividly remembered the sensations that had overwhelmed him the first time he'd seen Charlotte holding Jeremy. Watching her play with his brother's son had left him breathless. Of course, being hit by a fast-moving Frisbee might have contributed to that.

Okay, so he wanted children. A man didn't marry a woman without giving the prospect some consideration. Since he was well past thirty, and fast approaching forty, he should start thinking along those lines soon. Charlotte was nearly thirty-six herself, and he knew it was safer for a woman to give birth before the age of forty.

Which meant he had to throw out his idea of waiting two or three years to get married. If he was serious, and he was, they should do it soon.

But three weeks was *too* soon....

He'd sleep on it, Jason decided, take his father's advice and give this whole wedding business some thought. But he could say right now, that on general principles alone, he was against it.

An hour later, after tossing and turning and wreaking havoc with his bedsheets, Jason knew. Knew it from the way he couldn't keep his hands from clenching. Knew it from the way his stomach tensed.

He was going to marry Charlotte Weston. The wedding was already scheduled.

Charlotte didn't know what was wrong with him. Jason had fidgeted all through dinner, although dinner had been his idea. He'd called her early that morning, before she'd left for work, and invited her out.

The invitation had sounded offhand, spur of the moment. Or that was how he'd apparently intended it to sound. But Charlotte wasn't fooled. His voice had tensed as though he wasn't sure she'd say yes—which was ridiculous. Surely he knew how crazy she was about him. Yet, when she assured him she'd be happy to join him for dinner, he hadn't seemed the least bit relieved.

She'd suggested Mr. Tamales, but he'd disagreed. Instead he'd chosen a fancy seafood restaurant near the harbor. She'd been looking forward to chicken enchiladas, but certainly wasn't disappointed with her shrimp Louis.

Charlotte could have sworn, however, that Jason hadn't eaten more than three bites of his wine-sautéed scallops. "Jason," she said after a long silence. "Is something bothering you?"

"No," he replied abruptly.

"You haven't said a word in the last five minutes. Aren't you feeling well?"

"My stomach's in knots." His reply was quick and short-tempered. He reached for his water glass, emptying ice chips into his mouth, then chewed on them fiercely.

"Do you want to leave?"

His eyes met hers and for an all-too-brief moment the tension eased from around his mouth. "Not yet."

"Okay," she said, wondering at his strange mood.

"How did everything go with your boss?" he asked, seeming to want to change the subject.

She'd already told him, but apparently he hadn't been paying attention. "He's angry, especially since two other people also gave their notice when they learned I wasn't changing my mind."

"Did he try to make staying worth your while?"

Charlotte nodded. "He offered me and the others a raise." Mr. Ward had called all three of them into his office, smugly claimed he was willing to overlook this small mutiny and offered them each a raise if they'd withdraw their resignations.

"You didn't take his bride—I mean bribe—did you?"

"No." Charlotte was still basking in the satisfaction she'd felt when she told Mr. Ward she wasn't interested in withdrawing her notice. Cheryl and Janice hadn't changed their minds, either. Mr. Ward had been stunned, but she knew that would soon pass.

Before the end of the two weeks, he'd try every manipulative tactic in the book. When she didn't give in, he'd try anger, his least effective tool.

She was through with a boss who was so angry and unreasonable. Through with guilt and regret and abuse. She already had a line on another job, although she would've enjoyed taking the summer off.

Unfortunately, she couldn't afford it. As it was, she only had two months' budget in her savings account, and it had taken her a year to accumulate that much. She called it her "attitude money." It was a whole lot easier to walk away from her position at the agency, knowing she had some cash to fall back on if she didn't get a job right away.

"How about dessert?" Jason suggested after the waitress had taken their dinner dishes away.

She shook her head. "No, thanks. I'm stuffed."

He looked disappointed at her response.

"You go ahead, though," she urged.

Jason immediately rejected the idea, proving her initial impression wrong. But if he *wasn't* craving dessert, what did he want? He seemed restless, yet obviously wasn't inclined to leave.

Whatever was bothering Jason wasn't trivial, Charlotte realized. Jason Manning wasn't a man easily unnerved. She wondered if it was something she'd done, something she'd said. She didn't know what to make of his behavior. Throughout dinner, she'd considered various explanations, none of which seemed all that logical.

The silence between them lingered as they sipped their after-dinner coffee. From the moment he'd picked her up, she'd been surprised that Jason was wearing a suit, the same attractive gray one he'd had on the night of the dance. His brother's suit. She knew very well that he didn't dress formally unless it was some important occasion. His entire wardrobe consisted of jeans and T-shirts.

He hated wearing a suit. Five minutes after they'd arrived at the dance, he'd loosened his tie, and had completely discarded it by the end of the evening. Why he'd worn one this evening remained a mystery.

Charlotte frowned, trying to analyze what was wrong. Waiting for Jason to tell her was making her nervous. He looked miserable, which made *her* increasingly miserable.

She felt close to Jason, closer than she'd felt to any man since Tom. She hadn't meant that to happen, and she didn't think Jason had, either. Their relationship had grown steadily more intense in the past weeks. She'd fallen in love—it was that simple—and thought he had, too.

But perhaps falling in love wasn't what Jason wanted. Perhaps he was trying to find a way to tell her they were in too deep, that he wanted out.

It made sense.

The fancy dinner, the hesitation and even regret. The fact that his eyes kept avoiding hers. The silence. That was the worst. The awkward silence, as though he couldn't bear to speak those final words.

"I'm ready to leave, if you are," she said with false enthusiasm.

He looked over at her, his expression uncertain. Perhaps he planned to tell her in the restaurant, in order to avoid a scene. She'd heard that was a popular tactic. All Charlotte wanted to do was leave, before she made a fool of herself by breaking into tears.

He was going to break up with her; she was sure of it. A hundred explanations crowded her mind. They'd gotten too close, too fast. It wasn't as if she was…unencumbered. True, she was single, but she had a child, and if a man was going to get serious with a woman, he'd prefer that she didn't bring along excess baggage. That was common knowledge. She'd heard it often enough from friends and acquaintances.

Jason's parents might have disapproved of her, too. It wasn't as if she came from a fine, upstanding family. His mother had asked her a number of questions Saturday morning about her parents and grandparents. Charlotte had found it difficult to explain that she had no idea where her father was, or even if he was still alive. Neither of the elder Mannings had seemed to disapprove of her openly. If anything, they'd been warm and gracious. But although they might have accepted her, even liked her, they might also think she was the wrong kind of woman for their son.

Jason paid the bill while Charlotte excused herself for a visit to the ladies' room, hoping to regain her composure.

He was waiting for her by the door when she returned.

Silence accompanied them into the parking lot.

Jason opened her door. By the time he'd walked around the front of his car, Charlotte's hold on her poise was tenuous. When he glanced in her direction, though, she managed a smile. Her pride demanded it.

Charlotte expected Jason to drive her directly to the apartment, since he hadn't been able to break the news to her at the restaurant. At least when he delivered the blow, it would be in the comfort of familiar surroundings.

But he drove to a deserted stretch of beach, then pulled off the road, climbed out of the car and came around to her side.

"It's late," she said, frowning at her watch. "I should be getting home. Carrie's by herself."

"In a minute." He wore a pensive frown, the same expression she'd seen all evening.

She gazed past him to the shoreline. Small breakers rolled onto the sand, their motion soothing. Charlotte wasn't soothed, however, and she looked away to the wide expanse of darkening sky. The scent of the sea hung in the air.

"Just say it," she muttered. Her patience had evaporated and she couldn't bear the painful silence anymore.

"You know?"

"Of course I know." She walked onto the sand, removed her shoes and purposefully forged ahead, stopping at a thick log that was charred at one end.

Swallowing a mouthful of self-pity, she looked over her shoulder to discover that Jason had followed her onto the beach. She almost wished he'd driven away, left her behind. It would've been easier that way.

Her legs didn't feel as if they'd support her much longer, so she sat on the log and stared sightlessly out at the horizon, waiting for him to begin his litany of excuses and stumbling explanations.

"Charlotte…I'm not very good at this sort of thing."

"Who is? Listen, it's been great." She strove to sound flippant and knew she'd failed. She lowered her gaze to her hands, forcing herself to continue. "I'll always be grateful for this time with you." Tears rolled down her cheeks and she brushed them aside, not daring to look at Jason. "But as we both know, all good things must come to an end…."

Jason said nothing. Not one word, and that made everything even more difficult.

His hands were buried in his pants pockets and when she glanced up at his face, she saw that his jaw was tightly clenched. She didn't understand his anger, not when she'd made it so easy for him.

"So you had me sit through that whole miserable dinner," he said with barely controlled antagonism. "Did you enjoy watching me squirm?"

"No."

"You know, Charlotte, if you weren't interested in marrying me in the first place you could have—"

"Marrying you!" Charlotte's head snapped up. "You planned on asking me to *marry* you?" For one wild second she was paralyzed with shock, unable to move or think. There must've been a mistake. It was a joke. Jason Manning was a confirmed bachelor, wasn't he? Despite her feelings for him, Charlotte had accepted that.

"Don't pretend you didn't know," he said.

"But I thought…I thought you wanted to stop seeing me."

He snickered as though he didn't believe her and turned away. "Why would I take you to a fancy restaurant if I wanted to say something as ridiculous as that?" He turned back, glaring at her.

"To let me down easy. What did you expect me to think, when you were in such a bad mood?"

"I already told you I'm no good at this sort of thing. If you want romance and a bunch of pretty words, you're going to have to marry someone else."

She was on her feet and not quite sure how she got there. "You honestly want to marry me?" she repeated as her eyes brimmed with tears. They were tears of relief. Tears of joy.

"Sit down," he said gruffly. "If I'm going to do this, I want to do it right."

Charlotte complied and was shocked when Jason got down on one knee directly in front of her. He cleared his throat. "I love you, Charlotte. I wasn't planning to fall in love with you, but I knew it was happening, and I let it happen because—well, I don't really know. It happened and I'm glad it did. I can't think of spending a day without you at my side. I can't imagine playing softball without you there. I love you. I love the chocolate chip cookies you bake. I admire you for the wonderful job you've done raising Carrie. I'm deeply impressed by your wisdom and courage."

"Oh, Jase." She blinked back her tears and brought her fingertips to her lips.

"You're the first woman I ever dated who let me be myself. You didn't feel obligated to clean up after me. You don't act as if my refrigerator's some kind of scary science experiment." He grinned, apparently pleased with his own wit. "You even like sports."

The lump in her throat made it impossible to speak. Tears ran unrestrained down her face. With all her heart she wanted to shout, "Yes, I'll marry you," and throw her arms around him. But she was afraid to believe Jason would continue to love her once he learned how inadequate she was, how worthless she was as a lover. She didn't know if she could bear to disappoint him.

"If it helps," he said in a low voice, "I talked to Carrie, and she's all for us getting married."

Charlotte sniffed tearfully. "You mean my daughter's given you her seal of approval?"

"Yup."

There was another silence. Then he said, "I don't mean to rush you, but I have this sore knee. I slid into first base last week and I've been in pain ever since. So, if you don't mind, I'd prefer a quick answer."

Before she could stop herself, before she could listen to her head instead of her heart, she nodded. It wasn't a very enthusiastic nod, perhaps, but Jason didn't seem to have any objections.

"Thank God," he murmured, awkwardly rising to his feet.

"You idiot. You didn't have to get down on your knee," she whispered through her tears.

"Yes, I did," he said, but he sounded grateful to be off

it as he sat down on the log beside her. A deep sigh rumbled through his chest. "It wasn't the most romantic proposal, was it?"

"Oh, Jase, it was perfect," she said, touching the side of his face and gazing into his eyes. Her throat was tight and constricted. "What you said about not being able to live without me…that's how I feel about you. Sharing cookies, going to ball games, walking the dog together—it all sounds wonderful. I guess I'm not much of a romantic, either," she said with a shy laugh.

"I didn't buy a diamond ring. I figured you'd want to pick a setting yourself."

A ring. Charlotte froze. Soon he'd want to discuss a wedding date. A chill worked its way through her, the same cold feeling she'd experienced whenever Tom wanted to make love. A sick sensation would build in the pit of her stomach and by the time they went to bed she'd feel encased in ice. All Tom had to do was kiss her and he'd know. Then the tirades would begin, the accusations, the ugliness.

Jason was going to kiss her, too. Now. His lips grazed hers. Briefly. Lightly. The cold fear melted as if it had never been. Charlotte groaned and slipped her arms around his neck.

He kissed her again, but this time the kiss blossomed into something wild and erotic that left Charlotte panting, seeking more.

They drew apart, and she rested her forehead against his. When he spoke, his voice was husky and warm, as warm as heated brandy and just as intoxicating.

"We're going to be very good in bed," he whispered.

Charlotte tensed, panic a heartbeat away, but she forced it down, focusing instead on how gentle he'd always been with her. How patient. With Jason, she'd felt a level of pleasure she'd never realized she was capable of reaching. When he kissed her she felt hot and quivery from the inside out. Maybe it would be different this time, with this man. Maybe. She prayed that was true.

"You're worried about making love, aren't you?"

She nodded.

"I'd never hurt you, Charlotte. I hope you understand that. Whatever the problem is, we'll work it out together."

"I'm grateful…for that." Despite the excitement she felt at his kisses, she had to fight back the fear that threatened to choke her every time he mentioned the physical aspects of their relationship.

Her only recourse was to insist on a long engagement. That way she could slowly, gradually, feel comfortable with their sexual relationship. After they made love… She hesitated. There'd been a time she wouldn't have thought that was possible, but Jason had given her hope.

"Do you want to set the wedding date?" she asked, deciding to broach the subject now.

"Yes, but…" He shrugged. "There's one small problem."

"What's that?"

"I'm going to let my parents tell you. It's only fair. They're at home, waiting for us now."

Eleven

"I don't believe this!" Jason muttered under his breath as they pulled into his parents' driveway.

"What are all these cars doing here?" Carrie asked from the backseat. Jason had insisted on going back to the apartment to pick her up.

"You'll see," he said grimly.

Either his parents owned a car dealership or they were entertaining a houseful of company.

"This is going to be a real circus." He sighed as he helped Charlotte out of the front seat. Carrie bounded out from the back.

Charlotte's nervousness, already heightened by the prospect of an audience, grew exponentially.

The door opened and Elizabeth Manning stepped out of the house. Jason's father and brothers, sisters-in-law and several children all crowded on the front porch behind her. The porch light revealed a variety of expressions, from amusement to elation.

"Well?" his mother asked as she walked toward them.

Jason slid his arm around Charlotte's waist and slowly, sweetly smiled down at her. In those brief seconds, Charlotte was comforted and reassured by his love. Her senses sang and her heart fluttered wildly.

Jason lowered his head. Charlotte wasn't sure that kissing in front of his parents, his whole family, was the best thing to do. Oh, what the heck. She was marrying Jason. They were in love, so a simple kiss shouldn't offend anyone.

Their lips met and she moaned a little with surprise and wonder at the ready response he never failed to evoke from her. Her hand crept up his chest and gripped the lapel of his suit jacket as his mouth made love to hers.

When he broke away, he was breathless. For that matter, so was Charlotte. She marveled that he was able to speak at all. "Does that answer your question, Mother?"

"Charlotte's agreed to marry you?"

"In a heartbeat," she answered for herself.

"Isn't it great!" Carrie shouted.

Spontaneous applause broke out from the porch, followed by several earsplitting whistles. Ryan and Ronnie were pounding their feet but she doubted the little boys understood exactly what the family was celebrating.

The evening was lovely; honeysuckle and roses scented the air. The sun had almost set, casting—literally—a rosy glow over the scene.

Jason bowed as though he were a knight and she his lady, accepting his family's enthusiasm.

"I hope you realize you're getting the runt of the litter," Paul told her, laughing.

"Hey," Rich put in. "Just be grateful that Charlotte's willing to put Jason out of his misery. He's been walking around like a lovesick puppy for weeks."

Jason glowered at his brothers, but she could tell he wasn't angry. He took their teasing in stride. From the time he'd brought her to that first softball game, Charlotte had envied him his family, especially the close relationship he shared with his brothers. The three were more than brothers; they were best friends. They looked out for one another and, just as important, they laughed together.

Leah and Jamie were best friends, too. Yet they seemed eager to extend that camaraderie to Charlotte. They'd gone out of their way to include her, to make her feel welcome, a part of the family. One of them.

Jason's mother came forward, tears in her eyes as she hugged Charlotte. "I couldn't be more pleased. Jason couldn't have chosen better."

"Thank you," Charlotte said, blushing. Doubt bobbed like a cork to the surface of her mind. Not that she didn't love Jason. She did, with all her heart, but she still wasn't sure whether she was the right woman for him.

"I'm so happy for you—and for us," Jamie said, hugging her next. "The two of you are perfect for each other. Leah and I agreed on that the minute we saw you together."

A warmth permeated Charlotte's heart. She wanted so badly to believe it was true.

"We'll be sisters now," Leah whispered, taking Charlotte's hands and lightly squeezing her fingers.

"I couldn't be marrying into a more wonderful family," Charlotte said to Jason as they made their way into the house. Carrie followed, carrying Jeremy, while the other children raced excitedly ahead.

His brothers congratulated Jason, slapping him on the back.

Once inside, Jason and Charlotte sat on the couch and the family gathered around them, making them the center of attention. Every eye was on Charlotte, smiling and happy, yet expectant. Puzzled, she glanced up at Jason, wondering if they wanted her to say something, to make some speech or pronouncement.

"Does she know yet?" Paul asked.

"No," Jason murmured. "I'm leaving the explanation up to Mom and Dad."

"Smart boy," Rich said, sitting on the armrest of the couch. He leaned forward eagerly, as though waiting for the opening act of an award-winning play.

"What's everyone talking about?" she asked.

"Mom?" Jason gestured eloquently toward his mother.

Elizabeth hesitated and turned to her husband. Eric Manning grinned and gave his wife a reassuring nod, which only compounded Charlotte's curiosity.

"As I said, I'm delighted that you've agreed to marry Jason," Elizabeth began. "He's waited all this time to meet the right woman and, frankly, Eric and I were beginning to wonder if that was ever going to happen. Now that we've met you, Charlotte, we're glad he waited so long. We understood the moment we saw you together how special you were to him."

A low murmuring chorus of assent brought a sheen of tears to Charlotte's eyes. If anyone should be grateful, it was her. Jason had changed her world, opened her mind to everything she'd believed was closed off to her. Love. Family. Joy. Partnership.

The room went strangely quiet. Charlotte looked around and, although everyone seemed genuinely pleased, there was a tension here, too.

"Just tell her, Mother," Jason advised. "No need to drag this out."

By now, Charlotte was more than curious. "Tell me what?"

"Don't rush me," Elizabeth said, chiding her son. "Charlotte," she began, "when Jason told us he'd fallen in love with you, his father and I naturally wondered about his intentions. Then he told us he intended to ask you to marry him, so we decided to do a bit of checking in regard to the arrangements. Weddings need to be planned."

Jason's fingers entwined with hers, his hold on her hand tightening.

Elizabeth paused as though she expected a response. "Well, yes," Charlotte said, since everyone was staring at her. "That's a practical thing to do."

"I learned some distressing news," his mother continued. "The yacht club, which we feel is the best place for the reception, is booked solid for the next twenty-three months."

Once again, like clockwork, all eyes in the room swiveled to Charlotte, awaiting her response. "I hope you put our name on a waiting list, then," she murmured.

Elizabeth brightened, and some of the tension lines on her forehead seemed to relax. "I did better than that. You see," she went on, her voice growing more confident, "there happened to be a cancellation, and so I asked they reserve that day for you and Jason."

"Wonderful."

"You're leaving out the most important part," Jason said, his lips barely moving.

"The date is July fourteenth," Elizabeth announced, folding her hands and nodding sagely. "Don't you think that's excellent timing?"

"That sounds fine," Charlotte agreed, when it was apparent once again that everyone was waiting for her to respond. A little more than a year would give her and Jason ample time to discover if a marriage between them was viable. By then, they'd certainly know if a sexual relationship was possible. A year gave them both an opportunity to adjust.

"It's not July fourteenth of *next* year," Jason filled in,

his gaze locking with hers. "Mother meant July fourteenth of *this* year."

Charlotte was too stunned to respond, other than with a gasp. Her mouth fell open in shock.

"What's the problem, Mom?" Carrie asked, looking surprised.

"But…but no one can plan a wedding of any size in that length of time," Charlotte managed after a moment. "It's…impossible."

"Not for Elizabeth," Leah said, her eyes sparkling with excitement. "Mom's been working on this since Jason mentioned the word *marriage*."

"But…"

"I've seen to everything," Elizabeth said confidently. "And it *is* possible, very possible—if you'll agree to such a quick wedding. I realize we're being unfair to you, and I do hope you'll find it in your heart to forgive me for taking over like this. The thing is, I know my son, and once he makes up his mind, that's the end of it. Jason wouldn't have been willing to wait almost two years."

"But…there are other places. Besides the yacht club, I mean."

"Yes, but none of them are as special."

"Charlotte," Jason said, raising her hand to his lips and kissing it. "I know it sounds crazy, but Mom's right. I wouldn't have wanted to wait just so my mother could put on a fancy wedding. At first I thought she'd gone berserk. The idea's preposterous, but the more I thought about it, the more I liked it."

"Leah and I will do anything we can to help," Jamie inserted. "If you want the truth, we're both thrilled."

"Taylor and Christy and their families are flying out. They've already made their reservations," Elizabeth added.

"But they can change them," Jason told her, frowning at his mother as if to say Charlotte was under enough pressure as it was.

And he was right. She felt as if a giant hammer was poised above her head, ready to smash down on her at any second. The entire family was waiting. Happy. Excited. Thrilled. Carrie's eyes begged her to say yes.

"Of course, Taylor and Christy can change their reservations, if necessary," someone said. That was Paul, and Charlotte wanted to thank him.

"Personally, I think it's wildly romantic," Leah added. She was sitting in the recliner, her hand resting on her swollen abdomen. Paul was sitting on the armrest, his arm wrapped around his wife's shoulders, his eyes filled with love as he gazed down on her.

"Naturally I haven't made any final decisions—that would be up to you," Elizabeth said.

"I…don't know what to say."

"You must think I'm a domineering old woman, and I suppose I am, but nothing's been finalized. I don't generally meddle in my children's lives, but—"

"Actually, if you want to be angry with anyone, it should be with the rest of us," Jamie told her. "Jason is the family's last chance for Mom to put on a big wedding. She'd been looking forward to it for years and we all disappointed her. She's always done a fabulous job with the receptions, though."

"We've had our hearts set on a formal wedding for so long," Eric said.

"But in three weeks?" Charlotte murmured.

"We'll all need to work together, of course, but we can do it." Jason's mother sounded utterly convinced of that. Her eyes sought out Charlotte's and, in their beautiful blue depths, Charlotte saw how much Elizabeth wanted this.

How much the entire family did. They all looked forward to contributing.

"Charlotte," Jason said softly, "would you like more time to decide?"

She glanced around; everyone was waiting. The room had gone completely silent; even the children were quiet. Charlotte didn't know how she could refuse. She closed her eyes and tried to think. If she postponed the wedding, the elder Mannings might hold it against her. It could taint their future relationship. The others were just as eager for this to happen. Each one felt guilty for cheating Eric and Elizabeth out of the family wedding they wanted.

Her whole future with the Manning family could be at stake, Charlotte thought.

"Do I…need to decide now?" she asked after an awkward moment.

"There's so little time," Elizabeth warned.

Charlotte glanced from one to the other and knew she couldn't refuse. She loved Jason and wanted to marry him more than she'd wanted anything in her life. She could be happy with him, happy in ways she'd hardly imagined before. And for the first time she and Carrie had the chance to be part of a real family.

If she were to marry Jason there was the possibility of her having another child. *If* she conquered her fear of sex. The hollow ache inside her intensified as she studied the soft swell of Leah's abdomen.

She turned to Jason, needing some kind of confirmation, some indication of what he was thinking. His eyes, so like his mother's, blue and intense, reflected his love for her. His faith in her. The desire to be part of *her* life. He believed their love was enough to overcome any obstacle. Their love was all that was necessary.

For now, because she wanted to believe it, too, that was enough for her, too.

"We have a lot to do, then, don't we?" she said, reluctantly dragging her gaze away from Jason and back to his mother.

"Does that mean you agree?"

She nodded and the entire family broke into cheers.

The excitement and the enthusiasm carried Charlotte for a full two weeks. Two of the busiest weeks of her life. When she wasn't putting in her final days at work, she was with Jason's mother.

During their first afternoon together, it became apparent that Elizabeth was a gifted organizer. She'd have to be in order to pull off a full-scale wedding in less than a month.

Ignorance had been bliss. Had Charlotte realized the sheer magnitude of what they needed to accomplish in such a short time, she would have refused.

Not a day passed that she didn't have some kind of appointment, some place to be, someone to meet, some decision to make. There were dressmakers, florists, photographers, caterers and printers. And countless decisions, all of which had to be dealt with right that minute. There wasn't time to ponder or reflect. As soon as one task was completed, Elizabeth steered her toward the next.

Carrie was delighted to be her mother's maid of honor. Charlotte's four soon-to-be sisters-in-law were to be her bridesmaids, and that meant frequent conference calls between Montana and Seattle.

When Charlotte somehow found time to see Jason, it was for a few moments, and then only in passing. He, too, was exceptionally busy.

Just when it looked like everything was falling neatly into place, and Charlotte would finally be able to return to a life of her own, a series of showers and parties began. Every night was busy with one event or another. Even the women in the office held a bridal shower for her on her last day with the agency.

The Mannings were a well-established, well-liked family. Three of Elizabeth's closest friends decided to honor Charlotte with a shower the Monday before the wedding.

"I can't believe how generous everyone is," Charlotte said to Carrie, who had just attended the shower with her. They were carrying the wide array of gifts from the car into the apartment.

"Those old ladies don't even know you," Carrie remarked, her voice filled with astonishment. "All these gifts! You don't suppose they'd throw a birthday party for me sometime, do you?"

"Carrie!"

"Just joking, Mom." She hurried past Charlotte and brought in a gaily decorated box that was still unopened. Charlotte had been told the gift was for Jason, therefore he should be the one to open it. The giver was his godmother, a spry older woman named Donna Bondi.

"You want me to see if Jason's home?" Carrie asked eagerly.

Charlotte, too, was curious to see what was inside. "Go ahead." It was almost ten, and under normal circumstances Charlotte would've been more concerned about getting to bed so she'd be ready for work in the morning, but her two-weeks' notice was up and she was officially among the unemployed.

She had the entire week free, or as free as any bride's time could be five days before her wedding.

Carrie returned a few minutes later with Jason in tow. He smiled when he saw her and kissed her lightly on the lips, then bent to stroke an ecstatic Higgins. "What's this I hear about Mrs. Bondi sending me a gift?"

"She insisted you open it yourself."

Jason's look was skeptical. "Is it a gag gift?"

"I don't know. Why don't you find out?" Charlotte leaned against the kitchen counter and crossed her arms. "When you're finished, I'll show you all the loot we collected. I had no idea everyone would be so extravagant."

"Don't get any ideas about spending our honeymoon writing thank-you notes," he warned. He was grinning but she caught a serious undertone.

The honeymoon.

She wanted to talk to Jason about that, *needed* to talk to him about it, but there'd been so little time. They'd each been caught up in a whirlwind of activity. Since the evening he'd taken her to dinner and proposed, she hadn't spent any uninterrupted time with him. Now wasn't good, either. He was tired and so was she. Perhaps they could arrange to have lunch one day later this week.

Jason tore at the paper.

"You wouldn't believe Mom," Carrie said, her hands on the back of a kitchen chair as she looked on excitedly. "She doesn't tear a single piece of wrapping paper."

"It's all so pretty," Charlotte defended herself. "And I can use it again."

"It takes her forever to unwrap anything. I had to help her tonight, or we'd still be there."

Jason paused when he uncovered a plain white box. He raised his eyes to Charlotte.

"Don't look at me. I have no idea what Mrs. Bondi sent you."

Carefully he raised the lid and folded back the white tissue paper, but Charlotte couldn't see what was inside with Carrie bending over the table.

"All right, Mrs. Bondi," Jason said, emitting a low whistle.

Carrie covered her mouth and giggled before glancing at her mother.

"What is it?" Charlotte asked.

"Wait until you see this, Mom."

Using both hands, holding on to the thin straps, Jason lifted the sheerest, slinkiest, blackest nightie Charlotte had ever seen.

Charlotte forced a smile but she felt as though the older woman had slapped her in the face.

Charlotte knew better than to even try to sleep.

The next morning she'd walk down the church aisle and pledge her life to Jason Manning. She would vow to love and honor this man who'd come to mean so much to her.

To love him….

What would happen if she couldn't love him properly? What would happen when he realized she was incapable of satisfying him sexually? Would he claim he'd been cheated the way Tom had? Would he seek out another woman who'd give him the gratification she couldn't?

Oh, please, not that, not again—she couldn't bear it.

Charlotte didn't know how Jason would react, but she knew she'd find out soon.

She stared at the bright green numbers on her clock radio as one in the morning became two and then three.

The alarm was set for six. Charlotte's stomach tightened and a cold sweat broke out on her forehead. Her happiness had been supplanted by her fears, her anxieties and the certainty that her heart would be broken once again.

She'd made an effort to talk to Jason several times, she reasoned. It wasn't like she'd *planned* it this way. In the past week alone she'd called him three times, but he'd been so busy with his practice, tying up the loose ends so he'd have two uninterrupted weeks for their honeymoon in Hawaii.

The honeymoon terrified her even more than the wedding.

What was she supposed to do? Wait for Jason to say "I do," before she whispered in his ear that she wasn't sure she could satisfy him? Or should she say something before he slipped the ring on her finger?

It seemed cruel to wait until they got to their honeymoon suite. How could she possibly tell him something like that wearing the sheer black nightie Mrs. Bondi had sent?

The tightening in her stomach grew worse, until she thought she might actually throw up.

She shouldn't have left it to the last minute like this, but she'd had no other options.

She'd tried to spend time alone with Jason, to talk to him, but they hadn't connected all week. Whenever she saw him, there were other people around. She'd decided to demand time with him after the wedding rehearsal. They had to talk.

Only that hadn't worked, either.

They'd sat next to each other at the rehearsal dinner, but before she could say more than a few words, his brothers had spirited him away for a bachelor party.

Although she hadn't been in any mood to socialize, Charlotte had pretended to have a good time with Leah, Jamie, Jason's two sisters from Montana and her future mother-in-law. If any of them noticed how distracted she was, they must have attributed it to nerves.

By now the bachelor party would be over, probably had been for hours.

What was she going to do?

Her dinner, what little she'd eaten, soured in her stomach and she thought she might be sick. Tossing back the sheets, she climbed out of bed, waiting for the nausea to subside, then wandered aimlessly into the living room.

Dragging the afghan from the back of the sofa, she wrapped it around her shoulders and huddled in the recliner, the dog at her feet. Carrie and Mandy, Russ Palmer's half sister, were in the bedroom down the hall sleeping soundly, unaware of her torment.

Jason knew so little about her first marriage. He hadn't asked for information, and she'd volunteered even less. Instead, he'd cautiously tried to learn the details, but she'd put off explaining, afraid she'd lose him.

Soon, within less than twenty-four hours, Jason would know for himself why Tom had gone to another woman. Charlotte would have to face her inadequacies all over again.

As she sat in the dark, the shadows from the street danced against the walls, taunting her, jeering, shouting that she was a fool to believe she could ever satisfy a man.

Another hour passed and still the trapped, restless feeling refused to leave her; if anything, it became more intense. If only she could sleep. If only she could disappear. Vanish. Go someplace where no one would find her.

Squeezing her eyes shut, she tried to force her body to relax, but closing her eyes was just one more mistake. In her mind, Tom rose, scorn engraved on his handsome features. A cocky smile lifted the edges of his mouth, as if to tell her this was exactly what he'd been waiting for. As soon as she tried to make love with another man, she'd know everything he'd told her was true. *He* wasn't the one to blame for the failure of their marriage; she was. Charlotte—a woman too cold, too stiff, too lacking in sensuality.

Her eyes shot open and hot tears dripped down her face.

A series of sobs racked her shoulders and took control of her body until she was trembling from head to foot.

She couldn't bear it, couldn't deal with it. Tom was right, he'd always been right. She was a fool to believe that a sexual relationship between her and Jason would be any different, any better. They could kiss without a problem, but after the wedding, he was going to expect a lot more than a few kisses.

Panic filled her lungs, and it was all she could do not to scream in sheer terror.

Jason was wrapped in a warm cocoon of blankets, but the irritating noise refused to go away. He reached out his hand to turn off the alarm, fumbling with the dials before he realized it wasn't his alarm.

Opening one eye, he read the digital readout and discovered it was only four. He was entitled to another couple of hours' sleep. His head throbbed. Who'd come up with the bright idea of a morning wedding, anyway? No one had asked *him* about it.

The noise increased. It was now a steady pounding.

Someone was at his door. If this was one of his brothers' idea of a joke, he wasn't amused. He'd only gotten a few hours' sleep so far. If anyone in his family was involved in this, he'd make his displeasure clear in no uncertain terms.

Apparently whoever was at his door wasn't leaving. Jason struggled out of bed, pulled on a pair of pants and walked blindly through his apartment.

"Who is it?" he demanded irritably, wiping a hand down his face.

"Carrie."

"And Mandy."

The two vaulted into the room as he opened the door.

"You've got to do something!" Carrie cried.

Although his vision was a bit fuzzy, he could tell that she'd been crying.

"We didn't know what to do," Mandy wailed.

"About what?"

"This." Carrie handed him an envelope with his name written across the front. He recognized the handwriting as Charlotte's, but her usually smooth script was jerky and uneven.

Puzzled that she'd resort to writing a letter and having it delivered in the wee hours of the morning by two worried teenagers, he removed the single piece of paper.

He read it quickly.

Jason,

I'm sorry seems so inadequate, but I can't go through with the wedding. Please, if you can, find it in your heart to forgive me.

She'd signed it with her name.

It was a joke. Not a very good one, but he'd laugh over it in a few minutes.

"Who put you two up to this?" he asked, using his sternest voice.

"No one!" Carrie sobbed. "It's true. I got up to go to the bathroom and Mom's bedroom light was on, so I went in to see what was wrong and she wasn't there. She wasn't anywhere."

"The car's gone, too," Mandy added.

The words galvanized Jason into action. He shook the hair out of his face.

"What are we going to do?" Carrie asked, still crying softly.

"*We* aren't doing anything," Jason answered firmly.

"But someone has to do something!"

"I'll take care of it," he assured them. "Don't breathe a word of this to anyone, understand?"

"But..."

"Just do as I say. There isn't time to argue. If I'm not back with Charlotte before the car comes to take her to the church, tell everyone she's with me."

"What are you going to do?" Mandy asked, her eyes following him as he trotted back to his bedroom. He turned back and grinned. "Do?" he repeated. "Find her, of course. She's got a wedding to attend."

Twelve

Jason couldn't even guess where Charlotte was. He finished dressing, grabbed his car keys and took off, determined to find her.

He drove around for an hour, considering various possibilities. He tried to think like she would. If he were a bride running away from a wedding, where would he go? But that didn't work; he'd never run away from anything in his life, certainly not a wedding.

Darned if he knew what Charlotte was thinking. He had difficulty enough understanding women under normal circumstances. Still, he'd thought Charlotte was different. He'd thought—he'd assumed, erroneously it seemed—that Charlotte was as eager for their wedding as he was. He was shocked that he'd been so blind to her doubts. She must be terrified to have run away like this. Terrified and alone.

He should've known something like this would happen. He'd backed her into a corner, pushed her into this wedding. He'd allowed his own needs, his own desires, to overrule hers.

As dawn streaked the horizon with lavender and pink, he found himself growing ever more concerned.

Where could she be?

His driving became increasingly reckless, his speed gaining as he raced desperately from one possible location to the next. Checking the time, he was nearly swallowed by panic.

There wasn't much time left. They were both supposed to be at the church in a couple of hours. The thought of hurrying back to his family and having to announce that Charlotte had run away filled him with a sick kind of dread. He wouldn't return, he decided, until he'd found her. Until he'd done whatever he could to calm her fears, to reassure her, convince her how much he loved her.

Jason wasn't sure what led him to the beach where he'd proposed to her.

When he saw her car parked haphazardly along the side of the road, he nearly collapsed in relief. A calmness took hold of him and his pulse slowed to an even, steady pace.

He parked behind her and rushed out of his car. The sound of the door closing must have been carried away with the wind, because she didn't turn around or give any indication that she realized he was there.

He paused for a few seconds, looking at her, his heart swelling with gratitude at finding her safe.

Charlotte sat on a log, facing the water. The same log he'd knelt in front of to ask her to marry him. He felt a stab of pain as he remembered that night and how ecstatic he'd been when she accepted his proposal. He didn't expect to feel that good again until they shared in the birth of a child.

Charlotte's shoulders were slumped forward and she seemed mesmerized by the gentle lapping of the water. The wind whipped her hair, which flew wildly about, but she didn't appear to notice. She wasn't wearing a sweater. She must be half freezing, Jason thought, peeling off his jacket.

He watched her for another moment, wondering exactly what he'd say. He'd had hours to prepare for this, hours to come up with the words to tell her how much he loved her and how sorry he was for the way everything had gone. Now he found himself speechless.

She didn't see him until he was almost upon her. When she happened to look up, he saw that her face, ravaged by tears, was as pale as moonlight. She blinked, then frowned as though she couldn't quite believe he was really there.

"Jason?"

"Funny meeting you here," he said, placing his jacket around her shoulders.

"I… How did you find me?"

"It took some effort. If you had any doubts, Charlotte, I wish you'd talked them over with me."

She frowned again. "There wasn't any time… I tried, honestly I did, but you were always so busy and the time went so fast, and now…" The rest of her words faded into nothingness, her gaze avoiding his.

"There's time now," he said, sitting down on the log beside her.

Her eyes widened. "I…can't go through with it."

"Why not?" he asked calmly.

She answered him with a wrenching sob. "Please…I can't. I don't love you…"

Jason tensed. "I don't believe that, Charlotte. There's something else."

"There is… I realize now that it's your family I love. I never had one of my own and it came to me that I was marrying you for all the wrong reasons. I…can't go through with the wedding… I just can't."

Jason felt as if someone had punched him. Hard. "My… family?"

"Yes," she cried. "They're all so wonderful and I…got carried away, thinking that if I married you…Carrie and I would be part of a large, loving family. Then I saw how unfair I was being to *you*...marrying you when I didn't love you."

A cold anger took hold of Jason. An anger rooted in pain and disillusionment.

"It's too bad you didn't think of that sooner, because all this soul-searching is a little too late." He grasped her arm and pulled her to her feet. She sagged against him, but he tugged at her and she straightened.

"Jason, please..."

"Shut up, Charlotte. Just shut up before I say something I'll regret." It was no comfort realizing she was the only woman who'd ever brought him willingly to his knees. He'd gone to her in love, a love so strong it had swept away his loneliness. Charlotte was throwing it all back at him now, rejecting his love, betraying him with her last-minute revelations.

Walking out on him at the eleventh hour like this couldn't be considered anything less. Nothing she could've done would have humiliated him more than to leave him standing at the altar.

"I can't be your wife... Don't you understand?"

Her voice was so weak he wasn't sure he'd heard her correctly. Not that it mattered; nothing she could have said would've had any effect on him after her confession. It didn't matter if he could hear her or not. She was mumbling, pleading with him, but he closed off his heart the same way he had his ears.

When they reached his car, he opened the passenger door and deposited her inside. He ran around to the driver's side, not knowing if he could trust her to stay put. He was mildly surprised that she didn't try to escape.

He started the engine and turned on the heater. A blast of warm air filled the car. She didn't seem to notice.

Neither spoke until they were close to the freeway entrance.

"Why are you doing this?" she demanded.

"I don't know," he answered. "But I do know you're going through with this wedding, if it's the last thing either of us ever does."

"But how can you force me to marry you, knowing what you do?"

"It must have something to do with saving my entire family from humiliation," he continued with the same chilly irony. "That family you claim to love so much. Maybe it's because I don't want my mother—who's worked day and night on this wedding for the past three weeks, who's looked forward to this day for years—to become an object of pity among her friends. Maybe it's because I'd have trouble looking my two sisters and their husbands in the eye, knowing they rearranged their entire summer, gave up their vacations, to fly out here for our wedding. Just maybe it's because I have an aversion to being ridiculed myself. I can't really tell you what else would reduce a man to drag a woman who's rejected him to the altar. But make no mistake, Charlotte, you will marry me."

"It isn't that I don't care for you," she whispered through her tears.

"Right. You care so deeply that you decided to go into hiding on our wedding day."

"I know you're angry…"

"You're damn right I'm angry."

"We can't go through with the wedding, Jason! We just can't."

"Oh, but we are, Charlotte."

"What will we do afterward? I mean, once we're married and—"

"Somehow we'll find a way to miss our flight to Hawaii, then, first thing Monday morning, I'll file for an annulment."

"But it doesn't make sense to go through with the wedding—"

"Yes, my darling Charlotte, it does. It makes a whole lot of sense."

Charlotte was determined to survive the day, although she wasn't sure how she'd manage. She'd been a fool to run off the way she had. A fool and a coward. She was an even bigger fool to think she'd appease Jason's anger by lying.

When she'd left, she hadn't thought about what she was doing to Jason or his family. She hadn't been thinking at all, overpowered instead by her own fears.

On the way back, she tried to tell Jason she was sorry, to apologize for the hurt and humiliation she'd caused, but each time he cut her off, saying he didn't want to hear it.

The ride back to her apartment was like living through the worst nightmare of her life. Jason was so cold, so furiously angry.

He dropped her off at her apartment, took her arm, leveled his steely blue eyes on her and said, "I'll be by to pick you up in forty minutes."

"I can't possibly be ready by then."

"You can and you will. And, Charlotte, don't even think about running away again. Do you understand me?"

Charlotte nodded and almost told him it was bad luck for the groom to see the bride before the wedding. Then she remembered the whole wedding was a farce, anyway.

"Fine. I'll be ready," she assured him calmly.

She showered, brushed her hair and dressed, but she wasn't conscious of doing any of those things. Carrie was with her, and Mandy, too, both silent and pale. Worried. What she'd done to them was terrible, Charlotte realized.

They were both too young to carry this secret, too young to bear the burden of her foolishness.

Neither girl asked her any questions, and for that, Charlotte was grateful. She didn't know what she would've told them if they had.

Leah and Jamie had arrived within minutes of Jason's bringing her home. They were both happy and excited. If her complete lack of emotion bewildered them, they didn't let it show. They chatted excitedly, recalling events at their own weddings, bubbling over with enthusiasm. Charlotte tried to smile, tried to pretend this was the happiest moment of her life. Leah and Jamie seemed to believe it, even if the girls had their doubts.

Jason arrived to escort her to the church, and her future sisters-in-law shooed him away. She wore the beautiful off-white dress Elizabeth Manning had insisted on buying her, and Leah had woven flowers in her hair.

Before she knew it, Charlotte was at the church. The number of guests surprised her. Tears clogged her throat when she reminded herself that she was playing a role. Tomorrow morning she'd go back to what her life had been before she met Jason Manning. Back to the emptiness. The loneliness.

At the appropriate moment, with organ music swirling around her, she walked dutifully down the aisle, aware every second of Jason standing at the front of the church. His eyes held hers as effectively as a vise, as though he suspected she might try to run even now. And if she tried, she didn't doubt for a second that he'd go after her.

With her morning little more than a vague memory, Charlotte found it ironic that the actual wedding ceremony was so clear to her.

Jason stood at her side, revealing no emotion, and calmly repeated his vows. Charlotte wondered why the minister didn't stop him. It was all too evident from the clipped, angry tone of his voice that he didn't mean what he was saying. He had no intention of loving her, of cherishing her, of allowing her ever to be important in his life. Not after what she'd done. Not after she'd led him to believe her motives were so deceitful. Not after she'd made him think she planned to ridicule him and his family. Whatever love he'd once felt for her was dead. He'd practically told her so himself.

When it was her turn to say her vows, Charlotte's voice was surprisingly strong. She would always love Jason, and she'd always treasure the months they'd shared. The sincerity in her voice must have caught his attention, because he looked at her for the first time since they'd approached the altar. His eyes narrowed scornfully. For a moment she nearly faltered, but decided she wouldn't let him intimidate her.

His eyes seemed to be laughing at her—a mocking laugh that told her she was the biggest hypocrite who'd ever lived. He could think what he wanted, but in her heart she knew the truth.

After the ceremony, they were whisked from the church to the reception at the yacht club.

For Charlotte, the lengthy reception was a thousand times worse than the ceremony. They stood, for what seemed like hours, with the members of their wedding party, while an endless line of guests paraded past.

Everyone was so thrilled for them, so happy, everyone except the two of them. From the moment they'd arrived at the reception, Charlotte was a heartbeat away from dissolving into tears. Heaven knew how she survived the ordeal.

Later they had to cut the cake. The photographer took picture after picture.

"Resist the urge to shove the cake in my face," Jason

whispered behind a smile, when she went to feed him a small piece for the camera, "and I'll do the same."

They ate, they danced, they opened gifts. Outwardly they were the perfect couple. Madly in love, solicitous of each other, eager to be alone. Eager to start their lives together.

Only Charlotte and Jason knew the reality beneath the pretense.

Despite herself, Charlotte was impressed by what a brilliant actor Jason was. He refrained from touching her, but when it was unavoidable, his arms were gentle, his look as tender as he could make it, although she knew that he seethed with outrage. She could feel his anger, hidden below the surface, out of everyone's sight but hers. At times Charlotte felt as if that anger would devour her whole.

"Just a few minutes longer," Jason whispered harshly while they were on the dance floor. "Then we can leave."

She relaxed. "Where are we going?"

"Not the airport, so don't worry about it."

"We need to talk."

"No, we don't. Everything's been said. I'll drop you off at your apartment and you can forget this day ever happened."

"But—"

"Like I said, don't worry about it. I'll arrange everything. Once this is over, we won't ever have to see each other again. Needless to say, I'll expect you to find a new place as soon as possible."

She nodded, knowing she'd brought this on herself. But when it was time to go, there was a surprise awaiting both of them. Jason's brothers and brothers-in-law had rented two limousines. The first to take them to the airport, Rich explained, grinning proudly. And the second limousine was so the entire wedding party could follow them and see them off with as much fanfare and enthusiasm as was allowed.

Jason's eyes sought out Charlotte's when she returned from changing her clothes. His gaze assured her not to worry. He wasn't any more willing to spend two weeks in her company than she'd been about going through with the wedding. She was sure he'd find some way to miss the flight.

Except that he didn't.

His mother waited with them at the airline counter, wiping the tears from her eyes as she hugged her son. Carrie was there, too, more relaxed now, excited that she and Higgins would be spending two weeks with Leah and Paul.

Charlotte hugged Jason's mother farewell, tears brimming in her eyes. "No woman ever had a more beautiful wedding," she whispered. "Thank you."

Her father-in-law was waiting when she'd finished, holding out his arms to her as though she were a small child needing reassurance. Nothing could be closer to the truth.

"Eric, thank you," she murmured, as she slipped into his embrace. This might well be the only opportunity she'd have to express her gratitude. Soon enough Jason's parents would know. She wouldn't be able to face them.

"You call me Dad," Eric said, hugging her close. "We already love you like a daughter, Charlotte."

Tears blurred her vision and when she turned, she nearly collided with Jason. He took her by the elbow, his fingers pinching her skin. "You're laying it on a bit thick, aren't you?"

She didn't answer him, couldn't have said a word if she'd tried. They got their boarding passes as everyone watched. They were going to Hawaii, like it or not.

Charlotte realized there was no escape for them, unless

they owned up to the truth immediately. Jason didn't look any more pleased than she did, but obviously didn't want to disillusion the family quite so soon.

As he led her into the security area, away from his family, he muttered, "I didn't plan this."

"I know," she said with a helpless sigh. "Oh—my car. I left it at the beach."

"Mandy's getting it for you."

His thoughtfulness surprised her. "Thank you."

"Don't mention it," he said sarcastically. "I wanted it back in the apartment lot so you wouldn't have any trouble leaving again. Next time you can go with my blessing."

Their seats were in business class and they were quickly served glasses of champagne that neither of them drank.

As the plane taxied away from the jetway and toward the airstrip, he closed his eyes, heaved a massive sigh and said, "Don't worry, I'll get us out of this yet."

Charlotte nodded and lowered her gaze. "I'll do everything I can to stay out of your way."

"That would be appreciated."

The flight was five hours, but it seemed closer to fifty. Jason didn't exchange one unnecessary word with Charlotte. At this rate, she didn't know how they'd be able to spend two weeks in each other's company.

Jason must have been thinking the same thing. "I'll see what I can do about arranging a flight back to Seattle as soon as we land," he told her briskly, without a shred of emotion. No regret, no disappointment, nothing.

Charlotte bit her lip. "I…I didn't pack much of anything…since the suitcase was just for show."

He didn't respond. By the time they landed and collected their luggage, Charlotte was falling asleep on her feet. Apparently Jason suspected as much, since he made some excuse about contacting the airlines from the hotel instead of rushing her onto a return flight. But she wasn't sure if this small kindness was for her benefit or his own, since he couldn't have had much more sleep than she had.

She barely noticed the scenery as the taxi carried them through town. Their hotel was on Waikiki Beach, built on white sands and surrounded by swaying palms.

When they went to check in at the front desk, Charlotte stepped back, letting Jason take care of the necessary paperwork. He was obviously upset about something, but she couldn't tell what.

"Is everything all right?" she asked, as they moved toward the elevator.

"I thought we could get a double room, but…" Jason rubbed a hand across his face, looking weary and defeated. "My parents booked us into the bridal suite."

"Oh." Charlotte didn't fully realize the implications of that until the bellman ushered them, with much fanfare, into the corner suite. There was one bed. A king-size bed that loomed before her.

Charlotte's startled gaze sought out Jason's as he paid the attendant and closed the door. The fear she'd managed to bury for hours spilled over now, but before she could say a word, he turned to her.

"Don't look so shocked. It isn't as if I intend to make love to you."

"But where will…we sleep?"

He laughed, the sound abrupt. "If you want to call down to the front desk and order a rollaway for the bridal suite, then by all means, be my guest. Frankly, I feel enough of a fool for one day, so I'll leave that option to you."

With no real alternative, she showered, put on an old T-shirt and crawled between the crisp sheets of the bed, making sure she was as far on her side as possible.

She was drifting off to sleep when Jason finished his

shower and returned to the bedroom. He stood for several minutes looking down at her. Her heart roared like a crazed animal as she wondered about his intentions. He could force her. Tom had often enough, using her body, leaving her feeling sick and abused afterward. She'd curl up tightly while he shouted how incompetent she was, how unattractive, how lacking. She'd lie there silently as the ugly, demeaning words rained down on her. When he was done with his tirade he'd leave.

The memories made her shiver with revulsion and fear.

"Charlotte."

She didn't answer, pretending to be asleep. Jason was angry with her, angrier than she'd ever seen him. Eyes closed, she lay still, her heart pounding with dread.

She heard Jason dressing, heard him pause and then, after a moment, heard him turn off the light and leave the room.

Abruptly Charlotte sat up. He'd left her, walked away just like Tom had, as though he couldn't bear to be in the same room with her. Like Tom, he couldn't wait to be rid of her.

He'd left without a word.

Wasn't that what she wanted? Then why did she feel so alone, so deserted and unloved, so empty inside?

The tears that had threatened most of the day broke free with a low, eerie wail. She tucked her knees against her chest as the sobs overtook her.

She wept for all she'd lost. Jason's love. Any chance of sharing their lives. The dream of having another child. The family she'd never had. It was gone now, crushed by her own hand.

It was too late to try and get any of it back. Jason hated her. She could never recapture what she'd destroyed with her fear. Never rebuild the trust she'd demolished when she'd run away.

She sobbed until the well of grief was emptied. Even that wasn't enough. She tore at the sheets, pulling the blankets from the bed and beating the pillows.

It didn't take long to exhaust what little energy she had, and she fell across the bed sobbing, then fell into a deep, troubled sleep.

Jason came back to the room an hour later, moving as silently as possible, not wanting to wake Charlotte. He wished he could hate his wife, punish her for what she'd done. She deserved to suffer, didn't she?

But if that was really the case, then why was *he* the one in pain? He saw her climb into bed and curl up, and it was all he could do not to dash across the room and take her in his arms. This woman had betrayed him, and yet he wanted to comfort her.

It was either leave the room or beg her forgiveness for forcing her to endure this day. She wasn't entitled to his forgiveness, he reminded himself, which meant there was only one option. He'd left.

He'd gone for a walk on the beach, which wasn't exactly how he'd expected to spend his wedding night. Not that he was any great shakes as a husband. A hundred times or more he'd gone over his own part in this fiasco. He'd rushed Charlotte into marriage and so had his family, not giving her a chance for second thoughts. Looking back, he understood now that it was the urgency of his mother's idea that he'd found so appealing. Now he understood why.

He'd rushed into marriage with Charlotte because, deep down, he'd been afraid that if she'd had the chance to change her mind, she would. And he'd been right.

Jason didn't know what lunacy had prompted him to

make her go through with the ceremony. To avoid embarrassment? Having their marriage annulled the following week would still embarrass him and his family. There was the problem, too, of returning all the wedding gifts. Eventually he'd have to face people. Make explanations.

He'd taken the easy way out, delaying the inevitable because of his pride.

Charlotte had wanted to cancel the wedding and he'd perversely refused to release her. So now they were stuck in Hawaii on a two-week honeymoon neither of them wanted. Stuck in each other's company, in the bridal suite no less, until he could find a flight back to Seattle.

Once his eyes had adjusted to the dark, Jason made his way across the elegant room. Charlotte was still curled up on the bed, but the sheets and blankets were strewn about as though a storm had raged through.

He discovered a second and a third pillow hurled across the room. One was on the floor, the other dangling from a chair. It looked as if his bride had thrown a temper tantrum.

So she hadn't liked it that he'd left. A smile played across his lips. It was the first time since he'd found her on the beach that she'd displayed any emotion.

The thought of Charlotte losing her temper pleased him, until he remembered she wasn't given to bouts of anger. He felt a pang of concern but brushed it aside—it belonged to the past, to the old Charlotte, the one he'd loved.

Exhausted and depressed, he gazed about the room and noted that the bed was all she'd bothered to disarrange. Everything else in the room remained untouched.

Not knowing what to think, and too tired to care, he quietly stripped off his clothes and slipped beneath a rumpled sheet. It didn't take him long to fall asleep, but his dreams were disturbing and he woke several times before morning.

Not once during the night did Charlotte move. She stayed on her side, facing away from him, never changing her position.

He woke in the morning, the bright sunshine slashing through the bedroom curtains. Charlotte was on her back, already awake. She shifted her head and stared at him with eyes so filled with pain that he hurt just looking at her.

"I lied when I said I didn't love you, Jason," she whispered and a tear rolled down the side of her face. "I do… so very much. I'm sorry…for everything I've done."

He nodded, his throat thick. "I'm sorry, too, Charlotte."

Thirteen

Charlotte closed her eyes because looking at Jason was so painful, knowing he hated her, knowing he'd never really forgive her for what she'd done.

"I lied when I said I wanted to marry you because of your family. I…ran away because I was afraid."

"Of me?"

Her pulse scampered. She should've told him the truth weeks earlier. She'd agreed to be his wife; he had a right to know. But the truth was so easy to put off, so easy to deny. So hard to explain.

There'd been opportunities to tell him, plenty of them, although she'd tried to convince herself otherwise. She'd been too much of a coward to present Jason with the truth. And then, when time ran out, she'd panicked.

"Charlotte?" Jason said in a low voice. "What are you afraid of?"

She couldn't explain that she was, to put it bluntly, afraid of sex. Of intimacy. That wasn't what a man wanted to hear. Not just Jason, but any man.

He deserved so much more than she was capable of giving him. He deserved a woman who was emotionally whole and healthy. A woman who was physically responsive. Not someone scared and battle-weary and all but dead to her own sexuality.

"I owe you an explanation…."

"I'd say so," he agreed, but his voice was devoid of the previous day's sarcasm, without a trace of anger.

"I meant to tell you sooner. To give you the choice of going through with the wedding or not. But as time went on I—I couldn't…and then it was too late."

"Tell me now."

Charlotte thought back to an age when she'd been innocent, vulnerable and naive. "My mother died while I was in high school. My father had abandoned us years earlier and I don't think my mother ever recovered. If he contacted her at any point after he left, I didn't know about it. She was different after he was gone. It was like she'd given up on life. She loved me, though—I know she did—and she'd been insightful enough to plan for my future."

Jason's hand reached across the bed for hers. Their fingers entwined and Charlotte was grateful for his touch.

"I met Tom my first year of college. He came from another state and was attending classes on a limited scholarship. He was intelligent and good-looking. When he asked me out, I was thrilled. He seemed to like me…. Later I realized it wasn't me that attracted him, but the insurance money I'd received when my mother died. After a few months, we made love and…and he asked me to marry him. I didn't have any family and…I desperately needed someone. I was too stupid to know why Tom really wanted to marry me. He saw marriage as a way of paying for his education without having to work for it.

"I dropped out of school after one semester and we got married. The money that was meant for my education went toward Tom's while I got a full-time job to pay our living expenses."

Jason's hand flinched, tightening around hers.

"I should've gotten out of the marriage as soon as I figured out he was using me. Instead, I compounded my mistake. I thought if I got pregnant it would make everything better. If Tom didn't love me, surely he'd love the baby."

"You've been so hard on yourself."

"I'll never regret having Carrie. She's been the best thing in my life…but Tom wasn't happy." She hesitated, reliving the terrible scene, so many years past, when she'd told Tom she was pregnant. He'd wanted her to have an abortion, even given her the money. She'd lied and told him she'd done it, hiding her pregnancy until it was too late. He'd been so furious that he'd hit her. The blow had been so hard, it had loosened three of her teeth.

"Go on," Jason prompted.

"I had Carrie and for a while I thought the marriage might work. Tom liked his little girl and was proud of her."

"You told me Tom was having an affair. When did this happen?"

"It started while I was pregnant. Tom enjoyed sex…and after a while he said I was too fat and ugly to make love to, and everything came to a stop." Charlotte remembered how relieved she was, how grateful because she no longer had to give in to his rough physical demands. She was working a forty-hour week, waiting tables, and was too exhausted at night to satisfy him. He'd been telling her for months that a man needed enthusiasm from his wife during sex, but Charlotte had never seemed able to rouse any. It was like making love to a corpse, he told her.

"I…I never was very good at sex," she continued in a tight voice. "And after Carrie was born, I lost all interest." Actually any pleasure in the physical aspects of their marriage had died months earlier, when Tom had demanded she have an abortion. After Carrie was born, she found herself unwilling to make any effort to please him physically.

"That was when the really bad fights began," she said as evenly as the remembered emotions would allow. "Tom claimed it was his right to make love to me whenever he wanted and…and…" Her throat closed up, forcing her to stop.

"Did he rape you, Charlotte?"

Biting her lower lip, she nodded. Only Tom hadn't called it rape; he'd said it was his right. He'd married her, hadn't he? That meant she'd given him the right to do whatever he wanted with her body the moment she'd signed the marriage document.

Jason moved closer and brought her into his arms, cradling her head against his shoulder, stroking her hair. His chest was heaving and Charlotte knew he was fighting his own anger.

Her eyes glazed over with tears as she struggled to hold back the fear, the memory of the violence, the feeling of powerlessness, the revulsion of those terror-filled episodes. Her breathing became labored.

"I…couldn't satisfy Tom," she admitted in a breathless whisper.

"That has everything to do with Tom—not with you." He paused. "Are you afraid you won't be able to satisfy me?"

She nodded through her tears.

"But, Charlotte," he said, raising himself on one elbow and gazing down at her, "how can you think that? Everything between us has always been so good. Or am I wrong? Haven't you enjoyed the times we kissed?"

She lowered her lashes. "Yes…but they've frightened me."

"I never forced you."

"I…I know that. You've been so patient and gentle. I almost convinced myself I could make love again…that I could erase those nightmare years with Tom and start all over…but I can't. That's why I ran away…that's the real reason, not what I told you earlier."

"Why couldn't you tell me this before?"

She wiped the tears from her face, and swallowed the bittersweet agony of the moment. "Because I love you so much."

Her words were met with a puzzled hesitation. "You wouldn't tell me because you love me?"

She nodded, and hiccuped a sobbing laugh. "It sounds ludicrous, I know, but it's true. Because I couldn't stand to lose you—not that way. Because if we ever did make love, you'd see—you wouldn't want me anymore."

"How could you think that?" Jason asked.

This was the moment she'd dreaded. The moment of truth. She turned her head away, unwilling to look at him, unwilling to let him see her face. A tightness gripped her chest, crushing her, the pressure so intense she could hardly breathe.

"Charlotte?"

It would've been easier if he hadn't been so gentle. She could deal with his anger and frustration, but not his tenderness. She didn't know how to respond to that in a man.

Shoving aside the blanket and sheet, she sat on the edge of the bed. When he caressed her back, she stood, unable to deal with being touched just then. Her arms were locked around her middle and the aching pressure in her chest rose, settling in her throat. Tears burned her eyes.

"Tell me," he demanded, not unkindly. "Just say it."

"I can't be your wife."

"It's too late for that," he murmured. "You already are."

"I'm not…not in the ways that matter to a man."

"Oh?"

"Don't you understand what I'm saying?" she cried. "Do I have to spell out every degrading detail? Is that what you want? Then fine, I'll say it. I can't be your wife because I can't make love." She gulped in a deep breath. "I'm frigid, Jason. The term might be out of fashion but it still applies."

There was a brief, shocked silence. Then Jason started to laugh.

"Don't you dare laugh at me! Don't you dare laugh." A fury rose inside Charlotte, one that had been years in the making, one so strong there was no holding back. She threw herself at him, arms swinging, feet kicking, fingers clawing, before he had a chance to react.

He caught her by the wrists. "Charlotte…I wasn't laughing at *you.*"

She barely heard his words, not that it mattered. She twisted and bucked in his hold. He twisted, too, and with the momentum of his weight they fell together on the bed. He was sprawled over her upper body, his thigh across her legs, holding her down.

Her chest was heaving, her shoulders jerking upward in an effort to escape.

"Charlotte, for heaven's sake, I wasn't laughing at you," he said again.

She gritted her teeth, refusing to answer him.

"Stop struggling, before you destroy any chance of my fathering our future child."

She went still, although the fight hadn't completely left her.

"Now let me explain."

There were too many years of agony inside her, too many insecurities to be soothed away with a few simple words. "No. Just let me go."

"In a minute. Then if you still want me to release you I will. You owe me this much. All right?"

She twisted her head away from him, still refusing to answer.

"I love you, Charlotte. I realized when we first started seeing each other that you'd been badly hurt by your ex-husband. I didn't understand the extent of it until now, but in some ways I think not knowing was for the best. It would have intimidated me in the beginning."

A sob tore through her throat.

"The first time we kissed…I wish I knew how to explain it, but I knew you were different. That moment was different than any I'd ever known before. Kissing you was so good."

Charlotte didn't respond, but she knew he was right. Their kisses *had* been good. Very good.

"It got even better, didn't it?"

She nodded, although only slightly.

"You're not frigid, or whatever term the psychologists prefer now. Not even close. What you are, my love, is afraid, and for a very legitimate reason. You've been sexually abused."

"I'm sexually…damaged. Forever."

"No, not forever. In time you'll heal. We'll heal together." He said it with such conviction, as though they faced only a small problem, when to her it was bigger than both of them. Bigger than even their love.

"But it isn't *you* who…can't make love," she sobbed. "It's me. You're not the one who has to heal…and I don't know if I can."

"We're in this together, Charlotte. Whatever it takes."

"There isn't any reason you should—"

"We can't heal," he interrupted, "unless we try. We can't sweep this under the carpet and ignore it. I'm not so stupid as to believe that all the pain and all the memories will go away simply because we make love and it's as good as our kisses have been."

"I…don't know if I'll ever be able to forget."

Jason rolled away from her, freeing her arms and legs. He stood and raked his hand through his hair. "The decision is yours, and I'll abide by whatever you want. I'm not going to force you to be my wife. I've made some mistakes in this relationship and just now was one of them. I'm sure I'll make more. You should know that."

"I don't understand what you're saying." She sat up and wiped the tears from her burning cheeks, her hands trembling. Jason had moved away from her and was staring out the window.

"Like I said, the decision is yours. If you want me to file for an annulment, then I will. I'll make the arrangements to get us off this island as quickly as possible. As soon as I can, I'll take care of all the legalities. In a few days there won't be anything to bind us together—if that's what you want."

"I see." Her heart filled with mourning.

"But there's something you should understand, Charlotte. If you decide you want to give this marriage a try, there'll be no turning back."

She did understand, and the thought filled her with panic.

"I'm willing to devote myself to you and the marriage, but I'll need the same kind of commitment from you. In other words, you're going to have to *want* to heal. It may mean counseling for you, for us both. We both have to be willing to do whatever it takes."

"I don't know if I could…ever tell anyone else about my marriage to Tom."

"That's your decision, too. If you want to stay my wife,

you have to realize that the time will come when we *will* make love—but only when you're ready. And when we do, it'll be good, Charlotte…I promise you that."

"How often?" It was probably a stupid question, but one she needed to know. She might be able to bear it if Jason wanted to make love occasionally. She might be able to overcome the terror if he wasn't too demanding.

"I can't answer that because I don't know."

"More than once a month?"

He turned away from her, but not before she saw his smile. "Yes, Charlotte, more than once a month."

"I see."

"It seems to me that you have some serious thinking to do. Perhaps it would be best if I left for a while. When I come back, you can tell me your thoughts. Does that sound fair?"

She waited until he turned to look at her before she nodded.

So this was what it meant to love someone, Jason thought as he left the hotel and headed for the beach. He felt as though a hole had been carved through the center of his life, and nothing—besides Charlotte—was capable of filling it. He wanted to believe she'd realize he wasn't another Tom. That didn't seem to be the case, however.

He'd felt a glimmer of hope when he'd first started talking, trying to get through to her, soothe her fears. The anger had drained from her eyes as she'd studied him, seeming to measure his words. He'd seen trust gradually replace that anger.

He hoped she'd be willing to give their marriage a chance. He loved her, but he wasn't naive or arrogant enough to believe his feelings for her could, on their own, heal the horror of her experience. She was going to need more than his love, more than his gentleness. Being tender and patient with her wasn't going to wipe out the trauma of having been raped by her own husband. No wonder she was so terrified.

Jason sensed that other things, maybe even worse than those he knew, had happened in her marriage. Things she hadn't told him yet.

Her marriage had been so ugly, so abusive. He marveled that she'd even considered remarrying. Knowing what he did now, it didn't surprise him that she'd run away at the eleventh hour. It wouldn't surprise him if she decided to go through with the annulment, either.

He'd given her the option, laid everything out on the table for her to examine. His love, his commitment, his willingness to do whatever he could to help her overcome her fears. But in light of what he'd learned, it seemed so little….

A couple of hours later, Jason returned to the hotel to confront Charlotte again. Two hours didn't seem like much time to come to such a monumental decision, but he wanted to be with her.

Perhaps it would be best if he waited for her to come to him, but he quickly rejected that idea as impractical. If he was going to waste precious time debating with himself, he should do it over something important, like how was he going to live without Charlotte. How was he going to let her go, the only woman he'd ever truly loved? Those were the questions he should be asking himself.

Charlotte sat in the darkened room, the drapes pulled against the brightness of the sun, waiting for Jason. Having carefully considered her husband's words, she knew with a clarity that defied explanation what she was meant to do. She *should* remain his wife. *Should* share his bed. *Should* share his life.

The heavy ache in her chest intensified. Fresh tears moistened her eyes. Jason had offered her his love, his devotion, and his wholehearted commitment. He'd done so with a courage that left her humbled. He was willing to help her heal, but Charlotte didn't know if it would be enough.

There was no guarantee the pain would ever end. No guarantee she'd ever feel whole again. Healing demanded courage. It meant reaching back into the past, into the pain, and reliving the nightmare. Wasn't enduring it *once* enough? Healing meant risking whatever serenity she'd found in the years since her divorce. Healing meant trusting a man again, trusting him enough to freely share her body.

Charlotte closed her eyes, wanting to blot everything out. She was such a coward. A world-class wimp. She knew what she *should* do, but it was so frightening. She wanted to run away, bury her feelings. Hide, the way she'd been doing for years. There was something so comfortable in denial.

There had to be more to life than this choking anger. More than this grief and fear.

With Jason's love there *was* more.

There was hope.

Charlotte must have fallen asleep. When she stirred she saw that the drapes were open and Jason was sitting on the lanai, sipping a glass of orange juice.

"Hello," he said with a smile.

"Hi." She felt a little shy as she slipped out of bed and rubbed her eyes. "What time is it?"

"Afternoon. I imagine you're starved."

Now that he mentioned it, she realized she was hungry. The last food she'd eaten had been at their wedding dinner, and that had been the day before.

"I took the liberty of ordering you lunch."

She smiled and joined him on the lanai. "I slept for so long."

"You needed the rest." He looked so familiar and handsome, sitting there in the sunlight with his baseball cap shading his eyes. His skin was bronzed, and his eyes, as blue as the Hawaiian sky, roamed over her with undisguised love and tenderness. "Listen, Charlotte, I was wrong."

"Wrong?"

"I shouldn't have given you an ultimatum. You're going to need more than a few hours to decide what you want. I made the same mistake earlier by rushing you into a marriage you didn't want and…"

"But I did want this marriage, very badly."

"Did," he repeated in a husky, regretful voice.

"Do," she corrected firmly.

For several minutes, he said nothing. "Even now, knowing what it'll mean?"

"Even now," she said, holding out her hand to him.

Jason held it fast. "I love you, Charlotte Manning."

"I know." Her voice broke, and she struggled not to break down and weep. Someday she'd tell him how close she'd come to walking away from the brightest promise of her life. She'd tell him how she'd finally decided that loving Jason, being his wife, sharing his life wasn't just something she *should* do, but something she *wanted* to do. *Ached* to do, with all her heart. Someday she'd tell him all of this.

"I don't want to live without you."

He reached for her, bringing her onto his lap, his mouth

instinctively finding hers. Everything she'd planned to say was caught between two hungry mouths. Trapped between two pounding hearts.

Fourteen

Several months later a storm, a Seattle cloudburst, woke Charlotte. Dawn was on the horizon, but very little light filtered through the gray clouds. The wind beat hard against the windows, rattling them until Charlotte feared they might break.

Gently setting aside the covers, she climbed out of bed and crept into the living room. Higgins was sleeping there, looking worried. She patted his head and offered him reassurances.

She opened the living-room drapes just in time to watch a bolt of lightning rip apart the night. For an hour or so afterward, smiling contentedly, she watched morning creep across the sky. Her life, inside and out, was everything she wanted it to be. Jason had moved into her apartment; they planned to buy a house in the spring. She was taking a break from work, enrolled in an advanced accounting course. Eventually she'd handle all of his bookkeeping and maybe look for a few other clients, too. Yes, life was full of new possibilities.

"Charlotte?" Jason murmured when she returned to bed. He reached for her and without a second's hesitation she slipped into his embrace.

"There's a storm," she whispered.

His smile was lazy, sleepy. "So I hear. Are you frightened?"

"Not anymore." There'd been a time when she would've been terrified, but that time was long past. She felt intensely alive, completely calm. The dangerous storms were gone from her life. She'd survived the raging wind, the drenching rain, the booming thunder. That was all in the past. Her future was holding her in his arms.

She sighed, cuddling close to her husband, suffused with a feeling of profound joy.

"I love you," she whispered.

"I know," he said without opening his eyes. "Believe me, I know."

She slid her arms up his shoulders and brought her mouth to his. He welcomed her kiss, which was slow and deep. Hot excitement poured into her blood. Soon the kiss was no longer slow, but hungry, needy.

Charlotte felt Jason's chest lift with a shuddering intake of breath.

"I want to make love," she said against his lips.

Jason went still. His hand, which was sliding up her thigh, stopped at her hip.

"You're sure?"

It was the first time she'd ever made the request, the first time she'd ever initiated their lovemaking.

"Yes."

Lightning briefly brightened the room, shadows frolicked and danced against the walls, followed by the roar of thunder. The bedroom vibrated with sound.

Jason, ever-sensitive to her moods, paused, but she refused to allow any hesitation. She drew his mouth down to hers and they kissed, until Charlotte's whole body seemed to throb with excitement.

Gently Jason removed her nightgown, pulling it over her head. He'd awakened her to an entire world of sensual pleasure in the months since their marriage, a world she wanted to explore *now.*

He hungrily covered her mouth with his own and her head spun, her nails digging into his back. Abruptly she broke off the kiss, her shoulders heaving. "Jason, please… I want you."

He didn't need any further encouragement….

"Okay so far?" he asked sometime later.

"Oh, yes," she whispered, smiling her assurance. The pleasure was so keen it was almost beyond bearing.

Lightning flashed and thunder rolled, punctuating their lovemaking. "Jason…oh, Jase," she cried out, her voice a trembling wail of pleasure as her senses caught fire, exploding into a mindless madness. Her body shuddered as she gave herself to the storm, to her husband, to the night.

Afterward, when he, too, had reached completion, they were both panting. Jason gathered her in his arms, and they were silent, words between them unnecessary.

Eventually their breathing steadied.

"I still have trouble believing how good this is," Charlotte whispered. "Making love, I mean."

Jason kissed the crown of her head. "It always has been."

"Not in the beginning."

"It was," he said. "Because you let me try to prove how much I love you."

Charlotte was quiet for a moment as she absorbed his words. Their first attempts at making love, on their honeymoon, had left her frustrated and in tears. She was convinced Jason had made a terrible mistake in marrying her. He wouldn't allow her to criticize herself, though.

His patience astonished her and gave her the courage to keep trying.

She'd struggled with her inadequacies, silently condemning herself, but on the seventh night of their stay, they'd broken through the restraints and made beautiful, intoxicating love. Charlotte had wanted everything to be magically different from then on, but that would have been unrealistic. Her fears were unpredictable and continued to be for weeks. But now, four months after their wedding, loving Jason was the most incredible experience of her life.

Tears slipped down Charlotte's cheeks as she recalled the first weeks of their marriage—his gentleness, his unwillingness to give up, his *love.*

"You're crying," he whispered, his lips against her hair.

"You're not supposed to notice."

"But I have. Are you going to tell me why?"

Emotion clogged her throat as she struggled to hold back the tears. "In a minute."

Jason's brow creased with a thoughtful frown. "Is it something that came from your meeting with Bill?"

Bill was her counselor; she saw him twice a week. She shook her head. "You promise you won't laugh?"

"I'll try."

"I'm crying because I'm so happy."

"Happy," Jason repeated slowly. "But if you cry when you're happy, what do you do when you're sad?"

"Cry," she returned with irrefutable logic. "Now aren't you going to ask me *why* I'm so happy?"

"I don't need to. It's obvious."

"It is?"

"Of course. You're married to me."

Charlotte laughed at his mock arrogance. "Carrie cried, too."

"Carrie's *that* happy?"

"It's the reason she's spending the night with a friend. I wanted the evening alone with you."

Jason snickered. "If that's the case, why'd you go to bed at six-thirty?"

"I didn't plan that," she murmured, "but I think it's going to be pretty much the norm for the next few months. I couldn't seem to get enough sleep when I was pregnant with Carrie, either."

"Cute, Charlotte, very cute. You couldn't possibly be—" He stopped cold, his eyes widening.

"It's true," she said, pressing her head to his chest. She smiled as the erratic beat of his heart sounded in her ear.

"How far…?"

"A month."

He shook his head as though in a trance.

"It was inevitable, you know," she told him, happiness spilling from her heart. "How could I not be pregnant? We've been making love for months. And we decided not to use birth control for this very reason."

"Yes, but…"

"When the lovemaking's this good, doesn't it make sense that the result will be equally beautiful?"

Jason kissed her again, his mouth worshipping hers. "I love you so much."

Charlotte sighed and closed her eyes, utterly content. She'd conquered her fears, begun to heal her pain. She'd survived the memories and triumphed over her past.

The future stretched before her, filled with bright promise. She wasn't going to miss a single moment.

* * * * *

MY HERO

One

The man was the source of all her problems, Bailey York decided. He just didn't cut it. The first time around he was too cold, too distant. Only a woman "who loved too much" could possibly fall for him.

The second time, the guy was a regular Milquetoast. A wimp. He didn't seem to have a single thought of his own. This man definitely needed to be whipped into shape, but Bailey wasn't sure she knew how to do it.

So she did the logical thing. She consulted a fellow romance writer. Jo Ann Davis and Bailey rode the subway together every day, and Jo Ann had far more experience in this. Three years of dealing with men like Michael.

"Well?" Bailey asked anxiously when they met on a gray, drizzly January morning before boarding San Francisco's Bay Area Rapid Transit system, or BART for short.

Jo Ann shook her head, her look as sympathetic as her words. "You're right—Michael's a wimp."

"But I've worked so hard." Bailey couldn't help feeling discouraged. She'd spent months on this, squeezing in every available moment. She'd sacrificed lunches, given up nighttime television and whole weekends. Even Christmas had seemed a mere distraction. Needless to say, her social life had come to a complete standstill.

"No one told me writing a romance novel would be so difficult," Bailey muttered, as the subway train finally shot into the station. It screeched to a halt and the doors slid open, disgorging a crowd of harried-looking passengers.

"What should I do next?" Bailey asked as she and Jo Ann made their way into one of the cars. She'd never been a quitter, and already she could feel her resolve stiffening.

"Go back to the beginning and start over again," Jo Ann advised.

"Again," Bailey groaned, casting her eyes about for a vacant seat and darting forward, Jo Ann close behind, when she located one. When they were settled, Jo Ann handed Bailey her battle-weary manuscript.

She thumbed through the top pages, glancing over the notes Jo Ann had made in the margins. Her first thought had been to throw the whole project in the garbage and put herself out of her misery, but she hated to admit defeat. She'd always been a determined person; once she set her mind to something, it took more than a little thing like characterization to put her off.

It was ironic, Bailey mused, that a woman who was such a failure at love was so interested in writing about it. Perhaps that was the reason she felt so strongly about selling her romance novel. True love had scurried past her twice, stepping on her toes both times. She'd learned her lesson the hard way. Men were wonderful to read about and to look at from afar, but when it came to involving herself in a serious relationship, Bailey simply wasn't interested. Not anymore.

"The plot is basically sound," Jo Ann assured her. "All you really need to do is rework Michael."

The poor man had been reworked so many times it was

a wonder Janice, her heroine, even recognized him. And if *Bailey* wasn't in love with Michael, she couldn't very well expect Janice to be swept off her feet.

"The best advice I can give you is to re-read your favorite romances and look really carefully at how the author portrays her hero," Jo Ann went on.

Bailey heaved an expressive sigh. She shouldn't be complaining—not yet, anyway. After all, she'd only been at this a few months, unlike Jo Ann, who'd been writing and submitting manuscripts for more than three years. Personally, Bailey didn't think it would take *her* that long to sell a book. For one thing, she had more time to write than her friend. Jo Ann was married, the mother of two school-age children, plus she worked full-time. Another reason Bailey felt assured of success was that she had a romantic heart. Nearly everyone in their writers' group had said so. Not that it had done her any good when it came to finding a man of her own, but in the romance-writing business, a sensitive nature was clearly an asset.

Bailey prayed that all her creative whimsy, all her romantic perceptions, would be brilliantly conveyed on the pages of *Forever Yours.* They were, too—except for Michael, who seemed bent on giving her problems.

Men had always been an enigma to her, Bailey mused, so it was unreasonable to expect that to be any different now.

"Something else that might help you..." Jo Ann began thoughtfully.

"Yes?"

"Writers' Input recently published a book on characterization. I read a review of it, and as I recall, the author claims the best way to learn is to observe. It sounded rather abstract at the time, but I've had a chance to think about it, and you know? It makes sense."

"In other words," Bailey mused aloud, "what I really need is a model." She frowned. "I sometimes think I wouldn't recognize a hero if one hit me over the head."

No sooner had the words left her mouth than a dull object smacked the side of her head.

Bailey let out a sharp cry and rubbed the tender spot, twisting around to glare at the villain who was strolling casually past. She wasn't hurt so much as surprised.

"Hey, watch it!" she cried.

"I beg your pardon," a man said crisply, continuing down the crowded aisle. He carried a briefcase in one hand, with his umbrella tucked under his arm. As far as Bailey could determine, the umbrella handle had been the culprit. She scowled after him. The least he could've done was inquire if she'd been hurt.

"You're coming to the meeting tonight, aren't you?" Jo Ann asked. The subway came to a stop, which lowered the noise level enough for them to continue their conversation without raising their voices. "Libby McDonald's going to be there." Libby had published several popular romances and was in the San Francisco area visiting relatives. Their romance writers' group was honored that she'd agreed to speak.

Bailey nodded eagerly. Meeting Jo Ann couldn't have come at a better time. They'd found each other on the subway when Bailey noticed they were both reading the same romance, and began a conversation. She soon learned that they shared several interests; they began to meet regularly and struck up a friendship.

A week or so after their first meeting, Bailey sheepishly admitted how much she wanted to write a romance novel herself, not telling Jo Ann she'd already finished and submitted a manuscript. It was then that Jo Ann revealed that she'd written two complete manuscripts and was working on her third historical romance.

In the months since they'd met, Jo Ann's friendship had been invaluable to Bailey. Her mentor had introduced her to the local writers' group, and Bailey had discovered others all striving toward the same ultimate goal—publishing their stories. Since joining the group, Bailey had come to realize she'd made several mistakes, all typical of a novice writer, and had started the rewriting project. But unfortunately that hadn't gone well, at least not according to Jo Ann.

Bailey leafed through her manuscript, studying the notes her friend had made. What Jo Ann said made a lot of sense. "A romance hero is larger than life," Jo Ann had written in bold red ink along one margin. "Unfortunately, Michael isn't."

In the past few months, Bailey had been learning about classic romance heroes. They were supposed to be proud, passionate and impetuous. Strong, forceful men who were capable of tenderness. Men of excellent taste and impeccable style. That these qualities were too good to be true was something Bailey knew for a fact. A hero was supposed to have a burning need to find the one woman who would make his life complete. That sounded just fine on paper, but Bailey knew darn well what men were *really* like.

She heaved an exasperated sigh and shook her head. "You'd think I'd know all this by now."

"Don't be so hard on yourself. You haven't been at this as long as I have. Don't make the mistake of thinking I have all the answers, either," Jo Ann warned. "You'll notice I haven't sold yet."

"But you will." Bailey was convinced of that. Jo Ann's historical romance was beautifully written. Twice her friend had been a finalist in a national writing competition, and everyone, including Bailey, strongly believed it was only a matter of time before a publishing company bought *Fire Dream.*

"I agree with everything you're saying," Bailey added. "I just don't know if I can do it. I put my heart and soul into this book. I can't do any better."

"Of course you can," Jo Ann insisted.

Bailey knew she'd feel differently in a few hours, when she'd had a chance to muster her resolve; by tonight she'd be revising her manuscript with renewed enthusiasm. But for now, she needed to sit back and recover her confidence. She was lucky, though, because she had Jo Ann, who'd taken the time to read *Forever Yours* and give much-needed suggestions.

Yet Bailey couldn't help thinking that if she had a model for Michael, her job would be much easier. Jo Ann used her husband, Dan. Half their writers' group was in love with him, and no one had even met the man.

Reading Jo Ann's words at the end of the first chapter, Bailey found herself agreeing once more. "Michael should be determined, cool and detached. A man of substance."

Her friend made it sound so easy. Again Bailey reflected on how disadvantaged she was. In all her life, she hadn't dated a single hero, only those who thought they were but then quickly proved otherwise.

Bailey was mulling over her dilemma when she noticed him. He was tall and impeccably dressed in a gray pinstriped suit. She wasn't an expert on men's clothing, but she knew quality when she saw it.

The stranger carried himself with an air of cool detachment. That was good. Excellent, in fact. Exactly what Jo Ann had written in the margin of *Forever Yours.*

Now that she was studying him, she realized he looked

vaguely familiar, but she didn't know why. Then she got it. This was "a man of substance." The very person she was looking for…

Here she was, bemoaning her sorry fate, when lo and behold a handsome stranger strolled into her life. Not just any stranger. This man was Michael incarnate. The embodiment of everything she'd come to expect of a romantic hero. Only this version was living and breathing, and standing a few feet away.

For several minutes, Bailey couldn't keep her eyes off him. The subway cars were crowded to capacity in the early-morning rush, and while other people looked bored and uncomfortable, her hero couldn't have been more relaxed. He stood several spaces ahead of her, holding the overhead rail and reading the morning edition of the paper. His raincoat was folded over his arm and, unlike some of the passengers, he seemed undisturbed by the train's movement as it sped along.

The fact that he was engaged in reading gave Bailey the opportunity to analyze him without being detected. His age was difficult to judge, but she guessed him to be in his mid-thirties. Perfect! Michael was thirty-four.

The man in the pin-striped suit was handsome, too. But it wasn't his classic features—the sculpted cheekbones, straight nose or high forehead—that seized her attention.

It was his jaw.

Bailey had never seen a more determined jaw in her life. Exactly the type that illustrated a touch of arrogance and a hint of audacity, both attributes Jo Ann had mentioned in her critique.

His rich chestnut-colored hair was short and neatly trimmed, his skin lightly tanned. His eyes were dark. As dark as her own were blue.

His very presence seemed to fill the subway car. Bailey was convinced everyone else sensed it, too. She couldn't understand why the other women weren't all staring at him just as raptly. The more she studied him, the better he looked. He was, without a doubt, the most masculine male Bailey had ever seen—exactly the way she'd always pictured her hero. Unfortunately she hadn't succeeded in transferring him from her imagination to the page.

Bailey was so excited she could barely contain herself. After months of writing and rewriting *Forever Yours,* shaping and reshaping the characters, she'd finally stumbled upon a real-life Michael. She could hardly believe her luck. Hadn't Jo Ann just mentioned this great new book that suggested learning through observing?

"Do you see the man in the gray pin-striped suit?" Bailey whispered, elbowing Jo Ann. "You know who he is, don't you?"

Jo Ann's eyes narrowed as she identified Bailey's hero and studied him for several seconds. She shook her head. "Isn't he the guy who clobbered you on the head with his umbrella a few minutes ago?"

"He is?"

"Who did you think he was?"

"You mean you don't know?" Bailey had been confident Jo Ann would recognize him as quickly as she had.

"*Should* I know him?"

"Of course you should." Jo Ann had read *Forever Yours*. Surely she'd recognize Michael in the flesh.

"Who do *you* think he is?" Jo Ann asked, growing impatient.

"That's Michael—my Michael," she added when Jo Ann frowned.

"Michael?" Jo Ann echoed without conviction.

"The way he was meant to be. The way Janice, my heroine, and I want him to be." Bailey had been trying to create him in her mind for weeks, and now here he was! "Can't you feel the sexual magnetism radiating from him?" she asked out of the corner of her mouth.

"Frankly, no."

Bailey decided to ignore that. "He's absolutely perfect. Can't you sense his proud determination? That commanding presence that makes him larger than life?"

Jo Ann's eyes narrowed again, the way they usually did when she was doing some serious contemplating.

"Do you see it now?" Bailey pressed.

Jo Ann's shoulders lifted in a regretful shrug. "I'm honestly trying, but I just don't. Give me a couple of minutes to work on it."

Bailey ignored her fellow writer's lack of insight. It didn't matter if Jo Ann agreed with her or not. The man in the gray suit was Michael. Her Michael. Naturally she'd be willing to step aside and give him to Janice, who'd been waiting all these weeks for Michael to straighten himself out.

"It hit me all of a sudden—what you were saying about observing in order to learn. I need a model for Michael, someone who can help me gain perspective," Bailey explained, her gaze momentarily leaving her hero.

"Ah..." Jo Ann sounded uncertain.

"If I'm ever going to sell *Forever Yours* I've got to employ those kinds of techniques." Bailey's eyes automatically returned to the man. Hmm, a little over six feet tall, she estimated. He really was a perfect specimen. All this time she'd been feeling melancholy, wondering how she could ever create an authentic hero, then, almost by magic, this one appeared in living color...

"Go on," Jo Ann prodded, urging Bailey to finish her thought.

"The way I figure it, I may never get this characterization down right if I don't have someone to pattern Michael after."

Bailey half expected Jo Ann to argue with her. She was pleasantly surprised when her friend agreed with a quick nod. "I think you're right. It's an excellent idea."

Grinning sheepishly, Bailey gave herself a mental pat on the back. "I thought so myself."

"What are you planning to do? Study this guy—research his life history, learn what you can about his family and upbringing? That sort of thing? I hope you understand that this may not be as easy as it seems."

"Nothing worthwhile ever is," Bailey intoned solemnly. Actually, how she was going to do any of this research was a mystery to her, as well. Eventually she'd come up with some way of learning what she needed to know without being obvious about it. The sooner the better, of course. "I should probably start by finding out his name."

"That sounds like a good idea," Jo Ann said as though she wasn't entirely sure this plan was such a brilliant one, after all.

The train came to a vibrating halt, and a group of people moved toward the doors. Even while they disembarked, more were crowding onto the train. Bailey kept her gaze on the man in the pin-striped suit for fear he'd step off the subway without her realizing it. When she was certain he wasn't leaving, she relaxed.

"You know," Jo Ann said thoughtfully once the train had started again. "My Logan's modeled after Dan, but in this case, I'm beginning to have—"

"Did you see that?" Bailey interrupted, grabbing her friend's arm in her enthusiasm. The longer she studied the stranger, the more impressed she became.

"What?" Jo Ann demanded, glancing around her.

"The elegant way he turned the page." Bailey was thinking of her own miserable attempts to read while standing in a moving train. Any endeavor to turn the unwieldy newspaper page resulted in frustration to her and anyone unfortunate enough to be standing nearby. Yet he did it as gracefully and easily as if he were sitting at his own desk, in his own office.

"You're really hung up on this guy, aren't you?"

"You still don't see it, do you?" Bailey couldn't help being disappointed. She would've expected Jo Ann, of all her friends, to understand that this stranger was everything she'd ever wanted in Michael, from the top of his perfect hair to the tip of his (probably) size-eleven shoe.

"I'm still trying," Jo Ann said squinting as she stared at Bailey's hero, "but I don't quite see it."

"That's what I thought." But Bailey felt convinced she was right. This tall, handsome man was Michael, and it didn't matter if Jo Ann saw it or not. She did, and that was all that mattered.

The subway train slowed as it neared the next stop. Once again, passengers immediately crowded the doorway. Her hero slipped the newspaper into his briefcase, removed the umbrella hooked around his forearm and stood back, politely waiting his turn.

"Oh, my," Bailey said, panic in her voice. This could get complicated. Her heart was already thundering like a Midwest storm gone berserk. She reached for her purse and vaulted to her feet.

Jo Ann looked at her as though she suspected Bailey had lost her wits. She tugged the sleeve of Bailey's coat. "This isn't our stop."

"Yes, I know," Bailey said, pulling an unwilling Jo Ann to her feet.

"Then what are you doing getting off here?"

Two

"You don't mean we're actually going to *follow* him?"

"Of course we are." They couldn't stand there arguing. "Are you coming or not?"

For the first time in recent history, Jo Ann seemed at a complete loss for words. Just when Bailey figured she'd have to do this on her own, Jo Ann nodded. The two dashed off the car just in time.

"I've never done anything so crazy in all my life," Jo Ann muttered.

Bailey ignored her. "He went that way," she said, pointing toward the escalator. Grabbing Jo Ann by the arm, she hurried after the man in the pin-striped suit, maintaining a safe distance.

"Listen, Bailey," Jo Ann said, jogging in order to keep up, but still two steps behind her. "I'm beginning to have second thoughts about this."

"Why? Not five minutes ago you agreed that modeling Michael on a real man was an excellent approach to characterization."

"I didn't know you planned to stalk the guy! Don't you think we should stay back a little farther?"

"No." Bailey was adamant. As it was, her hero's long,

powerful strides were much faster than Bailey's normal walking pace. Jo Ann's short-legged stride was even slower.

By the time they reached the corner, Jo Ann was panting. She leaned against the street lamp and placed her hand over her heart, inhaling deeply. "Give me a minute, would you?"

"We might lose him." The look Jo Ann gave her suggested that might not be so bad. "Think of this as research," Bailey added, looping her arm through Jo Ann's again and dragging her forward.

Staying in the shadow of the buildings, the two trailed Bailey's hero for three more blocks. Fortunately he was walking in the direction of the area where Bailey and Jo Ann both worked.

When he paused for a red light, Bailey stayed several feet behind him, wandering aimlessly toward a widow display while glancing over her shoulder every few seconds. She didn't want to give him an opportunity to notice her.

"Do you think he's married?" Bailey demanded of her friend.

"How would I know?" Jo Ann snapped.

"Intuition."

The light changed and Bailey rushed forward. A reluctant Jo Ann followed on her heels. "I can't believe I'm doing this."

"You already said that."

"What am I going to tell my boss when I'm late?" Jo Ann groaned.

Bailey had to wait when Jo Ann came to a sudden halt, leaned against a display window and removed her high heel. She shook it out, then hurriedly put it back on.

"Jo Ann," Bailey said in a heated whisper, urging her friend to hurry.

"There was something in my shoe," she said from between clenched teeth. "I can't race down the streets of San Francisco with a stone in my shoe."

"I don't want to lose him," Bailey stopped abruptly, causing Jo Ann to collide with her. "Look, he went into the Cascade Building."

"Oh, good," Jo Ann muttered on the tail end of a sigh that proclaimed relief. "Does that mean we can go to work now?"

"Of course not." It was clear to Bailey that Jo Ann knew next to nothing about detective work. She probably didn't read mysteries. "I have to find out what his name is."

"What?" Jo Ann sounded as though Bailey had suggested they climb to the top of Coit Tower and leap off. "How do you plan to do that?"

"I don't know. I'll figure it out later." Clutching her friend's arm, Bailey urged her forward. "Come on, we can't give up now."

"Sure we can," Jo Ann muttered as they entered the Cascade Building.

"Hurry," Bailey whispered, releasing Jo Ann's elbow. "He's getting into the elevator." Bailey slipped past several people, mumbling, "Excuse me, excuse me," as she struggled to catch the same elevator, Jo Ann stumbling behind her.

They managed to make it a split second before the doors closed. There were four or five others on board, and Jo Ann cast Bailey a frown that doubted her intelligence.

Bailey had other concerns. She tried to remain as unobtrusive as possible, not wanting to call attention to herself or Jo Ann. Her hero seemed oblivious to them, which served her purposes nicely. All she intended to do was find out his name and what he did for a living, a task that shouldn't require the FBI.

Jo Ann jerked Bailey's sleeve and nodded toward the stranger's left hand. It took Bailey a moment to realize her friend was pointing out the fact that he wasn't wearing a wedding ring. The realization cheered Bailey and she made a circle with thumb and finger, grinning broadly.

As the elevator sped upward, Bailey saw Jo Ann anxiously check her watch. Then the elevator came to a smooth halt. A few seconds passed before the doors slid open and two passengers stepped out.

Her hero glanced over his shoulder, then moved to one side. For half a second, his gaze rested on Bailey and Jo Ann.

Half a second! Bailey straightened, offended at the casual way in which he'd dismissed her. She didn't want him to notice her, but at the same time, she felt cheated that he hadn't recognized the heroine in her—the same way she'd seen the hero in him. She was, after all, heroine material. She was attractive and… Well, attractive might be too strong a word. Cute and charming had a more comfortable feel. Her best feature was her thick dark hair that fell straight as a stick across her shoulders. The ends curved under just a little, giving it shape and bounce. She was taller than average, and slender, with clear blue eyes and a turned-up nose. As for her personality, she had spunk enough not to turn away from a good argument and spirit enough to follow a stranger around San Francisco.

Bailey noted that once again his presence seemed to fill the cramped quarters. His briefcase was tucked under his arm, while his hand gripped the curved handle of his umbrella. For all the notice he gave those around him, he might have been alone.

When Bailey turned to her friend, she saw that Jo Ann's eyes were focused straight ahead, her teeth gritted as though she couldn't wait to tell Bailey exactly what she thought of this crazy scheme. It *was* crazy, Bailey would be the first to admit, but these were desperate times in the life of a budding romance writer. She would stop at nothing to achieve her goal.

Bailey grinned. She had to agree that traipsing after her hero was a bit unconventional, but *he* didn't need to know about it. He didn't need to ever know how she intended to use him.

Her gaze moved from Jo Ann, then to the man with the umbrella. The amusement drained out of her as she found herself staring into the darkest pair of eyes she'd ever seen. Bailey was the first to look away, her pulse thundering in her ears.

The elevator stopped several times until, finally, only the three of them were left. Jo Ann had squeezed into the corner. Behind the stranger's back she mouthed several words that Bailey couldn't hope to decipher, then tapped one finger against the face of her watch.

Bailey nodded and raised her hand, fingers spread, to plead for five more minutes.

When the elevator stopped again, her hero stepped out, and Bailey followed, with Jo Ann trailing behind her. He walked briskly down the wide hallway, then entered a set of double doors marked with the name of a well-known architectural firm.

"Are you satisfied now?" Jo Ann burst out. "Honestly, Bailey, have you gone completely nuts?"

"You told me I need a hero who's proud and determined and I'm going to find one."

"That doesn't answer my question. Has it occurred to you yet that you've gone off the deep end?"

"Because I want to find out his name?"

"And how do you plan to do that?"

"I don't know yet," Bailey admitted. "Why don't I just

ask?" Having said that, she straightened her shoulders and walked toward the same doors through which the man had disappeared.

The pleasant-looking middle-aged woman who sat at the reception desk greeted her with a warm smile. "Good morning."

"Good morning," Bailey returned, hoping her smile was as serene and trusting as the older woman's. "This may seem a bit unusual, but I…I was on the subway this morning and I thought I recognized an old family friend. Naturally I didn't want to make a fool of myself in case I was wrong. He arrived in your office a few minutes ago and I was wondering… I know it's unusual, but would you mind telling me his name?"

"That would be Mr. Davidson. He's been taking BART the last few months because of the freeway renovation project."

"Mr. Davidson," Bailey repeated slowly. "His first name wouldn't be Michael, would it?"

"No." The receptionist frowned slightly. "It's Parker."

"Parker," Bailey repeated softly. "Parker Davidson." She liked the way it sounded, and although it wasn't a name she would've chosen for a hero, she could see that it fit him perfectly.

"Is Mr. Davidson the man you thought?"

It took Bailey a second or two to realize the woman was speaking to her. "Yes," she answered with a bright smile. "I do believe he is."

"Why, that's wonderful." The woman was obviously delighted. "Would you like me to buzz him? I'm sure he'd want to talk to you himself. Mr. Davidson is such a nice man."

"Oh, no, please don't do that." Bailey hoped she was able to hide the panic she felt at the woman's suggestion.

"I wouldn't want to disturb him and I really have to be getting to work. Thank you for your trouble."

"It was no trouble whatsoever." The receptionist glanced down at her appointment schedule and shook her head. "I was going to suggest you stop in at noon, but unfortunately Mr. Davidson's got a lunch engagement."

Bailey sighed as though with regret and turned away from the desk. "I'll guess I'll have to talk to him another time."

"That's really too bad. At least give me your name." The woman's soft brown eyes went from warm to sympathetic.

"Janice Hampton," Bailey said, mentioning the name of her heroine. "Thank you again for your help. You've been most kind."

Jo Ann was in the hallway pacing and muttering when Bailey stepped out of Parker's office. She stopped abruptly as Bailey appeared, her eyes filled with questions. "What happened?"

"Nothing. I asked the receptionist for his name and she told me. She even let it slip that he's got a lunch engagement..."

"Are you satisfied *now?*" Jo Ann sounded as though she'd passed from impatience to resignation. "In case you've forgotten, we're both working women."

Bailey glanced at her watch and groaned. "We won't be too late if we hurry." Jo Ann worked as an insurance specialist in a doctor's office and Bailey was a paralegal.

Luckily their office buildings were only a few blocks from the Cascade Building. They parted company on the next corner and Bailey half jogged the rest of the way.

No one commented when she slipped into the office ten minutes late. She hoped the same held true for Jo Ann, who'd probably never been late for work in her life.

Bailey settled down at her desk with her coffee and her

files, then hesitated. Jo Ann was right. Discovering Parker's name was useless unless she could fill in the essential details about his life. She needed facts. Lots of facts. The kinds of people he associated with, his background, his likes and dislikes, everyday habits.

It wasn't until later in the morning that Bailey started wondering where someone like Parker Davidson would go for lunch. It might be important to learn that. The type of restaurant a man chose—casual? elegant? exotic?—said something about his personality. Details like that could make the difference between a sale and a rejection, and frankly, Bailey didn't know if Michael could tolerate another spurning.

At ten to twelve Bailey mumbled an excuse about having an appointment before she headed out the door. Her boss gave her a funny look, but Bailey made sure she escaped before anyone could ask any questions. It wasn't like Bailey to take her duties lightly.

Luck was with her. She'd only been standing at the street corner for five minutes when Parker Davidson came out of the building. He was deeply involved in conversation with another man, yet when he raised his hand to summon a taxi, one appeared instantly, as if by magic. If she hadn't seen it with her own eyes, Bailey wouldn't have believed it. Surely this was the confidence, the command, others said a hero should possess. Not wanting to miss a single detail, Bailey took a pen and pad out of her purse and started jotting them down.

As Parker's cab slowly pulled away, she ventured into the street and flagged down a second cab. In order to manage that, however, she'd had to wave her arms above her head and leap up and down.

She yanked open the door and leapt inside. "Follow that cab," she cried, pointing toward Parker's taxi.

The stocky driver twisted around. "Are you serious? You want me to follow that cab?"

"That's right," she said anxiously, afraid Parker's taxi would soon be out of sight.

Her driver laughed outright. "I've been waiting fifteen years for someone to tell me that. You got yourself a deal, lady." He stepped on the accelerator and barreled down the street, going well above the speed limit.

"Any particular reason, lady?"

"I beg your pardon?" The man was doing fifty in a thirty-mile-an-hour zone.

"I want to know why you're following that cab." The car turned a corner at record speed, the wheels screeching, and Bailey slid from one end of the seat to the other. If she'd hoped to avoid attention, it was a lost cause. Parker Davidson might not notice her, but nearly everyone else in San Francisco did.

"I'm doing some research for a romance novel," Bailey explained.

"You're doing *what?*"

"Research."

Apparently her answer didn't satisfy him, because he slowed to a sedate twenty miles an hour. "Research for a romance novel," he repeated, his voice flat. "I thought you were a private detective or something."

"I'm sorry to disappoint you. I write romance novels and— Oh, stop here, would you?" Parker's cab had pulled to the curb and the two men were climbing out.

"Sure, lady, don't get excited."

Bailey scrambled out of the cab and searched through her purse for her money. When she couldn't find it, she slapped the large bag onto the hood of the cab and sorted through its contents until she retrieved her wallet. "Here."

"Have a great day, lady," the cabbie said sardonically,

setting his cap farther back on his head. Bailey offered him a vague smile.

She toyed with the idea of following the men into the restaurant and having lunch. She would have, too, if it weren't for the fact that she'd used all her cash to pay for the taxi.

But there was plenty to entertain her while she waited—although Bailey wasn't sure exactly what she was waiting for. The streets of Chinatown were crowded. She gazed about her at the colorful shops with their produce stands and souvenirs and rows of smoked ducks hanging in the windows. Street vendors displayed their wares and tried to coax her to come examine their goods.

Bailey bought a fresh orange with some change she scrounged from the bottom of her purse. Walking across the street, she wondered how long her hero would dawdle over his lunch. Most likely he'd walk back to the office. Michael would.

His lunch engagement didn't last nearly as long as Bailey had expected. When he emerged from the restaurant, he took her by surprise. Bailey was in the process of using her debit card to buy a sweatshirt she'd found at an incredibly low price and had to rush in an effort to keep up with him.

He hadn't gone more than a couple of blocks when she lost him. Stunned, she stood in the middle of the sidewalk, wondering how he could possibly have disappeared.

One minute he was there, and the next he was gone. Tailing a hero wasn't nearly as easy as she'd supposed.

Discouraged, Bailey clutched her bag with the sweatshirt and slung her purse over her shoulder, then started back toward her office. Heaven only knew what she was going to say to her boss once she arrived—half an hour late.

She hadn't gone more than a few steps when someone

grabbed her arm and jerked her into the alley. She opened her mouth to scream, but the cry died a sudden death when she found herself staring up at Parker Davidson.

"I want to know why the hell you're following me."

Three

"Ah... Ah..." For the life of her, Bailey couldn't string two words together.

"Janice Hampton, I presume?"

Bailey nodded, simply because it was easier than explaining herself.

Parker's eyes slowly raked her from head to foot. He obviously didn't see anything that pleased him. "You're not an old family friend, are you?"

Still silent, she answered him with a shake of her head.

"That's what I thought. What do you want?"

Bailey couldn't think of a single coherent remark.

"Well?" he demanded since she was clearly having a problem answering even the most basic questions. Bailey had no idea where to start or how much to say. The truth would never do, but she didn't know if she was capable of lying convincingly.

"Then you leave me no choice but to call the police," he said tightly.

"No...please." The thought of explaining everything to an officer of the law was too mortifying to consider.

"Then start talking." His eyes were narrow and as cold as the January wind off San Francisco Bay.

Bailey clasped her hands together, wishing she'd never given in to the whim to follow him on his lunch appointment. "It's a bit…complicated," she mumbled.

"Isn't it always?"

"Your attitude isn't helping any," she returned, straightening her shoulders. He might be a high-and-mighty architect—and her behavior might have been a little unusual—but that didn't give him the right to treat her as if she were some kind of criminal.

"*My* attitude?" he said incredulously.

"Listen, would you mind if we shorted this inquisition?" she asked, checking her watch. "I've got to be back at work in fifteen minutes."

"Not until you tell why you've been my constant shadow for the past hour. Not to mention this morning."

"You're exaggerating." Bailey half turned to leave when his hand flew out to grip her shoulder.

"You're not going anywhere until you've answered a few questions."

"If you must know," she said at the end of a protracted sigh, "I'm a novelist…"

"Published?"

"Not yet," she admitted reluctantly, "but I will be."

His mouth lifted at the corners and Bailey couldn't decide if the movement had a sardonic twist or he didn't believe a word she was saying. Neither alternative did anything to soothe her ego.

"It's true!" she said heatedly. "I am a novelist, only I've been having trouble capturing the true nature of a classic hero and, well, as I said earlier, it gets a bit involved."

"Start at the beginning."

"All right." Bailey was prepared now to do exactly that. He wanted details? She'd give him details. "It all began several months back when I was riding BART and I met Jo

Ann—she's the woman I was with this morning. Over the course of the next few weeks I learned that she's a writer, too, and she's been kind enough to tutor me. I'd already mailed off my first manuscript when I met Jo Ann, but I quickly learned I'd made some basic mistakes. All beginning writers do. So I rewrote the story and—"

"Do you mind if we get to the part about this morning?" he asked, clearly impatient.

"All right, fine, I'll skip ahead, but it probably won't make much sense." She didn't understand why he was wearing that beleaguered look, since he was the one who'd insisted she start at the beginning. "Jo Ann and I were on the subway this morning and I was telling her I doubted I'd recognize a hero. You see, Michael's the hero in my book and I'm having terrible problems with him. The first time around he was too harsh, then I turned him into a wimp. I just can't seem to get him to walk the middle of the road. He's got to be tough, but tender. Strong and authoritative, but not so stubborn or arrogant the reader wants to throttle him. I need to find a way to make Michael larger than life, but at the same time the kind of man any woman would fall in love with and—"

"Excuse me for interrupting you again," Parker said, folding his arms across his chest and irritably tapping his foot, "but could we finish this sometime before the end of the year?"

"Oh, yes. Sorry." His sarcasm didn't escape her, but she decided to be generous and overlook it. "I was telling Jo Ann I wouldn't recognize a hero if one hit me over the head, and no sooner had I said that than your umbrella whacked me." The instant the words were out, Bailey realized she should have passed over that part.

"I like the other version better," he said with undisguised contempt. He shook his head and stalked past her onto the busy sidewalk.

"What other version?" Bailey demanded, marching after him. She was only relaying the facts, the way *he'd* insisted!

"The one where you're an old family friend. This nonsense about being a novelist is—"

"The absolute truth," she finished with all the dignity she could muster. "You're the hero—well, not exactly the hero, don't get me wrong, but a lot like my hero, Michael. In fact, you could be his twin."

Parker stopped abruptly and just as abruptly turned around to face her. The contempt in his eyes was gone, replaced by some other emotion Bailey couldn't identify.

"Have you seen a doctor?" he asked gently.

"A doctor?"

"Have you discussed this problem with a professional?"

It took Bailey a moment to understand what he was saying. Once she did, she was so furious she couldn't formulate words fast enough to keep pace with her speeding mind.

"You think…mental patient…on the loose?"

He nodded solemnly.

"That's the most ridiculous thing I've ever heard in my life!" Bailey had never been more insulted. Parker Davidson thought she was a crazy person! She waved her arms haphazardly as she struggled to compose her thoughts. "I'm willing to admit that following you is a bit eccentric, but…but I did it in the name of research!"

"Then kindly research someone else."

"Gladly." She stormed ahead several paces, then whirled suddenly around, her fists clenched. "You'll have to excuse me, I'm new to the writing game. There's a lot I don't know yet, but obviously I have more to learn than I realized. I was right the first time—you're no hero."

Not giving him the opportunity to respond, she rushed back to her office, thoroughly disgusted with the man she'd assumed to be a living, breathing hero.

Max, Bailey's cat, was waiting anxiously for her when she arrived home that evening, almost an hour later than usual since she'd stayed to make up for her lengthy lunch. Not that Max would actually deign to let her think he was pleased to see her. Max had one thing on his mind and one thing only.

Dinner.

The sooner she fed him, the sooner he could go back to ignoring her.

"I'm crazy about you, too," Bailey teased, bending over to playfully scratch his ears. She talked to her cat the way she did her characters, although Michael had been suspiciously quiet of late—which was fine with Bailey, since a little time apart was sure to do them both good. She wasn't particularly happy with her hero after the Parker Davidson fiasco that afternoon. Once again Michael had led her astray. The best thing to do was lock him in the desk drawer for a while.

Max wove his fat fluffy body between Bailey's legs while she sorted through her mail. She paused, staring into space as she reviewed her confrontation with Parker Davidson. Every time she thought about the things he'd said, she felt a flush of embarrassment. It was all she could do not to cringe at the pitying look he'd given her as he asked if she was seeking professional help. Never in her life had Bailey felt so mortified.

"Meow." Max seemed determined to remind her that he was still waiting for his meal.

"All right, all right," she muttered, heading for the refrigerator. "I don't have time to argue with you tonight. I'm going out to hear Libby McDonald speak." She removed the can of cat food from the bottom shelf and dumped the contents on the dry kibble. Max had to have his meal moistened before he'd eat it.

With a single husky purr, Max sauntered over to his dish and left Bailey to change clothes for the writers' meeting.

Once she was in her most comfortable sweater and an old pair of faded jeans, she grabbed a quick bite to eat and was out the door.

Jo Ann had already arrived at Parklane College, the site of their meeting, and was rearranging the classroom desks to form a large circle. Bailey automatically helped, grateful her friend didn't question her about Parker Davidson. Within minutes, the room started to fill with members of the romance writers' group.

Bailey didn't know if she should tell Jo Ann about the meeting with Parker. No, she decided, the whole sorry episode was best forgotten. Buried under the heading of Mistakes Not to Be Repeated.

If Jo Ann did happen to ask, Bailey mused, it would be best to say nothing. She didn't make a habit of lying, but her encounter with that man had been too humiliating to describe, even to her friend.

The meeting went well, and although Bailey took copious notes, her thoughts persisted in drifting away from Libby's speech, straying to Parker. The man had his nerve suggesting she was a lunatic. Who did he think he was, anyway? Sigmund Freud? But then, to be fair, Parker had no way of knowing that Bailey didn't normally go around following strange men and claiming they were heroes straight out of her novel.

Again and again throughout the talk, Bailey had to stubbornly refocus her attention on Libby's speech. When Libby finished, the twenty or so writers who were gathered applauded enthusiastically. The sound startled Bailey, who'd been embroiled in yet another mental debate about the afternoon's encounter.

There was a series of questions, and then Libby had to leave in order to catch a plane. Bailey was disappointed that she couldn't stay for coffee. It had become tradition for a handful of the group's members to go across the street to the all-night diner after their monthly get-together.

As it turned out, everyone else had to rush home, too, except Jo Ann. Bailey was on the verge of making an excuse herself, but one glance told her Jo Ann was unlikely to believe it.

They walked across the street to the brightly lit and almost empty restaurant. As they sat down in their usual booth, the waitress approached them with menus. Jo Ann ordered just coffee, but Bailey, who'd eaten an orange for lunch and had a meager dinner of five pretzels, a banana and two hard green jelly beans left over from Christmas, was hungry, so she asked for a turkey sandwich.

"All right, tell me what happened," Jo Ann said the moment the waitress left their booth.

"About what?" Bailey tried to appear innocent as she toyed with the edges of the paper napkin. She carefully avoided meeting Jo Ann's eyes.

"I phoned your office at lunchtime," her friend said in a stern voice. "Do I need to go into the details?" She studied Bailey, who raised her eyes to give Jo Ann a brief look of wide-eyed incomprehension. "Beth told me you'd left before noon for a doctor's appointment and weren't back yet." She paused for effect. "We both know you didn't have a doctor's appointment, don't we?"

"Uh..." Bailey felt like a cornered rat.

"You don't need to tell me where you were," Jo Ann went on, raising her eyebrows. "I can guess. You couldn't leave it alone, could you? My guess is that you followed Parker Davidson to his lunch engagement."

Bailey nodded miserably. So much for keeping one of her most humiliating moments a secret. She hadn't even told Max! Her cat generally heard everything, but today's encounter was best forgotten.

If only she could stop thinking about it. For most of the afternoon she'd succeeded in pushing all thoughts of that man, that unreasonable insulting architect, out of her mind. Not so this evening.

"And?" Jo Ann prompted.

Bailey could see it was pointless to continue this charade with her friend. "And he confronted me, wanting to know why the hell I was following him."

Jo Ann closed her eyes, then slowly shook her head. After a moment, she reached for her coffee. "I can just imagine what you told him."

"At first I had no idea what to say."

"That part I can believe, but knowing you, I'd guess you insisted on telling him the truth and nothing but the truth."

"You're right again." Not that it had done Bailey any good.

"And?" Jo Ann prompted again.

Bailey's sandwich arrived and for a minute or so she was distracted by that. Unfortunately she wasn't able to put off Jo Ann's questions for long.

"Don't you dare take another bite of that sandwich until you tell me what he said!"

"He didn't believe me." Which was putting it mildly.

"He didn't believe you?"

"All right, if you have to know, he thought I was an escaped mental patient."

Anger flashed in Jo Ann's eyes, and Bailey was so grateful she could have hugged her.

"Good grief, why'd you do anything so stupid as to tell him you're a writer?" Jo Ann demanded vehemently.

So much for having her friend champion her integrity, Bailey mused darkly.

"I can't understand why you'd do that," Jo Ann continued, raking her hand furiously through her hair. "You were making up stories all over the place when it came to discovering his name. You left me speechless with the way you walked into his office and spouted that nonsense about being an old family friend. Why in heaven's name didn't you make up something plausible when he confronted you?"

"I couldn't think." That, regrettably, was the truth.

Not that it would've made much difference even if she'd been able to invent a spur-of-the-moment excuse. She was convinced of that. The man would have known she was lying, and Bailey couldn't see the point of digging herself in any deeper than she already was. Of course she hadn't had time to reason that out until later. He'd hauled her into the alley and she'd simply followed her instincts, right or wrong.

"It wasn't like you didn't warn me," Bailey said, half her turkey sandwich poised in front of her mouth. "You tried to tell me from the moment we followed him off the subway how dumb the whole idea was. I should've listened to you then."

But she'd been so desperate to get a real hero down on paper. She'd been willing to do just about anything to straighten out this problem of Michael's. What she hadn't predicted was how foolish she'd end up feeling as a result. Well, no more—she'd learned her lesson. If any more handsome men hit her on the head, she'd hit them back!

"What are you going to do now?" Jo Ann asked.

"Absolutely nothing," Bailey answered without a second's hesitation.

"You mean you're going to let him go on thinking you're an escaped mental patient?"

"If that's what he wants to believe." Bailey tried to create the impression that it didn't matter to her one way or the other. She must have done a fairly good job because Jo Ann remained speechless, raising her coffee mug to her mouth three times without taking a single sip.

"What happens if you run into him on the subway again?" she finally asked.

"I don't think that'll be a problem," Bailey said blithely, trying hard to sound unconcerned. "What are the chances we'll be on the same car again at exactly the same time?"

"You're right," Jo Ann concurred. "Besides, after what happened today, he'll probably go back to driving, freeway renovation or not."

It would certainly be a blessing if he did, Bailey thought.

He didn't.

Jo Ann and Bailey were standing at the end of the crowded subway car, clutching the metal handrail when Jo Ann tugged hard at the sleeve of Bailey's bulky-knit cardigan.

"Don't turn around," Jo Ann murmured.

They were packed as tight as peas in a pod, and Bailey had no intention of moving in any direction.

"He's staring at you."

"Who?" Bailey whispered back.

She wasn't a complete fool. When she'd stepped onto the train earlier, she'd done a quick check and was thankful to note that Parker Davidson wasn't anywhere to be seen. She hadn't run into him in several days and there was no reason to think she would. He might have continued to take BART, but if that was the case their paths had yet to cross, which was fine with her. Their second encounter would likely prove as embarrassing as the first.

"He's here," Jo Ann hissed. "The architect you followed last week."

Bailey was convinced everyone in the subway car had turned to stare at her. "I'm sure you're mistaken," she muttered, furious with her friend for her lack of discretion.

"I'm not. Look." She motioned with her head.

Bailey did her best to be nonchalant about it. When she did slowly twist around, her heart sank all the way to her knees. Jo Ann was right. Parker stood no more than ten feet from her. Fortunately, they were separated by a number of people—which didn't disguise the fact that he was staring at Bailey as if he expected men in white coats to start descendingon her.

She glared back at him.

"Do you see him?" Jo Ann asked.

"Of course. Thank you so much for pointing him out to me."

"He's staring at you. What else was I supposed to do?"

"Ignore him," Bailey suggested sarcastically. "I certainly intend to." Still, no matter how hard she tried to concentrate on the advertising posted above the seats, she found Parker Davidson dominating her thoughts.

A nervous shaky feeling slithered down her spine. Bailey could *feel* his look as profoundly as a caress. This was exactly the sort of look she struggled to describe in *Forever Yours.*

Casually, as if by accident, she slowly turned her head and peeked in his direction once more, wondering if she'd imagined the whole thing. For an instant the entire train seemed to go still. Her blue eyes met his brown ones, and an electric jolt rocked Bailey, like nothing she'd ever felt before. A breathless panic filled her and she longed to drag her eyes away, pretend she didn't recognize him, anything to escape this fluttery sensation in the pit of her stomach.

This was exactly how Janice had felt the first time she met Michael. Bailey had spent days writing that scene, studying each word, each phrase, until she'd achieved the right effect. That was the moment Janice had fallen in love with Michael. Oh, she'd fought it, done everything but stand on her head in an effort to control her feelings, but Janice had truly fallen for him.

Bailey, however, was much too wise to be taken in by a mere look. She'd already been in love. Twice. Both times were disasters and she wasn't willing to try it again soon. Her heart was still bleeding from the last go-round.

Of course she was leaping to conclusions. She was the one with the fluttery stomach. Not Parker. He obviously hadn't been affected by their exchange. In fact, he seemed to be amused, as if running into Bailey again was an unexpected opportunity for entertainment.

She braced herself, and with a resolve that would've impressed Janice, she dropped her gaze. She inhaled sharply, then twisted her mouth into a sneer. Unfortunately, Jo Ann was staring at her in complete—and knowing—fascination.

"What's with you—and him?"

"Nothing," Bailey denied quickly.

"That's not what I saw."

"You're mistaken," Bailey replied in a voice that said the subject was closed.

"Whatever you did worked," Jo Ann whispered a couple of minutes later.

"I don't know what you're talking about."

"Fine, but in case you're interested, he's coming this way."

"I beg your pardon?" Bailey's forehead broke out in a cold sweat at the mere prospect of being confronted by Parker Davidson again. Once in a lifetime was more than enough, but twice in the same week was well beyond her capabilities.

Sure enough, Parker Davidson boldly stepped forward and squeezed himself next to Bailey.

"Hello again," he said casually.

"Hello," she returned stiffly, refusing to look at him.

"You must be Jo Ann," he said, turning his attention to Bailey's friend.

Jo Anne's eyes narrowed. "You told him my name?" she asked Bailey in a loud distinct voice.

"I… Apparently so."

"Thank you very much," she muttered in a sarcastic voice. Then she turned toward Parker and her expression altered dramatically as she broke into a wide smile. "Yes, I'm Jo Ann."

"Have you been friends with Janice long?"

"Janice? Oh, you mean…" Bailey quickly nudged her friend in the ribs with her elbow. "Janice," Jo Ann repeated in a strained voice. "You mean *this* Janice?"

Parker frowned. "So that was a lie, as well?"

"As well," Bailey admitted coolly, deciding she had no alternative. "That was my problem in the first place. I told you the truth. Now, for the last time, I'm a writer and so is Jo Ann." She gestured toward her friend. "Tell him."

"We're both writers," Jo Ann confirmed with a sad lack of conviction. It wasn't something Jo Ann willingly broadcast, though Bailey had never really understood why. She supposed it was a kind of superstition, a fear of offending the fates by appearing too presumptuous—and thereby ruining her chances of selling a book.

Parker sighed, frowning more darkly. "That's what I thought."

The subway stopped at the next station, and he moved toward the door.

"Goodbye," Jo Ann said, raising her hand. "It was a pleasure to meet you."

"Me, too." He glanced from her to Bailey; she could have sworn his eyes hardened briefly before he stepped off the car.

"You told him your name was Janice?" Jo Ann cried the minute he was out of sight. "Why'd you do that?"

"I…I don't know. I panicked."

Jo Ann wiped her hand down her face. "Now he *really* thinks you're nuts."

"It might have helped if you hadn't acted like you'd never heard the word 'writer' before." Before Jo Ann could heap any more blame on her shoulders, Bailey had some guilt of her own to spread around.

"That isn't information I tell everyone, you know. I'd appreciate if you didn't pass it out to just anyone."

"Oh, dear," Bailey mumbled, feeling wretched. Not only was Jo Ann annoyed with her, Parker thought she was a fool. And there was little she could do to redeem herself in his eyes. The fact that it troubled her so much was something for the men with chaise longues in their offices to analyze. But trouble her it did.

If only Parker hadn't looked at her with those dark eyes of his—as if he was willing to reconsider his first assessment of her.

If only she hadn't looked back and felt that puzzling sensation come over her—the way a heroine does when she's met the man of her dreams.

The weekend passed, and although Bailey spent most of her time working on the rewrite of *Forever Yours,* she couldn't stop picturing the disgruntled look on Parker's face as he walked off the subway car. It hurt her pride that he assumed she was a liar. Granted, introducing herself as Janice Hampton had been a lie, but after that, she'd told only the truth. She was sure he didn't believe a single word she'd said. Still, he intrigued her so much she spent a couple of precious hours on Saturday afternoon on the Internet, learning everything she could about him, which unfortunately wasn't much.

When Monday's lunch hour arrived, she headed directly for Parker's building. Showing up at his door should merit her an award for courage—or one for sheer stupidity.

"May I help you?" the receptionist asked when Bailey walked into the architectural firm's outer office. It was the same woman who'd helped her the week before. The nameplate on her desk read Roseanne Snyder. Bailey hadn't noticed it during her first visit.

"Would it be possible to see Mr. Davidson for just a few minutes?" she asked in her most businesslike voice, hoping the woman didn't recognize her.

Roseanne glanced down at the appointment calendar. "You're the gal who was in to see Mr. Davidson the first part of last week, aren't you?"

So much for keeping her identity a secret. "Yes." It was embarrassing to admit that. Bailey prayed Parker hadn't divulged the details of their encounter to the firm's receptionist.

"When I mentioned your name to Mr. Davidson, he didn't seem to remember your family."

"Uh… I wasn't sure he would," Bailey answered vaguely.

"If you'll give me your name again, I'll tell him you're here."

"Bailey. Bailey York," she said with a silent sigh of relief. Parker didn't know her real name; surely he wouldn't refuse to see her.

"Bailey York," the friendly woman repeated. "But aren't you—?" She paused, staring at her for a moment before she pressed the intercom button. After a quick exchange, she nodded, smiling tentatively. "Mr. Davidson said to go right in. His office is the last one on the left," she said, pointing the way.

The door was open and Parker sat at his desk, apparently engrossed in studying a set of blueprints. His office was impressive, with a wide sweeping view of the Golden Gate Bridge and Alcatraz Island. As she stood in the doorway, Parker glanced up. His smile faded when he recognized her.

"What are you doing here?"

"Proving I'm not a liar." With that, she strode into his office and slapped a package on his desk.

"What's that?" he asked.

"Proof."

Four

Parker stared at the manuscript box as though he feared it was a time bomb set to explode at any moment.

"Go ahead and open it," Bailey said. When he didn't, she lifted the lid for him. Awkwardly she flipped through the first fifteen pages until she'd gathered up the first chapter, which she shoved into his hands. "Read it."

"Now?"

"Start with the header," she instructed, and then pointed to the printed line on the top right-hand side of each page.

"York...*Forever Yours*...Page one," he read aloud, slowly and hesitantly.

Bailey nodded. "Now move down to the text." She used her index finger to indicate where she wanted him to read.

"Chapter one. Janice Hampton had dreaded the business meeting for weeks. She was—"

"That's enough," Bailey muttered, ripping the pages out of his hands. "If you want to look through the rest of the manuscript, you're welcome to."

"Why would I want to do that?"

"So you no longer have the slightest doubt that I wrote it," she answered in a severe tone. "So you'll believe that I *am* a writer—and not a liar or a maniac. The purpose of this visit, though, why I find it necessary to prove I'm telling you the truth, isn't clear to me yet. It just seemed… important."

As she spoke, she scooped up the loose pages and stuffed them back into the manuscript box, closing it with enough force to crush the lid.

"I believed you before," Parker said casually, leaning back in his chair as if he'd never questioned her integrity. Or her sanity. "No one could've made up that story about being a romance writer and kept a straight face."

"But you—"

"What I didn't appreciate was the fact that you called yourself by a false name."

"You caught me off guard! I gave you the name of my heroine because…well, because I saw you as the hero."

"I see." He raised one eyebrow—definitely a hero-like mannerism, Bailey had to admit.

"I guess you didn't appreciate being followed around town, either," she said in a small voice.

"True enough," he agreed. "Take my advice, would you? The next time you want to research details about a man's life, hire a detective. You and your friend couldn't have been more obvious if you'd tried."

Bailey's ego had already taken one beating from this man, and she wasn't game for round two. "Don't worry, I've given up the chase. I've discovered there aren't any real heroes left in this world. I thought you might be one, but—" she shrugged elaborately "—alas, I was wrong."

"Ouch." Parker placed his hand over his heart as though her words had wounded him gravely. "I was just beginning to feel flattered. Then you had to go and ruin it."

"I know what I'm talking about when it comes to this hero business. They're extinct, except between the pages of women's fiction."

"Correct me if I'm wrong, but do I detect a note of bitterness?"

"I'm not bitter," Bailey denied vehemently. But she didn't mention the one slightly yellowed wedding dress hanging in her closet. She'd used her savings to pay for the elegant gown and been too mortified to return it unused. She tried to convince herself it was an investment, something that would gain value over the years, like gold. Or stocks. That was what she told herself, but deep down she knew better.

"I'm sorry to have intruded upon your busy day," she said, reaching for her manuscript. "I won't trouble you again."

"Do you object to my asking you a few questions before you go?" Parker asked, standing. He walked around to the front of his desk and leaned against it, crossing his ankles. "Writers have always fascinated me."

Bailey made a show of glancing at her watch. She had forty-five minutes left of her lunch hour; she supposed she could spare a few moments. "All right."

"How long did it take you to write *Forever and a Day?*"

"Forever Yours," Bailey corrected. She suspected he was making fun of her. "Nearly six months, but I worked on it every night after work and on weekends. I felt like I'd completed a marathon when I finished." Bailey knew Janice and Michael were grateful, too. "Only I made a beginner's mistake."

"What's that?"

"I sent it off to a publisher."

"That's a mistake?"

Bailey nodded. "I should've had someone read it first, but I was too new to know that. It wasn't until later that I met Jo Ann and joined a writers' group."

Parker folded his arms across his broad chest. "I'm not

sure I understand. Isn't having your work read by an editor the whole point? Why have someone else read it first?"

"Every manuscript needs a final polishing. It's important to put your best foot forward."

"I take it *Forever Yours* was rejected."

Bailey shook her head. "Not yet, but I'm fairly certain it will be. It's been about four months now, but meanwhile I've been working on revisions. And like Jo Ann says—no news is no news."

Parker arched his brows. "That's true."

"Well," she said, glancing at her watch again, but not because she was eager to leave. She felt foolish standing in the middle of Parker's plush office talking about her novel. Her guard was slipping and the desire to secure it firmly in place was growing stronger.

"I assume Jo Ann read the manuscript after you mailed it off?"

"Yes." Bailey punctuated her comment with a shrug. "She took it home and returned it the next morning with margin notes and a list of comments three pages long. When I read them over, I could see how right she was and, well, mainly the problem was with the hero."

"Michael?"

Bailey was surprised he remembered that. "Yes, with Michael. He's a terrific guy, but he needs a little help figuring out what women—in this case Janice Hampton—want."

"That's where I came in?"

"Right."

"How?"

Bailey made an effort to explain. "A hero, at least in romantic fiction, is determined, forceful and cool. When I saw you the first time, you gave the impression of being all three."

"Was that before or after I hit you in the head?"

"After."

Parker grinned. "Did you ever consider that my umbrella might have caused a temporary lack of, shall we say, good judgment? My guess is that you don't normally follow men around town, taking notes about their behavior, do you?"

"No, you were my first," she informed him coldly. This conversation was becoming downright irritating.

"I'm pleased to hear that," he said with a cocky grin.

"Perhaps you're right. Perhaps I *was* hit harder than I realized." Just when she was beginning to feel reasonably comfortable around Parker, he'd do or say something to remind her that he was indeed a mere mortal. Any effort to base Michael's personality on his would only be a waste of time.

Bailey clutched her manuscript to her chest. "I really have to go now. I apologize for the intrusion."

"It's fine. I found our discussion…interesting."

No doubt he had. But it didn't help Bailey's dignity to know she was a source of amusement to one of the city's most distinguished architects.

"What else did he say?" Jo Ann asked early the following morning as they sat side by side on the crowded subway car.

Even before Bailey could answer, Jo Ann asked another question. "Did you get a chance to tell him that little joke about your story having a beginning, a *muddle* and an end?"

Jo Ann's reaction had surprised her. When Bailey admitted confronting Parker with her completed manuscript, Jo Ann had been enthusiastic, even excited. Bailey had supposed that her friend wouldn't understand her need to see Parker and correct his opinion of her. Instead, Jo Ann had been approving—and full of questions.

"I didn't have time to tell Parker any jokes," Bailey answered. "Good grief, I was only in his office, I don't know, maybe ten minutes."

"Ten minutes! A lot can happen in ten minutes."

Bailey crossed her long legs and prayed silently for patience. "Believe me, nothing happened. I accomplished what I set out to prove. That's it."

"If you were in there a full ten minutes, surely the two of you talked."

"He had a few questions about the business of writing."

"I see." Jo Ann nodded slowly. "So what did you tell him?"

Bailey didn't want to think about her visit with Parker. Not again. She'd returned from work that afternoon and, as was her habit, went directly to her computer. Usually she couldn't wait to get home to write. But that afternoon, she'd sat there, her hands poised on the keys, and instead of composing witty sparkling dialogue for Michael and Janice, she'd reviewed every word of her conversation with Parker.

He'd been friendly, cordial. And he'd actually sounded interested—when he wasn't busy being amused. Bailey hadn't expected that. What she'd expected was outright rejection. She'd come prepared to talk to a stone wall.

Michael, the first time around, had been like that. Gruff and unyielding. Poor Janice had been in the dark about his feelings from page one. It was as though her hero feared that revealing emotion was a sign of weakness.

In the second version Michael was so…amiable, so pleasant, that any conflict in the story had been watered down almost to nonexistence.

"As you might have guessed," Jo Ann said, breaking into her thoughts, "I like Parker Davidson. You were right when you claimed he's hero material. You'll have to forgive me for doubting you. It's just that I've never followed a man around before."

"You like Parker?" Bailey's musing about Michael and his shifting personality came to a sudden halt. 'You're married," Bailey felt obliged to remind her.

"I'm not interested in him for *me,* silly," Jo Ann said, playfully nudging Bailey with her elbow. "He's all yours."

"Mine!" Bailey couldn't believe what she was hearing. "You're nuts."

"No, I'm not. He's tall, dark and handsome, and we both know how perfect that makes him for a classic romance. And the way you zeroed in on Parker the instant you saw him proves he's got the compelling presence a hero needs."

"The only *presence* I noticed was his umbrella's! He nearly decapitated me with the thing."

"You know what I think?" Jo Ann murmured, nibbling on her bottom lip. "I think that something inside you, some innate sonar device, was in action. You're hungering to find Michael. Deep within your subconscious you're seeking love and romance."

"Wrong!" Bailey declared adamantly. "You couldn't be more off course. Writing and selling a romance are my top priorities right now. I'm not interested in love, not for myself."

"What about Janice?"

The question was unfair and Bailey knew it. So much of her own personality was invested in her heroine.

The train finally reached their station, and Bailey and Jo Ann stood up and made their way toward the exit.

"Well?" Jo Ann pressed, clearly unwilling to drop the subject.

"I'm not answering that and you know why," Bailey said, stepping onto the platform. "Now kindly get off this subject. I doubt I'll ever see Parker Davidson again, and if I do I'll ignore him just the way he'll ignore me."

"You're sure of that?"

"Absolutely positive."

"Then why do you suppose he's waiting for you? That *is* Parker Davidson, isn't it?"

Bailey closed her eyes and struggled to gather her wits. Part of her was hoping against hope that Parker would saunter past without giving either of them a second's notice. But another part of her, a deep womanly part, hoped he was doing exactly what Jo Ann suggested.

"Good morning, ladies," Parker said to them as he approached.

"Hello," Bailey returned, suspecting she sounded in need of a voice-box transplant.

"Good morning!" Jo Ann said with enough enthusiasm to make up for Bailey's sorry lack.

Parker bestowed a dazzling smile on them. Bailey felt the impact of it as profoundly as if he'd bent down and brushed his mouth over hers. She quickly shook her head to dispel the image.

"I considered our conversation," he said, directing his remark to Bailey. "Since you're having so many problems with your hero, I decided I might be able to help you, after all."

"Is that right?" Bailey knew she was coming across as defensive, but she couldn't seem to help it.

Parker nodded. "I assume you decided to follow me that day to learn pertinent details about my habits, personality and so on. How about if the two of us sit down over lunch and you just ask me what you want to know?"

Bailey recognized a gift horse when she saw one. Excitement welled up inside her; nevertheless she hesitated.

This man was beginning to consume her thoughts already, and she'd be asking for trouble if she allowed it to continue.

"Would you have time this afternoon?"

"She's got time," Jo Ann said without missing a beat. "Bailey works as a paralegal and she can see you during her lunch hour. This afternoon would be perfect."

Bailey glared at her friend, resisting the urge to suggest *she* have lunch with Parker since she was so keen on the idea.

"Bailey?" Parker asked, turning his attention to her.

"I…suppose." She didn't sound very gracious, and the look Jo Ann flashed her told her as much. "This is, um, very generous of you, Mr. Davidson."

"Mr. Davidson?" Parker said. "I thought we were long past being formal with each other." He dazzled her with another smile. It had the same effect on Bailey as before, weakening her knees—and her resolve.

"Shall we say noon, then?" Parker asked. "I'll meet you on Fisherman's Wharf at the Sandpiper."

The Sandpiper was known for its wonderful seafood, along with its exorbitant prices. Parker might be able to afford to eat there, but it was far beyond Bailey's meager budget.

"The Sandpiper?" she repeated. "I…I was thinking we could pick up something quick and eat on the wharf. There are several park benches along Pier 39…"

Parker frowned. "I'd prefer the Sandpiper. I'm doing some work for them, and it's good business practice to return the favor."

"Don't worry, she'll meet you there," Jo Ann assured Parker.

Bailey couldn't allow her friend to continue speaking for her. "Jo Ann, if you don't mind, I'll answer for myself."

"Oh, sure. Sorry."

Parker returned his attention to Bailey, who inhaled sharply and nodded. "I can meet you there." Of course it would mean packing lunches for the next two weeks and cutting back on Max's expensive tastes in gourmet cat food, but she supposed that was a small sacrifice.

Parker was waiting for Bailey when she arrived at the Sandpiper at a few minutes after noon. He stood when the maitre d' ushered her to his table. The room's lighting, its thick dark red carpet and rich wood created a sense of intimacy and warmth that appealed to Bailey despite her nervousness.

She'd been inside the Sandpiper only once before, with her parents when they were visiting from Oregon. Her father had wanted to treat her to the best restaurant in town, and Bailey had chosen the Sandpiper, renowned for its elegance and its fresh seafood.

"We meet again," Parker said, raising one eyebrow—that hero quirk again—as he held out her chair.

"Yes. It's very nice of you to do this."

"No problem." The waiter appeared with menus. Bailey didn't need to look; she already knew what she wanted. The seafood Caesar salad, piled high with shrimp, crab and scallops. She'd had it on her last visit and thoroughly enjoyed every bite. Parker ordered sautéed scallops and a salad. He suggested a bottle of wine, but Bailey declined. She needed to remain completely alert for this interview, so she requested coffee instead. Parker asked for the same.

After they'd placed their order, Bailey took a pen and pad from her purse, along with her reading glasses. She had a list of questions prepared. "Do you mind if we get started?"

"Sure," Parker said, leaning forward. He propped his

elbows on the table and stared at her intently. "How old are you, Bailey? Twenty-one, twenty-two?"

"Twenty-seven."

He nodded, but was obviously surprised. "According to Jo Ann you work as a paralegal."

"Yes." She paused. "You'll have to excuse Jo Ann. She's a romantic."

"That's what she said about *you*—that you're a romantic."

"Yes, well, I certainly hope it works to her advantage *and* to mine."

"Oh?" His eyebrows lifted.

"We're both striving to becoming published novelists. It takes a lot more than talent, you know."

Hot crisp sourdough rolls were delivered to the table and Bailey immediately reached for one.

"The writer has to have a feel for the genre," she continued. "For Jo Ann and me, that means writing from the heart. I've only been at this for a few months, but there are several women in our writers' group who've been submitting their work for five or six years without getting published. Most of them are pragmatic about it. There are plenty of small successes we learn to count along the way."

"Such as?"

Bailey swallowed before answering. "Finishing a manuscript. There's a real feeling of accomplishment in completing a story."

"I see."

"Some people come into the group thinking they're going to make a fast buck. They think anyone should be able to throw together a romance. Generally they attend a couple of meetings, then decide writing is too hard, too much effort."

"What about you?"

"I'm in this for the long haul. Eventually I will sell because I won't stop submitting stories until I do. My dad claims I'm like a pit bull when I want something. I clamp on and refuse to let go. That's how I feel about writing. I'm going to succeed at this if it's the last thing I ever do."

"Have you always wanted to be a writer?" Parker helped himself to a roll.

"No. I wasn't even on my high-school newspaper, although now I wish I had been. I might not have so much trouble with sentence structure and punctuation if I'd paid more attention back then."

"Then what made you decide to write romances?"

"Because I read them. In fact, I've been reading romances from the time I was in college, but it's only been in the past year or so that I started creating my own. Meeting Jo Ann was a big boost for me. I might have gone on making the same mistakes for years if it wasn't for her. She encouraged me, introduced me to other writers and took me under her wing."

The waiter arrived with their meals and Bailey sheepishly realized that she'd been doing all the talking. She had yet to ask Parker a single question.

The seafood Caesar salad was as good as Bailey remembered. After one bite she decided to treat herself like this more often. An expensive lunch every month or so wouldn't sabotage her budget.

"You were telling me it only took you six months to write *Forever Yours,*" Parker commented between forkfuls of his salad. "Doesn't it usually take much longer for a first book?"

"I'm sure it does, but I devoted every spare minute to the project."

"I see. What about your social life?"

It was all Bailey could do not to snicker. What social

life? She'd lived in San Francisco for more than a year, and this lunch with Parker was as close as she'd gotten to a real date. Which was exactly how she wanted it, she reminded herself.

"Bailey?"

"Oh, I get out occasionally," but she didn't mention that it was always with women friends. Since her second broken engagement, Bailey had given up on the opposite sex. Twice she'd been painfully forced to accept that men were not to be trusted. After fifteen months, Tom's deception still hurt.

Getting over Tom might not have been so difficult if it hadn't been for Paul. She'd been in love with him, too, in her junior year at college. But like Tom, he'd found someone else he loved more than he did her. The pattern just kept repeating itself, so Bailey, in her own sensible way, had put an end to it. She no longer dated.

There were times she regretted her decision. This afternoon was an excellent example. She could easily find herself becoming romantically interested in Parker. She wouldn't, of course, but the temptation was there.

Parker with his coffee-dark eyes and his devastating smile. Fortunately Bailey was wise to the fickle hearts of men. Of one thing she was sure: Parker Davidson hadn't reached his mid-thirties, still single, without breaking a few hearts along the way.

There were other times she regretted her decision to give up on dating. No men equaled no marriage. And no children. It was the children part that troubled her most, especially when she was around babies. Her decision hit her hard then. Without a husband she wasn't likely to have a child of her own, since she wasn't interested in being a single mother. But so far, all she had to do was avoid places where she'd run into mothers and infants. Out of sight, out of mind....

"Bailey?"

"I'm sorry," she mumbled, suddenly aware that she'd allowed her thoughts to run unchecked for several minutes. "Did I miss something?"

"No. You had a...pained look and I was wondering if your salad was all right?"

"Yes. It's wonderful. As fantastic as I remember." She briefly relayed the story of her parents treating her to dinner at the Sandpiper. What she didn't explain was that their trip south had been made for the express purpose of checking up on Bailey. Her parents were worried about her. They insisted she worked too hard, didn't get out enough, didn't socialize.

Bailey had listened politely to their concerns and then hugged them both, thanked them for their love and sent them back to Oregon.

Spotting her pad and pen lying beside her plate, Bailey sighed. She hadn't questioned Parker once, which was the whole point of their meeting. Glancing at her watch, she groaned inwardly. She only had another fifteen minutes. It wasn't worth the effort of getting started. Not when she'd just have to stop.

"I need to get back to the office," she announced regretfully. She looked around for the waiter so she could ask for her check.

"It's been taken care of."

It took Bailey a moment to realize that Parker was talking about her meal. "I can't let you do that," she insisted, reaching for her purse.

"Please."

If he'd argued with her, shoveled out some chauvinistic challenge, Bailey would never have allowed him to pay. But that one word, that one softly spoken word, was her undoing.

"All right," she agreed, her own voice just as soft.

"You didn't get a chance to ask your questions."

"I know." She found that frustrating, but had no one to blame but herself. "I got caught up talking about romance fiction and writing and—"

"Shall we try again? Another time?"

"It looks like we'll have to." She needed to be careful that lunch with Parker didn't develop into a habit.

"I'm free tomorrow evening."

"Evening?" Somehow that seemed far more threatening than meeting for lunch. "Uh…I generally reserve the hours after work for writing."

"I see."

Her heart reacted to the hint of disappointment in his voice. "I might be able to make an exception." Bailey was horrified as soon as the words were out. She couldn't believe she'd said that. For the entire hour, she'd been lecturing herself about the dangers of getting close to Parker. "No," she said firmly. "It's crucial that I maintain my writing schedule."

"You're sure?"

"Positive."

Parker took a business card from his coat pocket. He scribbled on the back and handed it to her. "This is my home number in case you change your mind."

Bailey accepted the card and thrust it into her purse, together with her notepad and pen. "I really have to write… I mean, my writing schedule is important to me. I can't be running out to dinner just because someone asks me." She stood, scraping back her chair in her eagerness to escape.

"Consider it research."

Bailey responded by shaking her head. "Thank you for lunch."

"You're most welcome. But I hope you'll reconsider having dinner with me."

She backed away from the table, her purse held tightly in both hands. "Dinner?" she echoed, still undecided.

"For the purposes of research," he added.

"It wouldn't be a *date*." It was important to make that point clear. The only man she had time for was Michael. But Parker was supposed to help her with Michael, so maybe… "Not a date, just research," she repeated in a more determined voice. "Agreed?"

He grinned, his eyes lighting mischievously. "What do you think?"

Five

Max was waiting at the door when Bailey got home from work that evening. His striped yellow tail pointed straight toward the ceiling as he twisted and turned between her legs. His not-so-subtle message was designed to remind her it was mealtime.

"Just a minute, Maxie," she muttered. She leafed through the mail as she walked into the kitchen, pausing when she found a yellow slip.

"Meow."

"Max, look," she said, waving the note at him. "Mrs. Morgan's holding a package for us." The apartment manager was always kind enough to accept deliveries, saving Bailey more than one trip to the post office.

Leaving a disgruntled Max behind, Bailey hurried down the stairs to Mrs. Morgan's first-floor apartment, where she was greeted with a warm smile. Mrs. Morgan was an older woman, a matronly widow who seemed especially protective of her younger tenants.

"Here you go, dear," she said, handing Bailey a large manila envelope.

Bailey knew the instant she saw the package that this

wasn't an unexpected surprise from her parents. It was her manuscript—rejected.

"Thank you," she said, struggling to disguise her disappointment. From the moment Bailey had read Jo Ann's critique she'd realized *Forever Yours* would probably be rejected. What she hadn't foreseen was this stomach-churning sensation, this feeling of total discouragement. Koppen Publishing had kept the manuscript for nearly four months. Jo Ann had insisted no news was no news, and so Bailey had begun to believe that the editor had held on to her book for so long because she'd seriously considered buying it.

Bailey had fully expected that she'd have to revise her manuscript; nonetheless, she'd *hoped* to be doing it with a contract in her pocket, riding high on success.

Once again Max was waiting by the door, more impatient this time. Without thinking, Bailey walked into the kitchen, opened the refrigerator and dumped food into his bowl. It wasn't until she straightened that she realized she'd given her greedy cat the dinner she was planning to cook for herself.

No fool, Max dug into the ground turkey, edging his way between her legs in his eagerness. Bailey shrugged. The way she was feeling, she didn't have much of an appetite, anyway.

It took her another five minutes to find the courage to open the package. She carefully pried apart the seam. Why she was being so careful, she couldn't even guess. She had no intention of reusing the envelope. Once the padding was separated, she removed the manuscript box. Inside was a short letter that she quickly read, swallowing down the emotion that clogged her throat. The fact that the letter was personal, and not simply a standard rejection letter, did little to relieve the crushing disappointment.

Reaching for the phone, Bailey punched out Jo Ann's

number. Her friend had experienced this more than once and was sure to have some words of wisdom to help Bailey through this moment. Jo Ann would understand how badly her confidence had been shaken.

After four rings, Bailey was connected to her friend's answering machine. She listened to the message, but didn't want to leave Jo Ann such a disheartening message, so she mumbled, "It's Bailey," and hung up.

Pacing the apartment in an effort to sort out her emotions didn't seem to help. She eyed her computer, which was set up in a corner of her compact living room, but the desire to sit down and start writing was nil. Vanished. Destroyed.

Jo Ann had warned her. So had others in their writers' group. Rejections hurt. She just hadn't expected it to hurt so much.

Searching in her purse for a mint, she felt her fingers close around a business card. *Parker's* business card. She slowly drew it out. He'd written down his phone number….

Should she call him? No, she decided, thrusting the card into her pocket. Why even entertain the notion? Talking to Parker now would be foolish. And risky. She was a big girl. She could take rejection. Anyone who became a writer had to learn how to handle rejection.

Rejections were rungs on the ladder of success. Someone had said that at a meeting once, and Bailey had written it down and kept it posted on the bottom edge of her computer screen. Now was the time to act on that belief. Since this was only the first rung, she had a long way to climb, but the darn ladder was much steeper than she'd anticipated.

With a fumbling resolve, she returned to the kitchen and reread the letter from Paula Albright, the editor, who wrote that she was returning the manuscript "with regret."

"Not as much regret as I feel," Bailey informed Max, who was busy enjoying *her* dinner.

"She says I show promise." But Bailey noted that she didn't say promise of what.

The major difficulty, according to the editor, was Michael. This wasn't exactly a surprise to Bailey. Ms. Albright had kindly mentioned several scenes that needed to be reworked with this problem in mind. She ended her letter by telling Bailey that if she revised the manuscript, the editorial department would be pleased to reevaluate it.

Funny, Bailey hadn't even noticed that the first time she'd read the letter. If she reworked Michael, there was still a chance.

With sudden enthusiasm, Bailey grabbed the phone. She'd changed her mind—calling Parker now seemed like a good idea. A great idea. He might well be her one and only chance to straighten out poor misguided Michael.

Parker answered on the second ring, sounding distracted and mildly irritated at being interrupted.

"Parker," Bailey said, desperately hoping she wasn't making a first-class fool of herself, "this is Bailey York."

"Hello." His tone was a little less disgruntled.

Her mouth had gone completely dry, but she rushed ahead with the reason for her call. "I want you to know I've…I've been thinking about your dinner invitation. Could you possibly meet me tonight instead of tomorrow?" She wanted to start rehabilitating Michael as soon as possible.

"This is Bailey York?" He sounded as though he didn't remember who she was.

"The writer from the subway," she said pointedly, feeling like more of an idiot with every passing second. She should never have phoned him, but the impulse had been so powerful. She longed to put this rejection behind her and write a stronger romance, but she was going to need his help. Perhaps she should call him later. "Listen, if now is inconvenient, I could call another time." She was about to hang up when Parker spoke.

"Now is fine. I'm sorry if I seem rattled, but I was working and I tend to get absorbed in a project."

"I do that myself," she said, reassured by his explanation. Drawing a deep breath, she explained the reason for her unexpected call. "*Forever Yours* was rejected today."

"I'm sorry to hear that." His regret seemed genuine, and the soft fluttering sensation returned to her stomach at the sympathy he extended.

"I was sorry, too, but it didn't come as a big shock. I guess I let my hopes build when the manuscript wasn't immediately returned, which is something Jo Ann warned me about." She shifted the receiver to her other ear, surprised by how much better she felt having someone to talk to.

"What happens when a publisher turns down a manuscript? Do they critique the book?"

"Heavens, no. Generally manuscripts are returned with a standard rejection letter. The fact that the editor took the time to personally write me about revising is sort of a compliment. Actually, it's an excellent sign. Especially since she's willing to look at *Forever Yours* again." Bailey paused and inhaled shakily. "I was wondering if I could take you up on that offer for dinner. I realize this is rather sudden and I probably shouldn't have phoned, but tonight would be best for me since…since I inadvertently gave Max my ground turkey and there's really nothing else in the fridge, but if you can't I understand…." The words had tumbled out in a nervous rush; once she'd started, she couldn't seem to make herself stop.

"Do you want me to pick you up, or would you rather meet somewhere?"

"Ah..." Despite herself, Bailey was astounded. She hadn't really expected Parker to agree. "The restaurant where you had lunch a couple of weeks ago looked good. Only, please, I insist on paying for my own meal this time."

"In Chinatown?"

"Yes. Would you meet me there?"

"Sure. Does an hour give you enough time?"

"Oh, yes. An hour's plenty." Once again Bailey found herself nearly tongue-tied with surprise—and pleasure.

Their conversation was over so fast that she was left staring at the phone, half wondering if it had really happened at all. She took a couple of deep breaths, then dashed into her bedroom to change, renew her makeup and brush her hair.

Bailey loved Chinese food, especially the spicy Szechuan dishes, but she wasn't thinking about dinner as the taxi pulled up in front of the restaurant. She'd decided to indulge herself by taking a cab to Chinatown. It did mean she'd have to take the subway home, though.

Parker, who was standing outside the restaurant waiting for her, hurried forward to open the cab door. Bailey was terribly aware of his hand supporting her elbow as he helped her out.

"It's good of you to meet me like this on such short notice," she said, smiling up at Parker.

"No problem. Who's Max?"

"My cat."

Parker grinned and, clasping her elbow more firmly, led her into the restaurant. The first thing that caught Bailey's attention was a gigantic, intricately carved chandelier made of dark polished wood. She'd barely had a chance to examine it, however, when they were escorted down a long hallway to a narrow room filled with wooden booths, high-backed and private, each almost a little room of its own.

"Oh, my, this is nice," she breathed, sliding into their booth. She slipped the bag from her shoulder and withdrew the same pen and notepad she'd brought with her when they'd met for lunch.

The waiter appeared with a lovely ceramic teapot and a pair of tiny matching cups. The menus were tucked under his arm.

Bailey didn't have nearly as easy a time making her choice as she had at the Sandpiper. Parker suggested they each order whatever they wished and then share. There were so many dishes offered, most of them sounding delectable and exciting, that it took Bailey a good ten minutes to make her selection—spicy shrimp noodles. Parker chose the less adventurous almond chicken stir-fry.

"All right," Bailey said, pouring them each some tea. "Now let's get down to business."

"Sure." Parker relaxed against the back of the booth, crossing his arms and stretching out his legs. "Ask away," he said, motioning with his hand when she hesitated.

"Maybe I'd better start by giving you a brief outline of the story."

"However you'd like to do this."

"I want you to understand Michael,' she explained. "He's a businessman, born on the wrong side of the tracks. He's a little bitter, but he's learned to forgive those who've hurt him through the years. Michael's in his mid-thirties, and he's never been married."

"Why not?"

"Well, for one thing he's been too busy building his career."

"As what?"

"He's in the exporting business."

"I see."

"You're frowning." Bailey hadn't asked a single one of

her prepared questions yet, and already Parker was looking annoyed.

"It's just that a man doesn't generally reach the ripe old age of thirty-five without a relationship or two. If he's never had any, then there's a problem."

"You're thirty-something and you're not married," she felt obliged to point out. "What's your excuse?"

Parker shrugged. "My college schedule was very heavy, which didn't leave a lot of time for dating. Later I traveled extensively, which again didn't offer much opportunity. Oh, there were relationships along the way, but nothing ever worked out. I guess you could say I haven't found the right woman. But that doesn't mean I'm not interested in marrying and settling down some day."

"Exactly. That's how Michael feels, except he thinks getting married would only complicate his life. He's ready to fall in love with Janice, but he doesn't realize it."

"I see," Parker said with a nod, "go on. I shouldn't have interrupted you."

"Well, basically, Michael's life is going smoothly until he meets Janice Hampton. Her father has retired and she's taking over the operation of his manufacturing firm. A job she's well qualified for, I might add."

"What does she manufacture?"

"I was rather vague about that, but I let the reader assume it has something to do with computer parts. I tossed in a word here and there to give that suggestion."

Parker nodded. "Continue. I'll try not to butt in again."

"That's okay," she said briskly. "Anyway, Janice's father is a longtime admirer of Michael's, and the old coot would like to get his daughter and Michael together. Neither one of them's aware of it, of course. At least not right away."

Parker reached for the teapot and refilled their cups. "That sounds good."

Bailey smiled shyly. "Thanks. One of the first things that happens is Janice's father maneuvers Michael and Janice under the mistletoe at a Christmas party. Everyone's expecting them to kiss, but Michael is furious and he—"

"Just a minute." Parker held up one hand, stopping her. "Let me see if I've got this straight. This guy is standing under the mistletoe with a beautiful woman and he's furious. What's wrong with him?"

"What do you mean?"

"No man in his right mind is going to object to kissing a beautiful woman."

Bailey picked up her teacup and leaned against the hard back of the wooden booth, considering. Parker was right. And Janice hadn't been too happy about the situation herself. Was that any more believable? Imagine standing under the mistletoe with a man like Parker Davidson. Guiltily she shook off the thought and returned her attention to his words.

"Unless..." he was saying pensively.

"Yes?"

"Unless he recognizes that he was manipulated into kissing her and resents it. He may even think she's in cahoots with her father."

Brightening, Bailey nodded, making a note on her pad. "Yeah, that would work." Parker was as good at tossing ideas around as Jo Ann, which was a pleasant surprise.

"Still..." He hesitated, sighing. "A pretty woman is a pretty woman and he isn't going to object too strongly, regardless of the circumstances. What happens when he does kiss her?"

"Not too much. He does it grudgingly, but I've decided I'm going to change that part. You're right. He shouldn't make too much of a fuss. However, this happens early on in the book and neither of them's aware of her father's scheme. I don't want to tip the reader off so soon as to what's happening."

Bailey's mind was spinning as she reworked the scene. She could picture Michael and Janice standing under the mistletoe, both somewhat uneasy with the situation, but as Parker suggested, not objecting too strongly. Janice figures they'll kiss, and that'll be the end of it…until they actually do the kissing.

That was the part Bailey intended to build on. When Michael's and Janice's lips met it would be like…like throwing a match on dry tinder, so intense would be the reaction.

The idea began to gather momentum in her mind. Then, not only would Janice and Michael be fighting her father's outrageous plot, they'd be battling their feelings for each other.

"This is great," Bailey whispered, "really great." She started to tell Parker her plan when they were interrupted by the waiter, who brought their dinner, setting the steaming dishes before them.

By then, Bailey's appetite had fully recovered and she reached eagerly for the chopsticks. Parker picked up his own. They both reached for the shrimp noodles. Bailey withdrew her chopsticks.

"You first."

"No, you." He waved his hand, encouraging her.

She smiled and scooped up a portion of the noodles. The situation felt somehow intimate, comfortable, and yet they were still basically strangers.

They ate in silence for several minutes and Bailey watched Parker deftly manipulate the chopsticks. It was the first time she'd dated a man who was as skilled at handling them as she was herself.

Dated a man.

The words leapt out at her. Bright red warning signs seemed to be flashing in her mind. Her head shot up and she stared wide-eyed at the man across the table from her.

"Bailey? Are you all right?"

She nodded and hurriedly looked away.

"Did you bite into a hot pepper?"

"No," she assured him, quickly shaking her head. "I'm fine. Really, I'm all right." Only she wasn't, and she suspected he knew it.

The remainder of their meal passed with few comments.

Naturally Parker had no way of knowing about her experiences with Paul and Tom. Nor would he be aware that there was an unused wedding dress hanging in her closet, taunting her every morning when she got ready for work. The wedding gown was an ever-present reminder of why she couldn't put any faith in the male of the species.

The danger came when she allowed her guard to slip. Before she knew it, she'd be trusting a man once again, and that was a definite mistake. Parker made her feel somehow secure; she felt instinctively that he was a man of integrity, of candor—and therein lay the real risk. Maybe he *was* a real live breathing hero, but Bailey had been fooled twice before. She wasn't going to put her heart on the line again.

They split the tab. Parker clearly wasn't pleased about that, but Bailey insisted. They were about to leave the restaurant when Parker said, "You started to say something about rewriting that scene under the mistletoe."

"Yes," she answered, regaining some of her former enthusiasm. "I'm going to have that kiss make a dynamite impact on them both. Your suggestions were very helpful. I can't tell you how much I appreciate your willingness to meet with me like this."

It was as though Parker hadn't heard her. His forehead

creased as he held open the door for her and they stepped onto the busy sidewalk.

"You're frowning again," Bailey noted aloud.

"Have you ever experienced that kind of intense sensation when a man kissed you?"

Bailey didn't have to think about it. "Not really."

"That's what I thought."

"But I like the idea of that happening between Janice and Michael," she argued. "It adds a whole new dimension to the plot. I can use that. Besides, there's a certain element of fantasy in a traditional romance novel, a larger-than-life perspective."

"Oh, I'm not saying a strong reaction between them shouldn't happen. I'm just wondering how you plan to write such a powerfully emotional scene without any real experience of it yourself."

"That's the mark of a good writer," Bailey explained, ignoring his less-than-flattering remark. She'd been kissed before! Plenty of times. "Being able to create an atmosphere of romance just takes imagination. You don't expect me to go around kissing strange men, do you?"

"Why not? You had no qualms about *following* a strange man. Kissing me wouldn't be any different. It's all research."

"Kissing you?"

"It'll add credibility to your writing. A confidence you might not otherwise have."

"If I were writing a murder mystery would you suggest I go out and kill someone?" Bailey had to argue with him before she found herself *agreeing* to this craziness!

"Don't be ridiculous! Murder would be out of the question, but a kiss…a kiss is very much within your grasp. It would lend authenticity to your story. I suggest we go ahead with it, Bailey."

They were strolling side by side. Bailey was deep in thought when Parker casually turned into a narrow alley. She guessed it was the same one he'd hauled her into the day she'd followed him.

"Well," he said, resting his hands on her shoulders and staring down at her. "Are you game?"

Was she? Bailey didn't know anymore. He was right; the scene would have far more impact if she were to experience the same sensations as Janice. Kissing Parker would be like Janice kissing Michael. The sale of her book could hinge on how well she developed the attraction between hero and heroine in that all-important first chapter.

"Okay," she said, barely recognizing her own voice.

No sooner had she spoken than Parker gently cupped her chin and directed her mouth toward his. "This is going to be good," she heard him whisper just before his lips settled over hers.

Bailey's eyes drifted shut. This *was* good. In fact, it was wonderful. So wonderful, she felt weak and dizzy—and yearned to feel even weaker and dizzier. Despite herself, she clung to Parker, literally hanging in his arms. Without his support, she feared she would have slumped to the street.

He tasted so warm and familiar, as if she'd spent a lifetime in his arms, as if she were *meant* to spend a lifetime there.

The fluttering sensation in her stomach changed to a warm heaviness. She felt strange and hot. Bailey was afraid that if this didn't end soon, she'd completely lose control.

"No more," she pleaded, breaking off the kiss. She buried her face in his shoulder and dragged in several deep breaths in an effort to stop her trembling.

It wasn't fair that Parker could make her feel this way. For Janice and Michael's sake, it was the best thing that could have happened, but for her own sake, it was the worst. She didn't *want* to feel any of this. The protective numbness around her heart was crumbling just when it was so important to keep it securely in place.

The hot touch of his lips against her temple caused her to jump away from him. "Well," she said, rubbing her palms briskly together once she found her voice. "That was certainly a step in the right direction."

"I beg your pardon?" Parker was staring at her as though he wasn't sure he'd heard her accurately.

"The kiss. It had pizzazz and a certain amount of charm, but I was looking for a little more…something. The kiss between Michael and Janice has got to have spark."

"Our kiss had spark." Parker's voice was deep, brooding.

"Charm," she corrected, then added brightly, "I will say one thing, though. You're good at this. Lots of practice, right?" Playfully she poked his ribs with her elbow. "Well, I've got to be going. Thanks again for meeting me on such short notice. I'll be seeing you around." Amazingly the smile on her lips didn't crack. Even more amazing was the fact that she managed to walk away from him on legs that felt like overcooked pasta.

She was about five blocks from the BART station, walking as fast as she could, mumbling to herself all the way. She behaved like an idiot every time she even came near Parker Davidson!

She continued mumbling, chastising herself, when he pulled up at the curb beside her in a white sports car. She didn't know much about cars, but she knew expensive when she saw it. The same way she knew his suit hadn't come from a department store.

"Get in," he said gruffly, slowing to a stop and leaning over to open the passenger door.

"Get in?" she repeated. "I was going to take BART."

"Not at this time of night you're not."

"Why shouldn't I?" she demanded.

"Don't press your luck, Bailey. Just get in."

She debated whether she should or not, but from the stubborn set of his jaw, she could see it would do no good to argue. She'd never seen a more obstinate-looking jaw in her life. As she recalled, it was one of the first things she'd noticed about Parker.

"What's your address?" he asked after she'd slipped inside.

Bailey gave it to him as she fiddled with the seat belt, then sat silently while he sped down the street, weaving his way in and out of traffic. He braked sharply at a red light and she glanced in his direction.

"Why are you so angry?" she demanded. "You look as if you're ready to bite my head off."

"I don't like it when a woman lies to me."

"When did I lie?" she asked indignantly.

"You lied a few minutes ago when you said our kiss was…lacking." He laughed humorlessly and shook his head. "We generated more electricity with that one kiss than the Hoover Dam does in a month. You want to kid yourself, then fine, but I'm not playing your game."

"I'm not playing any game," she informed him primly. "Nor do I appreciate having you come at me like King Kong because my assessment of a personal exchange between us doesn't meet yours."

"A personal exchange?" he scoffed. "It was a kiss, sweetheart."

"I only agreed to it for research purposes."

"If that's what you want to believe, fine, but we both know better."

"Whatever," she muttered. Parker could think what he

wanted. She'd let him drive her home because he seemed to be insisting on it. But as far as having anything further to do with him—out of the question. He was obviously placing far more significance on their kiss than she'd ever intended.

Okay, so she *had* felt something. But to hear him tell it, that kiss rivaled the great screen kisses of all time.

Parker drove up in front of her apartment building and turned off the engine. "All right," he said coolly. "Let's go over this one last time. Do you still claim our kiss was merely a 'personal exchange'? Just research?"

"Yes," she stated emphatically, unwilling to budge an inch.

"Then prove it."

Bailey sighed. "How exactly am I supposed to do that?"

"Kiss me again."

Bailey could feel the color drain out of her face. "I'm not about to sit outside my apartment kissing you with half the building looking on."

"Fine, then invite me in."

"Uh…it's late."

"Since when is nine o'clock late?" he taunted.

Bailey was running out of excuses. "There's nothing that says a woman is obligated to invite a man into her home, is there?" she asked in formal tones. Her spine was Sunday-school straight and her eyes were focused on the street ahead of her.

Parker's laugh took her by surprise. She twisted around to stare at him and found him smiling roguishly. "You little coward," he murmured, pulling her toward him for a quick peck on the cheek. "Go on. Run home before I change my mind."

Six

"I like it," Jo Ann said. "The way you changed that first kissing scene under the mistletoe is a stroke of genius." She smiled happily. "This is exactly the kind of rewriting you'll need to turn that rejection into a sale. You've taken Michael and made him proud and passionate, but very real and spontaneous. He's caught off guard by his attraction to Janice and is reacting purely by instinct." Jo Ann tapped her fingers on the top page of the revised first chapter. "This is your most powerful writing yet."

Bailey was so pleased she could barely restrain herself from leaping up and dancing a jig down the center of the congested subway-car aisle. Through sheer determination, she managed to confine her response to a smile.

"It's interesting how coming at this scene from a slightly different angle puts everything in a new light, isn't it?"

"It sure is," Jo Ann concurred. "If the rest of the book reads as well as this chapter, I honestly think you might have a chance."

It was too much to hope for. Bailey had spent the entire weekend in front of her computer. She must have rewritten the mistletoe scene no less than ten times, strengthening emotions, exploring the heady response Michael and Janice had toward each other. She'd worked hard to capture the incredulity they'd experienced, the shock of their unexpected fascination. Naturally, neither one could allow the other to know what they were feeling yet—otherwise Bailey wouldn't have any plot.

Michael had been dark and brooding afterward. Janice had done emotional cartwheels in an effort to diminish the incident. But neither of them could forget it.

If the unable-to-forget part seemed particularly realistic, there was a reason. Bailey's reaction to Parker had been scandalously similar to Janice's feelings about Michael's kiss. The incredulity was there. The wonder. The shock. And it never should have happened.

Unfortunately Bailey had suspected that even before she'd agreed to the "research." Who did she think she was fooling? Certainly not herself. She'd wanted Parker to kiss her long before he'd offered her the excuse.

Halfway through their dinner, Bailey had experienced all the symptoms. She knew them well. The palpitating heart, the sweating palms, the sudden loss of appetite. She'd tried to ignore them, but as the meal had progressed she'd thought of little else.

Parker had gone suspiciously quiet, too. Then, later, he'd kissed her and everything became much, much worse. She'd felt warm and dizzy. A tingling sensation had slowly spread through her body. It seemed as though every cell in her body was aware of him. The sensations had been so overwhelming, she'd had to pretend nothing had happened. The truth was simply too risky.

"What made you decide to rework the scene that way?" Jo Ann asked, breaking into her thoughts.

Bailey stared at her friend and blinked rapidly.

"Bailey?" Jo Ann asked. "You look as if your mind's soaring through outer space."

"Uh…I was just thinking."

"A dangerous habit for a writer. We can't seem to get our characters out of our minds, can we? They insist on following us everywhere."

Characters, nothing! It was Parker Davidson she couldn't stop thinking about. As for the *following* part… Had her thoughts conjured him up? There he was, large as life, casually strolling toward them as though he'd sought her out. He hadn't, she told herself sternly. Nonetheless she searched for him every morning. She couldn't seem to help it. She'd never been so frighteningly aware of a man before, so eager—yet so reluctant to see him. Often she found herself scanning the faces around her, hoping to catch a glimpse of him.

Now here he was. Bailey quickly looked out the window into the tunnel's darkness, staring at the reflections in the glass.

"Good morning, ladies," Parker said jovially, standing directly in front of them, his feet braced slightly apart. The morning paper was tucked under his arm, and he looked very much as he had the first time she'd noticed him. Forceful. Appealing. Handsome.

"Morning," Bailey mumbled. She immediately turned back to the window.

"Hello again," Jo Ann replied warmly, smiling up at him.

For one wild second Bailey experienced a flash of resentment. Parker was *her* hero, not Jo Ann's! Her friend was greeting him like a long-lost brother or something. But what bothered Bailey even more was how delighted *she* felt. These were the very reactions she'd been combating all weekend.

"So," Parker said smoothly, directing his words to

Bailey, "have you followed any strange men around town lately?"

She glared at him, annoyed at the way his words drew the attention of those sitting nearby. "Of course not," she snapped.

"I'm glad to hear it."

She'd just bet! She happened to glance at the man standing next to Parker. He was a distinguished-looking older gentleman who was peeking at her curiously over the morning paper.

"Did you rewrite the kissing scene?" Parker asked next.

The businessman gave up any pretense of reading, folded his paper and studied Bailey openly.

"She did a fabulous job of it," Jo Ann said with a mentor's pride.

"I was sure she would," Parker remarked. A hint of a smile raised the corners of his mouth and made his eyes sparkle. Bailey wanted to demand that he cease and desist that very instant. "I suspect it had a ring of sincerity to it," Parker added, his eyes meeting Bailey's. "A depth, perhaps, that was missing in the first account."

"It did," Jo Ann confirmed, looking mildly surprised. "The whole scene is beautifully written. Every emotion, every sensation, is right there, so vividly described it's difficult to believe the same writer is responsible for both versions."

Parker's expression reminded Bailey of Max when he'd discovered ground turkey in his dish instead of soggy cat food. His full sensuous mouth curved with satisfaction.

"I only hope Bailey can do as well with the dancing scene," Jo Ann said.

"The dancing scene?" Parker asked intently.

"That's several chapters later," Bailey explained, jerking the manuscript out of Jo Ann's lap. She shoved it inside a folder and slipped it into her spacious shoulder bag.

"It's romantic the way it's written, but there's something lacking," said Jo Ann. "Unfortunately I haven't been able to put my finger on what's wrong."

"The problem is and always has been Michael," Bailey inserted, not wanting the conversation to continue in this vein. She hoped her hero would forgive her for blaming her shortcomings as a writer on him.

"You can't fault Michael for the dancing scene," Jo Ann disagreed. "Correct me if I'm wrong, but as I recall, Michael and Janice were manipulated—by Janice's father—into attending a Pops concert. The only reason they went was that they couldn't think of a plausible excuse."

"Yes," she admitted grudgingly. "A sixties rock group was performing."

"Right. Then, as the evening went on, several couples from the audience started to dance. The young man sitting next to Janice asked her—"

"The problem is with Michael," Bailey insisted again. She glanced hopefully at the older gentleman, but he just shrugged, eyes twinkling.

"What did Michael do that was so wrong?" Jo Ann asked with a puzzled frown.

"He...he should never have let Janice dance with another man," Bailey said in a desperate voice.

"Michael couldn't have done anything else," Jo Ann argued, "otherwise he would've looked like a jealous fool." She turned to Parker for confirmation.

"I may be new to this hero business, but I can't help agreeing."

Bailey was irritated with both of them. This was *her* story and she'd write it as she saw fit. However, she refrained from saying so—just in case they were right. She needed time to mull over their opinions.

The train screeched to a halt and people surged toward the door. Bailey noted, gratefully, that this was Parker's stop.

"I'll give you a call later," he said, looking directly into Bailey's eyes. He didn't wait for a response.

He knew she didn't want to hear from him. She was frightened. Defensive. Guarded. With good reason. Only he didn't fully understand what that reason was. But a man like Parker wouldn't let her attitude go unchallenged.

"He's going to call you." Jo Ann sighed enviously. "Isn't that thrilling? Doesn't that excite you?"

Bailey shook her head, contradicting everything she was feeling inside. "Excite me? Not really."

Jo Ann frowned at her suspiciously. "What's the matter?"

"Nothing," Bailey answered with calm determination. She'd strolled down the path of romantic delusion twice before, but this time her eyes were wide open. Romance was wonderful, exciting, inspiring—and it was best limited to the pages of a well-crafted novel. Men, at least the men in her experience, inevitably proved to be terrible disappointments. Painful disappointments.

"Don't you like Parker?" Jo Ann demanded. "I mean, who wouldn't? He's hero material. You recognized it immediately, even before I did. Remember?"

Bailey wasn't likely to forget. "Yes, but that was in the name of research."

"Research?" Jo Ann cocked her eyebrows in flagrant disbelief. "Be honest, Bailey. You saw a whole lot more than Michael in Parker Davidson. You're not the type of woman who dashes off subways to follow a man. Some deep inner part of your being was reaching out to him."

Bailey forced a short laugh. "I hate to say it, Jo Ann, but I think you've been reading too many romances lately."

Jo Ann shrugged in a lie-to-yourself-if-you-insist manner. "Maybe, but I doubt it."

Nevertheless, her friend had given Bailey something to ponder.

The writing didn't go well that evening. Bailey, dressed in warm gray sweats, sans makeup and shoes, sat in front of her computer, staring blankly at the screen. "Inspiration is on vacation," she muttered, and that bit of doggerel seemed the best she could manage at the moment. Her usual warmth and humor escaped her. Every word she wrote sounded flat. She was tempted to erase the entire chapter.

Max, who had appointed himself the guardian of her printer, was curled up fast asleep on top of it. Bailey had long ago given up trying to keep him off. She'd quickly surrendered and taken to folding a towel over the printer to protect its internal workings from cat hair. Whenever she needed to print out a chapter, she nudged him awake; Max was always put out by the inconvenience and let her know it.

"Something's wrong," she announced to her feline companion. "The words just aren't flowing."

Max didn't reveal the slightest concern. He stretched out one yellow striped leg and examined it carefully, then settled down for another lengthy nap. He was fed and content and that was all that mattered.

Crossing her ankles, Bailey leaned back and clasped her hands behind her head. Chapter two of *Forever Yours* was just as vibrant and fast-paced as chapter one. But chapter three… She groaned and reread Paula Albright's letter for the umpteenth time, wanting desperately to capture the feelings and emotions the editor had suggested.

The phone rang in the kitchen, startling her. Bailey sighed irritably, then got up and rushed into the other room.

"Hello," she said curtly, realizing two important things at the same time. The first was how unfriendly and unwelcoming she sounded, and the second…the second was that she'd been unconsciously anticipating this call the entire evening.

"Hello," Parker returned in an affable tone. He didn't seem at all perturbed by her disagreeable mood. "I take it you're working, but from the sound of your voice I'd guess the rewrite isn't going well."

"It's coming along nicely." Bailey didn't know why she felt the need to lie. She was immediately consumed by guilt, then tried to disguise that by being even less friendly. "In fact, you interrupted a critical scene. I have so little time to write as it is, and my evenings are important to me."

There was an awkward silence. "Then I won't keep you," Parker said with cool politeness.

"It's just that it would be better if you didn't phone me." Her explaining didn't seem to improve the situation.

"I see," he said slowly.

And Bailey could tell that he *did* understand. She'd half expected him to argue, or at least attempt to cajole her into a more responsive mood. He didn't.

"Why don't you call me when you have a free moment," was all he said.

"I will," she answered, terribly disappointed and not sure why. It *was* better this way, with no further contact between them, she reminded herself firmly. "Goodbye, Parker."

"Goodbye," he said after another uncertain silence.

Bailey was still gripping the receiver when she heard a soft click followed by the drone of the disconnected line. She'd been needlessly abrupt and standoffish—as if she was trying to prove something. Trying to convince herself that she wanted nothing more to do with Parker.

Play it safe, Bailey. Don't involve your heart. You've learned your lesson. Her mind was constructing excuses for her tactless behavior, but her heart would accept none of it.

Bailey felt wretched. She went back to her chair and stared at the computer screen for a full five minutes, unable to concentrate.

He's only trying to help, her heart told her.

Men aren't to be trusted, her mind said. *Haven't you learned that yet? How many times does it take to teach you something?*

Parker isn't like the others, her heart insisted.

Her mind, however, refused to listen. *All men are alike.*

But if she'd done the right thing, why did she feel so rotten? Yet she knew that if she gave in to him now, she'd regret it. She was treading on thin ice with this relationship; she remembered how she'd felt when he kissed her. Was she willing to risk the pain, the heartache, all over again?

Bailey closed her eyes and shook her head. Her thoughts were hopelessly tangled. She'd done what she knew was necessary, but she didn't feel good about it. In fact, she was miserable. Parker had gone out of his way to help her with this project, offering her his time and his advice. He'd given her valuable insights into the male point of view. And when he kissed her, he'd reminded her how it felt to be a desirable woman....

Bailey barely slept that night. On Tuesday morning she decided to look for Parker, even if it meant moving from one subway car to the next, something she rarely did. When she did run into him, she intended to apologize, crediting her ill mood to creative temperament.

"Morning," Jo Ann said, meeting her on the station platform the way she did every morning.

"Hello," Bailey murmured absently, scanning the windows of the train as it slowed to a stop, hoping to spot Parker. If Jo Ann noticed anything odd, she didn't comment.

"I heard back from the agent I wrote to a couple of months back," Jo Ann said, grinning broadly. Her eyes fairly sparkled.

"Irene Ingram?" Bailey momentarily forgot about Parker as she stared at her friend. Her sagging spirits lifted with the news. For weeks Jo Ann had been poring over the agent list, trying to decide whom to approach first. After much deliberation and thought, Jo Ann had decided to aim high. Many of the major publishers were no longer accepting non-agented material, and finding one willing to represent a beginner had been a serious concern. Irene was listed as one of the top romance-fiction agents in the industry. She represented a number of prominent names.

"And?" Bailey prompted, although she was fairly sure the news was positive.

"She's read my book and—" Jo Ann tossed her hands in the air "—she's crazy about it!"

"Does that mean she's going to represent you?" They were both aware how unusual it was for an established New York agent to represent an unpublished author. It wasn't unheard of, but it didn't happen all that often.

"You know, we never got around to discussing that—I assume she is. I mean, she talked to me about doing some minor revisions, which shouldn't take more than a week. Then we discussed possible markets. There's an editor she knows who's interested in historicals set in this time period. Irene wants to send it to her first, just as soon as I've finished with the revisions."

"Jo Ann," Bailey said, clasping her friend's hands tightly, "this is fabulous news!"

"I'm still having trouble believing it. Apparently Irene phoned while I was still at work and my eight-year-old answered. When I got home there was this scribbled message that didn't make any sense. All it said was that a lady with a weird name had phoned."

"Leave it to Bobby."

"He wasn't even home for me to question."

"He didn't write down the phone number?" Bailey asked.

"No, but he told Irene I was at work and she phoned me at five-thirty, our time."

"Weren't you the one who told me that being a writer means always knowing what time it is in New York?"

"The very one," Jo Ann teased. "Anyway, we spoke for almost an hour. It was crazy. Thank goodness Dan was home. I was standing in the kitchen with this stunned look on my face, frantically taking down notes. I didn't have to explain anything. Dan started dinner and then raced over to the park to pick up Bobby from Little League practice. Sarah set the table, and by the time I was off the phone, dinner was ready."

"I'm impressed." Several of the women in their writers' group had complained about their husbands' attitudes toward their creative efforts. But Jo Ann was fortunate in that department. Dan believed in her talent as strongly as Jo Ann did herself.

Jo Ann's dream was so close to being realized that Bailey could feel her own excitement rise. After three years of continuous effort, Jo Ann deserved a sale more than anyone she knew. She squeezed her writing in between dental appointments and Little League practices, between a full-time job and the demands of being a wife and mother. In addition, she was the driving force behind their writers' group. Jo Ann Webster had paid her dues, and Bailey sincerely hoped that landing Irene Ingram as her agent would be the catalyst to her first sale.

"I refuse to get excited," Jo Ann said matter-of-factly.

Bailey stared at her incredulously. "You're kidding, aren't you?"

"I suppose I am. It's impossible not to be thrilled, but there's a saying in the industry we both need to remember. Agents don't sell books, good writing does. Plotting and characterization are what interest an editor. Agents negotiate contracts, but they don't sell books."

"You should've phoned and told me she called," Bailey chastised.

"I meant to. Honest, I did, but when I'd finished the dinner dishes, put the kids to bed and reviewed my revision notes, it was too late. By the way, before I forget, did Parker call you?"

He was the last person Bailey wanted to discuss. If she admitted he had indeed phoned her, Jo Ann was bound to ask all kinds of questions Bailey preferred not to answer. Nor did she want to lie about it.

So she compromised. "He did, but I was writing at the time and he suggested I call him back later."

"Did you?" Jo Ann asked expectantly.

"No," Bailey said in a small miserable voice. "I should have, but…I didn't."

"He's marvelous, you know."

"Would it be okay if we didn't discuss Parker?" Bailey asked. She'd intended to seek him out, but she decided against it, at least for now. "I've got so much on my mind and I…I need to clear away a few cobwebs."

"Of course." Jo Ann's look was sympathetic. "Take your time, but don't take too long. Men like Parker Davidson don't come along often. Maybe once in a lifetime, if you're lucky."

This wasn't what Bailey wanted to hear.

Max was curled up on Bailey's printer later that same evening. She'd worked for an hour on the rewrite and wasn't entirely pleased with the results. Her lack of satisfaction could be linked, however, to the number of times she'd inadvertently typed Parker's name instead of Michael's.

That mistake was simple enough to understand. She was tired. Parker had been in her thoughts most of the day. Good grief, when *wasn't* he in her thoughts?

Then, when she decided to take a break and scan the evening paper, Parker's name seemed to leap right off the page. For a couple of seconds, Bailey was convinced the typesetter had made a mistake, just as she herself had a few minutes earlier. Peering at the local-affairs page, she realized that yes, indeed, Parker was in the news.

She sat down on the kitchen stool and carefully read the brief article. Construction crews were breaking ground for a high-rise bank in the financial district. Parker Davidson was the project's architect.

Bailey read the item twice and experienced a swelling sense of pride and accomplishment.

She had to phone Parker. She owed him an explanation, an apology; she owed him her gratitude. She'd known it the moment she'd abruptly ended their conversation the night before. She'd known it that morning when she spoke with Jo Ann. She'd known it the first time she'd substituted

Parker's name for Michael's. Even the afternoon paper was telling her what she already knew.

Something so necessary shouldn't be so difficult, Bailey told herself, standing in front of her telephone. Her hand still on the receiver, she hesitated. What could she possibly say to him? Other than to apologize for her behavior and congratulate him on the project she'd read about, which amounted to about thirty seconds of conversation.

Max sauntered into the kitchen, no doubt expecting to be fed again.

"You know better," she muttered, glaring down at him.

Pacing the kitchen didn't lend her courage. Nor did examining the contents of her refrigerator. The only thing that did was excite Max, who seemed to think she'd changed her mind, after all.

"Oh, for heaven's sake," she muttered, furious with herself. She picked up the phone, punched out Parker's home number—and waited. The phone rang once, twice, three times.

Parker was apparently out for the evening. Probably with some tall blond bombshell, celebrating his success. Every woman's basic nightmare. Four rings. Well, what did she expect? He was handsome, appealing, generous, kind—

"Hello?"

He caught her completely off guard. "Parker?"

"Bailey?"

"Yes, it's me," she said brightly. "Hello." The things she'd intended to say had unexpectedly disintegrated.

"Hello." His voice softened a little.

"Am I calling at a bad time?" she asked, wrapping the telephone cord around her index finger, then her wrist and finally her elbow. "I could call back later if that's more convenient."

"Now is fine."

"I saw your name in the paper and wanted to congratulate you. This project sounds impressive."

He shrugged it off, as she knew he would. Silence fell between them, the kind of silence that needed to be filled or explained or quickly extinguished.

"I also wanted to apologize for the way I acted last night, when you phoned," Bailey said, the cord so tightly drawn around her hand that her fingers had gone numb. She loosened it now, her movements almost frantic. "I was rude and tactless and you didn't deserve it."

"So you ran into a snag with your writing?"

"I beg your pardon?"

"You're having a problem with your novel."

Bailey wondered how he knew that. "Uh…"

"I suggest it's time to check out the male point of view again. Get my insights. Am I right or wrong?"

"Right or wrong? Neither. I called to apologize."

"How's the rewrite coming?"

"Not too well." She sighed.

"Which tells me everything I need to know."

Bailey was mystified. "If you're implying that the only reason I'm calling is to ask for help with *Forever Yours* you couldn't be more mistaken."

"Then why *did* you call?"

"If you must know, it was to explain."

"Go on, I'm listening."

Now that she had his full attention, Bailey was beginning to feel foolish. "My mother always told me there's no excuse for rudeness, so I wanted to tell you something—something that might help you understand." Suddenly she couldn't utter another word.

"I'm listening," Parker repeated softly.

Bailey took a deep breath and closed her eyes. "Uh,

maybe you *won't* understand, but you should know there's…there's a slightly used wedding dress hanging in my closet."

Seven

Of all the explanations Bailey could have given, all the excuses she could have made to Parker, she had no idea why she'd mentioned the wedding dress. Sheer embarrassment dictated her next action.

She hung up the phone.

Immediately afterward it started ringing and she stared at it in stupefied horror. Placing her hands over her ears, she walked into the living room, sank into the overstuffed chair and tucked her knees under her chin.

Seventeen rings.

Parker let the phone ring so many times Bailey was convinced he was never going to give up. The silence that followed the last peal seemed to reverberate loudly through the small apartment.

She was just beginning to gather her thoughts when there was an impatient pounding on her door.

Max imperiously raised his head from his position on her printer as though to demand she do something. Obviously all the disruptions this evening were annoying him.

"Bailey, open this door," Parker ordered in a tone even she couldn't ignore.

Reluctantly she got up and pulled open the door, knowing intuitively that he would've gotten in one way or another. If she'd resisted, Parker would probably have had Mrs. Morgan outside her door with a key.

He stormed into her living room as though there was a raging fire inside that had to be extinguished. He stood in the center of the room and glanced around, running his hand through his hair. "What was that you said about a wedding dress?"

Bailey, who still clutched the doorknob, looked up at him and casually shrugged. "You forgot the slightly used part."

"Slightly used?"

"That's what I tried to explain earlier," she returned, fighting the tendency to be flippant.

"Are you married?" he asked harshly.

The question surprised her, although she supposed it shouldn't have. After all, they were talking about wedding dresses. "Heavens, no!"

"Then what the hell did you mean when you said it was slightly used?"

"I tried it on several times, paid for it, walked around in it. I even had my picture taken in it, but that dress has never, to the best of my knowledge, been inside a church." She closed the door and briefly leaned against it.

"Do you want to tell me what happened?"

"Not particularly," she said, joining him in the middle of the room. "I really don't understand why I even brought it up. But now that you're here, do you want a cup of coffee?" She didn't wait for his response, but went into her kitchen and automatically took down a blue ceramic mug.

"What was his name?"

"Which time? The first time around it was Paul. Tom followed a few years later," Bailey said with matter-of-fact sarcasm as she filled the mug and handed it to him. She poured a cup for herself.

"I take it you've had to cancel two weddings, then?"

"Yes," she said leading the way back into her living area. She curled up on the couch, her feet tucked beneath her, leaving the large overstuffed chair for Parker. "This isn't something I choose to broadcast, but I seem to have problems holding on to a man. To be accurate, I should explain I bought the dress for Tom's and my wedding. He was the second fiancé. Paul and I hadn't gotten around to the particulars before he…left." The last word was barely audible.

"Why'd you keep the dress?" Parker asked, his dark eyes puzzled.

Bailey looked away. She didn't want his pity any more than she needed his tenderness, she told herself. But if that was the case, why did she feel so cold and alone?

"Bailey?"

"It's such a beautiful dress." Chantilly lace over luxurious white silk. Pearls along the full length of the sleeves. A gently tapered bodice; a gracefully draped skirt. It was the kind of dress every woman dreamed she'd wear once in a lifetime. The kind of dress that signified love and romance…

Instead of leaving the wedding gown with her parents, Bailey had packed it up and transported it to San Francisco. Now Parker was asking her why. Bailey supposed there was some psychological reason behind her actions. Some hidden motive buried in her subconscious. A reminder, perhaps, that men were not to be trusted?

"You loved them?" Parker asked carefully.

"I thought I did," she whispered, staring into her coffee. "To be honest, I…I don't know anymore."

"Tell me about Paul."

"Paul," she repeated in a daze. "We met our junior year of college." That seemed like a lifetime ago now.

"And you fell in love," he finished for her.

"Fairly quickly. He intended to go into law. He was bright and fun and opinionated. I could listen to him for hours. Paul seemed to know exactly what he wanted and how to get it."

"He wanted you," Parker inserted.

"At first." Bailey hesitated, struggling against the pain before it could tighten around her heart the way it once had. "Then he met Valerie. I don't think he intended to fall in love with her." Bailey had to believe that. She knew Paul had tried to hold on to his love for her, but in the end it was Valerie he chose. "I dropped out of college afterward," she added, her voice low and trembling. "I couldn't bear to be there, on campus, seeing the two of them together." It sounded cowardly now. Her parents had been disappointed, but she'd continued her studies at a business college, graduating as a paralegal a year later.

"I should've known Paul wasn't a hero," she said, glancing up at Parker and risking a smile.

"How's that?"

"He drank blush wine."

Parker stared at her a moment without blinking. "I beg your pardon?"

"You prefer straight Scotch, right?"

"Yes." Parker was staring at her. "How'd you know?"

"You also get your hair cut by a real barber and not a hairdresser."

He nodded.

"You wear well-made conservative clothes and prefer socks with your shoes."

"That's all true," Parker agreed, as though he'd missed

the punch line in a joke. "But how'd you know?" he asked again.

"You like your coffee in a mug instead of a cup."

"Yes." His voice was even more incredulous.

"You're a hero, remember?" She sent him another smile, pleased with how accurately she'd assessed his habits. "At least I've learned one thing in all of this, and that's how to recognize a real man."

"Paul and Tom weren't real men?"

"No, they were costly imitations. Costly to my pride, that is." She altered her position and pulled her knees beneath her chin, wrapping her arms around her legs. She'd consciously assumed a defensive position—just in case he felt the need to comfort her. "Before you leap to conclusions, I think you should know that the only reason I need a hero is for the sake of *Forever Yours.* You're perfect as a model for Michael."

"But you don't want to become personally involved with me."

"Exactly." Now that everything was out in the open, Bailey felt an immediate sense of relief. Now that Parker understood, the pressure would be gone. There would be no unrealistic expectations. "I write romances and you're a hero type. Our relationship is strictly business. Though of course I'm grateful for your…friendship," she added politely.

Parker seemed to mull over her words for several seconds before shaking his head. "I could accept that—except there's one complication."

"Oh?" Bailey's gaze sought Parker's.

"The kiss."

Abruptly she dropped her gaze as a chill raced up her spine. "Foul!" she wanted to yell. "Unfair!" Instead, she muttered, "Uh, I don't think we should discuss that."

"Why not?"

"It was research," she said forcefully. "That's all." She was working hard to convince herself. Harder still at smiling blandly in his direction, hoping all the while he'd leave her comment untouched.

He didn't.

"Well, then it wouldn't hurt to experiment a second time, would it?" he argued. Unfortunately she had to acknowledge the logic of that—but she wouldn't admit it.

"No, please, there isn't any need," she told him, neatly destroying her own argument with her impassioned plea.

"I disagree," Parker said, standing up and striding toward her.

"Ah..." She clasped her bent legs even more tightly.

"There's nothing to worry about," Parker assured her.

"Isn't there? I mean...of course, there isn't. It's just that kissing makes me uncomfortable."

"Why's that?"

Couldn't the man accept a simple explanation? Just once?

Bailey sighed. "All right, you can kiss me if you insist," she said ungraciously, dropping her feet to the floor. She straightened her sweatshirt, dutifully squeezed her eyes shut, puckered her lips and waited.

And waited.

Finally she grew impatient and opened her eyes to discover Parker sitting next to her, staring. His face was inches from her own. A smile nipped at the corners of his mouth, making his lips quiver slightly.

"I amuse you?" she asked, offended. He was the one who'd requested this demonstration in the first place. He was the one who'd demanded proof.

"Not exactly *amuse,*" Parker said, but from the gleam

in his eyes she suspected he was fighting the urge to laugh out loud.

"I think we should forget the whole thing." She spoke with as much dignity as possible then got up to carry her cup into the kitchen. Turning to collect Parker's mug from the living room, she walked headlong into his arms.

His hands rested on her shoulders. "Both of those men were fools," he whispered, his gaze warm, his words soft.

Trapped between his body and the kitchen counter, Bailey felt the flutterings of panic. Her heart soared to her throat, beating wildly. He'd had his chance to kiss her, to prove his point. He should've done it then. Not now. Not when she wasn't steeled and ready. Not when his words made her feel so helpless and vulnerable.

Gently his mouth claimed hers. The kiss was straightforward, uncomplicated by need or desire. A tender kiss. A kiss to erase the pain of rejection and the grief of loss.

Bailey didn't respond. Not at first. Then her lips trembled to life in a slow awakening.

Like the first time Parker had kissed her, Bailey felt besieged by confusion and a sense of shock. She wasn't ready for this! She jerked herself free of his arms and twisted around. "There!" she said, her voice quavering. "Are you happy?"

"No," he answered starkly. "You can try to fool yourself if you want, but we both know the truth. You've been burned."

"Since I can't stand the heat," she said in a reasonable tone, "I got out of the kitchen." The fact that she'd just been kissed by him *in* the kitchen only made her situation more farcical. She brushed the hair back from her forehead, managed a false smile and turned around to face him. "I should never have said anything about the wedding dress.

I don't know why I did. I'm not even sure what prompted that display of hysteria."

"I'm glad you did. And, Bailey, don't feel you have to apologize to me."

"Thank you," she mumbled, leading the way to her door.

Parker stopped to pat Max, who didn't so much as open his eyes to investigate. "Does he always sleep on your printer?"

"No, he sometimes insists on taking up a large portion of my pillow, generally when I'm using it myself."

Parker grinned. Bailey swore she'd never met a man with a more engaging smile. It was like watching the sun break through the clouds after a heavy downpour. It warmed her spirit, and only with the full strength of her will was she able to look away.

"I'll be seeing you," he said, pausing at the door.

"Yes," she whispered, yearning to see him again, yet in the same heartbeat hoping it wouldn't be soon.

"Bailey," Parker said, pressing his hand to her cheek, "just remember you haven't been the only one betrayed by love. It happens to all of us."

Perhaps, Bailey thought, but Parker was a living, breathing hero. The type of man women bought millions of books a year to read about, to dream about. She doubted he knew what it was like to have love humiliate him and break his heart.

"You look like you don't believe me."

Bailey stared at him, surprised he'd read her reaction so clearly.

"You're wrong," he said quietly. "I lost someone I loved, too." With that he dropped his hand and walked out, closing the door behind him.

By the time Bailey had recovered her wits enough to race after him, question him, the hallway was empty.

Parker had lost at love, too? No woman in her right mind would walk away from Parker Davidson.

He was a hero.

"I'm afraid I did it again," Bailey announced to Jo Ann as they walked briskly toward their respective office buildings. The noise on the subway that morning had made private conversation impossible.

"Did what?"

"Put my foot in my mouth with Parker Davidson. He—"

"Did you see his name in the paper last night?" Jo Ann asked excitedly, cutting her off. "It was a small piece in the local section. I would've phoned you, but I knew I'd see you this morning and I didn't want to interrupt your writing time."

"I saw it."

"Dan was impressed that we even knew Parker. Apparently he's made quite a name for himself in the past few years. I never pay attention to that sort of thing. If it doesn't have to do with medical insurance or novel-writing, it's lost on me. But Dan's heard of him. He would, being in construction and all. Did you know Parker won a major national award for an innovative house he designed last year?"

"N-no."

"I'm sorry, I interrupted you, didn't I?" Jo Ann said, stopping midstride. "What were you about to say?"

Bailey wasn't sure how much she should tell her. "He stopped by my apartment—"

"Parker came to your place?" Jo Ann sounded awestruck, as though Bailey had experienced a heavenly visitation.

Bailey didn't know what was wrong with Jo Ann. She wasn't letting her get a word in edgewise. "I made the mistake of telling him about the wedding dress in my closet. And at first I think he assumed I was married."

Jo Ann came to an abrupt halt. Her eyes narrowed. "There's a wedding dress in your closet?"

Bailey had forgotten she'd never told Jo Ann about Paul and Tom. She felt neither the inclination nor the desire to explain now, especially on a cold February day in the middle of a busy San Francisco sidewalk.

"My, my, will you look at the time?" Bailey muttered, staring down at her watch. It was half-past frustration and thirty minutes to despair. The only way she could easily extricate herself from this mess was to leave—now.

"Oh, no, you don't, Bailey York," Jo Ann cried, grasping her forearm. "You're not walking away from me yet. Not without filling me in first."

"It's nothing. I was engaged."

"When? Recently?"

"Yes and no," Bailey responded cryptically with a longing glance at her office building two blocks south.

"What does that mean?" Jo Ann demanded.

"I was engaged to be married twice, and both times the man walked out on me. All right? Are you satisfied now?"

Her explanation didn't seem to appease Jo Ann. "Twice? But what's any of this got to do with Parker? It wasn't his fault those other guys dumped you, was it?"

"Of course not," Bailey snapped, completely exasperated. She'd lost her patience. It had been a mistake to ever mention the man's name. Jo Ann had become Parker's greatest advocate. Never mind that she was also *her* good friend and if she was going to champion anyone, it should be Bailey. However, in Jo Ann's starry-eyed view, Parker apparently could do no wrong.

"He assumed you were married?"

"Don't worry, I explained everything," she said calmly.

"Listen, we're going to be late for work. I'll talk to you later."

"You bet you will. You've got a lot more explaining to do." She took a couple of steps, walking backward, staring at Bailey. "You were engaged? To different men each time?" she repeated. "Two different men?"

Bailey nodded and held up two fingers as they continued to back away from each other. "Two times, two different men."

Unexpectedly Jo Ann's face broke into a wide smile. "You know what they say, don't you? Third time's the charm, and if Parker Davidson is anything, it's charming. Talk to you this evening." With a quick wave, her friend turned and hurried down the street.

By lunchtime, Bailey decided the day was going to be a disaster. She'd misfiled an important folder, accidentally disconnected a client on the phone and worst of all spent two hours typing up a brief, then pressed the wrong key and lost the entire document. Following the fiasco with the computer, she took an early lunch and decided to walk off her frustration.

Either by accident or unconscious design—she couldn't decide which—Bailey found herself outside Parker's office building. She gazed at it for several minutes, wavering with indecision. She wanted to ask him what he'd meant about losing someone he loved. It was either that or spend the second half of the day infuriating her boss and annoying important clients. She was disappointed in Parker, she decided. He shouldn't have walked away without explaining. It wasn't fair. He'd been willing enough to listen to the humiliating details of *her* love life, but hadn't shared his own pain.

Roseanne Snyder, the firm's receptionist, brightened when Bailey walked into the office. "Oh, Ms. York, it's good to see you again."

"Thank you," Bailey answered, responding naturally to the warm welcome.

"Is Mr. Davidson expecting you?" The receptionist was flipping through the pages of the engagement calendar. "I'm terribly sorry if I—"

"No, no," Bailey said, stepping close to the older woman's desk. "I wasn't even sure Parker would be in."

"He is, and I know he'd be pleased to see you. Just go on back and I'll tell him you're coming. You know the way, don't you?" She turned in her chair and pointed down the hallway. "Mr. Davidson's office is the last door on your left."

Bailey hesitated, more doubtful than ever that showing up like this was the right thing to do. She would have left, crept quietly away, if Roseanne hadn't spoken into the intercom just then and gleefully announced her presence.

Before Bailey could react, Parker's office door opened. He waited there, hands in his pockets, leaning indolently against the frame.

Fortifying her resolve, she hurried toward him. He moved aside and closed the door when she entered. Once again she was struck by the dramatically beautiful view of the bay, but she couldn't allow that to deter her from her purpose.

"This is an unexpected surprise," Parker said.

Her nerves were on edge, and her words were more forceful than she intended. "That was a rotten thing you did."

"What? Kissing you? Honestly, Bailey are we going to go through all that again? You've got to stop lying to yourself."

"My day's a complete waste," she said, clenching her hands, "and this has nothing to do with our kiss."

"It doesn't?"

She sank down in a chair. "I dragged my pride through the mud of despair for you," she said dramatically.

He blinked as though she'd completely lost him.

"All right," she admitted with a flip of her hand, "that may be a little on the purple side."

"Purple?"

"Purple prose." Oh, it was so irritating having to explain everything to him. "Do you think I enjoy sharing my disgrace? It isn't every woman who'd willingly dig up the most painful episodes in her past and confess them to you. It wasn't easy, you know."

Parker walked around to his side of the desk, sat down and rubbed the side of his jaw. "Does this conversation have anything to do with the slightly used wedding dress?"

"Yes," she returned indignantly. "Oh, it was perfectly acceptable for me to describe how two—not one, mind you, but two—different men dumped me practically at the altar steps."

The amusement faded from Parker's eyes. "I realize that."

"No, you don't," she said, "otherwise you'd never have left on that parting shot."

"Parting shot?"

She shut her eyes for a moment and prayed for patience. "As you were leaving, you oh-so-casually mentioned something about losing someone you loved. Why was it fine for me to share my humiliation but not for you? I'm disappointed and—" Her throat closed before she could finish.

Parker was strangely quiet. His eyes held hers, his look somber. "You're right. That was rude of me, and I don't have any excuse."

"Oh, but you do," she said dryly. She should have known. He was a hero, wasn't he? She shook her head, angry with herself as much as with him.

"I do?" Parker countered.

"Yes, I should've figured it out sooner. Heroes often have a difficult time exposing their vulnerabilities. Obviously this…woman you loved wounded your pride. She unmasked your vulnerability. Believe me, I know about that from experience. You don't have to explain it to me." She stood up to go, guiltily aware that she'd judged Parker too harshly.

"But you're right," he argued. "You shared a deep part of yourself and I should have been willing to do the same. It was unfair of me to leave the way I did."

"Perhaps, but it was true to character." She would have said a quick goodbye and walked out the door if not for the pain that suddenly entered his eyes.

"I'll tell you. It's only fair that you know. Sit down."

Bailey did as he requested, watching him carefully.

Parker smiled, but this wasn't the winsome smile she was accustomed to seeing. This was a strained smile, almost a grimace.

"Her name was Maria. I met her while I was traveling in Spain about fifteen years ago. We were both so young and in love. I wanted to marry her, bring her back with me to the States, but her family…well, suffice it to say her family didn't want their daughter marrying a foreigner. Several hundred years of tradition and pride stood between us, and when Maria was forced to choose between her family and me, she chose to remain in Madrid." He paused, shrugging one shoulder. "She did the right thing, I realize that now, much as it hurt at the time. I also realize how difficult her decision must have been. I learned a few months later that she'd married someone far more acceptable to her family than an American student."

"I'm sorry."

He shook his head as though to dispel the memories. "There's no reason you should be. Although I loved her a great deal, the relationship would never have lasted. Maria would've been miserable in this country. I understand now how perceptive she was."

"She loved you."

"Yes," he said. "She loved me as much as she dared, but in the end duty and family were more important to her than love."

Bailey didn't know what to say. Her heart ached for the young man who had lost his love, and yet she couldn't help admiring the brave woman who had sacrificed her heart for her family and her deepest beliefs.

"I think what hurt the most was that she married someone else so soon afterward," Parker added.

"Paul and Tom got married, too…I think." Bailey understood his pain well.

The office was quiet for a moment, until Parker broke the silence. "Are we going to sit around and mope all afternoon? Or are you going to let me take you to lunch?"

Bailey smiled. "I think you might be able to talk me into it." Her morning had been miserable, but the afternoon looked much brighter now. She got to her feet, still smiling at Parker. "One thing I've learned over the years is that you can't allow misery to interfere with mealtimes."

Parker laughed and the robust sound of it was contagious. "I have a small surprise for you," he told her, reaching inside his suit pocket. "I was going to save it for later, but now seems more fitting." He handed her two tickets.

Bailey stared at them, speechless.

"The Pops concert," Parker said. "They're having a rock group from the sixties perform. It seems only fitting that Janice and Michael attend."

Eight

It wasn't until they'd finished lunch that Bailey noticed what a good time she was having with Parker. They'd sat across the table from each other and chatted like old friends. Bailey had never felt more at ease with him, nor had she ever allowed herself to be more open. Her emotions had undergone a gradual but profound change.

Fear and caution had been replaced by genuine contentment. And by hope.

After lunch they strolled through Union Square tossing breadcrumbs to the greedy pigeons. The early-morning fog had burned away and the sun was out in a rare display of brilliance. The square was filled with tourists, groups of old men and office workers taking an outdoor lunch. Bailey loved Union Square. Being there now, with Parker, seemed especially…fitting. And not just because Janice and Michael did the same thing in chapter six!

He was more relaxed with her, as well. He talked freely about himself, something he'd never done before. He was the oldest of three boys and the only one still unmarried.

"I'm the baby of the family," Bailey explained. "Pampered and spoiled. Overprotected, I'm afraid. My parents tried hard to dissuade me from moving to California." She paused.

"What made you leave Oregon?"

Bailey waited for the tightness that always gripped her heart when she thought of Tom, but it didn't come. It simply wasn't there anymore.

"Tom," she admitted, glancing down at the squawking birds, fighting over crumbs.

"He was fiancé number two?" Parker's hands were locked behind his back as they strolled along the paved pathway.

Bailey couldn't resist wondering if he'd hidden his hands to keep from touching her. "I met Tom a couple of years after…Paul. He was, is, a junior partner in the law firm where I worked as a paralegal. We'd been dating off and on for several months, nothing serious for either of us. Then we got involved in a case together and ended up spending a lot of time in each other's company. Within three months we were engaged."

Parker placed his hand lightly on her shoulder as though to lend her support. She smiled up at him in appreciation. "Actually it doesn't hurt as much to talk about it now." Time did heal all wounds, or as she preferred to think, time wounds all heels.

"I'm not sure when he met Sandra," she continued. "For all I know, they might have been childhood sweethearts. What I do remember is that we were only a few weeks away from the wedding. The invitations were all finished and waiting to be picked up at the printer's when Tom told me there was someone else."

"Were you surprised?"

"Shocked. In retrospect, I suppose I should have recognized the signs, but I'd been completely wrapped up in preparing for the wedding—shopping with my bridesmaids for their dresses, arranging for the flowers, things like that. In fact, I was so busy picking out china patterns I didn't even notice that my fiancé had fallen out of love with me."

"You make it sound as though it was your fault."

Bailey shrugged. "In some ways I think it was. I'm willing to admit that now, to see my own faults. But that doesn't make up for the fact that he was engaged to me and seeing another woman on the sly."

"No, it doesn't," Parker agreed. "What did you say when he told you?" By now, his hand was clasping her shoulder and she was leaning into him. The weight of her humiliation no longer seemed as crushing, but it was still there, and talking about it produced a flood of emotions she hadn't wanted to face. It was ironic that she could do so now, after all this time, and with another man.

"Have you forgiven him?"

Bailey paused and nudged a fallen leaf with the toe of her shoe. "Yes. Hating him, even disliking him, takes too much energy. He was truly sorry. By the time he talked to me, I think poor Tom was completely and utterly miserable. He tried so hard to avoid doing or saying anything to hurt me. I swear it took him fifteen minutes to get around to telling me he wanted to call off the wedding and another thirty to confess that there was someone else. I remember the sick feeling in my stomach. It was like coming down with a bad case of the flu, having all the symptoms hit me at once." Her mind returned to that dreadful day and how she'd sat and stared at Tom in shocked disbelief. He'd been so uncomfortable, gazing at his hands, guilt and confusion muffling his voice.

"I didn't cry," Bailey recalled. "I wasn't even angry, at least not at first. I don't think I felt any emotion." She gave Parker a chagrined smile. "In retrospect I realize my pride wouldn't allow it. What I do remember is that I said the most nonsensical things."

"Like what?"

Bailey's gaze wandered down the pathway. "I told him I expected him to pay for the invitations. We'd had them embossed with gold, which had been considerably more expensive. Besides, I was already out the money for the wedding dress."

"Ah, the infamous slightly used wedding dress."

"It was expensive!"

"I know," Parker said, his eyes tender. "Actually you were just being practical."

"I don't know what I was being. It's crazy the way the mind works in situations like that. I remember thinking that Paul and Tom must have been acquainted with each other. I was convinced the two of them had plotted together, which was utterly ridiculous."

"I take it you decided to move to San Francisco after Tom broke the engagement."

She nodded. "Within a matter of hours I'd given my notice at the law firm and was making plans to move."

"Why San Francisco?"

"You know," she said, laughing lightly, "I'm not really sure. I'd visited the area several times over the years and the weather was always rotten. Mark Twain wrote somewhere that the worst winter he ever spent was a summer in San Francisco. I guess the city, with its overcast skies and foggy mornings, suited my mood. I couldn't have tolerated bright sunny days and moonlit nights in the weeks after I left Oregon."

"What happened to Tom?"

"What do you mean?" Bailey cocked her head to look up at him, taken aback by the question.

"Did he marry Sandra?"

"Heavens, I don't know."

"Weren't you curious?"

Frankly she hadn't been. He obviously hadn't wanted *her,* and that was the only thing that mattered to Bailey. She'd felt betrayed, humiliated and abandoned. If Tom ever regretted his decision or if things hadn't worked out between him and Sandra, she didn't know. She hadn't stuck around to find out. Furthermore, she wouldn't have cared, not then, anyway.

She'd wanted out. Out of her job, Out of Oregon. Out of her dull life. If she was going to fall in love, why did it have to be with weak men? Men who couldn't make up their minds. Men who fell in and out of love, men who were never sure of what they wanted.

Perhaps it was some flaw in her own character that caused her to choose such men. That was the very reason she'd given up on relationships and dating and the opposite sex in general. And she knew it was also why she enjoyed reading romances, why she enjoyed writing them. Romance fiction offered her the happy ending that had been so absent in her own life.

The novels she read and wrote were about men who were *real* men—strong, traditional, confident men—and everyday women not unlike herself.

She'd been looking for a hero when she stumbled on Parker Davidson. Yes, she could truly say her heart was warming toward him. Warming, nothing! It was *on fire* and had been for weeks, although she'd refused to acknowledge that until now.

Parker's dark eyes caressed hers. "I'm glad you moved to the Bay area."

"So am I."

"You won't change your mind, will you?" he asked as they began to walk back. He must have read the confusion in her eyes because he added, "The concert tonight? It's in honor of Valentine's Day."

"No, I'm looking forward to going." She hadn't even realized what day this was. Bailey suddenly felt a thrill of excitement at the thought of spending the most romantic evening of the year with Parker Davidson. Although of course it would mean no time to work on *Forever Yours*…

"Think of the concert as research," Parker said, grinning down at her.

"I will." A woman could be blinded by eyes as radiant as Parker's. They were alight with the sensitivity and strength of his nature.

"Goodbye," she said reluctantly, lifting her hand in a small wave.

"Until tonight," Parker said, sounding equally reluctant to part.

"Tonight," she repeated softly. She'd seen her pain reflected in his eyes when she told him about Tom. He understood what it was to lose someone you loved, regardless of the circumstances. She sensed that in many ways the two of them were alike. During that short walk around Union Square, Bailey had felt a closeness to Parker, a comfortable and open honesty she'd rarely felt with anyone before.

"I'll pick you up at seven," he said.

"Perfect." Bailey was convinced he would have kissed her if they hadn't been standing in such a public place. And she would have let him.

The afternoon flew by. Whereas the morning had been excruciatingly slow, filled with one blunder after another, the hours after her lunch with Parker were trouble free. No sooner had she returned to the office than it seemed time to pack up her things and head for the subway.

True to form, Max was there to greet her when she

walked in the door. She set her mail, two bills and an ad for the local supermarket, on the kitchen counter, and quickly fed him. Max seemed mildly surprised at her promptness and stared at his food for several minutes, as though he was hesitant about eating it.

Grumbling that it was impossible to please the dratted cat, Bailey stalked into her bedroom, throwing open the closet door.

For some time she did nothing but stare at the contents. She finally made her decision, a printed dress she'd worn when she was in college. The paisley print was bright and cheerful, the skirt widely pleated. The style was slightly dated, but it was the best she could do. If Parker had given her even a day's notice she would have gone out and bought something new. Something red in honor of Valentine's Day.

The seats Parker had purchased for the concert at Civic Center were among the best in the house. They were situated in the middle about fifteen rows from the front.

The music was fabulous. Delightful. Romantic. There were classical pieces she recognized, interspersed with soft rock, and a number of popular tunes and "golden oldies."

The orchestra was spectacular, and being this close to the stage afforded Bailey an opportunity so special she felt tears of appreciation gather in her eyes more than once. Nothing could ever duplicate a live performance.

The warm generous man in her company made everything perfect. At some point, early in the program, Parker reached for her hand. When Bailey's heartbeat finally settled down to a normal rate, she felt an emotion she hadn't experienced in more than a year, not since the day Tom had called off their wedding.

Contentment. Complete and utter contentment.

She closed her eyes to savor the music and when she

opened them again, she saw Parker studying her. She smiled shyly and he smiled back. And at that moment, cymbals clanged. Bailey jumped in her seat as though caught doing something illegal. Parker chuckled and raised her hand to his lips, gently brushing her knuckles with a kiss.

The second group, Hairspray, performed after the intermission. Bailey found their music unfamiliar with the exception of two or three classic rock numbers. But the audience responded enthusiastically to the group's energy and sense of fun. Several people got to their feet, swaying to the music. After a while some couples edged into the aisles and started dancing. Bailey would have liked to join them, but Parker seemed to prefer staying where they were. She couldn't very well leave him sitting there while she sought out a partner. Especially when the only partner she wanted was right beside her.

Eventually nearly everyone around them rose and moved into the aisle, which meant a lot of awkward shifting for Parker and Bailey. She was convinced they were the only couple in the section not on their feet.

She glanced at Parker, but he seemed oblivious to what was happening around them. At one point she thought she heard him grumble about not being able to see the band because of all those people standing.

"Miss?" An older balding man moved into their nearly empty row and tapped Bailey on the shoulder in an effort to get her attention. He wore his shirt open to the navel and had no less than five pounds of gold draped around his neck. Clearly he'd never left the early seventies. "Would you care to dance?"

"Uh..." Bailey certainly hadn't been expecting an invitation. She wasn't entirely confident of the protocol. She'd come with Parker and he might object.

"Go ahead," Parker said, reassuring her. He actually seemed relieved someone else had asked her. Perhaps he was feeling guilty about not having done so himself, Bailey mused.

She shrugged and stood, glancing his way once more to be sure he didn't mind. He urged her forward with a wave of his hand.

Bailey was disappointed. She wished with all her heart that it was Parker taking her in his arms. Parker, not some stranger.

"Matt Cooper," the man with the gold chains said, holding out his hand.

"Bailey York."

He grinned as he slipped his arm around her waist. "There must be something wrong with your date to leave you sitting there."

"I don't think Parker dances."

It had been a long while since Bailey had danced, and she wasn't positive she'd even remember how. She needn't have worried. The space was so limited that she couldn't move more than a few inches in any direction.

The next song Hairspray performed was an old rock song from the sixties. Matt surprised her by placing two fingers in his mouth and whistling loudly. The piercing sound cut through music, crowd noises and applause. Despite herself, Bailey laughed.

The song was fast-paced and Bailey began swaying her hips and moving to the beat. Before she was sure how it had happened, she was quite a distance from her friend. She found herself standing next to a tall good-looking man about Parker's age, who was obviously enjoying the group's performance.

He smiled at Bailey and she smiled shyly back. The next

song was another oldie, one written with young lovers in mind and perfect for slow dancing.

Bailey tried to make it down the aisle to Parker's seat, but the row was empty. Although she glanced all around she couldn't locate him.

"We might as well," the good-looking man said, holding out his hands to her. "My partner has taken off for parts unknown."

"Mine seems to have disappeared, too." Scanning the crowd, she still couldn't find Parker but then, the area was so congested it was impossible to see anyone clearly. A little worried, she wondered how they'd ever find each other when the concert was over.

She and her new partner danced two or three dances without ever exchanging names. He twirled her about with an expertise that masterfully disguised her own less-inspired movements. They finished a particularly fast dance, and Bailey fanned her face, flushed from the exertion, with one hand.

When Hairspray introduced another love ballad, it seemed only natural for Bailey to slip into her temporary partner's arms. He said something and laughed. Bailey hadn't been able to make out his words, but she grinned back at him. She was about to say something herself when she saw Parker edging toward them, scowling.

"My date's here," she said, breaking away from the man who held her. She gave him an apologetic look and he released her with a decided lack of enthusiasm.

"I thought I'd lost you," she said when Parker made it to her side.

"I think it's time we left," he announced in clipped tones.

Bailey blinked, surprised by his irritation. "But the concert isn't over yet." Cutting a path through the horde of dancers would be difficult, perhaps impossible. "Shouldn't we at least stay until Hairspray is finished?"

"No."

"What's wrong?"

Parker shoved his hands in his pockets. "I didn't mind you dancing with that Barry Gibb look-alike, but the next thing I know, you've taken off with someone else."

"I didn't *take off* with anyone," she said, disliking his tone as much as his implication. "We were separated by the crowds."

"Then you should've come back to me."

"You didn't honestly expect me to fight my way through this mass of humanity, did you? Can't you see how crowded the aisles are?"

"I made it to you."

Bailey sighed, fighting the urge to be sarcastic. And lost. "Do you want a Boy Scout award? I didn't know they issued them for pushing and shoving."

Parker's eyes flashed with resentment. "I didn't push anyone. I think it would be best if we sat down," he said, gripping her by the elbow and leading her back into a row, "before you make an even greater spectacle of yourself."

"A spectacle of myself," Bailey muttered furiously. "If anyone was a spectacle, it was you! You were the only person in ten rows who wasn't dancing."

"I certainly didn't expect my date to take off with another man." He sank down in a seat and crossed his arms as though he had no intention of continuing this discussion.

"Your date," she repeated, struggling to hold on to her temper by clenching her fists. "May I remind you this entire evening was for the purposes of research and nothing more?"

Parker gave a disbelieving snort. "That's not how I remember it. At the time, you seemed eager enough." He laughed, a cynical, unpleasant sound. "I'm not the one who chased after you."

Standing there arguing with him was attracting more attention than Bailey wanted. Reluctantly she sat down, primly folding her hands in her lap, and stared directly ahead. "I didn't chase after you," she informed him through gritted teeth. "I have *never* chased after any man."

"Oh, forgive me, then. I could have sworn it was you who followed me off the subway. Were you aware that someone who closely resembles you stalked me all the way into Chinatown?"

"Oh-h-h," Bailey moaned, throwing up her hands, "you're impossible."

"What I am is correct."

Bailey didn't deign to reply. She crossed her legs and swung her ankle ferociously until the concert finally ended.

Parker didn't say a word as he escorted her to his car, which was fine with Bailey. She'd never met a more unreasonable person in her life. Less than an hour earlier, they'd practically been drowning in each other's eyes. She'd allowed herself to get caught up in the magic of the moment, that was all. Some Valentine's Day!

They parted with little more than a polite goodnight. Bailey informed him there was no need to see her to her door. Naturally he claimed otherwise, just to be obstinate. She wanted to argue, but knew it would be a waste of breath.

Max was at the door to greet her, his tail waving in the air. He stayed close to her, rubbing against her legs, and Bailey nearly tripped over him as she hurriedly undressed. She started to tell him about her evening, changed her mind and got into bed. She pulled the covers up to her chin, forcing the cantankerous Parker Davidson from her mind.

* * *

Jo Ann was waiting for her outside the BART station the following morning. "Well?" she said, racing to Bailey's side. "How was your date?"

"What date? You couldn't possibly call that outing with Parker a date."

"I couldn't?" Jo Ann was clearly puzzled.

"We attended the Pops Concert—"

"For research," Jo Ann finished for her. "I gather the evening didn't go well?" They filed through the turnstile and rode the escalator down to the platform where they'd board the train.

"The whole night was a disaster."

"Tell Mama everything," Jo Ann urged.

Bailey wasn't in the mood to talk, but she made the effort to explain what had happened and how unreasonable Parker had been. She hadn't slept well, convinced she'd made the same mistake with Parker as she had with the other men in her life. All along she'd assumed he was different. Not so. Parker was pompous, irrational and arrogant. She told Jo Ann that. "I was wrong about him being a hero," she said bleakly.

Jo Ann frowned. "Let me see if I've got this straight. People started dancing. One man asked you to dance, then you got separated and danced with another guy and Parker acted like a jealous fool."

"Exactly." It infuriated Bailey every time she thought about it, which she'd been doing all morning.

"Of course he did," Jo Ann said enthusiastically, as though she'd just made an important discovery. "Don't you see? He was being true to character. Didn't more or less the same thing happen between Janice and Michael when they went to the concert?"

Bailey had completely forgotten. "Now that you mention it, yes," she admitted slowly.

The train arrived. When the screeching came to a halt, Jo Ann said, "I told Parker all about that scene myself, remember?"

Bailey did, vaguely.

"When you sit down to rewrite it, you'll know from experience exactly what Janice was feeling and thinking because those were the very thoughts you experienced yourself. How can you be angry with him?"

Bailey wasn't finding it difficult.

"You should be grateful."

"I should?"

"Oh, yes," Jo Ann insisted. "Parker Davidson is more of a hero than either of us realized."

Nine

"Don't you understand what Parker did?" Jo Ann asked when they met for lunch later that same day. The topic was one she refused to drop.

"You bet I understand. He's a…Neanderthal, only he tried to be polite about it. As if that makes any difference."

"Wrong," Jo Ann argued, looking downright mysterious. "He's given you some genuine insight into your character's thoughts and actions."

"What he did," Bailey said, waving her spoon above her cream-of-broccoli soup, "was pretty well ruin what started out as a perfect evening."

"You said he acted like a jealous fool, but you've got to remember that's exactly how Michael reacted when Janice danced with another man."

"Then he went above and beyond the call of duty, and I'm not about to reward that conduct in a man, hero or not." She crumbled her soda crackers into her soup, then brushed her palms free of crumbs.

Until Bailey accepted the invitation to dance, her evening with Parker had been wonderfully romantic. They'd sat together holding hands, while the music swirled and floated around them. Then the dancing began and her knight in shining armor turned into a fire-breathing dragon.

"You haven't forgotten the critique group is meeting tonight, have you?" Jo Ann asked, abruptly changing the subject.

Bailey's head was so full of Parker that she had, indeed, forgotten. She'd been absentminded lately. "Tonight?"

"Seven, at Darlene's house. You'll be there, won't you?"

"Of course." Bailey didn't need to think twice. Every other week, women from their writing group took turns hosting a session in which they evaluated one another's work.

"Oh, good. For a moment I wondered whether you'd be able to come."

"Why wouldn't I?" Bailey demanded. She was as dedicated as the other writers. She hadn't missed a single meeting since the group was formed two months ago.

"Oh, I thought you might be spending the evening with Parker. You two need to work out your differences. You're going to be miserable until this is resolved."

Bailey slowly lowered her spoon. "Miserable?" she repeated, giving a brief, slightly hysterical laugh. "Do I look like I'm the least bit heartbroken? Honestly, Jo Ann, you're making a mountain out of a molehill. The two of us had a falling out. I don't want to see him, and I'm sure he feels the same way. I won't have any problem making the group tonight."

Jo Ann calmly drank her coffee, then just as calmly stated, "You're miserable, only you're too proud to admit it."

"I am *not* miserable," Bailey asserted, doing her utmost to smile serenely.

"How much sleep did you get last night?"

"Why? Have I got circles under my eyes?"

"No. Just answer the question."

Bailey swallowed uncomfortably. "Enough. What's with you? Have you taken up writing mystery novels? Parker Davidson and I had a parting of the ways. It would have happened eventually. Besides, it's better to learn these sorts of things in the beginning of a…relationship." She shrugged comically. "A bit ironic to have it end on Valentine's Day."

"So you won't be seeing him again?" Jo Ann made that sound like the most desolate of prospects.

"We probably won't be able to avoid a certain amount of contact, especially while he's taking the subway, but for the record, no. I don't intend to ever go out with him again. He can save his caveman tactics for someone else."

"Someone else?" Jo Ann filled the two words with tearful sadness. Until Parker, Bailey had seen only the tip of the iceberg when it came to her friend's romantic nature.

Bailey finished her soup and, glancing at her watch, realized she had less than five minutes to get back to the office.

"About tonight—I'll give you a ride," Jo Ann promised. "I'll be by to pick you up as close to six-thirty as I can. It depends on how fast I can get home and get everyone fed."

"Thanks," Bailey said. "I'll see you then."

They parted and Bailey hurried back to her office. The large vase of red roses on the reception desk was the first thing she noticed when she walked in.

"Is it your birthday, Martha?" she asked as she removed her coat and hung it on the rack.

"I thought it must be yours," the secretary replied absently.

"Mine?"

"The card has your name on it."

Bailey's heart went completely still. Had Parker sent

her flowers? It seemed too much to hope for, yet… "My name's on the card?"

"A tall good-looking man in a suit delivered them not more than ten minutes ago. He seemed disappointed when I said you'd taken an early lunch. Who is that guy, anyway? He looks vaguely familiar."

Bailey didn't answer. Instead she removed the envelope and slipped out the card. It read, "Forgive me, Parker."

She felt the tightness around her heart suddenly ease.

"Oh, I nearly forgot," Martha said, reaching for a folded slip of paper next to the crystal vase. "Since you weren't here, he left a message for you."

Carrying the vase with its brilliant red roses in one hand and her message in the other, Bailey walked slowly to her desk. With eager fingers, she unfolded the note.

"Bailey," it said. "I'm sorry I missed you. We need to talk. Can you have dinner with me tonight? If so, I'll pick you up at seven. Since I'll be tied up most of the afternoon, leave a message with Roseanne."

He'd written down his office number. Bailey reached for the phone with barely a thought. The friendly—and obviously efficient—receptionist answered on the first ring.

"Hello, Roseanne, this is Bailey York."

"Oh, Bailey, yes. It's good to hear from you. Mr. Davidson said you'd be phoning."

"I missed him by only a few minutes."

"How frustrating for you both. I've been concerned about him this morning."

"You have?"

"Why, yes. Mr. Davidson came into the office and he couldn't seem to sit still. He got himself a cup of coffee, then two minutes later came out again and poured a second cup. When I pointed out that he already had coffee, he seemed surprised. That was when he started muttering under his breath. I've worked with Mr. Davidson for several years now and I've never known him to mutter."

"He was probably thinking about something important regarding his work." Bailey was willing to offer a face-saving excuse for Parker's unprecedented behavior.

"That's not it," the woman insisted. "He went into his office again and came right back out, asking me if I read romance novels. I have on occasion, and that seemed to satisfy him. He pulled up a chair and began asking me questions about a hero's personality. I answered him as best I could."

"I'm sure you did very well."

"I must have, because he cheered right up and asked me what kind of flowers a woman enjoys most. I told him roses, and a minute later, he's looking through my phone book for a florist. Unfortunately no florist could promise a delivery this morning, so he said he'd drop them off personally. He phoned a few minutes ago to tell me you'd be calling in sometime today and that I should take a message."

"I just got back from lunch."

So Parker's morning hadn't gone any better than her own, Bailey mused, feeling almost jubilant. She'd managed to put on a good front for Jo Ann, but Bailey had felt terrible. Worse than terrible. She hadn't wanted to discuss her misery, either. It was much easier to pretend that Parker meant nothing to her.

But Jo Ann had been right. She *was* miserable.

"Could you tell Mr. Davidson I'll be ready at seven?" She'd call Jo Ann later and tell her she wouldn't be able to make the critique group, after all.

"Oh, my, that *is* good news," Roseanne said, sounding absolutely delighted. "I'll pass the message along as soon as he checks in. I'm so pleased. Mr. Davidson is such a dear man, but he works too hard. I've been thinking he needed to meet a nice girl like you. Isn't it incredible that the two of you have known each other for so long?"

"We have?"

"Oh, yes, don't you remember? You came into the office that morning and explained how Mr. Davidson is a friend of your family's. You must have forgotten you'd told me that."

"Oh. Oh, yes," Bailey mumbled, embarrassed by the silly lie. "Well, if you'd give him the message, I'd be most grateful."

"I'll let Mr. Davidson know," Roseanne said. She hesitated, as though she wanted to add something else and wasn't sure she should. Then, decision apparently made, the words rushed out. "As I said before, I've been with Mr. Davidson for several years and I think you should know that to the best of my knowledge, this is the first time he's ever sent a woman roses."

For the rest of the afternoon, Bailey was walking on air. At five o'clock, she raced into the department store closest to her office, carrying one long-stemmed rose. Within minutes she found a lovely purple-and-gold silk dress. Expensive, but it looked wonderful. Then she hurried to the shoe department and bought a pair of pumps. In accessories, she chose earrings and a matching gold necklace.

From the department store she raced to the subway, clutching her purchases and the single red rose. She'd spent a fortune but didn't bother to calculate how many "easy monthly installments" it would take to pay everything off. Looking nice for Parker was worth the cost. No man had ever sent her roses, and every time she thought about it, her heart positively melted. It was such a *romantic* thing to do. And to think he'd conferred with Roseanne Snyder.

By six-thirty she was almost ready. She needed to brush her hair and freshen her makeup, but that wouldn't take long. She stood in front of the mirror in a model's pose, one hand on her hip, one shoulder thrust forward, studying the overall effect, when there was a knock at the door.

Oh, no! Parker was early. Much too early. It was either shout at him from this side of the door to come back later, or make the best of it. Running her fingers through her hair, she shook her head for the breezy effect and opted to make the best of it.

"Are you ready?" Jo Ann asked, walking inside, her book bag in one hand and her purse in the other. She gaped openly at Bailey's appearance. "Nice," she said, nodding, "but you might be a touch overdressed for the critique group."

"Oh, no, I forgot to call you." How could she have let it slip her mind?

"Call me?"

Bailey felt guilty—an emotion she was becoming increasingly familiar with—for not remembering tonight's arrangement. It was because of Parker. He'd occupied her thoughts from the moment he'd first kissed her.

There had been no kiss last night. The desire—no, more than desire, the *need*—for his kiss, his touch had flared into urgent life. Since the breakup with Tom she'd felt frozen, her emotions lying dormant. But under the warmth of Parker's humor and generosity, she thawed a little more each time she saw him.

"Someone sent you a red rose," Jo Ann said matter-of-factly. She walked farther into the room, lifting the flower to her nose and sniffing appreciatively. "Parker?"

Bailey nodded. "There were a dozen waiting for me when I got back to the office."

Jo Ann's smile was annoyingly smug.

"He stopped by while I was at lunch—we'd missed each other..." Bailey mumbled in explanation.

Jo Ann circled her, openly admiring the dress. "He's taking you to dinner?" Her gaze fell to the purple suede pumps that perfectly matched the dress.

"Dinner? What gives you that idea?"

"The dress is new."

"This old thing?" Bailey gave a nervous giggle.

Jo Ann tugged at the price tag dangling from Bailey's sleeve and pulled it free.

"Very funny!" Bailey groaned. She glanced at her watch, hoping Jo Ann would take the hint.

Jo Ann was obviously pleased about Parker's reappearance. "So, you're willing to let bygones be bygones?" she asked in a bracing tone.

"Jo Ann, he's due here any minute."

Her friend disregarded her pleas. "You're really falling for this guy, aren't you?"

If it was any more obvious, Bailey thought, she'd be wearing a sandwich board and parading in front of his office building. "Yes."

"Big time?"

"Big time," Bailey admitted.

"How do you feel about that?"

Bailey was sorely tempted to throw up her arms in abject frustration. "How do you think it makes me feel? I've been jilted twice. I'm scared to death. Now, isn't it time you left?" She coaxed Jo Ann toward the door, but when her friend ignored that broad hint, Bailey gripped her elbow. "Sorry you had to leave so soon, but I'll give your regards to Parker."

"All right, all right," Jo Ann said, sighing, "I can take a hint when I hear one."

Bailey doubted it. "Tell the others that...something

came up, but I'll be there next time for sure." Her hands were at the small of Jo Ann's back, urging her forward. "Goodbye, Jo Ann."

"I'm going, I'm going," her friend said from the other side of the threshold. Suddenly earnest, she turned to face Bailey. "Promise me you'll have a good time."

"I'm sure we will." *If* she could finish getting ready before Parker arrived. *If* she could subdue her nerves. *If...*

Once Jo Ann was gone, Bailey slammed the door and rushed back to her bathroom. She was dabbing cologne on her wrists when there was a second knock. Inhaling a calming breath, Bailey opened the door, half expecting to find Jo Ann on the other side, ready with more advice.

"Parker," she whispered unsteadily, as though he was the last person she expected to see.

He frowned. "I did get the message correctly, didn't I? You were expecting me?"

"Oh, yes, of course. Come inside, please."

"Good." His face relaxed.

He stepped into the room, but his eyes never left hers. "I hope I'm not too early."

"Oh, no." She twisted her hands, staring down at her shoes like a shy schoolgirl.

"You got the roses?"

"Oh, yes," she said breathlessly, glancing at the one she'd brought home from her office. "They're beautiful. I left the others on my desk at work. It was so sweet of you."

"It was the only way I could think to apologize. I didn't know if a hero did that sort of thing or not."

"He...does."

"So once again, I stayed in character."

"Yes. Very much so."

"Good." His mouth slanted charmingly with the slight smile he gave her. "I realize this dinner is short notice."

"I didn't mind changing my plans," she told him. The critique group was important, but everyone missed occasionally.

"I suppose I should explain we'll be eating at my parents' home. Do you mind?"

His parents? Bailey's stomach tightened instantly. "I'd enjoy meeting your family," she answered, doing her best to reassure him. She managed a fleeting smile.

"Mom and Dad are anxious to meet you."

"They are?" Bailey would have preferred not to know that. The fact that Parker had even mentioned her to his family came as a surprise.

"So, how was your day?" he asked, walking casually over to the window.

Bailey lowered her gaze. "The morning was difficult, but the afternoon…the afternoon was wonderful."

"I behaved like a jealous fool last night, didn't I?" He didn't wait for her to respond. "The minute I saw you in that other man's arms, I wanted to get you away from him. I'm not proud of how I acted." He shoved his fingers through his hair, revealing more than a little agitation. "As I'm sure you've already guessed, I'm not much of a dancer. When that throwback from the seventies asked you to dance with him, I had no objections. If you want the truth, I was relieved. I guess men are supposed to be able to acquit themselves on the dance floor, but I've got two left feet. No doubt I've blown this whole hero business, but quite honestly that's the least of my worries. I know it matters to you, but I can't change who I am."

"I wouldn't expect you to."

He nodded. "The worst part of the whole evening was the way I cheated myself out of what I was looking forward to the most."

"Which was?"

"Kissing you again."

"Oh, Parker…"

He was going to kiss her. She realized that at about the same time she knew she'd cry with disappointment if he didn't. Bailey wasn't sure who reached out first. What she instantly recognized was the perfect harmony between them, how comfortable she felt in his arms—as though they belonged together.

His mouth found hers with unerring ease. A moan of welcome and release spilled from her throat as she began to tremble. An awakening, slow and sure, unfolded within her like the petals of a hothouse rose.

That sensation was followed by confusion. She pulled away from Parker and buried her face in his strong neck. The trembling became stronger, more pronounced.

"I frighten you?"

If only he knew. "Not in the way you think," she said slowly. "It's been so long since a man's held me like this. I tried to convince myself I didn't want to feel this way ever again. I didn't entirely succeed."

"Are you saying you *wanted* me to kiss you?"

"Yes." His finger under her chin raised her eyes to his. Bailey thought they would have gone on gazing at each other forever if Max hadn't chosen that moment to walk across the back of the sofa, protesting loudly. This was his territory and he didn't take kindly to invasions.

"We'd better leave," Parker said reluctantly.

"Oh, sure…" Bailey said. She was nervous about meeting Parker's family. More nervous than she cared to admit. The last set of parents she'd been introduced to had been Tom's. She'd met them a few days before they'd announced their engagement. As she recalled, the circumstances were somewhat similar. Tom had unexpectedly declared that it was time to meet his family. That was when Bailey had realized how serious their relationship had grown. Tom's family was very nice, but Bailey had felt all too aware of being judged and, she'd always suspected, found wanting.

Bailey doubted she said more than two words as Parker drove out to Daley City. His family's home was an elegant two-story white stone house with a huge front garden.

"Here we are," Parker said needlessly, placing his hand on her shoulder when he'd helped her out of the car.

"Did you design it?"

"No, but I love this house. It gave birth to a good many of my ideas."

The front door opened and an older couple stepped outside to greet them. Parker's mother was tall and regal, her white hair beautifully waved. His father's full head of hair was a distinguished shade of gray. He stood only an inch or so taller than his wife.

"Mom, Dad, this is Bailey York." Parker introduced her, his arm around her waist. "Bailey, Yvonne and Bradley Davidson, my parents."

"Welcome, Bailey," Bradley Davidson said with a warm smile.

"It's a pleasure to meet you," Yvonne said, walking forward. Her eyes briefly connected with Parker's before she added, "at last."

"Come inside," Parker's father urged, leading the way. He stood at the door and waited for them all to walk into the large formal entry. The floor was made of black-and-white squares of polished marble, and there was a long circular stairway on the left.

"How about something to drink?" Bradley suggested. "Scotch? A mixed drink? Wine?" Bailey and Parker's mother both chose white wine, Parker and his father, Scotch.

"I'll help you, Dad," Parker offered, leaving the two women alone.

Yvonne took Bailey into the living room, which was strikingly decorated in white leather and brilliant red.

Bailey sat on the leather couch. "Your home is lovely."

"Thank you," Yvonne murmured. A smile trembled at the edges of her mouth, and Bailey wondered what she found so amusing. Perhaps there was a huge run in her panty hose she knew nothing about, or another price tag dangling from her dress.

"Forgive me," the older woman said. "Roseanne Snyder and I are dear friends, and she mentioned your name to me several weeks back."

Bailey experienced a moment of panic as she recalled telling Parker's receptionist that she was an old family friend. "I…guess you're wondering why I claimed to know Parker."

"No, although it did give me a moment's pause. I couldn't recall knowing any Yorks."

"You probably don't." Bailey folded her hands in her lap, uncertain what to say next.

"Roseanne's right. You really are a charming young lady."

"Thank you."

"I was beginning to wonder if Parker was ever going to fall in love again. He was so terribly hurt by Maria, and he was so young at the time. He took it very hard…" She hesitated, then spoke briskly. "But I suppose that's neither here nor there."

Bailey decided to ignore the implication that Parker had fallen in love with her. Right now there were other concerns to face. "Did Parker tell you how we met?" She said a silent prayer that he'd casually mentioned something about the two of them bumping into each other on the subway.

"Of course I did," Parker answered for his mother, as he walked into the room. He sat on the arm of the sofa and draped his arm around Bailey's shoulders. His laughing eyes held hers. "I did mention Bailey's a budding romance writer, didn't I, Mom?"

"Yes, you did," his mother answered. "I hope you told her I'm an avid reader."

"No, I hadn't gotten around to that."

Bailey shifted uncomfortably in her chair. No wonder Yvonne Davidson had trouble disguising her amusement if Parker had blabbed about the way she'd followed him off the subway.

Parker's father entered the room carrying a tray of drinks, which he promptly dispensed.

Then he joined his wife, and for some time, the foursome chatted amicably.

"I'll just go and check on the roast," Yvonne said eventually.

"Can I help, dear?"

"Go ahead, Dad," Parker said, smiling. "I'll entertain Bailey with old family photos."

"Parker," Bailey said once his parents were out of earshot. "How *could* you?"

"How could I what?"

"Tell your mother how we met? She must think I'm crazy!"

Instead of revealing any concern, Parker grinned widely. "Honesty is the best policy."

"In principle I agree, but our meeting was a bit…unconventional."

"True, but I have to admit that being described as classic hero material was flattering to my ego."

"I take everything back," she muttered, crossing her legs.

Parker chuckled and was about to say something else

when his father came into the room carrying a bottle of champagne.

"Champagne, Dad?" Parker asked when his father held out the bottle for Parker to examine. "This is good stuff."

"You're darn right," Bradley Davidson said. "It isn't every day our son announces he's found the woman he wants to marry."

Ten

Bailey's gaze flew to Parker's in shocked disbelief. She found herself standing, but couldn't remember rising from the chair. The air in the room seemed too thin and she had difficulty catching her breath.

"Did I say something I shouldn't have?" Bradley Davidson asked his son, distress evident on his face.

"It might be best if you gave the two of us a few minutes alone," Parker said, frowning at his father.

"I'm sorry, son, I didn't mean to speak out of turn."

"It's fine, Dad."

His father left the room.

Bailey walked over to the massive stone fireplace and stared into the grate at the stacked logs and kindling.

"Bailey?" Parker spoke softly from behind her.

She whirled around to face him, completely speechless, able only to shake her head in bemused fury.

"I know this must come as…something of a surprise."

"Something of a surprise?" she shrieked.

"All right, a shock."

"We…we met barely a month ago."

"True, but we know each other better than some couples who've been dating for months."

The fact that he wasn't arguing with her didn't comfort Bailey at all. "I… Isn't it a bit presumptuous of you…to be thinking in terms of an engagement?" She'd made it plain from the moment they met that she had no intention of getting involved with a man. Who could blame her after the experiences she'd had with the opposite sex? Another engagement, even with someone as wonderful as Parker, was out of the question.

"Yes, it was presumptuous."

"Then how could you suggest such a thing? Engagements are disastrous for me! I won't go through that again. I won't!"

He scowled. "I agree I made a mistake."

"Obviously." Bailey stalked to the opposite side of the room to stand behind a leather-upholstered chair, one hand clutching its back. "Twice, Parker, twice." She held up two fingers. "And both times, *both* times, they fell out of love with me. I couldn't go through that again. I just couldn't."

"Let me explain," Parker said, walking slowly toward her. "For a long time now, my parents have wanted me to marry."

"So in other words, you used me. I was a decoy. You made up this story? How courageous of you."

She could tell from the hard set of his jaw that Parker was having difficulty maintaining his composure. "You're wrong, Bailey."

"Suddenly everything is clear to me." She made a sweeping gesture with her hand.

"It's obvious that nothing is clear to you," he countered angrily.

"I suppose I'm just so naive it was easy for me to fall in with your…your fiendish plans."

"*Fiendish* plans? Don't you think you're being a bit melodramatic?"

"Me? You're talking to a woman who's been jilted. Twice. Almost every man I've ever known has turned into a fiend."

"Bailey, I'm not using you." He crossed the room, stood directly in front of her and rested his hands on her shoulders. "Think what you want of me, but you should know the truth. Yes, my parents are eager for me to marry, and although I love my family, I would never use you or anyone else to satisfy their desires."

Bailey frowned uncertainly. His eyes were so sincere, so compelling.… "Then what possible reason could you have for telling them you'd found the woman you want to marry?"

"Because I have." His beautiful dark eyes brightened. "I'm falling in love with you. I have been almost from the moment we met."

Bailey blinked back hot tears. "You may believe you're in love with me now," she whispered, "but it won't last. It never does. Before you know it, you'll meet someone else, and you'll fall in love with her and not want me anymore."

"Bailey, that's not going to happen. You're going to wear that slightly used wedding dress and you're going to wear it for me."

Bailey continued to stare up at him, doubtful she could trust what she was hearing.

"The mistake I made was in telling my mother about you. Actually Roseanne Snyder couldn't wait to mention you to Mom. Next thing I knew, my mother was after me to bring you over to the house so she and Dad could meet you. To complicate matters, my father got involved and over a couple of glasses of good Scotch I admitted that my intentions toward you were serious. Naturally both my parents were delighted."

"Naturally." The sinking feeling in her stomach refused to go away.

"I didn't want to rush you, but since Dad's brought everything out into the open, maybe it's best to clear the air now. My intentions are honorable."

"Maybe they are now," she argued, "but it'll never last."

Parker squared his shoulders and took a deep breath. "It will last. I realize you haven't had nearly enough time to figure out your feelings for me. I'd hoped—" he hesitated, his brow furrowed "—that we could have this discussion several months down the road when our feelings for each other had matured."

"I'll say it one more time—engagements don't work, at least not with me."

"It'll be different this time."

"If I was ever going to fall in love with anyone, it would be you. But Parker, it just isn't going to work. I'm sorry, really I am, but I can't go through with this." Her hands were trembling and she bit her lower lip. She was in love with Parker, but she was too frightened to acknowledge it outside the privacy of her own heart.

"Bailey, would you listen to me?"

"No," she said. "I'm sorry, but everything's been blown out of proportion here. I'm writing a romance novel and you...you're the man I'm using for the model." She gave a resigned shrug. "That's all."

Parker frowned. "In other words, everything between us is a farce. The only person guilty of using anyone is you."

Bailey clasped her hands tightly in front of her, so tightly that her nails cut deep indentations in her palms. A cold sweat broke out on her forehead. "I never claimed anything else."

"I see." The muscles in his jaw tightened again. "Then

all I can do is beg your forgiveness for being so presumptuous."

"There's no need to apologize." Bailey felt terrible, but she had to let him believe their relationship *was* a farce, otherwise everything became too risky. Too painful.

A noise, the muffled steps of Parker's mother entering the room, distracted them. "My dears," she said, "dinner's ready. I'm afraid if we wait much longer, it'll be ruined."

"We'll be right in," Parker said.

Bailey couldn't remember a more uncomfortable dinner in her life. The tension was so thick, she thought wryly, it could have been sliced and buttered.

Parker barely spoke during the entire meal. His mother, ever gracious, carried the burden of conversation. Bailey did her part to keep matters civilized, but the atmosphere was so strained it was a virtually impossible chore.

The minute they were finished with the meal, Parker announced it was time to leave. Bailey nodded and thanked his parents profusely for the meal. It was an honor to have met them, she went on, and this had been an exceptionally pleasant evening.

"Don't you think you overdid that a little?" Parker muttered once they were in the car.

"I had to say something," she snapped. "Especially since you were so rude."

"I wasn't rude."

"All right, you weren't rude, you were completely tactless. Couldn't you see how uncomfortable your father was? He felt bad enough about mentioning your plans. You certainly didn't need to complicate everything with such a rotten attitude."

"He deserved it."

"That's a terrible thing to say."

Parker didn't answer. For someone who, only hours before, had declared tender feelings for her, he seemed in an almighty hurry to get her home, careering around corners as though he were in training for the Indianapolis 500.

To Bailey's surprise he insisted on walking her to the door. The night before, he'd also escorted her to the door, and after a stilted good-night, he'd left. This evening, however, he wasn't content to leave it at that.

"Invite me in," he said when she'd unlatched the lock.

"Invite you in," Bailey echoed, listening to Max meowing plaintively on the other side.

"I'm coming in whether you invite me or not." His face was devoid of expression, and Bailey realized he would do exactly as he said. Her stomach tightened with apprehension.

"All right," she said, opening the door. She flipped on the light and removed her coat. Max, obviously sensing her state of mind, immediately headed for the bedroom. "I'd make some coffee, but I don't imagine you'll be staying that long."

"Make the coffee."

Bailey was grateful to have something to do. She concentrated on preparing the coffee and setting out mugs.

"Whatever you have to say isn't going to change my mind," Bailey told him. She didn't sound as calm and controlled as she'd hoped.

Parker ignored her. He couldn't seem to stand still, but rapidly paced her kitchen floor, pausing only when Bailey handed him a steaming mug of coffee. She'd seen Parker when he was angry and frustrated, even when he was jealous and unreasonable, but she'd never seen him quite like this.

"Say what you want to say," she prompted, resting her hip against the kitchen counter. She held her cup carefully in both hands.

"All right." Parker's eyes searched hers. "I resent having to deal with your irrational emotions."

"My irrational emotions!"

"Admit it, you're behaving illogically because some other man broke off his engagement to you."

"Other *men,*" Bailey corrected sarcastically. "Notice the plural, meaning more than one. Before you judge me too harshly, *Mr.* Davidson, let me remind you that every person is the sum of his or her experiences. If you stick your hand in the fire and get burned, you're not as likely to play around the campfire again, are you? It's as simple as that. I was fool enough to risk the fire twice, but I'm not willing to do it a third time."

"Has it ever occurred to you that you weren't in love with either Paul or Tom?"

Bailey blinked at the unexpectedness of the question. "That's ridiculous. I agreed to marry them. No woman does that without being in love."

"They both fell for someone else."

"How kind of you to remind me."

"Yet when they told you, you did nothing but wallow in your pain. If you'd been in love, deeply in love, you would've done everything within your power to keep them. Instead you did nothing. Absolutely nothing. What else am I to think?"

"Frankly I don't care what you think. I know what was in my heart and I was in love with both of them. Is it any wonder I refuse to fall in love again? An engagement is out of the question!"

"Then marry me now."

Bailey's heart leapt in her chest, then sank like a dead weight. "I—I'm not sure I heard you correctly."

"You heard. Engagements terrify you. I'm willing to

accept that you've got a valid reason, but you shouldn't let it dictate how you live the rest of your life."

"In other words, bypassing the engagement and rushing to the altar is going to calm my fears?"

"You keep repeating that you refuse to go through another engagement. I can understand your hesitancy," he stated calmly. "Reno is only a couple of hours away." He glanced at his watch. "We could be married by this time tomorrow."

"Ah..." Words twisted and turned in her mind, but no coherent thought emerged.

"Well?" Parker regarded her expectantly.

"I...we...elope? I don't think so, Parker. It's rather... heroic of you to suggest it, actually, but it's an impossible idea."

"Why? It sounds like the logical solution to me."

"Have you stopped to consider that there are other factors involved in this? Did it occur to you that I might not be in love with you?"

"You're so much in love with me you can't think straight," he said with ego-crushing certainty.

"How do you know that?"

"Easy. It's the way you react, trying too hard to convince yourself you don't care. And the way you kiss me. At first there's resistance, then gradually you warm to it, letting your guard slip just a little, enough for me to realize you're enjoying the kissing as much as I am. It's when you start to moan that I know everything I need to know."

A ferocious blush exploded in Bailey's cheeks. "I do not moan," she protested heatedly.

"Do you want me to prove it to you?"

"No," Bailey cried, backing away.

A smug smile moved over his mouth, settling in his eyes.

Bailey's heart felt heavy. "I'm sorry to disappoint you,

Parker, but I'd be doing us both a terrible disservice if I agreed to this."

Parker looked grim. She stared at him and knew, even as she rejected his marriage proposal, that if ever there was a man who could restore peace to her heart, that man was Parker. But she wasn't ready yet; she still had healing and growing to do on her own. But soon… Taking her courage in both hands, she whispered, "Couldn't we take some time to decide about this?"

Parker had asked her to be his wife. Parker Davidson, who was twice the man Paul was and three times the man Tom could ever hope to be. And she was so frightened all she could do was stutter and tremble and plead for time.

"Time," he repeated. Parker set his mug down on the kitchen counter, then stepped forward and framed her face in his large hands. His thumbs gently stroked her cheeks. Bailey gazed up at him, barely breathing. Warm anticipation filled her as he lowered his mouth.

She gasped sharply as his lips touched hers, moving over them slowly, masterfully. A moan rose deep in her throat, one so soft it was barely audible. A small cry of longing and need.

Parker heard it and responded, easing her closer and wrapping her in his arms. He kissed her a second time, then abruptly released her and turned away.

Bailey clutched the counter behind her to keep from falling. "What was that for?"

A slow easy grin spread across his face. "To help you decide."

"The worst part of this whole thing is that I haven't written a word in an entire week," Bailey complained as she sat on her living-room carpet, her legs pulled up under her chin. Pages of Jo Ann's manuscript littered the floor.

Max, who revealed little or no interest in their writing efforts, was asleep as usual atop her printer.

"In an entire week?" Jo Ann sounded horrified. Even at Christmas neither of them had taken more than a three-day break from writing.

"I've tried. Each and every night I turn on my computer and then I sit there and stare at the screen. This is the worst case of writer's block I've ever experienced. I can't seem to make myself work."

"Hmm," Jo Ann said, leaning against the side of the couch. "Isn't it also an entire week since you saw Parker? Seems to me the two must be connected."

She nodded miserably. Jo Ann wasn't telling her anything she didn't already know. She'd relived that night in her memory at least a dozen times a day.

"You've never told me what happened," Jo Ann said, studying Bailey closely.

Bailey swallowed. "Parker is just a friend."

"And pigs have wings."

"My only interest in Parker is as a role model for Michael," she tried again, but she didn't know who she was trying to convince, Jo Ann or herself.

She hadn't heard from him all week. He'd left, promising to give her the time she'd requested. He'd told her the kiss was meant to help her decide if she wanted him. Wanted him? Bailey didn't know if she'd ever *stop* wanting him, but she was desperately afraid that his love for her wouldn't last. It hadn't with Paul or Tom, and it wouldn't with Parker. And with Parker, the pain of rejection would be far worse.

Presumably Parker had thought he was reassuring her by suggesting they skip the engagement part and rush into a Nevada marriage. What he didn't seem to understand, what she couldn't seem to explain, was that it wouldn't make any difference. A wedding ring wasn't a guarantee. Someday, somehow, Parker would have a change of heart; he'd fall out of love with her.

"Are you all right?" Jo Ann asked.

"Of course I am." Bailey managed to keep her voice steady and pretend a calm she wasn't close to feeling. "I'm just upset about this writer's block. But it isn't the end of the world. I imagine everything will return to normal soon and I'll be back to writing three or four pages a night."

"You're sure about that?"

Bailey wasn't sure about anything. "No," she admitted.

"Just remember I'm here any time you want to talk."

A trembling smile touched the edges of Bailey's mouth and she nodded.

Bailey saw Parker three days later. She was waiting at the BART station by herself—Jo Ann had a day off—when she happened to glance up and see him walking in her direction. At first she tried to ignore the quaking of her heart and focus her attention away from him. But it was impossible.

She knew he saw her, too, although he gave no outward indication of it. His eyes met hers as though challenging her to ignore him. When she took a hesitant step toward him, his mouth quirked in a mocking smile.

"Hello, Parker."

"Bailey."

"How have you been?"

He hesitated a split second before he answered, which made Bailey hold her breath in anticipation.

"I've been terrific. How about you?"

"Wonderful," she lied, astonished that they could stand so close and pretend so well. His gaze lingered on her lips and she felt the throb of tension in the air. Parker must have rushed to get to the subway—his hair was slightly mussed and he was breathing hard.

He said something but his words were drowned out by the clatter of the approaching train. It pulled up and dozens of people crowded out. Neither Parker nor Bailey spoke as they waited to board.

He followed her inside, but sat several spaces away. She looked at him, oddly shocked and disappointed that he'd refused to sit beside her.

There were so many things she longed to tell him. Until now she hadn't dared admit to herself how much she'd missed his company. How she hungered to talk to him. They'd known each other for such a short while and yet he seemed to fill every corner of her life.

That, apparently, wasn't the case with Parker. Not if he could so casually, so willingly, sit apart from her. She raised her chin and forced herself to stare at the advertising panels that ran the length of the car.

Bailey felt Parker's eyes on her. The sensation was so strong his hand might as well have touched her cheek, held her face the way he had when he'd last left her. When she could bear it no longer, she turned and glanced at him. Their eyes met and the hungry desire in his tore at her heart.

With every ounce of strength she possessed, Bailey looked away. Eventually he would find someone else, someone he loved more than he would ever love her. Bailey was as certain of that as she was of her own name.

She kept her gaze on anything or anyone except Parker. But she felt the pull between them so strongly that she had to turn her head and look at him. He was staring at her, and the disturbing darkness of his eyes seemed to disrupt the very beat of her heart. A rush of longing jolted her body.

The train was slowing and Bailey was so grateful it was her station she jumped up and hurried to the exit.

"I'm still waiting," Parker whispered from directly behind her. She was conscious as she'd never been before of the long muscled legs so close to her own, of his strength and masculinity. "Have you decided yet?"

Bailey shut her eyes and prayed for the courage to do what was right for both of them. She shook her head silently; she couldn't talk to him now. She couldn't make a rational decision while the yearning in her heart was so great, while her body was so weak with need for him.

The crowd rushed forward and Bailey rushed with them, leaving him behind.

The writers' group met the following evening, for which Bailey was thankful. At least she wouldn't have to stare at a blank computer screen for several hours while she tried to convince herself she was a writer. Jo Ann had been making headway on her rewrite, whereas Bailey's had come to a complete standstill.

The speaker, an established historical-romance writer who lived in the San Francisco area, had agreed to address their group. Her talk was filled with good advice and Bailey tried to take notes. Instead, she drew meaningless doodles. Precise three-dimensional boxes and neat round circles in geometric patterns.

It wasn't until she was closing her spiral notebook at the end of the speech that Bailey realized all the circles on her page resembled interlocking wedding bands. About fifteen pairs of them. Was her subconscious sending her a message? Bailey had given up guessing.

"Are you going over to the diner for coffee?" Jo Ann asked as the group dispersed. Her eyes didn't meet Bailey's.

"Sure." She studied her friend and knew instinctively that something was wrong. Jo Ann had been avoiding her most of the evening. At first she'd thought it was her imagination, but there was a definite strain between them.

"All right," Bailey said, once they were outside. "What is it? What's wrong?"

Jo Ann sighed deeply. "I saw Parker this afternoon. I know it's probably nothing and I'm a fool for saying anything but, Bailey, he was with a woman and they were definitely more than friends."

"Oh?" Bailey's legs were shaky as she moved down the steps to the street. Her heart felt like a stone in the center of her chest.

"I'm sure it doesn't mean anything. For all I know, the woman could be his sister. I…I hadn't intended on saying a word, but then I thought you'd want to know."

"Of course I do," Bailey said, swallowing past the tightness in her throat. Her voice was firm and steady, revealing none of the chaos in her thoughts.

"I think Parker saw me. In fact, I'm sure he did. It was almost as if he *wanted* me to see him. He certainly didn't go out of his way to disguise who he was with—which leads me to believe it was all very innocent."

"I'm sure it was," Bailey lied. Her mouth twisted in a wry smile. She made a pretense of looking at her watch. "My goodness, I didn't realize it was so late. I think I'll skip coffee tonight and head on home."

Jo Ann grabbed her arm. "Are you all right?"

"Of course." But she was careful not to look directly at her friend. "It really doesn't matter, you know—about Parker."

"Doesn't matter?" Jo Ann echoed.

"I'm not the jealous type."

Her stomach was churning, her head spinning, her

hands trembling. Fifteen minutes later, Bailey let herself into her apartment. She didn't stop to remove her coat, but walked directly into the kitchen and picked up the phone.

Parker answered on the third ring. His greeting sounded distracted. "Bailey," he said, "it's good to hear from you. I've been trying to call you most of the evening."

"I was at a writers' meeting. You wanted to tell me something?"

"As a matter of fact, yes. You obviously aren't going to change your mind about the two of us."

"I…"

"Let's forget the whole marriage thing. There's no need to rush into this. What do you think?"

Eleven

"Oh, I agree one hundred percent," Bailey answered. It didn't surprise her that Parker had experienced a change of heart. She'd been expecting it to happen sooner or later. It was a blessing that he'd recognized his feelings so early on.

"No hard feelings then?"

"None," she assured him, raising her voice to a bright confident level. "I've gotten used to it. Honestly, you don't have a thing to worry about."

"You seem…cheerful."

"I am," Bailey answered, doing her best to sound as though she'd just won the lottery and was only waiting until she'd finished with this phone call to celebrate.

"How's the writing going?"

"Couldn't be better." Couldn't be worse actually, but she wasn't about to admit that. Not to Parker, at any rate.

"I'll be seeing you around then," he said.

"I'm sure you will." Maintaining this false enthusiasm was killing her. "One question."

"Sure."

"Where'd you meet her?"

"Her?" Parker hesitated. "You must mean Lisa. We've known each other for ages."

"I see." Bailey had to get off the phone before her facade cracked. But her voice broke as she continued, "I wish you well, Parker."

He paused as though he were debating whether or not to say something else. "You, too, Bailey."

Bailey replaced the receiver, her legs shaking so badly she stumbled toward the chair and literally fell into it. She covered her face with her hands, dragging deep gulps of air into her lungs. The burning ache in her stomach seemed to ripple out in hot waves, spreading to the tips of her fingers, to the bottoms of her feet.

By sheer force of will, Bailey lifted her head, squared her shoulders and stood up. She'd been through this before. Twice. Once more wouldn't be any more difficult than the first two times. Or so she insisted to herself.

After all, this time there was no ring to return, no wedding arrangements to cancel, no embossed announcements to burn.

No one, with the exception of Jo Ann, even knew about Parker, so the embarrassment would be kept to a minimum.

Getting over Parker should be quick and easy.

It wasn't.

A hellishly slow week passed and Bailey felt as if she were living on another planet. Outwardly nothing had changed, and yet the world seemed to be spinning off its axis. She went to work every morning, discussed character and plot with Jo Ann, worked an eight-hour day, took the subway home and plunked herself down in front of her computer, working on her rewrite with demonic persistence.

She appeared to have everything under control. Yet her life was unfolding in slow motion around her, as though she was a bystander and not a participant.

It must have shown in her writing because Jo Ann

phoned two days after Bailey had given her the complete rewrite.

"You finished reading it?" Bailey couldn't hide her excitement. If Jo Ann liked it, then Bailey could mail it right off to Paula Albright, the editor who'd asked to see the revised manuscript.

"I'd like to come over and discuss a few points. Have you got time?"

Time was the one thing Bailey had in abundance. She hadn't realized how large a role Parker had come to play in her life or how quickly he'd chased away the emptiness. The gap he'd left behind seemed impossible to fill. Most nights she wrote until she was exhausted. But because she couldn't sleep anyway, she usually just sat in the living room holding Max.

Her cat didn't really care for the extra attention she was lavishing on him. He grudgingly endured her stroking his fur and scratching his ears. An extra serving of canned cat food and a fluffed-up pillow were appreciated, but being picked up and carted across the room to sit in her lap wasn't. To his credit, Max had submitted to two or three sessions in which she talked out her troubles, but his patience with such behavior had exhausted itself.

"Put on a pot of coffee and I'll be over in a few minutes," Jo Ann said, disturbing Bailey's musings.

"Fine. I'll see you when I see you," Bailey responded, then frowned. My goodness, *that* was an original statement. If she was reduced to such a glaring lack of originality one week after saying farewell to Parker, she hated to consider how banal her conversation would be a month from now.

Jo Ann arrived fifteen minutes later, Bailey's manuscript tucked under her arm.

"You didn't like it," Bailey said in a flat voice. Her friend's expression couldn't have made it any plainer.

"It wasn't that, exactly," Jo Ann told her, setting the manuscript on the coffee table and curling up in the overstuffed chair.

"What seems to be the problem this time?"

"Janice."

"Janice?" Bailey cried, restraining the urge to argue. She'd worked so hard to make the rewrite of *Forever Yours* work. "I thought *Michael* was the source of all the trouble."

"He was in the original version. You've rewritten him just beautifully, but Janice seemed so—I hate to say this—weak."

"Weak?" Bailey shouted. "Janice isn't weak! She's strong and independent and—"

"Foolish and weak-willed," Jo Ann finished. "The reader loses sympathy for her halfway through the book. She acts like a robot with Michael."

Bailey was having a difficult time not protesting. She knew Jo Ann's was only one opinion, but she'd always trusted her views. Jo Ann's evaluation of the manuscript's earlier versions had certainly been accurate.

"Give me an example," Bailey said, making an effort to keep her voice as even and unemotional as possible.

"Everything changed after the scene at the Pops concert."

"Parker was a real jerk," Bailey argued. "He deserved everything she said and did."

"Parker?" Jo Ann's brows arched at her slip of the tongue.

"Michael," Bailey corrected. "You know who I meant!"

"Indeed I did."

During the past week, Jo Ann had made several awkward attempts to drop Parker's name into conversation, but Bailey refused to discuss him.

"Michael did act a bit high-handed," Jo Ann continued, "but the reader's willing to forgive him, knowing he's discovering his true feelings for Janice. The fact that he felt jealous when she danced with another man hit him like an expected blow. True, he did behave like a jerk, but I understood his motivation and was willing to forgive him."

"In other words, the reader will accept such actions from the hero but not the heroine?" Bailey asked aggressively.

"That's not it at all," Jo Ann responded, sounding surprised. "In the original version Janice comes off as witty and warm and independent. The reader can't help liking her and sympathize with her situation."

"Then what changed?" Bailey demanded, raising her voice. Her inclination was to defend Janice as she would her own child.

Jo Ann shrugged. "I wish I knew what happened to Janice. All I can tell you is that it started after the scene at the Pops concert. From that point on I had problems identifying with her. I couldn't understand why she was so willing to accept everything Michael said and did. It was as if she'd lost her spirit. By the end of the book, I actively disliked her. I wanted to take her by the shoulders and shake her."

Bailey felt like weeping. "So I guess it's back to the drawing board," she said, putting on a cheerful front. "I suppose I should be getting used to that."

"My best advice is to put the manuscript aside for a few weeks," Jo Ann said in a gentle tone. "Didn't you tell me you had another plot idea you wanted to develop?"

Bailey nodded. But that was before. Before almost all her energy was spent just surviving from day to day. Before she'd begun pretending her life was perfectly normal although the pain left her barely able to function. Before she'd lost hope…

"What will putting it aside accomplish?" she asked.

"It will give you perspective," Jo Ann advised. "Look at Janice. Really look at her. Does she deserve a man as terrific as Michael? You've done such a superb job writing him."

It went without saying that Parker had been the source of her inspiration.

"In other words Janice is unsympathetic?"

Jo Ann's nod was regretful. "I'm afraid so. But remember that this is strictly my opinion. Someone else may read *Forever Yours* and feel Janice is a fabulous heroine. You might want to have some of the other writers in the group read it. I don't mean to be discouraging, Bailey, really I don't."

"I know that."

"It's only because you're my friend that I can be so honest."

"That's what I wanted," Bailey admitted slowly. Who was she kidding? She was as likely to become a published writer as she was a wife. The odds were so bad it would be a sucker's bet.

"I don't want to discourage you," Jo Ann repeated in a worried voice.

"If I'd been looking for someone to tell me how talented I am, I would've given the manuscript to my mother."

Jo Ann laughed, then glanced at her watch. "I've got to scoot. I'm supposed to pick up Dan at the muffler shop. The station wagon's beginning to sound like an army tank. If you have any questions give me a call later."

"I will." Bailey led the way to the door and held it open as Jo Ann gathered up her purse and coat. Her friend paused, looking concerned. "You're not too depressed about this, are you?"

"A little," Bailey said. "All right, a lot. But it's all part of the learning process, and if I have to rewrite this manuscript a hundred times, then I'll do it. Writing isn't for the faint of heart."

"You've got that right."

Jo Ann had advised her to set the story aside but the instant she was gone, Bailey tore into the manuscript, leafing carefully through the pages.

Jo Ann's notes in the margins were valuable—and painful. Bailey paid particular attention to the comments following Michael and Janice's fateful evening at the concert. It didn't take her long to connect this scene in her novel with its real-life equivalent, her evening with Parker.

She acts like a robot with Michael, Jo Ann had said. As Bailey read through the subsequent chapters, she couldn't help but agree. It was as though her feisty, spirited heroine had lost the will to exert her own personality. For all intents and purposes, she'd lain down and died.

Isn't that what you've done? her heart asked.

But Bailey ignored it. She'd given up listening to the deep inner part of herself. She'd learned how painful that could be.

"By the end of the book I actively disliked her." Jo Ann's words resounded like a clap of thunder in her mind. Janice's and Bailey's personalities were so intimately entwined that she no longer knew where one stopped and the other began.

"Janice seemed so…so weak."

Bailey resisted the urge to cover her ears to block out Jo Ann's words. It was all she could do not to shout, "You'd be spineless too if you had a slightly used wedding dress hanging in your closet!"

When Bailey couldn't tolerate the voices any longer, she reached for her jacket and purse and escaped. Anything was better than listening to the accusations echoing in her mind. The apartment felt unfriendly and confining. Even Max's narrowed green eyes seemed to reflect her heart's questions.

The sky was overcast—a perfect accompaniment to Bailey's mood. She walked without any real destination until she found herself at the BART station and her heart suddenly started to hammer. She chided herself for the small surge of hope she felt. What were the chances of running into Parker on a Saturday afternoon? Virtually none. She hadn't seen him in over a week. More than likely he'd been driving to work to avoid her.

Parker.

The pain she'd managed to hold at bay for several days bobbed to the surface. Tears spilled from her eyes. She kept on walking, her pace brisk as though she was in a hurry to get somewhere. Bailey's destination was peace and she had yet to find it. Sometimes she wondered if she ever would.

Men fell in love with her easily enough, but they seemed to fall out of love just as effortlessly. Worst of all, most demeaning of all, was the knowledge that there was always another woman involved. A woman they loved more than Bailey. Paul, Tom and now Parker.

Bailey walked for what felt like miles. Somehow, she wasn't altogether shocked when she found herself on Parker's street. He'd mentioned it in passing the evening they'd gone to the concert. The condominiums were a newer addition to the neighborhood, ultramodern, ultra-expensive, ultra-appealing to the eye. It wouldn't surprise her to learn that Parker had been responsible for their design. Although the dinner conversation with his parents had been stilted and uncomfortable, Parker's mother had taken delight in highlighting her son's many accomplishments. Parker obviously wasn't enthusiastic about his mother's bragging, but Bailey had felt a sense of pride in the man she loved.

The man she loved.

Abruptly Bailey stopped walking. She closed her eyes and clenched her hands into tight fists. She did *not* love Parker. If she did happen to fall in love again, it wouldn't be with a man as fickle or as untrustworthy as Parker Davidson, who apparently fell in and out of love at the drop of a—

You love him, you fool. Now what are you going to do about it?

Bailey just wanted these questions, these revelations, to stop, to leave her alone. Alone in her misery. Alone in her pain and denial.

An anger grew in Bailey. One born of so much strong emotion she could barely contain it. Without sparing a thought for the consequences, she stormed into the central lobby of the condominium complex. The doorman stepped forward.

"Good afternoon," he said politely.

Bailey managed to smile at him. "Hello." Then, when she noticed that he was waiting for her to continue, she added, "Mr. Parker Davidson's home, please," her voice remarkably calm and impassive. They were going to settle this once and for all, and no one, not a doorman, not even a security guard, was going to stand in her way.

"May I ask who's calling?"

"Bailey York," she answered confidently.

"If you'll kindly wait here," He was gone only a moment. "Mr. Parker says to send you right up. He's in unit 204."

"Thank you." Bailey's determination hadn't dwindled by the time her elevator reached the second floor.

It took Parker a couple of minutes to answer his door. When he did, Bailey didn't wait for an invitation. She marched into his apartment, ignoring the spectacular view and the lush traditional furnishings of polished wood and rich fabric.

"Bailey." He seemed surprised to see her.

Standing in the middle of the room, hands on her hips, she glared at him with a week's worth of indignation flashing from her eyes. "Don't Bailey me," she raged. "I want to know who Lisa is and I want to know *now.*"

Parker gaped at her as though she'd taken leave of her senses.

"Don't give me that look." She walked a complete circle around him; he swiveled slowly, still staring. "There's no need to stand there with your mouth hanging open. It's a simple question."

"What are you doing here?"

"What does it look like?"

"Frankly I'm not sure."

"I've come to find out exactly what kind of man you are." That sounded good, and she said it in a mocking challenging way bound to get a response.

"What kind of man I am? Does this mean I have to run through a line of warriors waiting to flog me?"

Bailey was in no mood for jesting. "It just might." She removed one hand from her hip and waved it under his nose. "I'll have you know Janice has been ruined and I blame you."

"Who?"

"My character Janice," she explained with exaggerated patience. "The one in my novel, *Forever Yours.* She's wishy-washy, submissive and docile. Reading about her is like…like vanilla pudding instead of chocolate."

"I happen to be partial to vanilla pudding."

Bailey sent him a furious look. "I'll do the talking here."

Parker raised both hands. "Sorry."

"You should be. So…exactly what kind of man *are* you?"

"I believe you've already asked that question." Bailey spun around to scowl at him. "Sorry," he muttered, his mouth twisting oddly. "I forgot you're doing the talking here."

"One minute you claim you're in love with me. So much in love you want me to marry you." Her voice faltered slightly. "And the next you're involved with some woman named Lisa and you want to put our relationship on hold. Well, I've got news for you, Mr. Unreliable. I refuse to allow you to play with my heart. You asked me to marry you…" Bailey paused at the smile that lifted the corners of his mouth. "Is this discussion amusing you?" she demanded.

"A little."

"Feel free to share the joke," she said, motioning with her hand.

"Lisa's my sister-in-law."

The words didn't immediately sink in. "Your what?"

"She's my brother's wife."

Bailey slumped into a chair. A confused moment passed while she tried to collect her scattered thoughts. "You're in love with your brother's wife?"

"No." He sounded shocked that she'd even suggest such a thing. "I'm in love with you."

"You're not making a lot of sense."

"I figured as much, otherwise—"

"Otherwise what?"

"Otherwise you'd either be in my arms or finding ways to inflict physical damage on my person."

"You'd better explain yourself," she said, frowning, hardly daring to hope.

"I love you, Bailey, but I didn't know how long it would take you to discover you love me, too. You were so caught up in the past—"

"With reason," she reminded him.

"With reason," he agreed. "Anyway I asked you to marry me."

"To be accurate, your father's the one who did the actual speaking," Bailey muttered.

"True, he spoke out of turn, but it was a question I was ready to ask…"

"But…" she supplied for him. There was always a "but" when it came to men and love.

"But I didn't know if your feelings for me were genuine."

"I beg your pardon?"

"Was it me you fell for or Michael?" he asked quietly.

"I don't think I understand."

"The way I figure it, if you truly loved me you'd do everything in your power to win me back."

"Win you back? I'm sorry, Parker, but I still don't get it."

"All right, let's backtrack a bit. When Paul announced he'd found another woman and wanted to break your engagement, what did you do?"

"I dropped out of university and signed up for paralegal classes at the business college."

"What about Tom?"

"I moved to San Francisco."

"My point exactly."

Bailey lost him somewhere between Paul and Tom. "*What* is your point exactly?"

Parker hesitated, then looked straight into her eyes. "I wanted you to love me enough to fight for me," he told her simply. "Don't worry. Lisa and I are not, repeat not, in love."

"You just wanted me to think so?"

"Yes," he said with obvious embarrassment. "She reads romances, too. Quite a few women do apparently. I was telling her about our relationship, and she came up with the idea of using the 'other woman' the way some romance novels do."

"That's the most underhand unscrupulous thing I've ever heard."

"Indulge me for a few more minutes, all right?"

"All right," she agreed.

"When Paul and Tom broke off their engagements to you, you didn't say or do anything to convince them of your love. You calmly accepted that they'd met someone else and conveniently got out of their lives."

"So?"

"So I needed you to want me so much, love me so much, that you wouldn't give me up. You'd put aside that damnable pride of yours and confront me."

"Were you planning to arrange a mud-wrestling match between Lisa and me?" she asked wryly.

"No!" He looked horrified at the mere thought. "I wanted to provoke you—just enough to come to me. What took you so long?" He shook his head. "I was beginning to lose heart."

"You're going to lose a whole lot more than your heart if you ever pull that stunt again, Parker Davidson."

His face lit up with a smile potent enough to dissolve her pain and her doubts. He opened his arms then, and Bailey walked into his embrace.

"I should be furious with you," she mumbled.

"Kiss me first, then be mad."

His mouth captured hers in hungry exultation. In a single kiss Parker managed to make up for the long cheerless days, the long lonely nights. She was breathless when he finally released her.

"You really love me?" she whispered, needing to hear him say it. Her lower lip trembled and her hands tightened convulsively.

"I really love you," he whispered back, smiling down at her. "Enough to last us two lifetimes."

"Only two?"

His hand cradled the back of her head. "At least four." His mouth claimed hers again, then he abruptly broke off the kiss. "Now, what was it you were saying about Janice? What's wrong with her?"

A slow thoughtful smile spread across Bailey's face. "Nothing that a wedding and a month-long honeymoon won't cure."

Epilogue

Bailey paused to read the sign in the bookstore window, announcing the autographing session for two local authors that afternoon.

"How does it feel to see your name in lights?" Jo Ann asked.

"You may be used to this, but I feel…I feel—" Bailey hesitated and flattened her palms on the smooth roundness of her stomach "—I feel almost the same as I did when I found out I was pregnant."

"It does funny things to the nervous system, doesn't it?" Jo Ann teased. "And what's this comment about me being used to all this? I've only got two books published to your one."

The bookseller, Caroline Dryer, recognized them when they entered the store and hurried forward to greet them, her smile welcoming. "I'm so pleased you could both come. We've had lots of interest." She steered them toward the front where a table, draped in lace, and two chairs were waiting. Several women were already lined up patiently, looking forward to meeting Jo Ann and Bailey.

They did a brisk business for the next hour. Family,

friends and other writers joined the romance readers who stopped by to wish them well.

Bailey was talking to an older woman, a retired schoolteacher, when Parker and Jo Ann's husband, Dan, casually strolled past the table. The four were going out for dinner following the autograph session. There was a lot to celebrate. Jo Ann had recently signed a two-book contract with her publisher and Bailey had just sold her second romance. After weeks of work, Parker had finished the plans for their new home. Construction was scheduled to begin the following month and with luck would be completed by the time the baby arrived.

"What I loved best about *Forever Yours* was Michael," the older woman was saying to Bailey. "The scene where he takes her in his arms right in the middle of the merry-go-round and tells her he's tired of playing childish games and that he loves her was enough to steal my heart."

"He stole mine, too," Bailey said, her eyes linking with her husband's.

"Do you think there are any men like that left in this world?" the woman asked. "I've been divorced for years, and now that I'm retired, well, I wouldn't mind meeting someone."

"You'd be surprised how many heroes there are all around us," Bailey said, her gaze still holding Parker's. "They take the subway and eat peanut-butter sandwiches and fall in love—like you and me."

"Well, there's hope for me, then," the teacher said jauntily. "And I plan to have a good time looking." She smiled. "That's why I enjoy romance novels so much. They give me encouragement, they're fun—and they tell me it's okay to believe in love," she confided. "Even for the second time."

"Or the third," Parker inserted quietly.

Bailey grinned. She couldn't argue with that!

* * * * *

In the Alaskan wilderness, love blooms in unlikely places—and between an unlikely couple...

Read on for a sneak peek at Alaska Reunion, *the newest book in Jennifer Snow's Wild River series.*

One

Alisha Miller has invited you to join the group Wild River High Class of 2011 Reunion.

For two days, Ellie Mitchell had stared at the notification. She'd hovered over the Accept button and then chickened out at least eighty-six times. High school felt like a million years ago. Did she really want to revisit that time in her life for one nostalgia-filled evening?

Now an emergency room nurse at Wild River Community Hospital, it made sense that Alisha wanted to have this reunion. She'd been captain of the cheerleading squad, senior class vice president (only because she'd opted not to run for president) and head of the debate team. Everyone loved her because she was that rare mix of popular, pretty *and* nice. She was always front and center at school events—not in a boastful, look-at-me way but in an uplifting, school spirit way.

Ellie had been more of a behind-the-scenes participant in school activities. She was a worker bee on student council and the school's event planning committee. She was the setup and takedown crew, never center stage. And she'd preferred it that way. Half of her classmates might even have forgotten she was in their graduating class. She hadn't exactly stood out.

At least not until senior year, when she'd stepped out and been noticed. But it had less to do with her and more to do with her dating Brent Lanigan, class president and star quarterback with big dreams for himself after graduation. Ellie still wasn't sure how it had even happened. One day she was tutoring him to ensure that his grades were high enough to keep playing football, the next he'd gone in for an unexpected kiss, and then the rest of the school year they were seeing one another.

She sighed. The reunion was tentatively scheduled for three weeks from now, and she could see that over half the class had RSVP'd already.

Brent hadn't yet. Would he attend? Would that affect her own decision? Probably. She was just that pathetic.

She tucked her cell phone into the back pocket of her jeans as the clock hit 9:00 a.m.

Time to open Flippin' Pages bookstore, the place where she'd worked since graduation. Having started as a clerk ten years ago, she was now the store manager, taking care of everything from ordering inventory, doing the bookkeeping and scheduling to running store events. Despite being a small town indie bookstore, it was actually one of the local hotspots thanks to their weekly book club meetings, author appearances and read-aloud story time for kids. Every week the place hosted something for locals, and things picked up even more during the tourist seasons.

Going to the front door, she flipped the Closed sign to Open and unlocked it. She flicked on the interior lights and a cozy, inviting feeling washed over her. Flippin' Pages was located in one of the older buildings along Main Street in Wild River, Alaska, and its historic charm was one of the things that drew people to the store. It was three stories high, with a magnificent spiral staircase leading to the upper floors, deep mahogany wood accents throughout, original hardwood flooring and patterned tin ceilings, and patrons admired the building's historic vibe as well as the impressive selection of books it housed.

Like the incredible delivery that had arrived the day before. Ellie couldn't wait to dig into the box of donated classics that had come in courtesy of the estate of an older man who'd died the previous weekend. Hyped books from fresh new authors were always exciting, but old, secondhand donations were Ellie's favorite.

Blame it on her old, romantic soul, maybe, but there was something magical about antiques and collectibles. Old items passed down through generations, that had a history…that had existed long before she had, held a mysterious quality that she was drawn to.

Grabbing a box cutter from behind the counter, she carefully sliced through the cardboard and opened the box of books. Reaching inside was like opening a present on Christmas morning. Joy and anticipation wrapped around her as she took one of the books out and turned it over in her hands.

A well-loved first edition of *The Scarlet Letter* by Nathaniel Hawthorne.

She ran a finger over the cover—octavo, original brown cloth, 1850 dated on the spine. There were only twenty-five hundred of these in the world, and it would sell for quite a nice price, but that wasn't what appealed to her most. She took a deep breath and carefully opened the flap to the inside page.

Yes! There was an inscription. That was always the best part. Almost as though she were eavesdropping on the past.

To My Dear Michael,
May this book take you on a fantastical journey.
All my love,
Rose

Ellie sighed. Michael and Rose. What had their lives been like back then? Who were they? What had they meant to one another? Relatives or secret lovers? She brought the book to her nose and inhaled deeply.

"Were you just smelling that book?" a male voice asked over the chime of the door opening.

Ellie quickly put the book on the New Antique Arrival shelf and turned as her coworker Callum McKendrick entered the bookstore. "I smell all the books," she said. "And you're late." He was always late. It was almost endearing how predictable his lateness was. Like if he ever arrived on time, she'd know something was wrong. He breezed through life without a care to societal conventions like being on time for work. And got away with it.

"Only four minutes," he said, checking an imaginary watch. "Better than yesterday."

She laughed and shook her head. "Better than yesterday."

"What have we got?" he asked, rolling up the sleeves of his light blue shirt and bending at the knees to peer inside the box. His thick, dark hair fell into his face and he pushed it back. Everyone in town called him Clark Kent because he looked exactly like the fictional superhero at six foot three, with a muscular build, wide shoulders and a broad chest. His jet-black hair was always slightly too long, and his dark-rimmed glasses did nothing to tame the sex appeal he radiated.

Ellie liked to believe that their regular customers came in for the literary experience and wide selection of art the bookstore provided, but it probably had more to do with the sexy bookseller.

"This is that estate donation from the lady who called yesterday," she said, making room on the shelf for the rest of the books. She couldn't believe the condition they were in. Someone must have cherished them enough to preserve them and take care of them. A lot of the old books that came into the store needed restoring, but not these.

"I can't believe none of his children or grandchildren wanted these," Callum said, taking out a copy of *Moby Dick.* "These look like they could be first editions."

"They are," she said, pointing to the date on the spine. "That's why we will be selling them for a small fortune."

"Also because you don't want anyone to actually buy them," he said with a wink.

No doubt that little flicker of an eyelid had women fainting in old 1800s fashion, but Ellie was immune to Callum's charm. He was at least several years younger than her and he flirted as often as he exhaled.

"I don't do that," she said.

"Yes you do."

"Fine. You know me too well," she said with a laugh, but her smile faded as her cell phone chimed in her pocket. Taking it out, she saw a new post in the reunion Facebook group, from Cheryl Kingsly—one of Alisha's longtime best friends. Cheryl was a personal trainer now, and Ellie often saw the two leaving the gym together.

Can't wait to be reunited with my Wild Cougar Family! Do we have a venue yet?

Immediately little dots appeared that showed someone was typing, and seconds later Alisha's reply appeared.

Not yet. You know me—brilliant ideas, zero execution skills.

Ellie shook her head. It was so like them to try to organize a last-minute event without actually organizing anything. Years ago, it was the same. The student council would meet and come up with great ideas, but then no one stepped up to do the actual work—besides her and a few others that no one gave credit to in the end when the events were a success.

Alisha hoped to do this in three weeks, and yet there was absolutely nothing planned yet. No venue, no discussion about food, no theme or decor… Ellie sighed.

"What's wrong?" Callum asked, handing her another book.

She studied the copy of Jane Austen's *Pride and Prejudice*, unable to fully appreciate it. Did she go to the reunion or didn't she? Would it make her feel better or worse about the direction her life had taken, catching up with her former classmates? "It's my ten-year high school reunion this year, and the populars are posting nonstop on the Facebook group page with updates."

Callum frowned. "The populars?"

"You know, the popular crowd in school. The ones who are still popular and want to show off how awesome their lives have turned out by forcing everyone to return to the scene of some of the most humiliating days of their lives and try to maintain chitchat while feeling the weight of judgment," she said.

What would they say about her? About the fact that, unlike so many of them, she hadn't become what her high school yearbook had claimed she'd wanted to be—a teacher. What would they whisper when she walked past?

Poor Ellie—still working in a bookstore.

Poor Ellie—not married, not engaged, not even having fantastic casual sex.

Poor Ellie—no kids yet. Didn't she say she wanted three? Better get on with that life plan before her ovaries completely dry up.

"I always thought reunions were just a fun way to catch up with people you haven't seen in years," Callum said with a shrug.

She eyed him. "Of course that's what it would be for *you*."

He faked a look of hurt. "What's that supposed to mean?"

"Look at you. You're gorgeous—tall, dark and handsome with muscles in places I didn't even think muscles could grow…or form…or whatever they do," she said casually. She wasn't hitting on him, just stating facts.

She knew better. Guys like Callum got the pretty girls, the athletic girls, the popular ones…like the ones she was wanting to avoid at this reunion. Ellie had been the book nerd even in high school. Not much had changed. Her idea of fun was a quiet night in, discussing a good book with close, like-minded friends while enjoying an amazing vintage wine. Going to an event to reminisce about the good old days with people who remembered high school a lot differently than she did wasn't her idea of an enjoyable time.

"You eyeballing me?" Callum asked, leaning against the shelf and flashing her his best flirty smile. She knew it was his best flirty smile because he used it on all the female customers, and their orders magically increased. As she was technically his boss—being the store manager—Ellie appreciated his sales abilities, but she knew not to read anything into the flirting.

"I'm saying that you wouldn't understand the intense pressure this event could have on a person," she said, taking the remaining books out of the box and shelving them without even opening the cover flaps to check for inscriptions. A serious sign that this whole reunion thing was stressing her out.

"What pressure? Explain it to me," Callum said, taking the empty box from her and breaking it down.

She sighed. "If I go, everyone will know that my life is just as boring now as it was back in high school. So, my choices are to skip it or go and invent a more exciting existence."

He frowned. "I thought you loved your life here in Wild River."

She did. It just wasn't newsworthy. Running the small bookstore on Main Street, living in the apartment upstairs wasn't exactly how she'd expected her life to turn out. Not that she had anything to prove or that there was anything wrong with her lifestyle…if she didn't know for a fact that Brent was a commercial pilot whose most recent serious relationship had been a six-month affair with a flight attendant who'd missed her calling as a Victoria's Secret model. Ellie had consumed countless tubs of ice cream while cyberstalking the two of them on Instagram.

Brent had been her first boyfriend and one true love. They'd started out as friends when she was assigned as his English tutor. At first she'd thought he would be just another jock who'd expect her to do his assignments for him, but he'd surprised her. He was actually interested in literature, he'd just suffered from assignment anxiety. Writer's block of sorts.

During their time together, she'd fallen hard and fast and he'd surprised her again with a spontaneous kiss and then asking her out on a date when he got a B in English on his midterm report card. The two had been inseparable until graduation, when Brent had made it clear he was planning on going away for university and flight school. It was his dream to become a commercial pilot and suddenly Ellie hadn't been a part of the future he saw for himself.

He'd left. She'd stayed.

He'd moved on. And she was still stuck in a heartbroken limbo of wanting to get over him and secretly hoping someday he'd come back to Wild River and tell her he still loved her.

Pathetic, but that's where she was.

"I do love my life." Most days. "I'm just dreading seeing certain people, that's all," she said honestly.

"Your ex Brent?"

She frowned. "How'd you know?"

"Because you talk about him as though you'd marry him and have a dozen children given the chance."

"Well, I would, but that's not going to happen because..." She opened her Instagram app and turned the phone toward Callum. "He's currently dating her." This new one was a waitress from Hawaii—beautiful, blonde, tanned with a breathtaking smile and perfect teeth. Apparently, flying commercial flights to the beach destination had more perks than just the round trips to paradise.

Callum squinted through his dark-rimmed glasses. "You're cuter."

She scoffed. "You're not getting a raise, so you can quit the compliments."

"I don't need a raise."

That's right. Callum was independently wealthy. His family were hotel owners, and the poshest hotel in Alaska was here in Wild River. It didn't quite fit the rest of the remote resort town's rugged mountain esthetic, but it catered to a different kind of tourist—ones with lots of money. The

Wild River Resort was located near the ski slopes and offered guests panoramic views of the mountains. A luxury spa and five-star restaurant were additional offerings that even had movie stars visiting the town. Or in the recent case of Selena Hudson, finding refuge from a stalker.

Callum didn't talk about his family much, but she could sense he wanted nothing to do with the hospitality industry or following in his father's and grandfather's footsteps of hotel ownership. He worked in the bookstore because he enjoyed books, and he hadn't told her, but she knew he donated his paycheck to the local animal shelter and the local school's love of reading program.

How he was still single, she had no idea.

Maybe it was hard for him to trust whether a woman was interested in him for himself or his trust fund and family status. Ellie thought he had nothing to worry about—he could be dirt poor, living in a van and women would still crave his attention.

"Anyway, I think you're worrying for nothing. He's probably off jetting around the world and won't even show up."

He hadn't RSVP'd one way or another yet, so Callum might be right. Brent rarely returned to Wild River now that both his parents had moved to Arizona to retire, and as an only child, he didn't have any other family to visit.

"Maybe," she said. She didn't want to go to the reunion, so why was she secretly hoping that Brent would say yes? If he did, there was no way she could *not* go. There hadn't been an opportunity to see him since he'd left Wild River. She wouldn't turn down the chance that maybe...

He'd see her and confess his undying love. Yeah, right.

Maybe it was time to lay off the romantic comedies for a while.

Don't miss Alaska Reunion,
available September 2021 wherever
Harlequin Books and ebooks are sold.

www.Harlequin.com